STAR TREK®

SPECTRE

Also by William Shatner

TekWar
TekLords
TekLab
Tek Vengeance
Tek Secret
Tek Power
Tek Money
Tek Kill
Man o' War
Believe (with Michael Tobias)
Star Trek Memories
Star Trek Movie Memories
The Ashes of Eden (with Judith and Garfield Reeves-Stevens)
The Return (with Judith and Garfield Reeves-Stevens)
Avenger (with Judith and Garfield Reeves-Stevens)

WILLIAM SHATNER

STAR TREK®

SPECTRE

with
Judith Reeves-Stevens &
Garfield Reeves-Stevens

POCKET BOOKS
New York   London   Toronto   Sydney   Tokyo   Singapore

POCKET BOOKS, a division of Simon & Schuster Inc.
1230 Avenue of the Americas, New York, NY 10020

 STAR TREK is a Registered Trademark of
Paramount Pictures.

This book is published by Pocket Books, a division of
Simon & Schuster Inc., under exclusive license from
Paramount Pictures.

ISBN: 0-671-00878-1

First Pocket Books hardcover printing May 1998

10 9 8 7 6 5 4 3 2 1

POCKET and colophon are registered trademarks of
Simon & Schuster Inc.

Printed in the U.S.A.

Star Trek has been good to me:
Fame, Fortune, Fantasy.
But most of all, Friendship.
My Friend, Leonard, my best man, *the* best man.
And the essential Southern gentleman, my Friend,
  DeForrest
And his devoted, loving, and lovely wife, Carolyn.
I dedicate this book to them and my delight in their
  friendship.

ACKNOWLEDGMENTS

Gar and Judy Reeves-Stevens are incredible. Their work speaks for itself. Their mastery of the legends of Star Trek is incomparable.

To John Ordover, Margaret Clark, and Gina Centrello for their expertise.

STAR TREK®

SPECTRE

PROLOGUE

☆

"He's still alive," the Vulcan said.

Though Kate heard the Vulcan's words, she didn't understand their significance. She leaned forward across the small table in the bar on *Deep Space Nine.* Some huge alien with a drooping face like a shriveled prune had just won a triple Dabo. He was making so much noise by the gaming table that normal conversation was impossible.

A nervous Ferengi scampered out from behind the bar, pushing his way through the noisy crowd, arms waving. "Morn! Morn! Put her down!"

The alien, Morn presumably, was performing some type of victory dance with a Dabo girl. As he spun her around in his embrace, her feet no longer touched the floor and she was precariously close to losing what little there was of her outfit.

With all eyes and other sensing organs in the bar on the dancing Morn, the Vulcan took advantage of the distraction to slip a small padd across the table to her human companion.

Kate palmed the flat device, cupped her hand around its miniature display, and activated it. She gasped as she recognized the face that appeared. The hatred that sprang to life within her was like a physical blow.

"James Tiberius Kirk," the Vulcan whispered. She kept one

1

hand—her real one—up by her face, half-covering her mouth. She was young, no more than twenty, Kate knew, but her eyes were older. Where she and the Vulcan came from, everyone's eyes were older.

"When was this image recorded?"

"A year ago," the Vulcan said. "During the virogen crisis, Kirk was arrested by port authorities at Vulcan. This is from a magistrate's hearing."

Instantly, Kate did the math. Kirk's birthdate, in the Earth year 2233, would be forever burned into her memory. "T'Val, that's impossible. This man is no more than sixty at most. But Kirk . . . today, he'd be . . . a hundred and forty-two years old."

A second Ferengi, in a Bajoran uniform, now joined the nervous one, and both took the place of the Dabo girl in Morn's arms. The lumbering alien was spinning the two Ferengi around as he hopped lightly from one foot to the other while bleating out a tuneless series of notes that sounded more like the mating call of a Yridian yak than the song of a sentient being.

The Vulcan, T'Val, sipped her water, using the moment to glance around the bar. "Eighty-two years ago, Kirk was presumed lost during the maiden voyage of a new starship from Earth. But in actuality, he was caught in a nonlinear temporal continuum."

Kate frowned. "I don't understand what that is," she said, staring once again at the monster on the padd display.

T'Val allowed a momentary flicker of shared confusion to play across her features, so subtle that none but another Vulcan, or Kate, would notice. Everyone else would be distracted by the flat red blister of a disruptor scar etched across the olive skin of her forehead. "Do not be troubled. No one does. But four years ago, Kirk was discovered within that continuum by . . ." T'Val's eyes scanned the nearby tables. Kate and she were in a corner, almost beneath the stairway that led to the second level and the notorious holosuites, but the Vulcan's attitude clearly stated that it paid to take no chances. T'Val dropped her voice to an even softer whisper. ". . . Starfleet Captain Jean-Luc Picard."

Kate's eyes widened. How could such a thing be possible? Even here?

T'Val continued. "After that, Kirk was once again thought to have perished almost immediately on the backwater planet where Picard retrieved him. But a year later, to everyone's surprise, he returned. A Romulan faction had used Borg technology to . . ." The Vulcan searched for the correct terminology.

"Bring him back to life?" Kate said.

But T'Val shook her head. "Logic dictates that because he lives today, he did not die then. It is more accurate to think of Kirk experiencing a momentary interruption in normal biological processes."

Kate had heard none of this before. "And then what?"

T'Val steepled her fingers, the fingertips of her natural right hand almost but not quite aligned with the crude bionic structure that served as her left hand. "And then, most of what followed is not part of the official record. It must be considered that, perhaps, Starfleet would prefer to keep the knowledge of Kirk's return a secret. Unofficially, it is known that two years ago, in a classified operation, Starfleet prevented a Borg-Romulan alliance from invading the Federation. They did so by undertaking an unprecedented preemptive assault on what they believed might have been the Borg homeworld. Last year, the Borg response to that assault was the launch of a desperate, single-ship attack on Earth in which, unconfirmed reports suggest, the Borg created a chronometric passage to Earth's past, and attempted to change that planet's history."

Her mind swimming with all she was learning, Kate sat back in her chair and watched as Morn was led from the bar by a security officer, also in a Bajoran uniform, who bore a strangely planed face, as if he were a sculpture half-completed. She was surprised to see the nervous Ferengi pat Morn on the back. The gesture seemed one of support, yet Kate saw its true intent as it diverted attention from the Ferengi's other hand slipping into the hulking alien's belt and reappearing with a bar of latinum.

Kate was not the only one to have noticed the maneuver. The smooth-faced security officer stopped, faced the Ferengi, and held out his hand with an expression of tired disgust.

The Ferengi feigned innocence for a few moments as he muttered something about "damages." Then, looking equally disgusted with the security officer and the universe in general, he shrugged and surrendered the latinum.

He doesn't know how good he's got it here, Kate thought. She looked around the bar. *None of these people do.*

"And Kirk survived all of that?" Kate asked.

"He was not involved in defending Earth from the Borg. But last year, again under strict conditions of secrecy, he played a key role in resolving the virogen crisis."

"And now . . . ?"

"And now, as best our sources can ascertain, he has withdrawn from all contact with the universe at large. Not even the war with the Dominion has drawn him out. In effect, he has retired. To a world named Chal."

Kate was intrigued. "A Klingon word?"

The Vulcan nodded. "'Heaven.' The one place where no one would expect to find Kirk. The colony on Chal was established more than a century ago by the Klingons and Romulans. A military installation to house a doomsday weapon, in case the empires lost what they expected to be an all-out war with the Federation."

Kate rubbed at a bead of moisture on the table. It was still a novelty to sit in a public place and not be afraid of being arbitrarily arrested. It was as refreshing as the new civilian clothes she wore, and the room she had rented in the habitat ring, a room she didn't have to share and where she could stand in the sonic shower all day if she wanted. The slight inconvenience of cutting her hair to bristle-short length and dyeing it flame red, as part of a disguise, was an inconsequential price to pay. She was certain that out of uniform, no one would recognize her, especially where they did not expect to find her. "If Kirk's retired, what makes our sources think that he has access to the material we need?"

"Starfleet honors its heroes."

Kate almost gagged at the term. "Hero? *Kirk?*"

"Remember where you are," T'Val cautioned her. "Following its standard policy to support personnel that have been temporally translocated, Starfleet stands ready to offer any aid and assistance to the famous Captain Kirk, at any time. Last year, he was even offered a position on the science vessel *Tobias.* He refused, but the Fleet would welcome a chance to reclaim one of its own, especially one with so much . . . experience."

Kate nodded, a sour smile on her face. All around her and T'Val, the bar was returning to normal. Or, at least, as normal as any bar run by a Ferengi could be. "If Kirk is such a hero, if he's held in such high regard, why don't we just *ask* him for what we need?"

The Vulcan raised a skeptical eyebrow. "Given all you know," she said, "would you trust him?"

"Hell, no. How could I?"

"Precisely. Thus, we must place Kirk in a situation in which he will have no choice but to accept the sincerity of our request, and the inevitability of his compliance."

Kate studied the image on the padd. Automatic waves of revulsion swept through her. "He was never the sort to respond to threats."

"Threats, no," the Vulcan agreed. "But logic, yes."

"T'Val, whatever else he is, Kirk is no Vulcan. What if logic doesn't work?"

The Vulcan's face became an impassive slate. "Logic *always* works. And since total secrecy—for ourselves and our activities—must be maintained, if James T. Kirk does not acquiesce to our requests, then we must do what logic demands."

Kate didn't need to have it explained to her. "We kill him."

"Precisely," the Vulcan said. "James Kirk has retired. For whatever reason, he has decided he has nothing else to contribute to this universe. But he can still serve us. And, if he will not, then he has no reason to live."

"I could have told you that." Kate stared down at the image of Kirk on the padd. "In a way, I hope he doesn't cooperate. I think I would enjoy killing him."

For the briefest of instants, T'Val's face was transformed by a remarkable expression of emotion—unfiltered hate and anger. "I understand," she said, and that emotion was in her voice as well as her eyes. Then, just as quickly, she regained her composure.

Kate held her finger above the padd's delete control, hesitated for just a moment of sweet anticipation, then pressed it. James T. Kirk was wiped from the device's memory as if he had been no more than a dream. Or a nightmare.

Erasing the detested image brought fierce pleasure. No question about it. For all he had done to her and her people, she would relish killing Kirk. She turned to her companion.

"Maybe after he's helped us," she said to T'Val, "you and I can kill him anyway."

The Vulcan's gaze was fixed on the blank padd display, and even Kate could read the un-Vulcanlike desire for revenge simmering beneath the surface. "Yes, we could," T'Val said. "One way or another, James Tiberius Kirk must die."

ONE

His shadow stretched before him in the blazing light of Chal's twin suns, but James T. Kirk stood alone.

For a year he had known that this day would come. This final moment when all he had worked for on this world would end in victory, or in final, ignominious defeat.

All or nothing.

It was the way Kirk liked it.

The hot suns of Chal burned at his back. But he did not let their assault deter him from what he must do—

Now!

With a sharp intake of breath, Kirk wrapped his arms around the wrinkled gray covering of his enemy—the beast that had relentlessly mocked him all through the year.

His muscles strained. Sweat poured from him.

His vision blurred with the effort.

All or nothing.

And then—

Movement!

He was doing it! He dug in his feet, struggled as he had never struggled in his life until—

—with a startling *crack* a band of fire shot through his

7

lower back like a phaser burst and he collapsed to the soil of
Chal, gasping in agony.

James T. Kirk's back had gone out.

Again.

And the malevolent tree stump, that last gnarled mound of
deadwood that was the final obstacle in the field he had
cleared, the field where his new house would be built and his
garden planted, remained in place. Mocking him still.

Kirk tried to sit up.

His back made him reconsider the idea.

He lay there for an endless time, finger tapping the soil. The
pain did not bother him so much as the forced inactivity.
Where's Dr. McCoy when you need him? he thought.

Then a shadow fell over him. A very short shadow. The
sound of its owner's approach so silent he had been taken by
surprise.

"What'sa matter, mister? You having a nap?"

Kirk raised his hand to shield his eyes as he stared up at . . .
The child's name escaped him.

"Who are you?" Kirk asked.

The young boy, no more than six, put one finger up his nose
as if performing exploratory brain surgery on himself.
"Memlon."

Kirk remembered him now. Memlon lived two farms along
the road to City. Like most of the people of Chal, his features
combined a suggestion of Klingon head ridges with a slight
Romulan point to his ears. Like those of most children
everywhere, the knees of his white trousers were smudged
with grass, his cheeks with dirt.

"Do your parents know where you are?" Kirk asked,
hoping to send him on his way.

"Uh-huh." Memlon nodded slowly as he withdrew his
finger from his nose to hold up his right hand to show Kirk his
subspace locator bracelet, a civilian spin-off from Starfleet's
communicators.

"Then isn't there something else you should be doing?"

Memlon wiped his finger on the white tunic he wore. The tunic showed evidence of previous similar maneuvers. The child shook his head. "What are *you* doing?"

Kirk sighed as he realized that his back still wasn't going to let him sit up. So he rolled onto his side and pushed himself into a sitting position . . . slowly. "I am trying . . . to remove that tree stump . . . from what will be my new dining room."

Memlon studied the twisted stump with the practiced eye of a six-year-old who had all the answers. "Don't you got a phaser?"

"No. I don't . . . got a phaser."

"My mom has a phaser." Memlon drew a bead on the stump with his finger, then did a remarkably realistic imitation of a phaser's transonic squeal, followed by a less-than-realistic "Pow!" The child looked back at Kirk with an expression of pity. "You want me to ask my mom if you can borrow it?"

"No. I am going to take that stump out by myself. With my own hands."

The child stared at Kirk as if the adult had suddenly begun speaking in an ancient Vulcan dialect. "Why?"

"Memlon," Kirk said. "Look around this field. Do you remember what it was like last year?"

Memlon held up his hand, fingers spread. "I'm six," he announced. As an afterthought, he held up one finger from his other hand as well.

Kirk took that to mean that Memlon had no memory of what this field used to look like. But Kirk did.

Three years ago, it had been like any other part of Chal's legendarily beautiful tropical islands: a slice of paradise, an Eden. Two years ago, the planet's plant life had been deliberately exposed to a virogen—a hideous disease organism which had reduced Chal's islands to an apocalyptic landscape of brown stubble and withered yellow vegetation. Not a flower had bloomed on the planet in more than a year.

But then, in that same year, Kirk had returned to this world eight decades after his "death" during the maiden voyage of the *Enterprise*-B. With Spock and McCoy, and with Captain Jean-Luc Picard and his new generation of Starfleet's finest, Kirk had discovered the conspiracy that had inflicted that hideous act of environmental terrorism on the worlds of the Federation. With the interplanetary civilizations of the Alpha and Beta Quadrants on the brink of environmental collapse, he and his allies had helped the Federation defeat the Vulcan Symmetrist movement. McCoy came up with an antivirogen, and the ecosystems of a hundred worlds were now being restored through their own natural healing processes.

Kirk had not saved the Federation, but he had bought it extra time to consider the fate that awaited it. In the next thirty years, he knew, and now others did too, that a new strategy of expansion and exploration must be embraced to allow humanity, and all the people of the galaxy, to live as *part* of the galactic ecology, not as its exploiters and spoilers. Otherwise, the next time environmental crisis struck, there would be no last-minute redemption.

But that was a challenge for Picard and his contemporaries. Kirk had fought his own war, too many times. So he had once again returned to Chal, and to his love, Teilani.

The spaceman had hung up his rockets. He was on this world to stay. To find a simpler life.

He had found it in this small patch of forest.

It was no more than a clearing in the midst of newly reborn vegetation, alive with birds and insects, ringed by vibrant green leaves, wreathed with flowers of uncountable colors. But it was Kirk's new home, new world, new universe.

A year ago, Teilani at his side, her hand in his, their hearts entwined, Kirk had stood in this clearing and, in an electrifying moment of self-realization, understood that he *was* Chal.

Born of conflict.

Subjected to incredible trials that had brought both to the edge of extinction.

And now, against all odds and expectations, reborn.

Kirk had never been one to waste the moments of his life, though he had too often been driven by his heart and by the moment, not by his intellect and reflection.

Here in this field, where his mind's eye in that instant had seen a simple wooden home, ringed by a veranda, powered by a simple windmill, and had seen the crops in the plots of soil to be carefully tended, Kirk resolved that his life would change.

Teilani had looked at him then, into his eyes, and so great was their love, so close their connection, that Kirk had not had to explain a word of what had arisen in his mind.

"You're right," Teilani had said with perfect understanding. "We'll build here. A house. A home."

And so in this field, Kirk had toiled.

Each tree he had cut down had been carefully stripped and planed to be used for that dwelling, so that nature's bounty wasn't squandered. Each tree had been replaced by a new seedling, precisely planted to provide shade for that dwelling and to maintain the balance of this world, so that nature was respected.

With a team of *ordovers*—the horned, horselike beasts of burden of Chal—pulling a hand-forged plow, Kirk had leveled the hillocks and filled in the depressions. He had carried the rocks that now strengthened the bank of the stream that flowed at the edge of the clearing. His skin had darkened beneath the suns of Chal, and since he no longer ate the precisely fortified and artificially enhanced foods of Starfleet, his hair had become threaded with silver. But each week, the rocks had become easier to lift, the ax easier to swing. New purpose had given him new strength and vitality.

The first time he had come to Chal, more than eighty years ago, he had believed his life to be at its end. The *Enterprise*-B was about to be launched. His career was over. The universe had seemed to have no more need for James T. Kirk. Had his life truly ended when history had first recorded it on that maiden flight of the new *Enterprise,* it would have been fitting. What additional contributions could be expected of him? How much more could the universe demand?

But as Spock was fond of reminding him, there were always possibilities. And Kirk felt certain that not even the Guardian of Forever could have predicted all the further adventures that had remained for him. Kirk himself still could not fully comprehend the gifts that life had bestowed upon him, and how his career had continued past any expectation or dream he had held at its beginning.

But, at last, even those adventures had come to an end, and it was to Chal he had come home.

Thus, where once he had roamed the galaxy, now he seldom strayed farther than the small cabin he shared with Teilani, and this field where he toiled. At this time in his life, after all he had accomplished, there was challenge here enough.

And the focus of that challenge was that one last miserable stump.

"Are you okay, mister?"

Kirk blinked at the little boy. "What?"

"Were you asleep?"

"I was thinking."

The child nodded sagely. "That's what my dad says when he lies on the hammock on the porch. He snores a lot when he thinks. Do you snore?"

Kirk was glad Teilani wasn't here to answer that question. "No," he said.

"We're you thinkin' about the stump?"

"I was."

"How come you don't blow it up?"

This time, Kirk thought about the problem at hand: how to explain to a child the reasoning of an adult. "Memlon, someday, when you're grown, you're going to pass by this field. And there will be a house built right where we're standing—"

"You're not standing, mister."

Kirk ignored him. "—where we are right now. And you'll see the crops, and the trees, and you'll be able to say to your children, Jim Kirk made that field the way it is. He planted every tree, took out every rock and stump, hammered every nail into every board of that house. That's Jim Kirk's field."

Kirk smiled as he contemplated that image. He wanted to build something with his own two hands. Create something that was uniquely his.

But Memlon frowned. "Who's Jim Kirk?"

Kirk sighed. He remembered speaking with computers that were as exasperating as this child. "I am."

The boy peered at him suspiciously. "Are you . . . *Cap'n* Kirk?"

Here we go, Kirk thought. Even after so many years, that old rank still followed him. Haunted him. The two great truths of the universe were that the future could never be foreseen, the past never escaped.

"Yes, I am," Kirk said.

Memlon didn't seem convinced. He leaned forward as if he might be able to see right through Kirk. "You don't *look* crazy."

Kirk tried to stand but his back screamed at him, making him grimace again. He coughed to cover the sudden expression of discomfort as he remained planted on the ground. "Who . . . says I'm crazy?"

Memlon shrugged. "Everybody."

"Why?"

The shrug became more exaggerated. "I dunno."

"Memlon . . ."

The sound of that new voice was like a wave of cool water to Kirk. He turned quickly, as if he were a teenager again, awaiting his first love at a secret rendezvous. "Teilani!"

And Teilani rode into the clearing, a vision, a dream come to life, her white wrap billowing from her as she sat bareback on Iowa Dream. The horse was a spectacular animal, a genetic re-creation of one of Earth's antique breeds, known as

13

a quarter horse. He had been a gift from Picard—a peace offering, Kirk suspected, considering the tension that had still remained between them after their last encounter.

Iowa Dream—the name chosen by Picard as well, in memory of an ancient champion and their own first meeting—stepped precisely from the trail to the center of the clearing, as magnificent as any other manifestation of nature on this planet.

Kirk didn't even bother to try to stand—he knew he couldn't make it—and he could see the look of amusement on Teilani's lovely face as she realized why he remained seated on the ground.

Memlon, on the other hand, shot off toward Teilani like a photon torpedo. *"ghojmoHwl'! ghojmoHwl'!"* he shouted. It was the Klingon word for "teacher," and Kirk realized that the child must be part of Teilani's weekly reading group.

Teilani expertly dismounted, her simple white leggings and tunic floating across her lithe body like wisps of clouds. Kirk had never seen anyone more beautiful, and in this setting, on this world, at this instant, his heart ached with his love for her.

Teilani walked over to Kirk, holding Memlon's hand, her bare feet sinking into the rich soil of Chal. She glanced at the stump. "The beast still mocks you?" she asked gravely.

"It started to move," Kirk said.

Teilani gave him a knowing smile. "But your back moved more?"

Kirk's face admitted the truth.

Teilani untangled her hand from Memlon's, then held out both to Kirk. "Keep it straight," she said with the voice of experience. "Use your legs."

Keeping his back rigid, Kirk pulled himself up with Teilani as his brace. Then his lips were only centimeters from hers, and it was as if time had stopped in that moment, each detail of her appearance only serving to entrance him once again.

In human terms, Teilani might appear to be fifty, though like that of a Vulcan's, her unique genetic heritage thoroughly concealed the fact that she had lived for more than a century. Her hair, tied back for riding, was even more silvered than Kirk's, though to his eyes, it was as if she were wreathed in stars.

From the subtle ridges of her brow, past an eye and across one cheek, the angry slash of a virogen scar still flared. The same genetic engineering that had enhanced her health and longevity had also served to make her flesh resistant to protoplaser treatment. McCoy had proposed an experimental grafting procedure that might reduce the raised evidence of the scar tissue, making it possible to disguise the disfigurement with makeup. But Teilani had told him, No.

Whether it was the Klingon in her that made her choose to wear the blemish to her beauty with honor, or that she had come to understand that outward appearance meant nothing when measured against those qualities that dwelt within a warrior's heart, Kirk didn't know. And he didn't care. For when he looked at Teilani, he no longer saw the scar, nor the silvered hair, nor the lines that age brought even to those of Chal.

He saw only the woman he loved. And no sight could be more beautiful.

Kirk leaned forward to brush his lips against hers.

And instantly tensed as his back went into a spasm of pain.

Teilani was not sympathetic. "Five minutes at the clinic could take care of that for the next five years."

"I'll keep doing my exercises," Kirk told her. "No more protoplasers, no more forcefield readjustments."

Teilani tapped his forehead. "No more sense."

He took her hand. Kissed her finger. Was sorry Memlon was here. This clearing held many special memories for Kirk and his love.

The child tugged on Teilani's tunic.

"Yes?" Teilani said with the forbearance of a born teacher.

"*ghojmoHwl'*, that's Cap'n Kirk!"

Teilani clapped her hands in surprise. "He is?"

Memlon nodded. "You be careful," he warned his teacher.

Teilani smiled at Kirk's look of consternation. "And why is that?" she asked with great seriousness.

"I'm crazy," Kirk explained.

He recognized the tremble that came to Teilani's lips when she tried not to laugh, and realized she had heard that conclusion before. "Who says?" she asked.

"Everyone," Kirk told her before Memlon could.

"I see. Well, if everyone says it, it must be true."

Memlon tugged on Teilani's tunic again.

"He doesn't got a phaser, neither."

"I know."

Memlon's eyes widened in surprise. "You do?"

"And he doesn't got a replicator," Teilani said. "No tricorder. No communicator. No computer."

Memlon's mouth hung open. "Not even a padd?"

Teilani shook her head. "Not even a padd."

Memlon gazed at Kirk as if trying to make sense of a creature from another dimension. "How come?"

"Because we depend too much on machines," Kirk told the boy. "We've given up too much of our independence, too much of our connection to the worlds around us. We've cut ourselves off from the experiences that make us human, from the knowledge that we are part of nature."

Memlon blinked, not a gram of comprehension in him.

"Do you understand a single word I've said?"

"Nope."

Teilani knelt down to hold the child's hands. "Memlon, it's getting close to supper time. I think you should be going home."

Memlon nodded. "All right, *ghojmoHwl'*." He drew his

16

hands away, hesitated, then threw his arms around Teilani's neck and hugged her.

Teilani hugged him back, gave him a kiss on his ridges, and stood up laughing as Memlon ran off toward the path.

Then she slipped her arm around Kirk—very carefully.

"Do they really think I'm crazy?" Kirk asked.

"Who?" Teilani replied innocently.

Kirk frowned. "Everyone."

"They don't understand you."

"But you do?"

Teilani lightly traced her fingers down the opening of Kirk's tunic. "I love you, James. But I'll never understand you."

Kirk took her errant hand before it could distract him further. "Why do they feel that way?"

Teilani seemed surprised he could even ask that question. "Because of the way you deny your past."

"I don't deny it."

"But you do. Across the Federation, children learn your name in school. Starfleet cadets study your logs from the first year of the Academy to their graduate studies. They've written books about you, created data tapes, there's even that opera on *Qo'Nos*—"

Kirk held up his hands, cutting off the recitation. "Those aren't me. They're reflections, interpretations. They've . . . taken on a life of their own."

"I know that. But they're also an indication of the effect you've had on the lives of millions, billions of beings. You can't deny that. And it's wrong of you to try."

"I don't . . . deny what I've done."

Teilani became serious, and Kirk recognized he was not looking into the eyes of his lover, but of Chal's greatest diplomat, the woman who had successfully brought this troubled world into the Federation.

"You do deny it, James. Every day."

Kirk said nothing.

"You've fought gods. You've changed the course of history. You've walked more worlds than most people will ever even see in tapes. And after all that, you've spent the last year of your life doing battle with . . . with a tree stump. A tree stump you could deal with in a second with a phaser, or in a minute with the same team of *ordovers* you used to level the field."

Kirk held out his hands to her. "I want this to be our home. A home that I build for us."

Teilani sighed as if this discussion were one they had had every day. In a way, it was. "James, *you* are my home. Where you are, my heart follows."

"And my heart is here, on Chal."

But Teilani, eyes full of love, shook her head. "I know that's what you tell yourself. But that's not what you believe. Not really."

Kirk was silent, not wanting to argue. It *was* what he believed. It *had* to be.

He felt Teilani's hand caress his cheek.

"I don't know which is more stubborn," she said. "You or that stump."

Kirk took her hand, looked at her again, afraid of what he must ask. "Are you telling me it's time to go?"

Of all the possible responses to that terrible question, Teilani chose to smile, with all the warmth of her planet's suns.

"Listen to you, James. It's always all or nothing. But life isn't like that. You have to find a balance."

Kirk didn't understand. "That's what I've found here."

"You mean, that's what you've sought. But you don't belong in this field any longer."

Kirk gazed around, seeing all his dreams in perfect completion. "This is my home."

"Your home will always be a place to return to, James."

Kirk didn't know if the sharp sorrow that now invaded him

was because of the thought of leaving Chal, and Teilani, or because, somehow, he knew she was right.

"There's nothing more for me to do out there, Teilani. They don't need me anymore. You do. Here."

Teilani pursed her lips in disbelief. "Must I also teach you to be selfish? Don't leave Chal or me because you feel you have to do something for someone. Leave for yourself."

"But where would I go?" he asked.

She spread her arms as if any part of the universe was his for the taking. "You get a hundred invitations every month. Choose one. Any one."

Kirk narrowed his eyes at Teilani. "You *are* trying to get rid of me." But then Kirk glimpsed in her the same sorrow he felt.

"James, I know you. If you don't go now, if you don't admit what's in your heart, then the restlessness and frustration will build in you, it will fester in you, until one day you will wake up and it will be all or nothing again. Then you'll turn your back on Chal, and on me, and leave us to search for something you still don't understand."

Kirk squeezed Teilani's hand as if to make his flesh fuse with hers. "Never."

"Balance, James. In your heart, there will always be room for Chal and me and . . ." She looked up, as if she could see the stars behind the brilliant blue sky of her world. ". . . all the rest. Go now, and you might learn that. Go later, and you never will."

"I don't want to leave you."

"I don't want you here until you understand that being here is right."

Kirk stared at the stump. It was gnarled and twisted, its spreading roots inseparable from the soil, powerfully linked with Chal.

It was also dead.

Is that why he had expended so much time on his battle

with the stump? Had his mind made it the symbol of his own battle to remain on Chal, accepting his new role as a man of quiet contemplation?

"Will you come with me?" he asked.

"Do *you* understand a single word *I've* said?"

Kirk smiled at her, tried a different, more playful tact. "Are you certain you can get along without me?"

Teilani gave a tug to the drawstring of his tunic, pulling it open, letting the breeze flutter over his chest, to be followed by her hand.

"I have a plan," she said.

"Do you?" Kirk asked as her other hand found her own drawstring, and opened that as well.

"You might be leaving Chal," she whispered as she drew near, "but you will always be here with me."

Kirk felt his breathing falter as she kissed his neck and her nails glided under his tunic, across his back. Then he glanced around, suddenly aware they were in the middle of the field.

Iowa Dream unconcernedly munched on some tufts of string grass, ignoring what his human companions were up to. But still, there might be other watchers.

"What about Memlon?" Kirk asked.

"He'll be halfway home," Teilani breathed into his ear as she tugged at the rest of his clothes. Then she straightened up, looked Kirk in his eyes. "What do you think of him?"

Kirk was surprised by the question. It wasn't what he was thinking about now. "He needs someone to explain things to him."

"You'd be good at that," Teilani said.

Kirk had no idea what she meant. And for the moment, he had no interest in pursuing the matter.

He cradled her head in his hands, kissed her head ridges, the points of her ears, inhaled the fragrant scent of her sun-warmed hair.

"I like this plan of yours," he said.

"I thought you'd approve."

"But maybe, with my back, this isn't the right time."

She smiled at him, eyes half open, breath shallow, lips parted. "Leave that to me." Then she smiled at him wickedly. "As someone once said, resistance is futile."

Kirk laughed. Beneath the suns of Chal, their shadows joined to become one. And he found peace in those timeless moments, a shield against the activity he must undertake in the next few days.

Because he knew Teilani was right. He needed to venture out into the universe again. Even though his secret fear was that there were no more challenges out there for him to face.

What need could the universe possibly have for a hero whose time had passed?

TWO

---☆---

Like a caged predator, Jean-Luc Picard paced the bridge of the *Enterprise,* ignoring the sporadic vibrations that shook it. Ten years ago, he might have accepted an assignment like this. But today, he could only see it as a waste. Of his ship, of his crew, and of his time.

And right now, to Picard, there was no commodity more precious.

As Picard strode along the raised deck encircling the bridge, another shudder passed through the *Enterprise.* The subspace pressure waves that pummeled the ship were not dangerous, merely annoying. Picard could ignore them, though he worried that they might be putting his crew on edge despite the monotony of their current duty. As the ship's artificial gravity field and inertial dampers compensated for the buffeting, Picard paused behind the sole member of his crew who did not appear to take umbrage at having the captain read over his shoulder. But this time even Data turned back to him from his science station.

"Captain, your observation of my sensor readings will not cause them to proceed more rapidly."

Picard nodded. When even an android reacted to his

impatience, he knew he had gone too far. "You're right, Data. A watched pot never boils."

Data observed the captain carefully. "Sir, at Commander Riker's suggestion, I once undertook a detailed analysis of that assumption. My research showed that at normal atmospheric pressure of seven hundred and sixty torr and in the presence of a heat source capable of delivering a temperature of one hundred Celsius degrees to an arbitrary mass of water, a watched pot *always* boils. At the macroscopic scale, the quantum-observer effect is trivial." Data paused, as if remembering something else from his detailed analysis. "Of course, if there is a defect in the observer's timing mechanism, from personal experience I can relate that subjective observations do appear to outweigh the empirical and—"

Picard knew when he had been told off. "Carry on, Mr. Data."

Data turned back to his sensor controls.

As Picard stepped away from Data's station, he caught Riker grinning at him. His executive officer was working at a secondary science station on the other side of the bridge. Picard walked toward him, tapping a clenched fist against the side of his leg.

"Don't tell me you're enjoying this duty," he said.

Riker's smile broadened. "I wasn't aware I had a choice, sir."

Picard didn't understand what was wrong with everyone. "Will, this is the flagship of the Fleet. The most sophisticated piece of machinery ever built by humanity. She's designed for . . . for exploration, blazing new ground, taking action."

"I think you're describing her captain."

But Picard was not to be swayed. He looked at the virtual main screen, where the Goldin Discontinuity was displayed in all its writhing, multicolored glory. Flashes of antiproton energy, appearing to be little more than lightning strikes despite their solar-system-size scale, flickered among the billowing plasma storms.

"This region of space is no different from a dozen others," Picard said. "Two science vessels could cover it more efficiently than even this ship. And they're built for it. This duty is what their crews train for."

Riker stood up and stretched, still watching the stream of data that played across his station's displays. "Sir, if this were just a science mission, you'd be right. But what if we find what we don't want to find?"

Picard had had this argument before. Specifically, with Fleet Admiral Alynna Nechayev at Starbase 310. With remarkable stubbornness, even for her, the admiral had insisted that the *Enterprise* be assigned to the Goldin Discontinuity. Picard had fought against that decision. And he had lost. He had no desire to suffer the same fate at the hands of his Number One. But he couldn't help himself.

"There're no Cardassians out there, Will."

"With the way the plasma storms disrupt our sensors, there could be an entire fleet riding our wake and we'd never know it."

"We're too deep within Federation territory. The Cardassians could never make the crossing undetected."

Riker didn't offer any more protestations, but Picard already knew how the rest of the argument would play out. Since the main hostilities of the war with the Dominion had appeared to be in momentary abeyance, some factions within the Cardassian ruling elite had become obsessed with finding a new wormhole passage to the Gamma Quadrant. During the war, Cardassia even had attempted to build an artificial wormhole, deep in Cardassian space.

Even if that attempt had been successful—and Picard and his crew had ensured that it was not—it would still have offered only a sporadic, partial connection to the Gamma Quadrant. All evidence supported the conclusion that only stable wormholes were useful for sustained transport, yet no theory had yet been accepted as to why the Bajoran wormhole should exist at all.

Certainly, the fact that intelligent beings dwelt within it—aliens or prophets depending on one's philosophical leanings—was considered a key factor in the wormhole's capabilities. But Starfleet scientists, charged with keeping current with Cardassian investigations, if not surpassing them, had recently begun to analyze the nature of space-time around the Bajoran system. As a result, several intriguing theories concerning the Badlands—a region of space near the Cardassian border, filled with plasma storms—had been developed.

It might be possible, both Starfleet and Cardassian scientists had concluded, that the presence of a Badlands-type section of space was an indication that the local continuum could maintain a stable wormhole. Thus, throughout the Alpha and Beta Quadrants, Starfleet was returning to previously mapped regions of plasma storms to see if more detailed study could reveal a connection between them and wormholes.

On the frontier, several Starfleet vessels had already had run-ins with Cardassian ships, leaving no doubt that the Cardassians were pursuing the same line of research. A new technological race had begun.

The Institute for Starfleet Strategic Initiatives had declared that the ability to create stable wormholes between any two points in space would be a development that could render the Cochrane drive—and, therefore, every warp vessel in Starfleet—obsolete.

Thus the *Enterprise* had been assigned to remap the Goldin Discontinuity, a task a dozen other vessels might have handled.

But only the *Enterprise,* Admiral Nechayev had argued in her most persuasive manner, could handle what might transpire if a Cardassian task force were discovered deep within Federation space.

This is the same Starfleet that didn't want me to take part in the defense of Earth when the Borg attacked, Picard had thought bitterly at the time. But he had accepted his orders. As Riker had said, it was not as if he had had a choice.

"Engineering to Captain Picard."

Geordi La Forge's voice over the bridge speakers was a welcome distraction to Picard. He turned away from Riker. "Picard here."

"Captain, the plasma storms are really eating into our shields. We could use another layover in normal space to recalibrate."

Picard looked ahead to Lieutenant Karo, the new Bolian conn officer. "Mr. Karo, what is current shield strength?"

"Eighty-four percent," the Bolian answered crisply.

"We do not appear to be in any immediate danger," Picard replied to La Forge.

"Not right now," the engineer answered. "But the way these storms work, we could experience a sudden drop to ten percent in less than a minute, with no warning."

Picard hesitated. As much as he wanted to warp out of the Goldin Discontinuity, he knew that each minute spent leaving and reentering the region of plasma storms delayed the ultimate conclusion of the mission.

Yet how could he put the *Enterprise* at risk for purely personal reasons?

"Very well," Picard said without enthusiasm. "Mr. Karo, plot a course to the closest clear region of space from our position at the end of this sector sweep." Picard read the figures on Riker's secondary science display. "That will allow us to leave the area in . . . fifteen minutes, Mr. La Forge. Will that be suitable?"

"Yes, sir. La Forge out."

Picard turned back to Riker. "I've just added a day to this interminable mission."

Riker's smile faded. "Sir, we've undertaken research like this a hundred times before. It's standard duty."

That was the point Picard had been trying to make to

anyone who would listen. "Exactly, Number One. But this is not a standard ship."

Riker appeared to misunderstand. "What I mean to say is, have you considered taking a few days off? Head out on a holodeck adventure. Dixon Hill, a cross-country ride, anything. I *can* mind the store, sir."

Picard didn't understand Riker's equanimity. "After all we've done, how can you stand this . . . inactivity?"

Riker stepped closer, lowered his voice. "Jean-Luc, it goes with the job. We can't fight the Borg every day."

Then what's the point? Picard wanted to say. If he wasn't out here accomplishing something worthwhile, something that demanded the best and the most of him and his crew, then what was the reason for being out here at all?

Riker seemed to sense the sudden resentment-filled frustration that had risen in his commanding officer. "Captain . . . you've been living in your ready room for weeks. You need to get off the bridge."

Picard's first impulse was to demand to know why Riker thought he could criticize his commanding officer. But he realized that knee-jerk reaction was born of something other than Riker's justifiable concern.

"You're right, Will," Picard forced himself to say, though he couldn't believe it. "I do need a change in routine. A few hours and—"

"A few days, sir. If anything happens, you're only as far as the turbolift."

Because Picard did not want to accept Riker's suggestion, he did accept it. A captain was only as good as his crew, and if he couldn't trust their judgment, then what were they doing on his ship?

"A day," Picard said in compromise.

"A day," Riker agreed. He put his hand on the back of his duty chair, about to sit in it again once the captain had left.

But Picard hesitated. He looked around the bridge, tugged on his uniform jacket.

Riker gestured to the closer turbolift, urging his captain on. "If we find Cardassians, you'll be the first to know."

Picard accepted that he couldn't put it off any longer. The bridge shook gently. It reminded him of being on the deck of an actual, seagoing vessel. Perhaps a holodeck cruise to the old South Pacific would be in order. "You have the bridge, Commander. I'll be in my quarters if you—"

Then Data's voice, calm yet urgent, cut off all other conversation on the bridge.

"Commander Riker—I have detected an antitachyon surge, bearing zero two eight, mark ten."

The deck pitched in response to a powerful pressure wave. Riker moved past Picard as if the captain had already left the bridge, and took up position in the center chair. "Distance?" he called out.

"There is so much subspace distortion, I cannot be certain," Data said. "But no farther than five hundred thousand kilometers."

Picard steadied himself against a railing as the bridge bucked up again, fighting for equilibrium.

Riker leaned forward, gripping the arms of the command chair. "Mr. Karo, adjust course to head for the source of the antitachyon surge, full impulse." He looked up to the bridge's curved ceiling. "Bridge to Engineering. Geordi, we're going to need stable shields for the next few minutes. If you see them weakening, go to auxiliary power."

La Forge responded that he was standing by.

Picard remained at the back of the bridge, watching in silent amazement as his executive officer polled the bridge crew, quickly giving them their tasks. He knew as well as Riker that an antitachyon surge could be an indication of a weakening in space-time, perhaps marking the initial appearance of a quantum fluctuation. And a large enough quantum fluctuation could give rise to a wormhole. It was exactly the phenomenon the *Enterprise* had been sent out here to find. To be superfluous on his own bridge, especially at a time like this, was more than he was willing to accept, even if he had already given Riker the conn.

He kept one hand on the railing as he stepped down to the main level. "I'll take over, Commander."

Picard was surprised by the flash in Riker's eyes, as if he had forgotten that his captain was present, or as if he resented giving up command. But without hesitation, Riker left the chair and took his position on the left.

Picard settled into the center chair, trying to ignore the sudden sensation that the *Enterprise* herself was trying to throw him from it by her shudderings.

"Readings, Mr. Data?"

"New surges, Captain. Whatever is happening, is increasing in strength. We could be witnessing a wormhole opening."

The shaking of the bridge was constant now. The background hum of the dampers and the structural-integrity field generators rose in a deep whine that hummed from the deck and the bulkheads.

Riker leaned closer. "Shall I ready the probes, sir?"

Picard nodded, eyes fixed on the screen. The closer they moved to the origin point of the antitachyon surges, the more scrambled the visual image ahead became. It was like looking through a flurry of visual static smeared by doubled images and ghostlike overlays.

La Forge suddenly broke in over the speakers. "Captain— shields are dropping. Twenty percent in the past ten seconds."

"We're so close," Picard murmured to himself. "How much longer do we have, Mr. La Forge?"

"If this keeps up, no more than two minutes, sir. And when I switch to auxiliary power, we'll be down to thirty seconds."

Picard glanced at Riker, wondering if the commander could appreciate the irony of the situation. Something had finally happened, and the *Enterprise* would not be able to stay in the area to witness it.

"Mr. Karo," Picard called out. "Lay in an immediate course out of the Discontinuity. Prepare to engage on my mark."

"Aye, sir," the Bolian answered.

Then the main screen flared with an explosion of deep violet light and the *Enterprise* angled wildly, as if she had hit a brick wall in space.

Picard didn't bother waiting for La Forge's report. "Mr. Karo, en—"

And then, the bridge was still.

On the screen, static and plasma clouds still writhed. But the *Enterprise* was as smooth and level as if she were warping through empty space.

"Data?" Picard asked. In the shorthand he used with his crew, no more detailed question was needed.

"The surges have stopped, sir. And . . . according to my readings . . . a wormhole *might* have opened."

Picard was on his feet. He moved quickly to Data's station. "What do you mean, 'might'?"

Data was clearly puzzled by the information on his screens. "Sensor distortion is so strong, many of these readings are suspect. But I am confident that some form of extradimensional rift did momentarily manifest."

"Any sign of it now?" Picard asked. A mystery was almost as good as action. At least, it gave him and his crew something to do, instead of just being passive recorders of sensor readings.

"No sign of . . ." Data stopped. Readjusted several sensitivity selectors.

"What is it?" Picard asked.

"It is . . . a . . . ship, sir." Data looked up at the captain, his emotion chip allowing his surprise to be clearly evident in his expression. "And I am receiving a standard Starfleet friend-or-foe automated transmission."

Picard turned to the main screen. "There are no other Starfleet vessels assigned to this area," he said.

Also on his feet, Riker peered up at the screen. Amid the wash of static and interference, an elongated sensor shadow was coming into view.

"Can you read the ID code?" Picard asked.

"No, sir," Data answered. "There is too much interference . . . too much . . ."

The image on the screen was growing, though it still wasn't detailed enough for Picard to identify. For a few moments, it was almost as if he was seeing the detached saucer hull of another Sovereign-class starship, identical to the *Enterprise*.

Data spoke again. "Captain . . . I am picking up the transmission now . . . NCC . . . seven . . . four six . . . five six?"

Picard stepped back as if the deck had pitched. The hair on the back of his neck bristled. He had wanted something to happen, but this . . . ?

"My God," Riker said as the ship on the screen at last came into view.

Picard understood the emotion Riker displayed, because he felt it, too.

The ship on the screen appeared in full detail now. The name across her battered hull clear and unmistakable.

Applause started on the bridge, soon followed by cheers.

Picard couldn't blame his crew.

This was truly a moment for celebration.

Five years after being lost with all hands in the Delta Quadrant, the *Starship Voyager* had at last come home.

THREE

☆

"Captain Kirk, for a man of your astoundingly advanced age, you're lookin' in fine fettle indeed."

Kirk shot his eyes sideways past his glass of iced mint tea, blinked as if what he saw couldn't be real, then opened his mouth in surprise. "Scotty?!"

The familiar face of Chief Engineer Montgomery Scott burst into a wide grin as he saw Kirk's expression. "You were expecting your great-aunt Mabel?"

For a person whose survival had often depended on his ability to talk his way out of an unexpected situation, Kirk was uncharacteristically speechless. He thought he had become fully acclimated to this new era in which he lived. He had grown used to the new wrinkles that creased Spock's taciturn features. He had come to accept McCoy's pure white hair. And he had learned to accept the inevitable loss of a lifetime of friends and family.

But to see Scotty before him, virtually unchanged from the last hour they had been together on the bridge of the *Enterprise*-B . . . For a moment, Kirk felt dizzy.

It's the gravity, Kirk told himself. After all, this *was* his first trip back to Earth since he had beamed up to the new *Enterprise,* with Chekov and Scott, eighty-three years ago.

Earth's gravity was slightly stronger than Chal's, so he was still getting used to it. That must be the reason for his sudden feeling of light-headedness. What else could it be?

"Cat got your tongue?" Scott asked, clearly enjoying Kirk's momentary silence.

Then Kirk found his way past his surprise. It no longer mattered that he was on Earth, in the city of Montreal, surrounded by more than a thousand other temporal translocatees who had gathered for this conference. All that mattered was he had found a friend he feared had been lost with so many others.

"Scotty, you . . . look wonderful."

Scott frowned in good-humored disbelief. "Aye, and might I add you don't look a day over one hundred and twenty yerself."

For a few moments, Kirk and Scott stared at each other, each with a glass in hand, both oblivious now to the gala party that swirled around them on the immense antigrav platform that floated through the night. But neither said anything more, as if there were so much to be said that the words had been caught in a monumental systems failure.

Captain Morgan Bateson disrupted the awkward silence. "I would think you two would have more to say to each other," he said. "How long were you shipmates?"

Kirk looked back at the officer to whom he had just been speaking, grateful for his assistance. "Scotty was with me on . . . on my first five-year mission." Kirk shook his head in wonder. How many years, how many light-years had they both traversed to come together in this present moment—a moment neither one would have believed if they had been told about it at their careers' beginning?

"Aye," Scott said pointedly. "The first five-year mission, and every mission thereafter." He stepped forward to offer his hand to Bateson. "Sometimes I suspect the captain has a wee bit o' trouble remembering that."

The tall, bearded captain shook Scott's hand, and as the

33

two men spoke Kirk was surprised to realize that they knew each other, and had even worked together. Bateson was also a Starfleet officer from Kirk's and Scott's era. But where Scotty had deliberately placed himself in a risky transporter loop in order to survive the seventy-five years it had taken to be rescued from his crashed ship, Bateson and his entire crew and starship, the *Bozeman,* had been trapped for ninety years in a temporal causality loop by accident. Whatever the differences in their journeys, though, both Scott and Bateson wore Starfleet's latest duty uniform, with gray on their shoulders and black for the rest.

Kirk, who wore the simple clothes of a Vulcan traveler, frowned as the greetings ended. "Scotty, that's not true. Where would I be without you?"

The engineer sipped his drink, something green, and gave Kirk a questioning look. "You'd be right here, sir. It's been how long now? More than three years since ye came outta that Nexus whozzit." Scott smiled, but there was a recriminatory undercurrent to it. "And look at you. . . . You never write. You never call."

Kirk understood Scott's exasperation, but there was another side to his complaint, as well. "Scotty, I was . . . busy."

"Aye. I've heard that before."

Kirk saw Bateson's look of amusement, and he suddenly realized that as annoyed as Scott appeared to be, the engineer was pushing the moment for their audience. Kirk and Scott had been through too many adventures together, too many good times—and bad—for the bond between them to be completely severed by the differing demands of their separate careers. At least, Kirk hoped that was the case.

He held up his glass, used it to indicate the holographic banner that floated above the Île Ste-Hélène and the meticulously reconstructed pavilions of Expo '67 they floated past— BIENVENU VOYAGEURS A TRAVERS LE TEMPS / WELCOME TIME TRAVELERS.

"Let's leave the past behind us, Mr. Scott. We're all of us on a journey to the future."

"Some of us faster than others," Bateson added with a smile.

"We should go forward together," Kirk continued. "Not stumble over what's happened in the past." He held out his glass to Scott, hoping the engineer would join him in a toast.

Scott leaned forward and made a show of sniffing Kirk's tea. "That's quite poetic. Have ye been into the Romulan Ale again?"

Kirk frowned at Scott. He was being serious, audience or no. "Mr. Scott . . . ?"

Scott smiled, clinked his glass to Kirk's. "To the future, then. Goodness knows we've made our living from it long enough."

"How about to friendship?" Kirk asked.

Scott winked at him. "That'll be a question for you to answer, sir."

Kirk sighed. Scott wasn't letting him off easy. "After eighty years, Mr. Scott, I think you can forgo the 'sir.'"

A devilish twinkle came to the Scotsman's eyes with that. "Right you are . . . Jimmy!" Then Scott downed the rest of his drink in a single swallow, beaming as Captain Bateson laughed.

Kirk did not join in the fun his two companions appeared to be sharing. He wondered what Teilani was doing that moment. This was the longest he had been apart from her for more than a year.

"I'm sorry," Bateson said, stifling his laughter. "But you two . . . you *must* have served a long time together."

Kirk nodded.

"Aye," Scott said.

"It's different for me," Bateson continued. "Mostly because Mr. Scott here helped me to accept this new age. And my whole crew came through the loop with me, so I don't feel as isolated in this time. Almost all of us are here tonight."

Kirk followed Bateson's gaze to the milling crowd behind him.

"Did you ever think there'd be so many people pulled from their own eras?" Kirk asked.

" 'Tis a growing concern," Scott said. "Cryoships from the twenty-first century. Colony sleeper ships from the twenty-second. Temporal rifts. Warp malfunctions." He looked meaningfully at Kirk. "I've heard rumors that Starfleet located another sleeper ship from the Eugenics Wars. Another batch of Khan's supermen, they say. Being 'reeducated' on Alpha Centauri II."

Kirk made no comment, sipped his tea. Those were the problems of this century. They weren't his. Instead, he wondered if Teilani was sleeping. He pictured the way the moonlight always caught her hair in the bed they shared. Once, she had wakened to find him transfixed by that sight, unable to sleep. But she had a way of dealing with that.

But Bateson seemed to have a direct connection to Kirk's thoughts. "It's a common experience, for those of us who've jumped ahead by more than our natural lifetimes, to consider that the challenges of the present day are no longer our concern."

Kirk eyed Bateson attentively. Those words had been far too formal. "Captain, you sound suspiciously like a man who wants to make a point."

Bateson smiled, caught in the act. "Then I'll make it. I have been asked by Fleet Admiral Alynna Nechayev herself, to personally invite you to return to Starfleet."

Kirk wasn't surprised, but Scott nearly spit out a mouthful of ale.

"Ye cannae be serious, lad."

"But I am, Mr. Scott. And so is Starfleet. To use the vernacular of the era in which this World's Fair was first built, Command wants James T. Kirk back in the saddle."

Scott looked puzzled. Kirk knew why.

"Actually," Kirk said, "this World's Fair is from the twentieth century. The 'back in the saddle' is from the nineteenth."

Bateson shrugged. "What's a century among friends? The point is, we can all learn a great deal from the past." He looked out past the railings of the antigrav platform to where a large geodesic sphere passed by them, glittering in the onslaught of dozens of searchlights. Kirk found it odd that a structure whose design was so old could look so familiar— Buckminster Fuller's ancient principles of geodesics were still used to build colony domes throughout the Federation.

"Consider this reconstruction," Bateson said. "The Montreal Historical Society has reproduced in exacting detail a moment in time. Nineteen sixty-seven. Before the first moon landing. One hundred and twenty separate governments taking part in a celebration of the full range of humanity's achievements of the day. Can you imagine? One planet but *one hundred and twenty* governing bureaucracies? No wonder it was an era of confusion."

Kirk chewed his lip in contemplation. Each moment of this return to Earth had brought new insight into his desire to remain on Chal. Why were so many people so intent on looking to the past? Teilani had been right to make him take this trip—it truly served to make him long for home. "If it was an era of confusion," he said, "then why return to it?" The best days were those to come, Kirk knew. Always.

But Bateson disagreed. "As the great Vulcan philosopher Surak once said, 'Those who do not understand history are condemned to repeat it.' "

"Surak and a dozen others at least," Kirk replied. He scanned the crowd, looking for a server. He'd like another iced tea, though the way Bateson was going on, he'd settle for his first whiskey in almost a century.

"Neural gel packs," Scott said out of nowhere.

Bateson blinked at him. "I beg your pardon."

37

Kirk saw a tray-bearing woman in a . . . tuxedo. He didn't know from where he had pulled that obscure term, but he knew it was the correct one for the antique black-and-white costume she wore. Yet, though servers in the second half of the twentieth century might very well have worn tuxedos as a uniform, Kirk had his doubts about this server's short, flame red hair. That seemed to be a fashion from another era. She was already heading in his direction and he raised his hand to attract her attention. She nodded. Her smile was quite charming. It made him think of Teilani again.

"Neural gel packs," Scott said again. "Have ye ever heard of them?"

Kirk realized the question had been directed at him. He had no idea what the engineer meant.

"I'm afraid I haven't."

Scott shrugged elaborately. "Och, well, there ye go then."

Now Bateson joined Kirk in waiting for Scott to make whatever point he seemed to be groping toward.

"There I go where?" Kirk asked.

"Well, in your day, it was duotronics. All the computers, most of the equipment, everything had duotronic circuitry at its core."

"Duotronics I know," Kirk said.

"My point precisely," Scott said. "But what about isolinear chips? What about—" He cleared his throat as if making a grand announcement. "—neural gel packs. They're the new heart of the computers these days. And you, my friend, don't know a thing about them."

Kirk shrugged. "You're right. I don't. At least, I don't think I do."

"Which proves my point. Ye have no intention of returning to Starfleet. Otherwise, ye'd never let things like that slip past you."

Kirk nodded, seeing no need to argue, and no point at all to it. He hadn't read a technical paper in more than a year, and he was glad of it. The time was right for moving on in his life. Starfleet had shown it could get along without him. His days of action and adventure were finally at an end, and he didn't miss them.

Kirk raised his glass in a toast. "For once, Scotty, we're in perfect agreement."

But with that, Scott suddenly looked concerned. "Hmm. Then p'raps I should reconsider my position."

"Captain Kirk," the server said as she approached him, holding out her tray of drinks.

Kirk smiled at her, finding her husky voice pleasing, wondering how she knew his name. There were more than a thousand attendees at this conference, most of them right here on the antigrav platform that slowly turned to take in the enormous ski-jump-type structure of a glass-covered pavilion. Kirk didn't recognize the hammer-and-sickle design on the pavilion's red flag. Another inconsequential detail lost in the mists of history.

Kirk checked the server's tray, sorry to see there were no teas or Vulcan waters. He shook his head to refuse her offer of a new drink. Then he glanced at Bateson, wondering if he would like to make a selection.

But Bateson's face was creased in concentration as he stared at the woman. "Excuse me, but has anyone ever told you you bear a remarkable resemblance to—"

The phaser beam hit Bateson square in the chest before he could finish.

Kirk stared in confusion as the Starfleet captain stumbled back with a moan. Part of him understood that the beam could only have come from a miniaturized weapon that the server held under her tray. But this was Earth, the safest planet in the Federation. This was the future, an era of peace that Kirk had helped to bring into being. Despite the evidence of his eyes, Kirk's only thought was *This isn't happening.*

Then the server tossed her tray aside to reveal the small

"cricket" phaser she held between thumb and forefinger, and she pushed it up under Kirk's jaw, close enough that even the mildest stun setting could be fatal.

Somehow by accident or excellent placement, the pressure of the phaser seemed to be cutting off the flow of blood to Kirk's neck. He was aware only of the slow fall of his glass of tea as it slipped from his hand, then shattered on the patio floor.

He had some dim perception of the people nearby calling out in alarm, but as his vision narrowed he was aware only of the server pulling close to him and wrapping a well-toned arm around him as she tapped a hidden communicator under her jacket.

"Janeway, here," the server said abruptly. "Two to beam up."

Then Kirk saw Scott and Bateson and the crowd of partygoers dissolve in the sparkle of a transporter beam.

This isn't *happening,* Kirk told himself uselessly. There was no more room for adventure in his life, and all he could think of was Teilani, and how much he wanted to go home.

But, as always, the universe had other plans for James T. Kirk.

FOUR

☆

On the *Enterprise*'s main viewer, the *Starship Voyager* slowly rotated, her inertial dampers apparently offline. The sudden elation that had swept Picard and his bridge crew vanished just as quickly, even before Data began reporting the results of his sensor scans.

"She is showing a great deal of battle damage, sir. Along with severe structural deformations consistent with passage through an unstable wormhole."

"A wormhole," Picard repeated as he stared at the blackened streaks of weapons' damage to the *Voyager*'s hull. The sight reawakened in him the terrible memories of seeing the battered saucer section of his own *Enterprise*-D on Veridian III, how he had felt as he had been forced to accept that his ship would never again move among the stars. He did not envy the *Voyager*'s commander now, nor had he when he had read the electrifying announcement that the ship's Emergency Medical Hologram had made contact with Starfleet through a mysterious alien communications array, only two months ago.

The remarkable story the EMH had told, of the *Voyager*'s sudden transit to the Delta Quadrant, the way her captain had combined her crew with the Maquis rebels she had hunted, and how they had since persevered to cross more

41

than ten thousand light-years on their journey home, had become an inspiration to all of Starfleet. And now, to have crossed the remaining sixty thousand light-years in only months, Picard knew he was looking at a ship full of heroes. "Mr. Data, what is the state of the crew?"

"Sensors show total crew complement of . . . thirty-two." Data glanced away from his station. "According to the status report filed by *Voyager*'s EMH, as of two months ago, her crew complement was one hundred and twenty."

Picard became aware of Riker moving forward to stand beside him.

"How are her shields?" Picard asked.

"Twenty-eight percent and fluctuating," Data answered. "Her warp engines are offline. She is running on emergency power. Life-support is functioning only on three of fifteen decks. And I am detecting evidence of inefficient repairs made with alien technology."

"They must have done whatever they had to to survive," Riker said softly, clearly as moved as Picard by the sight of the crippled ship.

Then a tremor made the bridge tilt, and Picard turned to Riker. "I think the first order of business is to remove her from these plasma storms."

"I agree," Riker said. "Mr. Karo, attach tractor beams to the *Voyager*. And treat her gently."

"Aye, sir," the Bolian acknowledged.

On the screen, three violet beams of focused gravitons reached out to the stricken starship.

"Any sign of them responding to our hails?" Picard addressed his query to Commander Zefram Sloane, the *Enterprise*'s security officer, who replied from his elevated station at the side of the bridge.

"I am certain they can hear us, Captain. There is a full crew and activity on the bridge, but there seems to be a problem with their subspace transmitters. I have informed them that we have received their standard ID transmission, so with luck they should be able to patch their communications through that system."

But Picard didn't believe in relying on luck. "Give them that suggestion, Mr. Sloane, and provide them with the appropriate circuitry diagrams. With almost eighty percent of their crew gone, they might not have a communications officer or engineer left."

Sloane immediately began to transmit the necessary information. He was a slightly built human who traced his ancestry back to one of the first families to settle the Alpha Centauri II system, and from there to Africa. Sloanes had been at the forefront of interstellar exploration from the days of Cochrane, and Picard was pleased that he was in the unique position to know why that should be so. More than three hundred years ago, he had had the singular pleasure of meeting Commander Sloane's great-great-great-to-the-ninth grandmother.

"Tractor beams engaged," Karo announced.

"Take us out of here," Picard ordered. "Warp factor one."

Instantly, the deep hum of the *Enterprise*'s engines pulsed through the bridge and, while the *Voyager* held her place in the viewer, the billowing, multicolored plasma storms of the Goldin Discontinuity fell away at the speed of light.

Picard returned to the center chair, guiltily relieved that this painfully dull assignment had become something vastly more important, though he was also saddened by the cost the *Voyager* apparently had paid for her journey here. He was mentally composing the historic message he would dispatch to Starfleet Command to advise them of his discovery, when Sloane reported that they were finally receiving a response from the *Voyager*.

Even as Picard gave the order to put the transmission onscreen, the haggard face of a Starfleet officer appeared there. He wore an older Starfleet uniform, with a red yoke and lavender shirt. Picard could see that the young man's collar was frayed and his uniform tunic was streaked with dirt.

"You're *Starfleet!*" the officer said in wonder.

Picard felt a wave of compassion as he realized what this officer and his crew must have gone through. The *Voyager* had once been the pride of Starfleet. Unlike the Defiant class of ships, or even this new *Enterprise, Voyager* was a vessel whose primary mission had been a return to the Federation's greatest ideals of pure exploration. The commander who had disappeared with her, Captain Kathryn Janeway, had come up through Starfleet's science ranks, not through the more traditional command route. Yet, in the appearance of *Voyager*'s current commander, Picard saw the end of the optimism with which the ship had been launched. *Voyager* was a dying vessel without even a replicator to provide fresh uniforms. The EMH had told a great deal of their travails, but in the time he had had, he had not been able to describe everything.

"I am Jean-Luc Picard of the *Enterprise.* And it is with heartfelt congratulations that my crew and I welcome you home. To whom do I have the honor of speaking?"

The young man's smile was instantaneous, but visibly tinged with exhaustion. "Commander Paris, sir. Tom Paris."

Mentally reproving himself, Picard nodded. He should have recognized the family resemblance at once. "Of course, Commander. I know your father, Owen. May I ask . . . is Captain Janeway among you?"

Paris shook his head. "She . . . she didn't make it, sir. Most of the crew . . ."

Picard interrupted, trying to ease the young man's burden. "We count thirty-two survivors, Commander. We can go into details later."

"Thank you, sir." Paris looked to the side, listening to a question asked out of range of his bridge audio pickups. He turned back to Picard. "Could you tell us where we are, sir? We're guessing we're somewhere in the Alpha Quadrant, but stellar cartography is completely offline."

"You are back in the Alpha Quadrant. You emerged from a wormhole in the Goldin Discontinuity, a few hundred light-years from the Vulcan Colonial Protectorates."

"The middle of the Federation," Paris said, obviously gratified.

"More or less," Picard confirmed. "May I ask how you managed to cross the remaining sixty thousand light-years since your EMH made contact with Starfleet?"

Paris sank back in his command chair, as if now was the first time in the past five years that he had been able to relax. "It's a long story, Captain. It might be a good idea to stabilize *Voyager* first, get medical attention for the crew. A hot meal and a shower would certainly be appreciated."

"It would be our pleasure," Picard said. "Your ship is safely in our tractor beams. We're ready to beam your entire crew aboard if you'd like."

"That would be . . . wonderful." Paris stood up. "We're ready to go, eager to go, any time. There are . . . a great many bad memories here."

"I understand," Picard said. "Have your people stand by for immediate transport."

"Paris, out." The viewer flickered back to show the *Voyager,* now in a stable orientation. The Goldin Discontinuity was taking on the appearance of a folded sheet of interstellar gas. The flight of the *Enterprise* was smooth, with no untoward vibrations.

"Mr. Data," Picard said, "arrange with transporter control to bring the commander's entire crew over. I'll want them all to have individual guest quarters, and unlimited replicator access with the captain's compliments. Inform Commander La Forge that I would like him to ascertain the status of the ship from her crew, and . . . apprise Counselor Troi and Dr. Crusher of our new arrivals. I imagine medical care and some counseling sessions might be in order."

Data began preparations at once.

"In addition to being a momentous rescue mission, sir," Riker said to Picard, "this could also validate the theories that had Starfleet investigating regions of plasma storms in the first place."

Picard wasn't quite sure what Riker meant.

"What if *Voyager* fell into a wormhole which reached from the Delta Quadrant to the Goldin Discontinuity? Depending on where they started from, this might rank as a discovery as valuable as the Bajoran wormhole."

"An interesting hypothesis," Picard agreed. "Mr. Data, is there any way to determine the extent of *Voyager*'s travels within a wormhole? How far? How long?"

Data took an unusually long time to respond. "Not really, sir. The deeper the meta-analysis of the ship's structural deformities goes, the more it seems I'm picking up interference in its structural-integrity field alone, and not actual physical damage at all."

Picard found that curious. He got up to read Data's science screens himself. "Are you suggesting the ship has been damaged only by faulty control settings?"

"That's one possibility," Data said, though he didn't sound convinced.

Picard read the details of the *Voyager*'s condition over the android's shoulder. If not for the visual appearance of *Voyager,* he would almost think he was looking at simulated battle damage from a Starfleet war-game scenario. "Is there any other indication that the damage is simulated, not physical?"

"No, sir. Unless . . ."

Picard had no patience for equivocation. Any ship of the complexity of the *Enterprise* ran by consensus, but that was impossible if any of her crew held back information, or even an opinion. "Mr. Data . . . ?"

Data sounded reluctant, but he continued. "Sir, I did take the liberty of analyzing their life-support systems. And even though sensors confirm only thirty-two humans on board, the levels of carbon dioxide, food, and heat waste handled by life-support indicate a larger crew complement."

Riker had joined Picard and Data. "How much larger?"

"If I had to guess, sir . . ."

"Consider it an order," Picard said.

"Two hundred. In addition to the thirty-two individuals that the sensors confirm being on board."

Riker rubbed at his beard in thought. "Is there any indication that life-support is one of the systems repaired with alien technology?"

"There are a great number of engineering anomalies in almost every system in the ship," Data said. "But not all of them are clearly alien. Some appear to be repairs made with . . . I would have to characterize it as less advanced human technology."

Picard thought there was an easy answer for that. "Is there any indication that *Voyager* has traveled in time? Perhaps to an earlier era where they had to adapt primitive materials?"

"An interesting proposal," Data responded. As the android realigned the sensors to determine an answer to Picard's question, La Forge announced that Commander Paris and the first of the *Voyager* crew had been beamed aboard.

"Escort them to the bridge before giving them quarters," Picard said. To Riker he added, "No doubt the commander will be able to answer a great many of our questions."

Riker looked concerned. "Sir . . . I wonder if we should consider mutiny as a cause of *Voyager*'s apparent condition?"

Picard remembered that that had been one of the theories advanced to account for the ship's loss, but that the EMH had firmly ruled it out. True, Tom Paris had been a member of the Maquis, and *Voyager* had been on a mission to capture a Maquis cell when she had vanished, but the EMH had claimed that all earlier animosity between the two opposing crews had vanished. Indeed, Picard—and most of Starfleet Command—had been startled to learn that Janeway had even invited a Borg to join her crew. The very idea raised the hair on the back of Picard's neck.

"Paris is wearing a Starfleet uniform," Picard noted. "But I shall keep in mind the possibility of trouble involving the crew." He looked back at the sensor displays. "Any progress, Mr. Data?"

"The effects of wormhole travel must be more complex than current theory suggests," the android said. "According to my preliminary temporal scans, more than ninety-three percent of the components on *Voyager* are less than eighteen months old."

"But, *Voyager* was at least a year old when she vanished," Riker said. "The hull plates alone would have been fabricated a year before that."

"As I said," Data repeated, "these readings are not in accordance to theory. It might be possible that the ship was subjected to an intense chroniton burst, though I doubt any member of her crew could have survived such an assault."

Riker looked meaningfully at Picard. "Captain, given the circumstances, I think it might be a wise precaution to keep our guests under observation."

Picard nodded. "I agree." He looked around for Commander Sloane, but Riker had more to say.

"And I don't think we should allow any of the *Voyager* crew on the bridge, or near any critical control facility."

"That seems rather harsh," Picard said, "but according to the EMH's description of life on board the ship, I suspect the crew will be more interested in any case in our food and recreation facilities. Commander Sloane, prepare a security detail—very discreet—to . . ." Picard stopped speaking as the starboard turbolift doors puffed open and Geordi La Forge appeared, accompanied by Tom Paris and five bedraggled Starfleet officers in old uniforms. Paris smiled broadly as he gazed around the expansive bridge.

"Your ship, Captain Picard, she's a wonder."

Picard leaned closer to Riker. "Will, see to the security detail," he said in a low voice. Then he approached Paris and the others from the *Voyager*.

"Welcome aboard, Commander. I hope you will treat the *Enterprise* as your new home."

Paris did something with his arm, as if flicking an object from his tunic's sleeve. "Don't worry, Captain, we intend to."

And then Picard saw in the young man's hand what could only be a weapon.

Riker moved forward at once to put himself between Paris and Picard. But Picard held up his hand. "It's all right, Will. Evidently, Commander Paris hasn't done his homework." He regarded the officer sternly. "The *Enterprise* computer will not allow a weapon to be fired on board this ship without command override. Mr. Sloane, prepare to fire on Commander Paris, heavy stun."

Paris crouched and spun, firing at Sloane before the security officer could rise from his chair. Picard heard a rush of air, but saw no energy beam leave the weapon.

Yet Sloane gasped and crashed back against his station as if he'd been blasted by disruptor fire.

The bridge crew were frozen in place, awaiting their orders, as all the others from the *Voyager* suddenly held similar weapons. One jammed her weapon against La Forge's temple.

"We *have* done our homework, Captain." Paris angled his weapon so Picard could better judge it. Constructed of a dark gray material, the device was no larger than a hand phaser, with no status lights apparent. "Mechanical springs that fire composite darts. Each tip coated with a Klingon nerve toxin. No high technology for your computer to suppress." He aimed once more at Sloane's unconscious form. "And two darts are fatal."

Data stood up. "Fortunately, I am not an organic being."

Paris swung his weapon around to Picard, as did four others of his crew. "But your captain is. If you think you can take us *all* out before we manage to hit him twice, feel free to try."

Data hesitated.

But Picard knew there was no need. Thirty-two humans were no match for the android. And the *Enterprise* always came first. "Computer," Picard said. "Emergency lockout! Picard Alpha One! Mr. Data—they are not to have this ship!"

That was all Data needed to hear, but as the android sprang forward with superhuman speed, Picard felt the first sting of a dart in his left shoulder.

As he fell back, stumbling against Mr. Karo, Picard saw Riker go down as well, clutching at a dart in his side. And even as Data smashed his fists into the third of Paris's crew, Picard saw La Forge drop with three darts in him, and felt another hit himself just below his sternum.

Picard collapsed to the deck, slumped against Mr. Karo's chair. The Bolian was already stretched out before him.

It was difficult to breathe, but Picard knew the risk had been worth it. Paris and all five of his accomplices were down, and Data was unharmed. Even as the bridge began to spin around him, Picard knew the *Enterprise* had been saved. In the end, that was all that mattered.

And then the port turbolift doors opened and Picard knew he was wrong.

Six more attackers stormed the bridge. Three Klingons. Three Cardassians. And whatever weapon they now fired at Data hurled the android into the engineering station in an explosion of transtator sparks.

Picard gazed up, unable to speak, unable to even focus his eyes as he saw the blurred image of a Cardassian female loom over him.

"Your Starfleet used the same weapons-override system for this ship that they used for *Voyager*," she said, in a voice that was drawn out and distorted. "An extremely shortsighted design flaw, wouldn't you agree?"

Using every bit of self-control he still possessed, Picard managed to gasp out, "Get off . . . my ship. . . ."

"There's just one problem, Picard. The *Enterprise* . . . she isn't yours anymore." The Cardassian bared her teeth at Picard as her image slowly dissolved into a featureless void of black. "She's *mine.*"

Then the emptiness of space reached out for Picard, to separate him forever from his ship . . . and his life.

FIVE

☆

Kirk tumbled downward through a tunnel of shimmering light, constantly aware of Janeway's firm, muscled body pressing closely against him. What at first had felt like a simple transport—a process that should have taken a few seconds at most—became drawn out and disorienting.

He tried to count the number of times he thought he felt solid ground materializing under his feet, only to be lost again. But each materialization seemed to bring a different gravity field whose effect served only to keep his balance unstable and his concentration distracted.

Finally, just as a section of solid flooring appeared beneath him and he tensed, waiting for it to dissolve again, Janeway suddenly shoved him forward.

Kirk reflexively spread out his arms, to absorb the impact of his fall.

But the impact didn't come.

He *was* falling forward toward the floor. But very slowly.

Before his fall ended, he had time to look around to see that he was in a small, metal-walled room, lit by sputtering light tubes, littered with garbage, reeking of sweat and something rotting, and *then* he hit the slick, wet floor. Gently.

Effortlessly, Kirk straightened up, and that was enough to

bring him back to his feet. He dried his hands on the edge of his Vulcan surplice as he slowly turned around, being careful to keep his feet in contact with the floor at all times.

He had felt this weakened gravitational field before, and he knew exactly where he was. His kidnapper had displayed an impressive technological feat, even for the twenty-fourth century.

Kirk faced Janeway, who remained on the portable transporter pad, raised a few feet above floor level. Her head was barely clear of the low, metal-ribbed ceiling plates.

She kept her small phaser trained on Kirk and pulled off her tuxedo jacket as if it were a constricting disguise. "I know all about you, Kirk. One wrong move, and you're a dead man."

But Kirk merely folded his hands behind his back, a reflection of the sudden sense of control he felt. His kidnapper had just revealed to him that he was not a random target. That meant someone wanted something from him. And that meant what had begun as a kidnapping now could play out as a negotiation.

"If you had wanted me dead, why go to all the trouble of a multiple-relay transport to get me to the moon?" Kirk asked, claiming the initial move in their exchange. After almost thirty years in the center chair of a starship, he was ready to pit his negotiating skills against any comers.

Janeway pulled at the waist of her black trousers and the loose garment broke apart, obviously intended to be quickly shed. Beneath her server's costume, she wore a sleek, black, one-piece combat suit. Kirk didn't recognize the design, but judging from the raised circuitry patterns that were woven through the garment, he presumed it would have phaser armor, as well as weaponry and communications capabilities built in.

"You think you're so clever," Janeway growled as she kicked off the shiny black shoes she had worn over her boots. They thudded into a dark corner of the room.

"No, but I believe *you* are. It shows a great deal of cleverness to devise a way to transport me from the Earth to the moon without being concerned that the authorities will track the multiple beampaths you must have used."

Janeway glared at him and Kirk understood that interference by Earth authorities was of definite concern to her. His response to that knowledge was to feel even more in control of the situation. So much so that there was not even any need for him to think of an escape strategy. Janeway's nervousness, despite her having accomplished a successful abduction, told Kirk that she was not the person in charge of whatever action was under way.

And if Janeway was just the middleman, following explicit orders, it meant she was essentially powerless.

Janeway stepped down from the transporter platform and gestured to a thick, armored pressure door. It was partially open, leading to a dark corridor beyond. From its construction, and the condition of its flaking paint, Kirk guessed they were in the abandoned service area of one of the first lunar colonies, dating back almost to Cochrane's time. He recalled that the moon had been terraformed in this new age, with its own free atmosphere and open bodies of water. Thus, the fact that he was in an area of the moon's natural low gravity suggested that he was either deep underground, below the range of the main gravity generators, or in an undeveloped region. In other words, this was a perfect location for a secret base in Earth's solar system.

"Through that door," Janeway ordered.

Kirk decided to see exactly how much latitude her orders gave her. He made no attempt to move. He only shook his head and said, "No." Then, inwardly, he smiled as he saw Janeway's expression of surprise. Kirk almost felt sorry for her. *Someone should tell her how much information she gives away just by not being aware of her own reactions.*

"You go out that door or I swear I'll stun you and drag you through it."

Kirk shrugged. "You could, but your commander ordered you not to." Otherwise, Kirk knew, Janeway would have stunned him at his first sign of obstruction.

Janeway looked startled, ready to blurt out a question, probably asking how Kirk could know what her commander had ordered her to do. But she didn't, showing she was capable of some self-control.

"My orders were not to hurt you . . ." She carefully aimed her phaser at Kirk. ". . . unless necessary."

Kirk had found one limit. He changed tactics to see if he could find another. "It won't be. I am willing to cooperate. But I want some assurances, first."

Janeway again gestured toward the doorway. "You're in no position to want anything."

"You haven't done this before, have you?"

Janeway stared at him, bewildered by his defiance. Kirk was clearly not behaving like a typical victim. For his own part, Kirk was finding it almost too easy to keep her off-balance.

"If you mean kidnapping, no," she said. "I usually just kill people."

Kirk read the truth in her eyes. She was a soldier of sorts, but experienced on the battlefield, not in covert operations. That told him a great deal about her superiors. And that knowledge gave him the strategy he needed to take control of the situation.

"Point that phaser away," Kirk said. He used what he had always thought of as his commander's voice—the tone he used on Academy cadets when it was important that they follow orders first and understand them later.

It had the appropriate effect. Janeway automatically deflected her aim by a few inches. He had her attention.

"I know all about you, too," Kirk continued, pressing his advantage. "You and your people are in trouble." *Why else would someone inexperienced in covert operations be given such an important task?* "And you think I can help you."

Which is why she had been ordered not to harm him. "But you don't have much time." *The authorities on Earth would eventually be able to trace the multiple transporter beams that had brought him here, and Janeway and her people knew it.* "And this base of yours is not secure." *Which is why she had made no attempt to use her communicator since they arrived. A stray subspace transmission could help the authorities locate this place even faster.* "So let's drop the theatrics, and the weapon. Since you apparently think you can convince me to help you without resorting to force, why waste time with a bluff you're not willing to carry out?"

Janeway's cheeks flushed red and she swung her arm out, directly at Kirk, thumb squeezing the phaser she held.

But Kirk didn't take his eyes from hers. Even as he stepped up to her, folded his hand around hers, and took the phaser away.

Whatever else this Janeway was, she was a good soldier. Her orders were clearly to deliver Kirk alive and unharmed. And she had followed them. Somewhere within her was a central core that understood and believed in duty and commitment.

He looked at the tiny weapon he had taken from her, pressed what he hoped was its safety lock, then slipped it inside a small pouch on his belt.

"That's better." He held out his hand. It was time to start again. "I'm Jim Kirk."

But his kidnapper was furious. She ignored his outstretched hand. He could tell she had no intention of acknowledging any sort of bond between them. She was, however, realistic enough to accept the situation. "Kathryn Janeway," she said icily.

The name seemed familiar to Kirk, but he couldn't place it.

She seemed to notice his attempt to recall her identity, didn't like it. "And I'm not who you think I am," she snapped.

"I . . . have no idea who I think you are."

"I'll bet," Janeway muttered. She stomped over to the pressure door, threw her shoulder against it to make it creak open, then gestured to the corridor outside. "Well?"

Kirk stared into the darkness. He could hear water dripping. Runoff from some ancient lunar ice mine, he decided. A relic of the pre-replicator past. Teilani enjoyed reading romance novels set in the early era of colonization, and Kirk thought she'd enjoy being able to visit this place. Though he doubted it would live up to her romantic ideals. "After you," he said.

Janeway exhaled angrily, but before she could step through the doorway, a deep voice spoke from the darkness. "You may remain where you are."

And at the sound of that voice, for the first time this evening, Kirk *was* surprised.

A tall, thin figure, wrapped in a simple dark cloak, stepped through the open doorway. His shoulders were stooped, his left leg stiff, but his distinctive silhouette was unmistakable.

"Spock?!" Kirk said.

The familiar figure limped from the shadow of the doorway, into the flickering light of the small room.

"Yes," he said. "And no."

For an instant, Kirk felt his world turn upside down. He had seen Spock only a year ago, at Mount Seleya on Vulcan. His friend was 145, middle-aged for a Vulcan, and though he had slowed down from his days on the *Enterprise,* he had been fit and hearty then and should be the same now.

But this Spock before him . . . he seemed another century older at least, as if in the past year some terrible illness had claimed him.

And then one key difference between this Spock and the Spock of Kirk's memory swam into view.

Spock's beard.

An elegant goatee, pure white to match the color of his traditional Vulcan bangs.

Kirk remembered the last time he had seen Spock with a beard.

Spock, and yet, not Spock.

As if he were a reflection cast in a dark, distorted mirror. This other Spock, this mirror Spock, raised an eyebrow at Kirk. "I see you recognize me," he said.

"How . . . could I forget?"

"Indeed." There was a tremor to this Spock, this spectre from the past. His head shook. One hand, his left, trembled. "One hundred and eight years ago, you challenged me, Captain Kirk."

The memory blazed in Kirk's consciousness. How he and McCoy, Scott and Uhura, had beamed up through an ion storm during that first five-year mission on the *Enterprise,* and somehow had traded places with their counterparts in a parallel universe. A version of Starfleet had existed there, as had the *Enterprise* herself, staffed by duplicates of Kirk's own crew.

Yet that other dimension, that mirror universe, was different—savage, brutal, a place where Starfleet officers advanced through the ranks by assassination. A place where Starfleet did not serve a benevolent Federation, but a repressive Empire that thought nothing of wiping out an entire race in retribution for a simple ineffectual act of defiance.

In the few hours Kirk had spent in that parallel existence, he had understood the truth of it.

The Empire would not endure. Within 240 years at most, an inevitable galactic revolt would overthrow it.

"The illogic of waste, Mr. Spock," Kirk had told this other Spock then. "The waste of lives, potential, resources, time. I submit to you that your Empire is illogical because it cannot endure. I submit that *you* are illogical to be a willing part of it."

Kirk still remembered the impassive face of the other Spock, as he had bluntly stated to Kirk, "One man cannot summon the future."

"But one man can change the present," Kirk had insisted. He had challenged the mirror Spock to take command of the mirror *Enterprise,* to find a way to change the Empire from within. "What will it be?" Kirk had demanded of him. "The past or the future? Tyranny or freedom? It's up to you."

That other Spock's expression had been unreadable, his thoughts unknowable, and Kirk had never known if his challenge had been accepted or rejected.

Now, here in this abandoned storeroom on the moon, in Kirk's own universe, that other Spock studied him in the inconstant light, as if he, too, shared the same precise memories of their first brief meeting. "You told me then," the mirror Spock said, " 'In every revolution, there is one man with a vision.' "

Kirk remembered that final exchange clearly. It was one of the handful of his missions from that earlier era which had remained alive within him. So much of those early days had been routine, easily forgotten unless prompted by a review of his old captain's logs. But his experience in the mirror universe, that had been intriguing and unique, a highlight of his career. "And you told me," Kirk replied, "that you would consider what I had said."

The two men faced each other as they had more than a century ago. "I've always wondered what you decided," Kirk said.

The other Spock looked away, as if lost in memory. He licked his dry lips. "I did more than consider your words, Captain. I . . . acted upon them."

"And . . . ?" Kirk asked, though he was suddenly aware of the only logical outcome of that action, given this Spock's condition and presence in this universe.

"And because I did what you had suggested," the mirror Spock said, "the Empire did fall. . . ." His face darkened, and the shaking of his head and hand became more pronounced. "And it was *replaced* by one even more abhorrent."

The mirror Spock limped closer, until he was mere inches from Kirk, allowing Kirk no escape or evasion. "In my universe today, the worlds of what you call the Federation are little more than prison camps. Crushed beneath the iron fist of the Alliance—a union of the Klingon and Cardassian people. Your Earth is a dying, devastated world, stripped of resources. My Vulcan is a slave compound, her libraries burned, her treasuries of art and science ransacked and mutilated."

This Spock's eyes were deeply shadowed, as if haunted by millennia of despair. His lips were dry and cracked, the thin, almost transparent skin above his sunken cheeks mottled by pale green spiderwebs of broken capillaries. "Tens of billions of humans and Vulcans live in abject slavery, Captain Kirk. Entire worlds have been moved from their orbits to fall into their suns as sport, extinguishing whole races and civilizations. 'Freedom' is a word which exists only as a forgotten whisper from the long-dead past. Hope is nonexistent."

The mirror Spock held a trembling finger before Kirk. It shook with age, with disease, and with outrage. "And these abominations and massacres and acts of depravity in my world—all this evil—exist because of *you!*"

Kirk stepped back, unable to deny his role in the horror this Spock had endured.

More than ever, he longed to return home. To Chal. To Teilani and the promise of their new life together.

More than ever, he knew that was no longer possible, and might never be again.

After a lifetime of looking to the possibilities of his future, Kirk now understood that the consequences of his past, at last and inevitably, had finally caught up with him.

SIX

☆

"Good thing you have an artificial heart."

Picard's eyes fluttered open and he was struck first by pain, and then by the sight of one of the more colorful aliens he had seen in his years in space.

The being had a high forehead and tall, concave temples, tinged by yellow and dappled with spots, topped by a crest of auburn hair that was in turn matched by muttonchops whiskers. He also had a deep cleft in his nose and a constant twitch under one eye.

"Hello," the alien said. "I could tell you were awake from the diagnostic readings."

Picard tried to swallow but his throat was dry. His head felt thick and every pulse of his heart sent a shock of pain through his skull. He whispered, "Hello," but that was all he could manage.

"I'll bet you're thirsty," the alien said. He scurried out of Picard's sight.

Picard tried to move, despite the deep ache in all of his muscles, but soon realized he was tied down by restraints on . . . he looked around, forcing his blurred vision to come into focus.

"Sickbay . . ." he croaked.

"That's right," the alien said cheerfully as he returned to Picard's medical bed. He carefully cradled a glass of water.

"Not . . . the *Enterprise,*" Picard said as he raised his head to the glass. This sickbay was smaller. The diagnostic wall to his side was gold, not blue. He was on a Federation starship, but he didn't know which one.

"Right again," the alien said as he slipped his hand helpfully behind Picard's neck. "You're on *Voyager.*"

Then Picard coughed as he tasted what he thought had been water. It was incredibly sweet, such a shocking flavor that he felt his eustachian tubes close and his jaw cramp.

"No, no," the alien said, keeping the glass to Picard's lips. "Torstolian elixir. Just the thing to help overcome the effects of that Klingon toxin. I make it myself," he added proudly.

Picard forced himself to swallow rapidly, trying to keep his tongue from making contact with the hideous clear liquid. "Are you . . . the doctor?" he asked.

The alien seemed bemused by the question. He held up the glass to be sure Picard had finished its contents. "Oh, no. I'm just the cook." He smiled at Picard, though not even that expression could erase the air of sadness about him. "I'm Neelix."

"Neelix," Picard said.

"I'm a Talaxian," Neelix explained. "I don't suppose you've met someone of my species before."

Picard shook his head, and was surprised that the movement was not as painful as he had feared. Perhaps there was something to that jarringly sweet elixir after all.

Then, as if his mind was clearing with the cessation of pain, so many questions came to Picard that he had trouble sorting them out. He seemed to recall Talaxians being mentioned in the report by the *Voyager*'s EMH. But his first priority was clear. "Where is the *Enterprise?*"

Neelix glanced to the side, as if expecting someone to interrupt. "As far as I know—which isn't a great deal—that ship is still beside us."

"How is her crew?" Picard didn't like the fact that there

was no one else being treated in this sickbay, even though Tom Paris and his accomplices had fired toxic darts at everyone on the *Enterprise*'s bridge.

Neelix looked away, and Picard judged him to be incapable of delivering bad news.

"Casualties?" Picard asked, fearing the answer.

"A . . . few. I think. But . . . no one tells me anything."

"Commander Riker?"

Neelix smiled apologetically as he shook his head. "I'm sorry, Captain. I don't know him."

It dawned on Picard that Neelix was not behaving as either a captor or a guard. Which left only one other conclusion.

"You're a prisoner here, too, aren't you, Neelix?"

The alien nodded with a quick jerky motion. The twitch under his eye was continuous. He reminded Picard of a mistreated animal who expected only the worst at the hands of his owners.

"Perhaps I can help you escape," Picard offered as he applied pressure to his restraints. "If you help me."

But at once, Picard saw that whatever spirit this alien might have had, it had long been beaten from him.

"Please don't ask me that, Captain. You . . . you don't know what these people are like. What they can do."

"What people, Neelix? Commander Paris?"

Neelix leaned forward, dropping his voice to a whisper. "He's a prisoner, too. All the Terrans on board are."

Picard slumped back, trying to process this new information. "The entire crew of the *Voyager,* taken prisoner by Klingons *and* Cardassians . . . ?" It made no sense. The Klingons were allied with the Federation. And just over a year ago, they had engaged the Cardassian Union in a devastating war. How could they possibly be allies? Unless . . . *Terrans?*

"The Alliance," Picard whispered, in shock. "Is that who the Klingons and Cardassians are? The Alliance?"

Neelix nodded as if he wasn't quite sure how to judge Picard's urgency. "That's right. *Voyager* is an Alliance vessel."

"No, she's not," Picard said. *"Voyager* is a Starfleet vessel that disappeared from the Alpha Quadrant five years ago. Somehow, in trying to find a fast way home, she must have been drawn into what we call the mirror universe." It all made sense to Picard now. When he had been a cadet, he had read about Captain Kirk's first encounter with that savage parallel dimension. And then, like almost every other officer in Starfleet, he had been startled when Dr. Bashir of *Deep Space Nine* and a Bajoran national had revisited that dimension just five years ago. Their classified logs of conditions in the mirror universe were tremendously disturbing. Starfleet had engaged the Seldon Institute of Psychohistory to determine exactly how the two universes might have diverged. If there was any chance that the fate which had befallen the Terran Empire, no matter how richly deserved, could also happen to the Federation, Starfleet wanted to be prepared.

But then Neelix destroyed Picard's careful chain of logic.

"Excuse me, Captain, but I don't think that's possible. According to what I've heard, *Voyager* is less than a year old. I mean, I was captured on her maiden flight and . . . that was only a few months ago."

"Where, exactly, were you captured?"

Neelix seemed to struggle with a painful memory. "You'd call it the Delta Quadrant."

Picard struggled to fit all the pieces together. "Which is where *Voyager* was lost, tens of thousands of light-years distant."

"Seventy thousand where I'm from," Neelix agreed. "I was a trader, you see. Poking through some old Kazon-Ogla ships—I don't suppose you know about the Kazon-Ogla?"

"The Kazon? Yes. There was something about them in the *Voyager* report."

"Well, there I was, and out of nowhere, literally, *Voyager* made contact with me. The Gul said she was lost."

"The Gul?"

"Gul Rutal. She's *Voyager*'s commander. She said they

were lost and they needed a guide and . . . well . . ." Neelix's eyes filled with tears. "I'm sorry. It's just such a terrible tale. They . . . *Voyager* was brought to my region of space by a displacement wave, generated by a venerable alien life-form." Neelix smiled wistfully. "The Caretaker, they called him. He was only attempting to provide for the Ocampa—a beautiful, peaceful race. Something could have been worked out. I'm just certain of it."

Picard listened carefully. Everything the alien told him was familiar, as if he were hearing a slightly different version of the *Voyager* report.

"But, in the end," Neelix continued, "Gul Rutal lied to me, betrayed the Ocampa, and allowed the Kazon-Ogla to destroy the alien's array, all so she could return *Voyager* to her own quadrant."

Picard had no idea what any of this had to do with the matter at hand. It was clear the Talaxian was confused. This vessel *was Voyager*—the history of the two universes had diverged so significantly since Kirk's experience there that no Starfleet existed on the other side, to design and build a duplicate of this ship. Somehow Captain Janeway had crossed over to the mirror universe, her ship been captured by the Alliance, and now had returned to this universe in order to—

Picard felt his breath grow short as he realized what Gul Rutal's mission must be.

"Gul Rutal wants to capture the *Enterprise.*"

"I already have," the Gul said.

Neelix jumped away from the treatment bed with a whimper of fear. But even in his injured state, Picard had enough self-control not to betray his own surprise. He turned his head toward the doctor's office built in to the side of the sickbay.

Gul Rutal, a tall, imposing Cardassian, stood there. She had been there from the beginning, Picard realized. She was the Cardassian who had claimed his bridge.

"You don't belong in this universe," Picard said, as if his restraints did not exist, as if he were not a prisoner.

Rutal smiled coldly at him, her dual, lateral spines giving her wide shoulders and thick neck the look of a cobra about to strike. "We are not doing anything here which you have not already done to us," she hissed.

"Your universe has been declared off-limits," Picard said. "Our Prime Directive prevents us from taking action there."

The Cardassian walked around Picard, appearing to judge him as if he were no more than a food animal tied down for sacrifice. "You Terrans can be so sanctimonious. The damage has already been done. So many of you crossed over into our universe that we established strict protocols to execute all such intruders at once."

Picard was sickened at the thought. "How many?"

The Cardassian shrugged. "Since your Kirk opened the doorway, at least twenty. But those deaths served to keep you under control like the vermin you are. Until you reached Terok Nor."

"Julian Bashir," Picard said.

A strange expression came to the Cardassian. "And Kira Nerys. We know everything about those 'visitors' from . . . this false reflection of reality where Terrans still rule. Those two were the first intruders since your Kirk to escape us. But before they left our world, they planted a seed." She leaned closer to Picard, so close Picard could smell the alien scent of her sweat. "Resistance. Rebellion. They left the Terrans of my universe with the ludicrous hope that they might actually succeed in overthrowing the Alliance. That's not quite in keeping with your famed Prime Directive, now, is it, Captain Picard?"

"Any oppressed people will fight for freedom." Picard glanced at Neelix, but Neelix remained with his head bowed at the foot of the diagnostic bed, refusing to meet Picard's gaze. "That idea did not originate with us."

"But the *Defiant* did." The Cardassian's gloved hand shot out and smashed against Picard's face in a painful blow.

Picard saw flashes of colors before his eyes. He tasted blood in his mouth.

"One of our Terran rebels downloaded your Starfleet's plans for an entire starship, Captain. And not just a starship—a *war*ship. The *Defiant*. That's what they're using against us now. The weaponry of your universe. In ours."

Mouth bloodied, Picard stared at the Cardassian, waiting for more explanation.

"You weren't aware of that?" Rutal said, suspicious of Picard's puzzled reaction. "That your peace-loving Federation has become a provider of weapons to our Terran Resistance?"

Picard shook his head. "The *Defiant*'s plans were stolen from us. To deliberately provide such technology would go against everything we believe in. You have my sympathy."

The Gul raised her fist again, but relented. Instead, she laughed, harshly. "Sympathy. From a Terran. How droll. But even the peace-loving Cardassian people can learn from human perfidy. Your interference left us no choice. As the Terran rebels had done, *we*—a group of Cardassian patriots—also penetrated your universe. Earth Station McKinley, to be precise."

Suddenly Picard understood the true origins of the ship he was in. Neelix was right. "That's where *Voyager* was built. And where you stole her plans."

Gul Rutal raised her hands to indicate the ship around her. "Not an exact duplicate of the craft in your universe, but . . . close enough to lure in an even bigger catch, wouldn't you say?"

Proudly, Picard stated the simple truth. "You can't have the *Enterprise*."

"Come now, Captain. Fair is fair. Even to a Terran male. Your universe provided the rebels of my universe with a starship to use against the Alliance. It is only fitting that now you provide us a starship to take back to our universe, for the Alliance to use against the rebels."

"The *Enterprise* is my ship. And I've locked out all her controls. Without my command codes, she's useless to you."

The Cardassian drew a single finger along Picard's temple.

"Believe me, Captain. Your command codes will be mine before a day has passed."

Picard clenched his fists. "I have been tortured by Cardassians before."

Gul Rutal's smile was unconcerned. "Correction. You have been tortured by your universe's weak and ineffectual version of Cardassians. Not *real* Cardassians, who have had almost a century to refine the art of extracting information from Terrans. When it comes to torture, you don't know the meaning of the word."

Picard did not avert his eyes from Gul Rutal's. He knew exactly what was in store for him. He had suffered terribly at the hands of another Cardassian Gul—Madred—and knew better than most beings what his true breaking point might be. But Starfleet was comprehensive in its tactics, and one of the command codes Picard possessed was specially developed to be given up under duress. The challenge would be to resist long enough that his captor would accept the false code as a legitimate one, and not suspect it had been extracted too easily.

Once that false code had been entered into the *Enterprise*'s computer, Picard's ship would know she had been taken over by a hostile force.

The computer would then set the ship on a course to the nearest starbase, transmit distress calls, and lock out all helm controls by explosively severing key ODN circuits.

Picard knew he might never reach home again. But his ship would. That was still all that mattered.

"Do your worst," Picard said defiantly, already preparing himself for the ordeal to come.

But Gul Rutal stepped back, raising her hands as if to distance herself from Picard's suggestion. "Oh, no, Captain. You misunderstand. A Cardassian would not stoop to . . . soiling her hands with the blood of a soulless Terran. In any event, I find it far more fitting that Cardassian expertise in these matters should be expressed by a hallmark of your own Terran technology—with some useful variations, of course."

Picard didn't understand.

The Cardassian glanced up at the ceiling. "Computer. Activate the EMH."

A third figure suddenly formed to Picard's side, and he recognized the familiar features of Dr. Lewis Zimmerman, the Starfleet physician who had used his own form as the template for the first of a series of artificially intelligent, holographic doctors designed to assist Starfleet medical crews during emergencies.

The holographic doctor wore an old-style Starfleet uniform, so Picard guessed its program had been stolen along with the plans for this duplicate *Voyager*.

In its typical brusque manner, the holographic doctor glanced at Gul Rutal, then down at Picard.

"Please state the nature of the interrogation requirements," the doctor said. With a bland expression, he held up a small device that looked as if a red triangle with rounded corners had been affixed to a dull silver box with two tiny wings at the top edge.

Gul Rutal gazed down at Picard. "As I said, Captain, this ship isn't an exact duplicate of your *Voyager* . . . but I'm sure you'll find our version has a unique nature all its own. To say nothing of its own supply of Terran-designed agonizers." She nodded at the doctor. "Carry on."

"Thank you," the doctor said dismissively.

Then the agonizer descended.

The last thing Picard saw was Neelix, as the trembling Talaxian covered his ears.

The last thing he knew was pain.

SEVEN

☆

Millennia ago, a vast comet had struck the moon, setting off the titanic upheaval that had led to the creation of the Sea of Serenity, one of the oldest of the dark lunar maria. Had there been any life on Earth to witness that stupendous impact, it would have seen fountains of incandescent liquid rock erupt into space, as if a quarter of the moon had been transformed into fire, blazing so brightly it outshone even the sun.

In the course of hours, as the immense crater formed by the comet fell in on itself, the scarred surface of the moon had healed in an outpouring of smooth lava. In the next few months, billions of tonnes of lunar ejecta would blaze through Earth's still-forming atmosphere. And in the next few centuries, a ring of debris would encircle the moon, slowly dissipating under the rhythmic tug of Earth's gravity. But in that instant of impact, when the ancient body of the comet had come to rest at last, its heart—one hundred million tonnes of interstellar ice older than the sun itself—had been forever captured by lunar rock.

That ice absorbed the heat of the comet's fiery death and was transformed into superheated steam in only minutes. But as the long centuries passed and the moon slowly radiated

69

that heat away, the steam became water, and in time the ice re-formed.

Protected from the vacuum of space by the chambers of rock which had solidified around it, the ice remained undisturbed until humanity's first wave of expansion from the planet of its birth. The lunar pioneers had found the ice and mined it—first to support their fragile, pressurized habitats, then to manufacture the antimatter used to fuel the new warp ships that would carry their species even farther from home.

Eventually, inevitably, easier methods of creating antimatter were discovered. More efficient means of obtaining water on the moon were engineered.

So the ice mines of Serenity closed, becoming as archaic and unnecessary as the abandoned oil fields of Earth, the need for their contents long ago supplanted by less disruptive forms of energy. Now the Serenity mines were simply remnants of a bygone age, old, and cold, and useless. And James T. Kirk walked through them as if they were the fitting home for his heart and for his soul.

The history that the other Spock related to him was that chilling.

At the branching of two rough-walled tunnels, in the dim blue light cast by flickering fusion globes that had burned for more than two hundred years, Kirk found he could go no farther. Not right now.

Janeway and the other Spock respected his request—though Janeway remained nervous, and kept checking a small tricorder.

Kirk reached out to a wall of rock to brace himself, to catch his breath, to try to comprehend the events he had set in motion so long ago.

The rock was textured with the melted cylindrical gouges created by a primitive drilling laser. The undulating surface was cold and made his fingers ache. But Kirk would not take his hand away, as if the pain could serve as penance for what he had done.

"You were supposed to be . . . invincible," Kirk said to the mirror Spock. His words escaped from him in clouds of vapor. His voice echoed in the lunar mines. "You were supposed to use the Tantalus Field."

That device had been an alien invention which had belonged to Kirk's counterpart on the other *Enterprise*. Hidden behind a wall panel in the mirror in Kirk's quarters was a display screen that could focus on any section of the starship. And any person or object at the center of that focus could be made to disappear, with only the touch of a finger on a button.

After the Tantalus Field had been used, there was no trace of an energy discharge that could be detected by investigators, no molecular residue from a corpse to linger in the air for a tricorder to sense. All that was left was a total absence of whatever had existed only an instant before.

The other Kirk had used the Tantalus Field to consolidate his power and maintain his command of the *Enterprise*. That Kirk's enemies had simply vanished. Kirk had told the mirror Spock to use the device for the same purpose.

"Did you?" Kirk asked.

"I did."

Kirk closed his eyes. Even in the weak gravity of the moon, he felt weighed down by the years. "Then what happened, Spock?"

"As you suggested, I found a way to spare the Halkans."

Kirk felt a momentary respite from his burden, thankful for that one small victory, at least.

The Halkans were a peaceful, ethically advanced race who, in Kirk's universe, had declined to allow the Federation to mine their dilithium. Despite the Federation's assurances, the Halkans feared their valuable crystals would one day be used to support acts of destruction.

Kirk had never been able to convince the Halkans to change their position, and so their dilithium had remained their own, yet the Federation and the Halkan people enjoyed a friendly and beneficial association to this day.

In the mirror universe, though, Starfleet Command had ordered the other Kirk to destroy the Halkan civilization as an example to any other race that might possibly consider refusing the Empire.

When Kirk had replaced his mirror-universe counterpart for those few hours, he had delayed implementing that deadly order, even though his defiance put him at risk of being killed by the mirror Sulu. Then, as Kirk had prepared to return to his own universe, he had told the other Spock to find some way to spare the Halkans from their fate.

"How did you manage it?" Kirk asked.

"I did not," the other Spock said. He explained that Kirk's counterpart had convinced Starfleet that the reports of the Halkans' dilithium reserves were a fabrication. A secret treaty supposedly existed between the Halkans and the Klingon Confederacy, so that if the Empire moved against that one planet, it would give the Klingons the excuse they needed to declare war. In the end, Kirk's counterpart received additional honors from the Empire for eluding such a devious trap.

But after all this time, the details of the Halkans' survival weren't important to Kirk. Another part of that story was. "I had always assumed . . . always thought it would be inevitable . . . that your first act would be to kill . . . my counterpart."

The flicker of a sad smile played over the other Spock, as if, like the Spock of this universe, he had found peace with his human heritage and occasionally allowed himself the freedom to express his emotions. "You forget the nature of my universe at that time. Had I killed my Captain Kirk upon his return to the *Enterprise,* my estimated lifetime would have been measured in days, if not hours. He was an extremely powerful and influential officer. The vendetta that would have ensued from his assassination would have been bloody and swift. I would not have survived it."

Kirk took his hand away from the wall of icy rock. He

flexed his frozen fingers, discovering in them a vestige of warmth. "Then . . . how did you take over your *Enterprise?*"

The other Spock seemed surprised by the question. "I did not do that, either."

"But I assumed . . ."

"Mere assumption does not make it so," the mirror Spock said. "As I told you at the time, I did not seek command. My captain did. Logic dictated that he be assisted in his endeavors, while I remain out of harm's way."

Kirk blew on his hand, rubbed it back to life. "You became the power behind the throne."

"Quite literally. Within five years, my Captain Kirk was commander in chief, Starfleet."

Janeway suddenly erupted at the mirror Spock, as if after a long struggle she had finally escaped from a gag. "Intendant Spock, how can you go on like this? As if this were some type of . . . of polite history lecture?" She wheeled to face Kirk, face suffused with anger, voice quavering. "Five years after becoming commander in chief, you—Captain Kirk—assassinated Androvar Drake and became *emperor!* Tiberius the First. The bloodiest, vilest, most depraved dictator in human history!"

Kirk stared accusingly at the mirror Spock. "How could you let that happen?"

But now there was anger even in that Spock, or perhaps frustration. "It had to happen. I needed power I could not obtain for myself. So I propelled my Kirk to the emperor's throne. And when he had taken it, *that* was when I moved against him."

Kirk didn't believe it. "If you couldn't stand up to him when he was a starship captain, how could you take him on when he had become a caesar?"

The mirror Spock stared fixedly at Kirk, dark eyes glittering with serious intent. "Because, *Captain,* I had spent ten years planning for that day, from the moment he returned to my

73

universe and I proposed our partnership based on what I had learned from you and your crew. For ten years, I orchestrated every alliance Tiberius made, brokered every treaty, managed every campaign. And when all the power I needed to reform the Empire was concentrated in Tiberius's hands, I took it."

Kirk studied the mirror Spock, wondering if that somber face was the last one his counterpart had seen before finally being assassinated, as he must have been. He wondered what it had taken for two universes to diverge so that here, he and Spock had become the closest of friends, and there, the deadliest of enemies. "And what happened to Tiberius?"

Janeway answered, filled with disgust. "Intendant Spock engineered the coup to be bloodless. It was. Tiberius escaped."

"And in the meantime," Kirk said, *"you* became emperor?"

"No. Again you make assumptions. That title was abolished at once. The first of many reforms. I remained subcommander, an appointed position, and then instituted the reforms that were necessary to allow each world within the Empire to select a representative to sit on a governing council." The other Spock rubbed his eyes with thumb and forefinger, as if he were feeling as tired as Kirk. "When you came to my universe, I mind-melded with Dr. McCoy. From him, I learned a great deal of your universe. And of the political organization of your Federation. It became my model."

Janeway slipped her small tricorder from an equipment pouch on her combat suit and checked its readout once again. "Intendant Spock, we must continue. The others will be waiting."

"Youth," the mirror Spock said. "So impatient."

Janeway aimed her tricorder down the tunnel, checking in the direction they had come. "For good reason, sir. Our transporter beams might as well have been beacons in this system."

That comment puzzled Kirk. If the transporter beams that had brought him to the moon were that easily traced, then it should only have taken a few seconds for Earth authorities to track him. Why the delay?

The other Spock indicated the sloping tunnel on the left. "Our destination is this way."

Kirk kept to the mirror Spock's side, both of them moving slowly to keep from bouncing too high in the low-ceilinged tunnel. Janeway remained a few paces behind. "How far did you get with your reforms?" Kirk asked.

"Quite far," the other Spock replied. "Within ten months of overthrowing Tiberius, the Imperial Senate met for the first time. Half the members had been selected through graft and corruption. Bribery was rampant. But, by the end of the session, because of the reforms I proposed, I was elected to a five-year term as commander in chief, and received unanimous support for ending the imperial tithe, and for unilaterally withdrawing occupation forces from more than fifty worlds."

"All in ten months," Kirk said, impressed. It appeared that the Spock of the mirror universe was as formidable as his own.

But the mirror Spock did not let Kirk hold that opinion for more than a few seconds. "Ten months which spelled the end of any chance the galaxy had of ever achieving the peace and security it has in your universe."

"Beam-ins!" Janeway suddenly announced.

"How many?" the other Spock asked.

Janeway read the tricorder. "Two so far . . . there's three . . . four . . ." She looked at the mirror Spock, her bristle-length hair almost black in the dim glow of the fusion globes, her eyes alive with the bright status lights of the tricorder. "We have less than five minutes before they track us."

The other Spock drew himself up. "It will be time enough."

Janeway held out her hand to Kirk. "In case it's not, I want my phaser back."

"I can handle this for you," Kirk said. "No charges, no complaints. The authorities will listen to me. Chances are, that's a Starfleet security team."

Janeway and the mirror Spock looked at each other, then at Kirk.

"Starfleet will have no idea where we've taken you," the other Spock said.

"We used transporters from our universe," Janeway added. "They're completely different from the type you use. Your sensors can't easily detect them."

"Then who's after us?" Kirk asked.

"The enemy," Janeway answered.

"The Alliance," Spock added. "The one element I did not include in my calculations."

"Small steps," Janeway said urgently. "Push forward, not up." She grabbed the mirror Spock's arm, and despite the Vulcan aversion to being touched, he did not protest.

Janeway and the other Spock began a series of slow shuffling steps along the tunnel floor that served to accelerate them as if they were running flat-out on Earth.

Kirk didn't see that he had a choice. He moved off after them, pleased that his Starfleet training for low-gravity environments came back to him so quickly.

He caught up to Janeway and the mirror Spock at another branch in the network of old mining tunnels. Whatever the motives of the visitors from the mirror universe, Kirk decided, this was the oddest kidnapping he had ever encountered, let alone personally experienced. He wondered what Teilani would make of it when he told her. And he had no doubt that sometime soon he *would* tell her. Any other possibility was unthinkable.

Kirk fell into step with his abductors. "Who or what is the Alliance?"

"The Cardassians," the mirror Spock said.

"And the Klingons," Janeway added.

"Working *together?*" Kirk asked. *Bizarre,* he thought.

"More than that," the mirror Spock explained. "They are a true political union, as consolidated as your own Federation."

Kirk struggled to keep his breathing controlled. He had no idea how long he'd be expected to keep up this pace. Janeway was handling it well. But the other Spock, so much weaker than the one he knew, was already fighting to catch his breath.

"I can't imagine what it would take to get the Klingons to ally their empire with another," Kirk said. He knew the Klingons. They had been his enemies for decades. They were not known for cooperation.

"But clearly you did imagine it," the mirror Spock said between gulps of air. "Because it was you who brought them together."

Janeway and the mirror Spock suddenly twisted to the right and Kirk skidded as he tried to match their trajectory—and missed. Instead, he hit another rocky wall. A vein of glistening ice ran through it.

He stumbled, regained his footing, then quickly retraced the three meters by which he had bypassed the turn.

The opening in the tunnel wall took him into a large grotto. One entire wall, ten meters high, fifty long, was solid ice. The chill in the large cavern was intense.

For a moment, Kirk paused at the opening, naturally averse to entering any new territory without checking for hidden dangers. But all he saw was a portable, field transporter platform, surrounded by newer, brighter fusion lights mounted on slender tripods. The mirror Spock and Janeway had already reached the platform, Intendant Spock clutching at his chest and leaning against Janeway for support.

A third figure was there as well. Another Vulcan, Kirk saw. A young woman with a disruptor scar on her forehead and a crude biomechanical hand.

Kirk ran to join them. He was unprepared for the look of disgust on the young Vulcan's face when she saw him.

"Jim Kirk," he said.

The Vulcan looked ready to strike him. "I know who you are."

Kirk ignored her. He turned to Janeway, pointed to the transporter platform. "Is that how we get out?"

"It's how we escape," Janeway said. "I—"

Then the electronic whine of a disruptor beam cut her off just as the female Vulcan flew screaming through the air, her body surrounded by a nimbus of crackling disruptor fire.

Escape was no longer possible.

James T. Kirk was at war again.

EIGHT

---- ☆ ----

Picard awoke to the smell of something burning. Or maybe it was the smell that had brought him from sleep.

He stirred against the comforter, peered out into the darkness of his room, but saw no sign of daylight through the draped window. It was still late. Still night. A comforting thought.

He yawned, stretched, sat up in the large soft bed, and sniffed the air again. He could smell apples, a hint of vanilla. *Marie's cooking,* he thought. His sister-in-law was so like his brother, so like his father. No replicators for them. Much better to spend hours in the kitchen, feeding wood to the impossibly old, cast-iron stove, chopping each ingredient by hand, ingredients grown here in the vineyard's gardens, or on one of the small farms nearby. *Not that I mind,* Picard thought. Marie's *tarte tatin* was exquisite, as good as his mother's. He remembered waking up in this same house to hear his mother at work in the kitchen, late at night, early in the morning. The house filled with the savory aroma of her culinary magic.

Picard smiled. At peace. This was his home. Where he had grown up, and to where he would return in time. To his home and family and all good things . . .

"Uncle!"

Picard was instantly alert. That had been René, his nephew, calling out. But from where? Across the hall? Downstairs? Somewhere out in the yard?

Picard threw back the comforter and slipped from the warmth of the bed. The smooth wood of the oak floor was icy cold, the air autumn brisk.

"Papa!"

René again—urgent. Frightened.

"René!"

And that was Robert, Picard's brother, shouting out in alarm.

They need me, Picard thought.

But that was all right. It was as it should be. He was a starship captain. No matter what difficulty or danger his family faced, Picard would be there to protect them.

He started toward the door, realized he was naked, looked around for his clothes, his uniform, but in the dark bedroom he could see nothing clearly, as if a fog had seeped in through the window.

"Jean-Luc! Hurry!"

Robert needed him. There was no time for delay. Picard ran across the room to the bedroom door. He put his hand on the brass knob, started to turn it—

—and lost his breath to pain as the flesh of his hand was seared by the burning metal.

"Uncle, please!"

René was near panic. Picard wouldn't let the pain stop him. He kept his hand in contact with the scorching knob, turned it, pulled open the door—

—and faced a wall of fire that stretched into distances beyond all reason.

The heat engulfed Picard and he raised an arm before his eyes, almost overcome by the gale of rushing smoke and the deafening roar of the flames.

Every instinct told him to step back inside the bedroom and close the door, to retreat to safety and sleep.

But René was somewhere inside those flames. An eleven-year-old child who wanted to be like his uncle Jean-Luc.

Picard could hear the boy.

Hear the boy calling for him.

Hear the boy screaming with agony for his uncle to save him.

Picard moved his arm and stared into the full fury of the all-devouring fire.

There! Before him! No more than a meter away!

René reached out to him . . . Robert beside him . . . flames eating at them . . . calling for him . . . always calling for him . . .

The starship captain.

Picard slapped at his chest. "Picard to *Enterprise!*" he cried.

But he wore no comm badge. There was no response. Even *she* had abandoned him.

As he had abandoned his family.

What Picard saw then he had no words to express. The way fire consumed a human body.

Until only a small blackened hand remained, still reaching out for him.

For Picard, this moment had moved beyond the physical. This moment had moved beyond any being's ability to endure.

In this dream, in this nightmare, there was only one thing left for Picard to do—

He *refused* to surrender. He threw himself into the flames, felt them boil away his flesh as still he struggled to reach through time itself to save his family, until—

It ended as it always did, and he awoke.

Except, this time, he was not in his cabin on the *Enterprise.* He was on the *Voyager.* Still in sickbay.

Neelix was there, a cool cloth in one hand, dabbing at Picard's forehead as Picard caught his breath.

"It's all right," Neelix said softly. "You're all right. You're safe. You're safe."

Picard grabbed Neelix's hand. He remembered the holographic doctor. The agonizer descending, and then . . .

"Neelix . . . what happened?"

"It's over," the Talaxian said. "That's all you need to know. It's over and everything's all right now."

Neelix left the cloth on Picard's forehead. He slid a hand beneath Picard's neck, raised his head. "This time, it's just water." He held a glass for Picard to drink from.

But even the water was like fire to Picard. His throat ached, as if he had inhaled acrid smoke. Every muscle in his body resisted the slightest movement. He slumped back to the bed, too overcome to even sip water.

"What . . . what did I tell them?"

Neelix waved his hands reassuringly. "Anyone would have talked. They have ways of getting inside what you're thinking. It's the agonizer. You can't blame yourself."

But Picard had no use for sympathy. "What did I tell them?"

"Well, codes . . . some numbers and letters . . . I don't know what they were. But the Gul hasn't come back, so I guess the codes did what she needed them to do."

Picard stared up at the ceiling. So much for Starfleet conditioning. If he had given Rutal the decoy code, the *Enterprise* would already have set her own course for the nearest starbase. Since the Cardassian had not returned to kill him, he could only assume she had succeeded in extracting the *real* codes from him.

Only a handful of hours ago, he had told Will Riker that the *Enterprise* was the most sophisticated piece of machinery ever built by humanity, and a simple, human intolerance to pain had resulted in him giving up *his ship* to the enemy.

"Neelix," Picard said in a tone that indicated he would allow no argument. "You must free me from these restraints."

"I . . . can't."

Picard had run out of patience. "Neelix, you don't have a choice!"

Neelix backed away. "But . . . where would you go?"

"To my ship. Release me, *now!*"

Neelix wrung his hands. The twitch under his eye grew so strong he was winking. "But . . . the *Enterprise* . . . Captain . . . Gul Rutal brought her crew aboard and . . . she took it. The *Enterprise* is gone."

Picard felt a stab of pain pierce his chest. She *had* abandoned him, just as in that terrible nightmare. "When?"

"An hour ago, maybe two. I was sitting here with you so I don't know."

"Where are they taking her?"

"I . . . don't know that, either."

All Picard's pent-up fury escaped him. "Do you know what that ship is capable of?"

Neelix covered his face with his hands, began sobbing. "Please . . . don't shout at me . . . please . . ."

This is useless, Picard thought in angry despair. Neelix was a broken person. Who knew how many times he had been subjected to what Picard had just experienced?

Picard took pity on him. Changed his tone. "It's all right, Neelix. I know what you're up against."

Neelix bobbed his head, appreciating Picard's understanding. He took a few deep breaths, calming himself. "I'd offer you something to eat, but . . . it's too soon. You have to take it easy for a day."

Picard forced himself to remain nonconfrontational. "Thank you."

A small anxious smile appeared on the Talaxian's face, as if he was relieved that Picard had decided to stop asking the impossible of him.

Picard looked around the sickbay. There had to be some way of getting free. Some way of contacting his crew. Suddenly, it came to him that since this duplicate ship was built according to Starfleet's designs . . .

"Computer," Picard said, "locate Commander William Riker."

The familiar female voice replied, "Commander Riker is being held in detention cell four."

Despite Neelix's look of horror, Picard continued. "Open a channel to him, please."

"Commander Riker is being held incommunicado. No channels are available."

Picard could accept that. At least he had learned that Riker was alive and on *Voyager.* That meant that his odds of escape had just doubled, at least.

"Computer, how many crew members from the *Enterprise* are currently on board *Voyager?*"

"Five hundred and eighty-three."

Picard was surprised. That was more than half. And *Voyager* was a much smaller ship.

"Where are they on *Voyager?*"

"Three hundred and twelve are in emergency-holding forcefields in the shuttlebay, deck ten. Two hundred and fifteen are confined to cargo bays two through twelve. Thirty-four are confined in the brig. Eight are under guard in engineering. Seven are in cryostasis awaiting burial. Two are on the bridge. And the remaining five individuals are under guard in the following locations: turbolift two, hydroponics, transporter control, corridor five on deck eight, and sickbay."

Picard took a steadying breath and asked for the names of the seven dead crew members. The computer recited them. He knew them all. But only the Bolian, Mr. Karo, was from his bridge crew.

Picard began quizzing the computer on the whereabouts of his other key command staff. Data and Troi also were being detained on *Voyager,* like Riker, unreachable through communications channels. Crusher and La Forge, though, had been kept on the *Enterprise* with the remainder of the crew. But there the computer's stream of information ended. Each inquiry Picard made about the *Enterprise*'s destination or mission, no matter how obliquely he phrased his request, was rebuffed with a curt request for his security-clearance code. Picard's own Starfleet codes were not accepted.

The only additional data Picard was able to obtain was the number of the *Voyager*'s current Alliance crew: thirty Klingons, forty-two Cardassians, three Bajorans, and twenty-four Thetas. The Thetas, Neelix explained, were Terran and Vulcan slaves who had earned trustee status. Their number included the mirror-universe counterpart of Tom Paris, who had posed as the *Voyager*'s commander.

As Picard paused to collect his thoughts, Neelix commented, "I never knew the ship's computer could do all that."

Picard was intrigued. "Have you never heard Gul Rutal address the computer?"

Neelix shook his head. "She gives it simple commands— activate this, initiate that—but to get information, she always uses a keypad or console."

Picard found that to be incredibly useful information. It was entirely possible that because the Alliance had built this duplicate from schematics they had had no role in creating, they might not be aware of all the subsystems and capabilities that were available to them. Clearly, they understood how the intraship communications system worked, because they had locked out the ability for prisoners to talk with each other.

But what other systems mightn't they understand? Or perhaps not even know about?

There was one quick way to find out.

"Computer," Picard said. "Activate the Emergency Medical Hologram."

Neelix stared at Picard in horror. "Are you mad?"

The holographic doctor resolved beside the diagnostic bed like a genie rising from a bottle.

"Please state the nature of your interrogation requirements," the doctor said brightly.

Here goes, Picard thought. "Your interrogation subroutine
is not required at this time. I need access to your main
medical routine."

The hologram nodded once. "Certainly." Then he gazed off
at nothing in particular for a moment, as if resetting something internal. "In that case, please state the nature of the
medical emergency."

Picard smiled. He had made the program cycle away from
whatever overlay the Alliance had added to make it an
implement of torture. A plan took form, but it all depended
on whether or not the Alliance had made other alterations in
the EMH program.

"Do you know who I am?" Picard asked.

The doctor appeared annoyed by the question. "According
to the ship's registry of senior Starfleet officers, you're Captain Jean-Luc Picard. Are you suffering from memory loss?"

"Who are you?"

The hologram narrowed his eyes in suspicion. "I am the
Emergency Medical Hologram. Are you experiencing difficul-
ties with your eyesight?"

"Where are we?"

With an expression of unalloyed exasperation, the doctor
picked up a medical tricorder and began to play it over
Picard. "We're on the *Starship Voyager.* Odd . . . I'm not
detecting any cranial injuries."

"You won't," Picard said, still wondering if his plan would
work. But since the EMH appeared to be functioning according to Starfleet design specs, he saw no reason why the plan
shouldn't. "I'm absolutely fine."

"I'll be the judge of that," the doctor said. He frowned at
the tricorder readings. "You're suffering from dehydration,
adrenaline intoxication . . . Your stress readings are off the
chart. . . ." The EMH peered at Picard in troubled concern.
"What have you been doing?"

Picard was intrigued. By stripping away the EMH's interrogation overlay, he apparently had erased the EMH's memory of having tortured him. Clearly the Alliance did not grasp Starfleet's methods of systems integration. "Can you give me anything?" Picard asked.

"Certainly. Sound medical advice. What you need is rest."

Keeping his voice under control, Picard gently asked, "Then, can I return to my quarters?"

"I see no reason why not." The EMH snapped his tricorder shut. "Perhaps next time you decide to waste my programming time, you could arrange to be in actual need of medical attention?"

"Ah, Doctor, just one thing. . . ."

The EMH sighed. "It's always one more thing with you people, isn't it?"

Picard moved his hands against his wrist restraints. "I need these taken off."

The doctor looked at the restraints. "May I ask why you're wearing them?"

Picard nodded his head at Neelix. "He did it. He claims it's . . . a new form of treatment for . . . stiff muscles."

The EMH glared at Neelix. "I see. And are you a physician?"

"No, sir," Neelix said nervously.

"Chiropractor? Physiotherapist? Somatician?"

"Oh, no, not at all."

"A Healer of the Vulcan School? Aural aligner? Midwife?"

Neelix's chin hung down on his chest. "No, sir. . . ."

"Dentist?"

Neelix silently shook his head, and Picard was grateful that the alien was going along with his ruse.

The EMH pressed the disconnect controls on the diagnostic bed's restraints. "Then I'd prefer you stay out of my sickbay with your . . . questionable theories."

Picard sat up, trying to keep his relief disguised. The last thing he needed was for the EMH to try and correlate the ship's registry of senior Starfleet officers with his medical records and stumble upon a reference to Picard, Jean-Luc, under "prisoners."

The EMH looked expectantly at Picard. "One more thing, perhaps?"

"No, that's fine. You've been very helpful."

The doctor frowned. "I live to serve. If it's not too much trouble . . . ?"

"Computer," Picard said as he at last stood up. "Deactivate the EMH."

"You're so kind," the doctor muttered, then rippled and faded from view.

Neelix stared at Picard in awe. "Very impressive, Captain."

"Let's hope *Voyager* has a few more surprises the Alliance doesn't know about." He straightened his tunic, paused a moment to see if the dizziness he felt would worsen. But it didn't. He felt light-headed, but it wasn't debilitating. He motioned for Neelix to come closer.

"What is it?" the alien asked.

"If I could get you off this ship, away from the Alliance, would you help me?"

Neelix rubbed at his twitching eye. "You don't even have to ask, Captain. You escaped while I was supposed to be guarding you. Gul Rutal . . . she'll kill me anyway."

Picard put his hand on the Talaxian's shoulder. "I promise you, she won't."

Neelix stood a little taller. "I'll do . . . whatever you say. Captain."

"Good man," Picard said. "Computer, who is the current captain of the *Voyager?*"

"Captain Kathryn Janeway has not yet reported for duty. No other officer has been assigned in her place."

Picard smiled. *All* of the *Voyager*'s programming had been built into this version. He was halfway home. "Computer, this is Picard, Jean-Luc. Activate Emergency Fleet Access Program Alpha Alpha One Alpha."

"Emergency Fleet Access Program initiated. You have one hour to comply with Starfleet regulations."

"All further communications with me are to be encrypted."

"Acknowledged."

Picard saw Neelix's questioning look.

"In times of war or other emergency," Picard explained, "ships can sometimes lose their command crews, and command crews can lose their ships. So Starfleet has established procedures by which crews can quickly shift command authority from ship to ship. Gul Rutal has made it much simpler by having never established her command posting with the computer according to Starfleet protocol. She just didn't know about it."

Neelix's eyes widened. "So *you've* taken control of *Voyager?* As quickly as that?"

"No," Picard said. "It's not that easy. Even without the computer acknowledging a previous commander for *Voyager,* I'll still need confirmation authority from Starfleet Command. Since the computer has given me an hour, that means there should be a starbase within thirty-minute, subspace-radio contact of our present position. But in the meantime, for the next hour at least, the computer will recognize me as *Voyager*'s acting captain and allow me to take certain limited actions in preparation of assuming full control."

"What sort of actions?" Neelix looked excited, and Picard decided it must be a Talaxian trait that their emotions were so clearly displayed, almost like Vulcans in reverse. He found it a refreshing characteristic.

Picard held up a finger, asking for Neelix's indulgence. "Computer, how many guards are posted within visual range of detention cell four?"

"No guards are currently posted within visual range of that cell."

Picard found that unusual. But then, only Neelix had been posted to guard him. Unless . . .

"Computer, is detention cell four under surveillance by security?"

"Affirmative."

Picard felt his stomach tighten. "Computer, is sickbay under surveillance by security?"

"Affirmative."

Picard's thoughts raced. Clearly, sickbay couldn't be under active surveillance, otherwise armed guards would have burst in within minutes of his having activated the EMH. But when the Cardassians and Klingons discovered he was missing and replayed the surveillance logs, they'd hear every word of explanation he had said to Neelix.

"Computer, delete all surveillance logs of sickbay, from the time code in which I was brought in."

"Unable to comply. Surveillance logs can only be deleted by order of Gul Rutal."

"Merde," Picard said. There had to be a way around that restriction. "Computer, as acting commander of the *Voyager,* I request that all surveillance logs of sickbay since my arrival here be encrypted, coded to my voiceprint alone. Can you comply?"

"Affirmative."

Picard felt he was riding a gravity whip at an amusement center. "Encrypt those logs. Also, encrypt all logs of detention cell four, from this time on."

"Logs encrypted."

"What are you doing?" Neelix asked.

"Being certain no one will be able to trace our movements," Picard explained. He took hold of Neelix's arm. "Computer, initiate site-to-site transport: Picard and Neelix to detention cell four, placing us outside the containment field."

"What's site-to-site transport?" Neelix asked.

Picard felt relieved that before he could answer, sickbay began to dissolve into the sparkling glow of the transporter effect.

A few moments later, the glow faded to be replaced by the bulkheads of *Voyager*'s brig.

Neelix seemed to lose his balance as he clutched at his chest. "In the name of the Great Forest . . ." he whispered.

But Picard ignored him. He looked to his right, where he saw the glow of a forcefield emitter. "Will!" he shouted as he saw Riker, standing up, as close as possible to the field, a handful of other *Enterprise* crew behind him.

And then Picard realized that Riker was not standing to welcome him, but to warn him.

"Captain! Behind you!"

Picard spun around, a confused Neelix still at his side, to face two Klingon warriors just entering from the corridor. One had already drawn his disruptor.

Picard had only time enough to think what a fool he had been to fall into this trap.

And then the Klingon fired.

NINE

Kirk grabbed the mirror Spock and leapt over the transporter pad to crouch behind it. Despite the weak gravity, the infirm Vulcan moaned as they landed. Kirk kept his head down, reached into his belt pouch for the small cricket phaser he had taken from Janeway.

Then Janeway was beside him, also crouching. She glanced at the tiny weapon. "That won't do any good. They're armored."

Before he could answer, a sparkling column of light formed to Kirk's other side. He glanced up in time to see a Cardassian materialize, a weapon already pointing straight down at Kirk.

No conscious thought was involved in what happened next. It didn't matter that Kirk had been little more than a gentleman farmer for the past year. He lunged up, arms crossed above his head to bring both forearms to bear against the Cardassian's throat.

He felt the heat of a disruptor blast as it fired past him, but it didn't strike.

In the lunar gravity, Kirk flew two meters in the air with the surprised Cardassian, and landed on top of him.

Then there was an explosion behind Kirk, a flare of golden

energy, and a blast of debris—the transporter pad, he knew. Whatever escape route Janeway had arranged was now cut off.

But that wasn't the crisis at hand. Kirk took care of that by driving his fist into the Cardassian's face, then swept aside the alien's hand, which still clutched the disruptor.

With his other hand, Kirk fired the small phaser at the Cardassian. The slender beam of phased energy flared against the large black breastplate of the Cardassian's uniform, but had no other effect. Kirk knew that not even a beam to his attacker's exposed head and neck would be effective as long as the antiphaser circuitry in the armor served to deflect the energy.

Then the Cardassian swung up his free hand and grabbed Kirk by the throat. Began to squeeze.

"Die, Terran!" the Cardassian snarled.

Kirk gasped for air but his throat was blocked. If he struck the Cardassian with his left hand, then the Cardassian would be free to use his disruptor. In his right hand, he held only the useless phaser. He was ready to toss it away so he could strike again at his attacker.

But then, Kirk knew, phasers were often good for more than just firing at the enemy.

As his vision clouded with growing darkness and he knew he had only seconds of consciousness remaining, Kirk fired the small phaser into the rocky ground *beside* the Cardassian.

Where the beam hit, a cloud of molten rock droplets sprayed out, some hitting the Cardassian's exposed flesh.

The alien screamed in pain, but it only served to strengthen his death grip around Kirk's throat.

Kirk heard his heart pounding, saw his field of vision collapsing to a narrow point of light.

There was only one last thing to try—and he didn't even know if it was still possible in this new age.

Kirk fumbled with the cricket phaser, pressed what he

still hoped was the safety interlock, then ran his thumb along its side to set it for full energy discharge.

Through the thunderous roar of his heartbeat, Kirk heard the telltale whine of an overload begin.

With the last of his strength, the last of his consciousness, Kirk jammed the small phaser down the gaping front of the Cardassian's chestplate.

Instantly, he felt the pressure on his neck disappear as the Cardassian bucked him off.

Kirk flailed through the air, rolled onto the freezing ground, saw the Cardassian tearing at his chestplate as the whine built and built and—

The Cardassian's armor bulged as if it had been suddenly overpressurized just as a flare of golden energy shot up through the neck opening.

The tiny phaser had exploded, and the Cardassian's armor had contained almost all of the phased energy of that burst, directing it inward.

As Kirk rubbed at his throat, he saw there was little of his attacker left, except for that smoking armor.

For an instant, he felt the familiar adrenal rush of knowing he had achieved victory—a response that was purely emotional. And then, unexpectedly, he was filled with regret.

Another intelligent being had just died at his hands.

Then Kirk felt another hand grip his shoulder and haul him to his feet, spinning him around so suddenly that a far-too-frequent shock of pain snapped through his lower back.

As Kirk faced the second Cardassian to grab him, he could make no effort to defend himself. The pain from his back was making it impossible to breathe, impossible to move.

The Cardassian raised a disruptor to Kirk's face, then hesitated.

The gray-skinned alien peered closely at Kirk, eyes opening wide.

"Tiberius . . . ?" he whispered.

Then Kirk's attacker's eyes rolled up in his head as he

dropped his disruptor and slumped to the ground, the mirror Spock's hand firmly gripping his shoulder.

Kirk winced in a spasm of pain, knowing that only the weak lunar gravity was allowing him to remain standing with what had happened to his back.

"Good work," Kirk gasped. He knew he should be looking around for other attackers, but he was a prisoner in his own body, completely immobilized.

The mirror Spock released the unconscious Cardassian at his feet, then flexed his hand as if he had strained it. He raised an eyebrow at Kirk. "Are you injured?"

"No," Kirk said, then flinched as he tried to nonchalantly shake his head. He could hear Teilani berating him for not taking better care of himself, for not trusting in modern medicine.

"Ah," the mirror Spock said, "your back."

"That's only two Cardassians," Kirk said, barely able to make his voice rise above a whisper. "Aren't there two more?"

Janeway stepped up beside Kirk, wiping the blood from a Klingon *mek'leth*. "Not anymore," she said. Then she expertly flipped the short sword around and slapped it against a sheath on her leg, so that the sheath closed over it like a thick liquid.

"How's your Vulcan friend?" Kirk asked.

"Her name is T'Val," Janeway said. "She'll recover."

"Good."

Janeway's eyes bore into Kirk's. "No thanks to you." She looked at the mirror Spock. "The platform is beyond repair. We're going to have to use the secondary—and quickly. Before someone realizes these four haven't reported in."

"We will need T'Val's medkit first," the mirror Spock said. "Captain Kirk is quite incapable of moving."

Janeway regarded Kirk as if he were a malingerer.

"My back," Kirk said, embarrassed by his weakness.

"Just a minute," Janeway sighed. Kirk heard her walk over

to the ruined transporter pad, but couldn't turn his head to watch her. So he and the mirror Spock stared at each other. Kirk could sense they shared the same sense of mystery and confusion. He kept reminding himself that this was not his old friend, and hoped that the mirror Spock kept reminding himself that Kirk was not his old enemy.

"I've dropped into the middle of a war, haven't I?" Kirk asked.

"A war of your causing, correct," the mirror Spock replied.

"Then 'dropped' isn't the word for it. You came looking for me."

"Correct again. I must say, I am impressed at your facility with logic."

Kirk raised an eyebrow at the Vulcan in what he hoped was a recognizable imitation. "Taught by an expert."

"Indeed." Then Kirk saw comprehension in the mirror Spock's eyes. "Ah, I see. In this universe, our friendship continued. What else does your logic tell you?"

"You want something from me, but I don't know what. And the Alliance knows you came looking for me, but doesn't want you to succeed."

"Almost flawless," the mirror Spock conceded. "The Vulcan resistance needs access to Starfleet databanks, which only you can provide for us. But the Alliance does not know that we have specifically sought you out for this. As a matter of course, they attempt to stop all our activities, wherever they uncover them."

Kirk heard Janeway returning with slow lunar steps. "But the Cardassians came after us so quickly here."

"They detected our transporters in use."

Kirk didn't like the implication hidden in that statement. "You mean, agents of the Alliance are already stationed in this solar system, in this universe, looking for signs of your activities?"

Before the mirror Spock could answer, Kirk shuddered as Janeway grabbed his shoulder from behind.

"Where?" she asked.

". . . lower . . . back . . ." It was all Kirk could say.

Then he felt a spot of heat deep within his back, just at his waist. Slowly it diffused along his entire spine. He took a deep breath, like breathing for the first time.

His back felt tender, almost as if a small object were being pressed a bit too tightly against his skin, but it no longer pained him.

Without meaning to, Kirk allowed a small moan of pleasure to escape. His back hadn't felt that good in a year, even under Teilani's ministrations.

And again, a moment after that purely visceral response to the change in his back, he felt that same regret he'd experienced while looking at the remains of the Cardassian he killed.

He turned to Janeway, took the flashing medical instrument from her hand. "What is it?"

"Standard tissue regenerator. Did it work?"

Kirk pressed the small control that turned the device off. He dropped it and it fell so slowly Janeway had ample time to pluck it from the air. "I promised myself I'd never use one of those things again."

"Fine," Janeway snapped. "When we're out of here, I'll remember to hit your back with the butt of a phaser rifle. Will that be better?"

If he hadn't seen her wipe the blood off her *mek'leth* himself, Kirk would never have believed this woman had the discipline to be a warrior. There was promise in her, if nothing else. But her temper would be a formidable barrier to her growth.

Kirk decided to show her how self-control was maintained.

"I'm sorry," he told her. "Thank you. My back feels much better and I appreciate what you've done."

Janeway said something under her breath that almost sounded Klingon—Kirk could only make out what seemed to be a reference to his mother. Then she added, "As soon as

T'Val's on her feet, we'll have to leave." She returned to the ruined transporter platform without waiting for a reply.

The mirror Spock spoke softly. "She doesn't know what to make of you, Captain. She knows only the Kirk of her universe. And she is one of the few Terrans to actually have a counterpart in this universe. That is always a difficult adjustment to make."

"I thought we all had counterparts," Kirk said.

"Since the time you crossed over, the universes have diverged even more. Our studies have shown that among those of our generation, yours and mine, more than eighty percent of the Terran and Vulcan populations were identical. But today, because history has progressed so differently in the two universes, many people born here, where the Terran and Vulcan populations are larger, were not born in my universe. Therefore, there is correspondingly less duplication."

Kirk read between the lines. "Why just Terran and Vulcan populations? Isn't the whole universe affected?"

The way the mirror Spock hesitated, Kirk could tell he was holding something back. "As far as I could ascertain from the comparisons I was able to make based on the information I absorbed from melding with your Dr. McCoy, our two universes were once virtually identical. Certainly, the alien cultures you encountered prior to your crossover were identical to their counterparts in my universe."

"But human—Terran, that is—and Vulcan history, that's where the difference lies? Only among those two people?"

"It is not a subject I have had time to explore in recent years," the mirror Spock said. "Suffice to say, when those of us who are little more than slaves or hunted fugitives in our own reality find out that we have a double who enjoys a life of privilege in this one, it can have an adverse emotional effect."

Kirk followed the mirror Spock's gaze to see Janeway using the medkit instruments on T'Val. The injured Vulcan female was sitting up, pale, but speaking. "What does her counterpart do?"

"To be precise, 'did.' In your universe, Kathryn Janeway became a starship captain."

Kirk was taken by surprise. He had seen the potential in Janeway, but to think she was that capable was a revelation. And then it hit him. Why her name had sounded familiar. "There was that starship I read about, the one that disappeared, that they just received some message from . . . *Voyager?*"

"Correct. Transported to your Delta Quadrant by an unknown alien technology."

"Then your Janeway has come out ahead." Kirk saw the mirror Spock's confusion. "She still has her life in the region she was born, not exiled to an unknown quadrant where she'll probably never see home again."

"It is hardly a life many would desire. To Janeway, she only knows that except for an accident of birth, she might have grown up without want, explored her love of science, of music. If the question had been put to her, as illogical as it might sound, she would have chosen a life such as that, even knowing it would end with exile, or even be cut short by early death, instead of what she endures today."

Kirk found that difficult to accept. Everything he had experienced in his own life had taught him that the one true, inarguable purpose of life was to *live.* Any other purpose was a matter for philosophers. Any other choice was escape, no different from choosing to cloud one's mind with chemicals or holographic fantasies or circuitry implants. With the exception of the decisions soldiers might make to risk their lives in pursuit of victory, Kirk could only imagine one possibility in which a person might willingly embrace death, and it left him saddened for Kathryn Janeway.

"You told me there was no hope left in your universe," Kirk said. "Can that be possible?"

"An insightful question," the mirror Spock said. "I trust the answer will provide even greater insight for you." He drew his cloak closer around his narrow shoulders. "In my universe,

Captain Kirk, the only hope left is what you now choose to bring to us."

Kirk had already guessed it would come to that. For whatever reason, this Spock was turning around their last conversation of more than a century ago. Then, Kirk had told the mirror Spock that one person with a vision could make a difference. Now, it was Kirk's turn. At least, according to this Spock.

"I take it you mean that the hope I could offer you is that information you want from the Starfleet databanks."

"And again, correct."

"What kind of information?"

"In the past century, your technology has advanced considerably faster than it has in my universe. We need weaponry. Ships. Faster and more powerful than anything the Alliance has. A cell of Terran rebels operating near Bajor has achieved great success with just such a strategy."

But Kirk wasn't interested in details. If technical specifications were all these people needed, he didn't understand why they had gone to such lengths to obtain them. More specifically, he didn't understand why they had come after *him.* "Given everything you've told me, I don't see how Starfleet could refuse you."

"Try the Prime Directive," T'Val said behind him.

Kirk was startled. He was so engrossed in his conversation with this other Spock that he had lost track of Janeway and her Vulcan accomplice.

"Starfleet has already placed our universe off limits," T'Val said bitterly. "They have washed their hands of us."

Hearing that explanation, Kirk smiled. He couldn't help it. *"That's* why you came to me? Because you needed someone who could break the Prime Directive for you?"

Janeway's voice was tight, the first tremors from a volcano about to explode. "This is not at all humorous."

"No," Kirk said, trying to put some of his own self-control to work. "I know it's not. But the irony of it. That's the one thing I kept doing that made Starfleet want to wash their hands of *me*. Breaking that damned directive. That *that* is the reason you've come looking for me . . . I mean, aren't there any other officers in Starfleet? How about Jean-Luc Picard? He knows the difference between right and wrong without being hobbled by Starfleet technicalities. You might not know it to look at him, but he'd cut through the regulations as fast as I would if he thought the end result was fair."

From their reactions to what he had said, Kirk saw some unspoken message pass between the three rebels from the mirror universe. But all the mirror Spock would say was "Jean-Luc Picard would not be suitable."

Kirk thought that was an odd reaction, and he suddenly wondered if there might be a Picard counterpart in the mirror universe.

Then Janeway checked her tricorder and announced that it was time to leave.

Kirk walked with them to the cavern's entrance, and followed them into the mine tunnels again.

As they proceeded in silence, moving again with the slow loping stride of lunar gravity, Kirk tried to decide why Picard wasn't right for what the rebels wanted, while he was. Then he remembered what this Spock had been saying to him earlier as they had hurried through the tunnels to the cavern.

"You're looking for justice, aren't you—all of you?" Kirk asked. "You've come to me to change the playing field because I, or my counterpart, at least, was the one who brought the Klingons and the Cardassians into their Alliance."

"No psychohistorian, on Earth or on Vulcan, could ever have predicted that impossible pairing," the mirror Spock answered. "It is in the Cardassian nature to seek allies. But it is not a common Klingon trait, except under exceptional circumstances. Yet somehow, Tiberius was able to go to the leaders of both groups, and convince them to follow him to reclaim the Terran Empire."

"The war," Kirk said, understanding. "The war of my causing."

They paused at another intersection as Janeway took readings.

"It was the most brutal war in the history of the known galaxy," the mirror Spock said, hugging his arms to his chest. This part of the mine was getting colder. Kirk could see that the mirror Spock had begun to shiver. It was such an unusual sight, a Vulcan who had lost control of his autonomic functions, that Kirk had to force himself not to stare. "It did not matter that under my rule the Terran Empire had withdrawn from the occupied worlds and was engaged in reparations. The legacy of hate the Empire had sewn was reaped a thousandfold. World after world joined the Alliance. Its only purpose, to erase Earth and Vulcan from the universe."

Again Kirk struggled to understand why everything in the mirror universe seemed to keep focusing on those two planets. Spock's world. Kirk's world. Why those two?

Janeway waved them down the tunnel to the left. It descended steeply and the fusion globes were farther apart, making each step treacherous.

T'Val took a hand torch from her combat suit and used her biomechanical hand to keep the beam focused on the tunnel floor before the mirror Spock.

As they continued down, Kirk began to learn why this Spock had aged so much more drastically than his own—his life had been much more difficult. "I faced Tiberius in battle a dozen times," the mirror Spock said, now openly breathing hard. "We held each other at bay as often as one or the other of us could declare victory. After so many years of working together, we had no secrets from one another. But then, the final battle came. Wolf 359. Seven point eight light-years from Earth. Strategically, the last major staging area before reaching Earth herself."

The mirror Spock halted momentarily, his gaze unfocused, as if reliving that battle in his troubled mind.

Janeway took his arm to urge him forward again. "The battle lasted three days," she told Kirk. "The combined Klingon/Cardassian Armada faced what remained of the Imperial Starfleet. Three hundred and ninety ships of the Terran Empire were lost. More than one hundred and ten thousand lives. Then the lines broke and there was nothing . . . nothing to stop the Armada from reaching Earth."

"The surface of the Earth was carved by particle beams," the mirror Spock said, "for no other reason than sheer hatred. For four days, a convoy of Klingon battlecruisers did nothing but fire their disruptors into the Great Lakes of North America, boiling them almost dry, forever changing the atmosphere of the Northern Hemisphere. The Cardassian fleet did the same to the Southern Hemisphere by burning the rain forests of South America and Asia. Then they poisoned the oceans so the biosphere of Earth could no longer produce enough oxygen to be self-sustaining."

Kirk's mouth was dry. This went beyond any act of war he could imagine. It was insanity, but at a level almost unbelievable. "What was Tiberius thinking . . . ?" he asked.

"I doubt Tiberius had anything to do with what happened to Earth," the mirror Spock said, almost wheezing. "By the time the Battle of Wolf 359 had ended, Tiberius was gone." The Vulcan continued to stumble forward—only, it seemed, by means of Janeway's assistance.

"What happened to him?"

"What didn't?" T'Val answered beside Kirk. Her artificial hand kept the hand torch trained on the ground ahead of Spock with the precision of a machine. "Some say his flagship was destroyed on the second day of battle. Some say as soon as the Imperial fleet was routed, the Klingons captured him and tortured him to death. Or threw him from an atmospheric cruiser twenty miles above the surface of the Earth."

"Some say the Cardassians captured him and sealed him in a hollow asteroid," Janeway said. Her voice bounced oddly off the icy rock walls of the dark corridor that surrounded them. "The only prisoner floating in absolute darkness, in a void a kilometer across." To Kirk, it sounded as if Janeway felt that would have been too easy a punishment for his counterpart. "Or else they dissected him over the course of a Cardassian year, keeping him alive and aware the whole time, until he was only a mesh of tissue and nerves and blood vessels to be offered to a pack of voles."

Kirk shivered at the level of revulsion his counterpart had inspired.

"Whatever his fate," the mirror Spock said, "after the fall of Earth, Tiberius was never seen again. Nor was he ever expected to be seen. It was quite clear that the Alliance, once formed, had no more use for him, and if he had survived the Alliance war to defeat the Empire, then he would have been assassinated as soon as his usefulness had ended."

Despite the atrocities Tiberius had committed, Kirk couldn't help feeling a pang of sorrow for his counterpart. Throughout his own life, Kirk had always fought to be the person in control. Yet Tiberius had been manipulated, first by Spock, then by the Alliance. In the end, he had lost everything to betrayal. *Dangerous thoughts,* Kirk suddenly told himself. How could he have sympathy for a monster like Tiberius?

"What happened to Vulcan?" Kirk asked.

The mirror Spock answered that question, for once all emotion driven from his tone, as if he were the Vulcan he had been a century ago. "My world did the logical thing. We surrendered. I negotiated the terms myself."

Kirk could guess what the result had been. This Spock had already described what his world was like today. "And the Alliance betrayed you."

"Vulcan was scourged," T'Val said. "Its biosphere was left intact, but nothing else was."

"But you escaped," Kirk said.

104

The mirror Spock merely nodded, as if he finally had no more breath to speak. Janeway's steady pace did not slacken.

"And ever since then," T'Val volunteered for the other Vulcan, "Spock has been a fugitive. Intendant of the Vulcan resistance."

They reached a level section of the tunnel. T'Val's torch beam found a narrow crevice in the tunnel wall. Janeway directed them through it.

A winding, cramped passageway led to a small chamber, littered with the remains of antique spacesuits. Kirk looked around and guessed that this had been a staging area for the ice miners. Another transporter platform was installed here, though it was smaller than the first he had seen.

"Is that powerful enough to take us to the surface?" Kirk asked. These portable models were generally used for short-distance transports in dangerous environments. He wasn't certain how deep they were, but he felt that the moon's surface must be several kilometers above them. And beaming through solid rock was much more energy-intensive than passing through vacuum.

But Janeway discounted Kirk's concerns. "It doesn't have to take us to the surface." She stepped up on the platform, then helped the mirror Spock up as well.

"Then, where will it take us?" Kirk asked. He took his position, too, and noticed that T'Val moved to stay out of contact with him. "To another cavern?"

"No," the mirror Spock said. "To another universe."

Kirk opened his mouth to object.

But he was too late.

The ice-mine chamber dissolved around him as, for the first time in a century and the second time in his life, James T. Kirk passed through the looking glass.

TEN

Neelix threw himself forward and took the first shot, doubling over soundlessly in the *Voyager*'s brig.

Picard wouldn't let the Talaxian's sacrifice be in vain.

He leapt up, slamming into the Klingon who had hit Neelix, spinning him around to smash into the second Klingon.

The second Klingon stumbled backward, raised his own disruptor, and fired from the hip.

Just as the misdirected beam hit the first Klingon, Picard released his hold and dropped him to the deck. Then, in the heartbeat before the second Klingon could fire again, Picard struck—a blow to the arm dropping the Klingon's weapon, a blow to the mouth breaking the Klingon's front teeth.

A fountain of pink blood sprayed into the air as the wounded warrior shook his massive head. Picard backed away as the Klingon fixed on his foe, snarling like a ravenous beast. Hair wild, blood from his torn mouth streaming down to his dull metal armor, the warrior pulled his *d'k tahg* from his belt in a single fluid movement, flicked open the weapon's side blades with an ominous click, and lunged for Picard.

No other human could have survived such an all-out attack.

But Jean-Luc Picard's greatest chief of security had been Klingon. And Picard had not wasted the opportunity to learn unarmed combat from one of the galaxy's most renowned masters of the art.

Thus Picard was not foolish enough to evade the charge—an action that would have made him instantly vulnerable. Instead, he swept his arm out to deflect the hand holding the three-bladed knife, locked his own hand around the Klingon's forearm, and pulled his attacker forward faster than the Klingon had planned.

Adeptly as a matador, Picard sidestepped as the Klingon lurched past him, arms outstretched, off balance, bellowing, his body propelled straight for the target Picard had selected.

The forcefield of detention cell four.

Because not only did the forcefield act to keep prisoners in, it acted to keep all else out.

As the Klingon hit the wall of energy, his nervous system short-circuited, and his cry of outrage was cut off, instantly. Amplified and rechanneled back into him, the inertial force of his impact threw him back in the opposite direction as if he had connected with a wall of hard rubber.

Sliding along the deck on his back, the Klingon warrior skidded to a stop at Picard's feet, unconscious.

But Picard had no time to savor his victory. If anyone on this ship's bridge was monitoring transporter use, he knew he had only moments before new guards arrived. He moved swiftly to the forcefield controls on the bulkhead beside cell four and input a standard override command. The field winked out.

At once, Riker and eight other members of the *Enterprise* crew charged out of the cell. Riker immediately directed some to the other detention cells to shut off those forcefields, as well, releasing all remaining crew members who had been held captive.

"Collect the Klingons' weapons," Picard instructed his

crew, "then block the doors. And find anything that might be a communicator so we can listen in on their transmissions."

Next Picard went back to Neelix and turned the small alien over, relieved and surprised to see that he was still breathing. Guessing that Talaxians must have natural immunity to Klingon disruptors, Picard waved over one of Dr. Crusher's nurses who was among the freed prisoners. Using a first-aid medkit he had taken from the brig's storage locker, the nurse began to treat Neelix.

Then a deep, guttural moaning turned Picard's attention to the Klingon who had been shot by his partner. He, too, was still alive.

This time, Picard called to Riker for help and together they tied and gagged the two Klingons and dragged them into a cell. "Why would Klingons have their disruptors set on stun?" Riker asked. As unlikely as it seemed, it was the only explanation for both shooting victims remaining alive.

"These aren't the same type of Klingons we're familiar with," Picard said.

Riker looked at his captain expectantly.

"This isn't the *Voyager,* Will. It's a duplicate, built in the quantum reality Starfleet calls the mirror universe."

Riker's mouth opened in surprise. "The one Kirk crossed into?"

Picard checked the gags on the two unconscious Klingons. "And the one Dr. Bashir and that Bajoran officer encountered just a few years ago."

"What are they doing here? And why build a *Voyager?*" Riker asked.

"Bait," Picard said, stepping out of the cell to reactivate the forcefield. He saw that the crew members who had been held in the brig had gathered together, awaiting orders. Commander Sloane and Lieutenant Stran, a young Vulcan scientist from Geology, stood to either side of the brig's main entrance doors, each with a Klingon disruptor in hand. Picard was pleased with his crew's initiative. Out of habit, born of too many dangerous away missions before he was a captain, he began a head count.

"But if they have the capability to build a *Voyager,* why not build their own *Enterprise,* too?" Riker asked.

Picard didn't answer. Frowning, he scanned the group assembled in the brig again. The computer had said that thirty-four members of the *Enterprise* crew were being held here. Picard counted all thirty-four standing before him.

And Riker made thirty-five.

"Captain?" Riker prompted.

"Is Deanna here?" Picard asked.

"I don't know where she is, sir."

Picard sensed the concern in his first officer. "I do know she is on this ship, Will, and she is all right, along with five hundred and seventy-five others from the crew. I obtained a report from the computer." Picard moved closer to Riker, angling so that the other crew members wouldn't be able to see or hear what he said next. "Someone in this room is an impostor. A mirror-universe counterpart. Someone who will look identical to a crew member we all know."

Picard watched Riker's reaction carefully, knowing full well that *he* might be the counterpart.

"That's why you wanted Deanna," Riker said. "She'd be able to sense the evasion in the impostor."

"In her absence, I'm open to suggestions," Picard said.

"You're sure there's only one impostor?"

"Unless someone else joined you in the past five minutes," Picard said.

"Only the Klingons, which makes it simple," Riker said. "We just have to find out which of the people in here arrived on his or her own."

That had been Picard's first strategy as well. But it didn't hold up. "Do *you* remember how you got here?" Picard asked.

He could see that Riker immediately grasped the dilemma. All those who were unconscious when they were brought on board this *Voyager* would be unable to recall exactly when or how any other crew member might have been added to the brig's detention cells.

But then Riker seemed to have a flash of inspiration. "This happened to Worf. When he went through that quantum fissure. What was it, five years ago?"

Picard saw the parallels, though not the exact application to what they faced now. "But Worf experienced an entire spectrum of alternate histories. Something on the order of two hundred and eighty-five thousand of them, I believe."

"Exactly," Riker said. "But each one of them had a unique quantum signature. That was how Worf managed to return to this reality."

Now Picard understood Riker's solution. "Of course. Everyone from the mirror universe will have a quantum signature unique to that reality, which we will be able to identify as different from our own."

"All we need is a tricorder."

Picard looked around the brig for a storage locker or—

"Over there," Picard said.

He and Riker immediately went to the replicator in the brig's far bulkhead. The main selection screen was set for food, and Picard was relieved to see that all the general settings were for standard Starfleet rations. The Klingons and Cardassians either had not bothered to reprogram the replicator system, or were unaware of how it functioned.

Picard entered his Emergency Fleet Access Code, then called up an equipment list, scrolling through it to see which models of tricorders were available.

"Was that a Fleet Access Code?" Riker asked.

"I believe the Alliance is unaware of many of the features of this ship," Picard said. "Gul Rutal never established herself as the commander, so the computer is prepared to accept me if Starfleet approves." He saw that the replicator banks contained the specs for a Type Ten tricorder and he ordered one.

Riker grinned. "I'd like to see the expression on the face of the communications officer who gets a message from *Voyager* asking for confirmation of your orders."

"With luck, Starfleet will know we're out here within the next hour," Picard said. On the replicator screen, a resource-conservation alert reminded him that eighty-five tricorders were already available in ship's stores, but Picard entered an override command.

With a flash of golden energy, the small tricorder appeared in the replicator receiving bay a few moments later. Picard handed it to Riker.

Riker flipped it open, switched it on, then paused. "Jean-Luc, does this strike you as being a bit too easy?"

Picard had wondered that himself, but had come up with an alternative explanation. "Counting their human slaves, there are ninety-nine Alliance crew on board to handle almost six hundred of us. The key Alliance command staff are on the *Enterprise,* and since no one has responded to my site-to-site transport, I can only conclude that the Alliance can't handle this ship."

"Let's hope you're right," Riker said. "Can you get that to produce phasers?"

Picard tried, but the screen display stated that his Fleet Access Code would not allow him to replicate weaponry until confirmation of his orders had been received. "Not yet," Picard said. "But let's see how I do with comm badges." He set the replicator to produce enough comm badges to replace the ones that had been removed from his crew's uniforms. They began to materialize in sets of six.

"Is the tricorder calibrated for quantum signatures?" Picard asked.

Riker pressed a final control, then nodded.

"Use it while you hand out the comm badges."

Riker took a handful of comm badges to the crew members

waiting in the center of the brig. Picard glanced at the doors, saw they were still guarded by Sloane and Stran, then went to the security station. There was a small desk there, with brig controls, a computer screen, and a communications console.

Picard remained standing, in case he had to move quickly, and logged on to the computer system. After entering his access code again, he asked the computer to list all the security systems currently in operation.

The screen displayed a short list of visual-sensor monitors, including the ones in sickbay and this brig. All were running on automatic. None were under live observation.

Picard didn't understand it. It was as if this ship were being run by cadets.

Riker came back to Picard, leaned over to read the screen. "Ensign Margaret Clark," he whispered.

Picard didn't look up. He knew the ensign, fair skin, dark hair, almost human, one of her grandparents a Vulcan, he recalled. She had been assigned to the *Enterprise* only three months ago. For a moment, he wondered how the Alliance had obtained their information about the ship's crew, how they knew that they could use Ensign Clark's counterpart to infiltrate the prisoners. That implied a certain level of sophistication that was missing from the way they ran this ship.

"How do you want me to handle it?" Riker asked.

Picard fixed Riker with a steady gaze. "How did you handle it when the *Pegasus* was lost?"

Riker blinked in momentary confusion. Then he frowned. "You want to know if I'm the counterpart."

"How did the warp-core breach happen, Will?" Picard waited, ready to drive his fist into William Riker's jaw if he had to. The *Pegasus* had been one of Riker's first assignments after graduating from the Academy. Seventeen years ago, the records stated, the experimental ship had exploded after the crew mutinied against Captain Erik Pressman. Pressman and Ensign Riker were among the nine survivors of the disaster.

And only those nine knew what the records didn't show—
what had really happened to their ship.

"There was no warp-core breach. The *Pegasus* was trapped
in an asteroid. Pressman was conducting a test of a cloaking
device, in violation of the Treaty of Algeron, and the crew
mutinied."

"That much is in Pressman's court-martial records," Picard said. "Tell me something that was withheld. The rank of
the Romulan spy we captured when we found the *Pegasus.*"

"We didn't capture any spies, Romulan or otherwise."

Picard smiled, mostly in relief. "Is there anything you'd
like to ask me?"

"No," Riker said. "You were the first person I scanned with
the tricorder."

Picard appreciated Riker's caution. "Clark's counterpart is
a slave in her reality. We might be able to get her to work with
us just as Neelix is."

"Neelix?"

Picard pointed over to where Neelix was still being treated
by the nurse. The Talaxian remained unconscious. "But get a
tranquilizer from the medkit. Just in case."

Riker went over to the nurse. After Picard had seen his
executive officer receive a hypospray, he called out for his
crew's attention. "We are in a critical situation," he told
them. "But by no means a desperate one. The Cardassians
and the Klingons who have captured us, and the *Enterprise,*
are not from our universe. They are counterparts from what
Starfleet has called the mirror universe."

Picard waited as murmured comments were passed back
and forth. He used the moment to move closer to the knot of
people standing next to Ensign Clark. Riker was approaching
her from behind.

"Right now, almost half the crew of the *Enterprise* is being
held on this ship, which is a duplicate of the *Voyager,* not the
Voyager herself. The good news is that we outnumber our

captors by almost six to one. The better news is that our captors are not fully aware of all the capabilities of this ship—capabilities which we can use to our advantage."

Now Riker was within arm's reach of Clark. Like the other, real members of the crew, she listened carefully to every word Picard said.

"However, we do face a unique challenge in dealing with these mirror counterparts. If you have kept up with Starfleet's situation reports, you will recall that many of us will have a counterpart in the mirror universe. A duplicate. Someone so perfectly identical that we will be at high risk of infiltration." Picard paused again while his crew exchanged suspicious glances with their neighbors. Except for Ensign Clark. She kept her eyes on Picard.

"However," Picard continued, "once again, we do have an advantage. In the mirror universe, humans are slaves. We can offer those humans who are on this ship, and on the *Enterprise,* their freedom. Consider this: We are deep within Federation territory; Starfleet is being apprised of our situation right now . . ." Picard paused as he saw Clark's eyes give away her surprise at what he had said. ". . . so there is no possible way that the Alliance of Klingons and Cardassians can succeed in their attempt to hijack our ship. Thus, I offer freedom, support, and a new life to any human from the mirror universe who wishes to help us."

Picard looked over his crew, then stopped on Clark. "Ensign Clark," Picard said kindly, "isn't that preferable to serving the Alliance?"

The ensign stiffened, as if she didn't understand why Picard was directing his comments to her.

Picard held out his hand to her. "Will you join us, Ensign?"

Clark frowned. "You think that *I'm* one of them?"

"We don't think. We know."

The ensign looked around nervously, obviously alarmed by the way everyone else in the brig was staring at her. Then she saw Riker standing behind her. She turned to run—but where she thought she might go, Picard had no idea.

Before she had completed a single step, Riker had grabbed her arm. Four other crew immobilized her.

"No!" she exclaimed.

Riker held up the hypospray, ready to tranquilize her. But Picard shook his head.

"You have no reason to fear us," Picard said. He didn't understand the captured counterpart's panic. Until she spoke.

"They'll kill my family!"

Now he had perfect understanding. And, perhaps, he could find a way to help. "Where are they?"

The woman's shoulders shook as her fear became manifest. "With the . . . with the hostages. . . ."

"What hostages?"

"The c-counterparts," Clark said, losing control of her words. "People like me, with a duplicate in your universe. They use us."

"For what?"

Clark stared at him as if she couldn't believe the question. "For *this*. To infiltrate you. To be spies for the Alliance."

Now Picard was growing alarmed. "How many of you are there?"

More confusion on Clark's features. "Where? On the *Enterprise?* In Starfleet?"

Picard saw his alarm mirrored in Riker. Could it be true that Starfleet itself had been compromised by mirror counterparts? "Let's start with the *Enterprise,"* he said.

Clark shook her head. "I don't know. They never tell us everything. So we can't be sure."

"Can you guess?"

Clark looked pained. "Five maybe. They came aboard at Starbase Three-Ten, just before you left for the Discontinuity."

Picard felt as if the deck were giving way beneath him. This attack on the *Enterprise* wasn't an isolated event. From what this frightened woman was saying, it seemed the Alliance had undertaken a long-term effort to infiltrate Starfleet. He was no longer dealing with an act of piracy.

The *Enterprise* had fallen victim to an act of war.

"Where is the real Margaret Clark?"

The woman looked at him in defiance. "I *am* the real Margaret Clark."

Picard forced himself not to argue with her. Of course she would think that this universe was but a reflection of her own. "Very well. Your counterpart. The Margaret Clark of this universe. When did you replace her?"

"A few hours ago. When they captured your ship."

"And what will happen to her now?"

Ensign Clark shrugged. "They'll hold her with the hostages. At least, that's what they do with the others. I don't know one way or the other."

"Where are the hostages? Have they been taken back to your universe?"

But Clark shook her head. "Not yet. Not till . . . not till the portal is completed."

For a moment, Picard felt overwhelmed by the woman's revelations. But they were so terrifyingly logical. "A portal. Between our universes."

Clark nodded, calmer now. She seemed to be adjusting to her changed situation.

"And that's where they're taking the *Enterprise.*"

"That's right."

Riker let go of Clark's arm, but kept the hypospray ready. "Where is the portal?" he asked.

"I don't know that, either. I came through it in the *Voyager.* There was an asteroid field. But there's no star nearby."

Riker looked at Picard. "We'll be able to check through Stellar Cartography." He turned back to Clark. "What was your transit time from the portal to the Goldin Discontinuity?"

Clark exhaled deeply. "A few days. I don't know." She looked at Picard, her anxiety now replaced by resignation. "We're slaves, Captain Picard. And that's how we're treated. We do what we're told, and we don't ask questions."

"That will change," Picard told her. Her puzzled reaction told him that it would be best if she learned what it meant to be a free person by experience, not by explanation. He resolved to treat her as he would a member of his crew. "Do you know where this *Voyager* is going now?"

"Back to the portal. With the *Enterprise.*"

Picard glanced at the bulkhead. "The *Enterprise* is . . . out there? Right now?"

"The last I heard," Clark said.

Picard was troubled by how quickly Clark had given up her information but was quickly able to confirm what she said by checking local sensor readings on the brig's computer. The *Enterprise* was only two kilometers away, still at relative rest with the *Voyager,* still near the Goldin Discontinuity.

Riker shared Picard's concern. "Didn't you say Neelix told you the *Enterprise* was gone?"

"He also said that he wasn't told everything."

Riker looked across the brig to see Clark still being held by four crew members. "She said the same."

"Do you think one of them is lying?" Picard asked. Certainly, he had not completely accepted anything Neelix had told him, except for what he had been able to confirm through the ship's computer.

"I think both of them are," Riker said. Then he tapped the computer display. "But it doesn't matter what Clark or Neelix say as long as we know the *Enterprise* is in range of the *Voyager*'s transporters. Once we're back onboard, we can check out everyone's story."

Picard felt a burden leave him. Will was right. It wasn't

necessary that he and his crew stage a takeover of this ship. Since they had access to the *Voyager*'s transporters, Picard could lead a team back to the *Enterprise.*

It took him only minutes to devise a plan with Riker. Two teams of six and one team of two—Picard and Riker—would be needed. The first team would beam directly to the *Enterprise*'s engineering section and attempt to shut down the warp core. The second team would beam to the bridge and attempt to overpower the Alliance crew they found there.

But, Picard told them, he was not expecting either team to be successful. In fact, he emphasized, they were to surrender almost at once. Their chief duty was simply to distract attention from what Picard and Riker would be doing in the *Enterprise*'s auxiliary bridge—reestablishing Picard's command authority over the ship.

Provided the computer network was still operational—and a ship as complex as the *Enterprise* could barely function without it—the procedure, he assured them, should take less than a minute. Then he would flood the ship with anesthezine gas, and set a maximum warp course to the nearest starbase. The *Voyager,* without a Starfleet engineering crew who knew how to coax the last millicochrane from her warp engines, would not be able to keep up.

Commander Sloane was to lead the bridge-assault team, and Picard told him to keep the Klingon disruptor he was using to guard the brig door. If the Alliance crew had not reset the weapon-suppression system, there was a chance he might be able to use it.

But the engineering assault team would not be armed—a stray disruptor beam near the warp core could be disastrous. Riker took that other disruptor.

Picard had the crew members who were not needed return to their detention cells, and then he adjusted the forcefield screens to their lowest setting before switching them back on. Should any other Alliance guards enter to check the prisoners in the brig, they would see the forcefields in operation. But in the event of an emergency, the crew could easily slip through the fields with little more discomfort than a mild electric shock.

Less than five minutes after Picard had confirmed that the *Enterprise* was within range, he stood in the center of the brig with Riker and the twelve other crew members who would help him retake his ship. "Are you ready?" he asked Riker.

"How about you?"

"I feel . . . fine," Picard said. Then he paused. Odd, he really did feel better. Not at all as he had felt after his experience with Gul Madred. Or with the Borg. *The heat of battle,* he decided. That must be what was masking the aftereffects of his torture at the hands of the EMH with the agonizer.

"Are you sure?" Riker asked, as if he sensed Picard's uncertainty.

"I want my ship back, Will." It was that simple. Everything else could wait until that had been accomplished. "Computer, is transporter room one staffed at this time?"

"Negative," the computer replied.

"Is transporter room one operational?"

"Affirmative."

"Initiate site-to-site transport. Picard and twelve others from the brig to transporter room one. Transport in groups of four, four, and five."

The computer did not bother to reply. Instead, Picard saw the brig dissolve into golden energy, then re-form as a transporter room very much like the ones on the *Enterprise*.

As the computer had said, the room was empty. Riker immediately ran to the corridor doors and sealed them.

Within another minute, all thirteen crew members were in the transporter room. And there was still no sign that anyone on this *Voyager*'s bridge was monitoring transporter usage. If the *Enterprise*'s new crew was equally deficient, Picard knew, retaking the ship was not going to present any difficulty.

At the transporter console, Picard locked in the coordinates for the three beam-ins, then set the controls on automatic cycling.

The engineering team beamed to the *Enterprise* first. Their presence would set off intruder-alert alarms and, Picard was confident, would cause a commotion on the bridge. Twenty seconds later, the bridge team beamed over to take advantage of that confusion and add to it.

Then it was just Picard and Riker.

They stood together on the transporter pad. Riker held his disruptor ready to fire. "This is why they warn you to be careful what you wish for," he told his captain.

"When I was complaining about our duty, Will, this wasn't what I had in mind to replace it."

Riker smiled at him. "Are you sure?"

Then the transporter effect played around them, and Picard had no opportunity to reply. But in the timeless moment of transport, he wondered if Riker was right.

Picard was in a life-or-death situation, fighting for his crew and his ship.

He couldn't deny the bracing sense of purpose this mission gave him.

To take action, to do something worthwhile, wasn't this why he had joined Starfleet in the first place? To be someone who could make a difference?

And then the auxiliary bridge of the *Enterprise* formed around him, every console in the compact control center coming online and powering up as the sensors detected his presence.

Riker spun around to cover the turbolift doors with the disruptor as Picard turned to the helm controls. Instantly, intuitively, he checked the status of his ship.

For a moment, he was puzzled to see that his lockout order, delivered in those final seconds when Tom Paris had arrived on his bridge, had yet to be overridden.

Then Picard felt a thrill of hope as he realized his situation might be better than he had anticipated. Either Neelix had lied or, more probably, had been misinformed about what Rutal had done with the *Enterprise.* Perhaps, Picard thought hopefully, he had *not* given up any access codes during his interrogation. Or, if he had, Rutal was still trying to determine if the codes she had obtained were real or decoys. Whatever the reason, it was going to be much simpler to retake control of the *Enterprise* than he first had thought.

"What's our status?" Riker asked him.

Picard called up the security displays. The plan was working perfectly. "Fighting in engineering and on the bridge," he reported. "The Alliance doesn't have any idea what's going on." Picard intended to keep it that way.

"Computer, this is Jean-Luc Picard. Confirm voiceprint identity."

"Voiceprint confirmed."

"Command authority Picard alpha null four four nine. Rescind operational lockout and restore full command capability."

"Command capability restored," the computer confirmed.

Picard jumped up and turned to face Riker. "We did it!"

Riker hurried to the environmental station. "I'll seal us off from main life-support." But before he could reach the raised deck ringing the auxiliary bridge, a dull thump vibrated through the bulkheads.

Riker halted, looking back at Picard in concern.

"Computer," Picard said at once. "Identify source of the tremor just experienced in the auxiliary bridge."

The computer didn't reply.

"Computer—this is Picard. Respond."

Nothing.

Picard turned back to the helm, punched in an access code for an automated damage report.

But the console displays did not change, as if the control surfaces had not detected his input.

"What is it?" Riker asked.

"We've been locked out," Picard said. But how could that be possible?

Then the auxiliary bridge's main viewer flickered into life, filling the small control room with baleful light.

Picard looked up at the screen.

It was Gul Rutal.

She was sitting on his bridge. In his chair.

Commanding his ship.

The Cardassian smirked at him. "Allow me to offer my thanks, Captain Picard. Without your assistance, I was told it might have taken us more than a month to establish manual control over the *Enterprise.*"

"Computer," Picard said. "Emergency lockout! Picard Alpha One!"

Gul Rutal shrugged elaborately. "That tremor you felt? We severed the ODN line connecting the auxiliary bridge to the ship's computer network. Your ship can't hear you."

Picard heard a faint hiss. He looked over at the air vents and saw a gentle cascade of white vapor begin. Anesthezine. His own plan was being used against him.

"Will! The turbolift door!"

Riker fired his disruptor at the turbolift door, but no beam was generated. Clearly, the weapon-suppression system was operational again. Every system that made it difficult for attackers to gain control of the ship would now be used to prevent Picard from reestablishing his own.

"You have to admit, Captain, that this is much more humane than torture."

Then Picard realized what he had missed. And he knew he should have realized it sooner. "You never interrogated me at all."

Rutal smiled, inclining her head as if to accept his acknowledgment of her cleverness. "Our sources suggested that you would be conditioned to give us false codes. If we input the wrong ones, significant damage to the ship might have resulted . . . and no one wished that. Least of all, you, I would think."

Picard felt himself begin to get dizzy.

"I'd sit down if I were you," Rutal said. "If you fall when that gas takes effect, you might be damaged as well."

Picard stumbled back to the center chair. Sat in it. Realized that he had seen all the clues—the Klingon darts that weren't fatal after all, no aftereffects from the torture, the ease with which he had been able to elude security on the duplicate *Voyager.*

"You led me through a maze . . ." Picard said faintly.

"On the contrary. We built the maze, and you ran through it. Eagerly. Of your own free will. Like a well-trained vole."

Picard felt the auxiliary bridge begin to spin around him. He saw Riker slump to the deck, eyes rolled up, unconscious.

Rutal was right. He had fallen for this trap without resistance. Believing he was on an important mission had kept him from stopping to consider all the inconsistencies, and from asking all the questions he should have.

But now there was no question. He had just delivered the *Enterprise* to his enemies.

"I must compliment you," he said stiffly.

"Before you think me too resourceful," Rutal said from the screen, "I must confess that I did have the assistance of an expert."

Picard blinked at the viewer, not understanding what Rutal meant.

"The only one who could build the maze that you would follow," the Gul said. "The only one who would know every tempting detail that would mislead and divert you."

Another figure stepped onto the screen. *A Klingon?* Picard thought, having trouble keeping his eyes focused. At least, whoever it was wore Klingon armor and his fringe of white hair was long, tied back in a warrior's queue.

But something was wrong. Picard strained to identify the figure on the screen.

The forehead and scalp of the figure was smooth. No Klingon ridges.

The figure was human.

As human as he was.

As familiar a face as if he were looking into a . . .

"Jean-Luc Picard," Gul Rutal said as Picard's vision faded to oblivion, "meet . . . Jean-Luc Picard."

ELEVEN

☆

At first he thought the transporter hadn't worked. The chamber Kirk materialized in had the same dimensions as the one he had just been in. But as the glow of the transporter effect faded, the differences became apparent.

Now the walls and debris were covered by thick layers of frost. Even the transporter platform was coated with ice—the few clear spots on it showing where heat leaked from its power units.

Then the major difference struck Kirk with the force of a body blow.

The cold.

So intense it was painful.

He shivered as he exhaled, mixing the air of one universe with that of another. His exhalation became a cloud of frozen vapor, swirling in the eddies caused by the way his arrival had disturbed the still air.

For a moment, he was uncertain what to do. The mirror Spock remained in place, pulling his cloak tightly around his thin shoulders. But Janeway and T'Val kicked off from the platform in a long and graceful lunar jump to land near a rime-encrusted crate.

Janeway tapped a code into the lockplate and the crate

hissed open. Kirk watched as they pulled out environmental suits. Their design was different from any he had seen. The outer covering was mottled with irregular splotches of grays and black. It was a few seconds before Kirk recognized the pattern as camouflage.

These were suits made for lunar combat. He was in a different universe.

Kirk saw the mirror Spock begin to shiver violently. He moved to help guide the Vulcan from the platform, toward the women and the crate.

"Why the temperature difference?" Kirk asked. He could feel his cheeks beginning to burn, recognized the sensation as the stage before frostbite.

T'Val assisted her intendant in putting on his suit. "Our moon isn't terraformed. There's no artificially maintained atmosphere to hold heat close to the surface."

As T'Val finished suiting up the mirror Spock, and as Janeway slipped into her own protective gear, Kirk studied the chamber, noting that the piles of debris were different here, as well. In the other chamber, in his own universe, it had consisted of discarded sections of environmental suits, left by ice miners, Kirk had guessed. But here, entire suits were scattered about.

Kirk looked more closely at one. Part of its chestpiece was missing. In the ragged opening, Kirk could see torn and mummified flesh and ice-covered ribs.

These weren't discarded suits. They were bodies.

"Who were they?" Kirk asked as Janeway handed him his own camouflaged suit.

"Who knows?" She looked, without interest, at the carcasses that surrounded them. "They've been here almost a century. They could be from the Alliance invasion. They could be victims of the Imperial Guard. It doesn't matter to them. It doesn't matter to me."

Kirk understood the flatness in Janeway's tone. As he had suspected, she was a battlefield soldier. For too many years.

The emotional distancing Vulcans strove all their lives to achieve, this human woman had attained by experiencing the horrors of war for too long and too closely.

Perhaps he *had* been responsible for Earth's downfall in this universe. But somehow, before he had crossed over, something else had happened here to make the Janeway of this universe a battle-hardened, emotionally scarred guerrilla warrior, while in his universe, her counterpart had become a starship captain—by all accounts a successful and resourceful one. What, he wondered again, besides his intrusion, had caused Earth and Vulcan to unite in a brutal Empire and not a peaceful Federation? And was it even possible that he could ever find the answer?

Kirk paused in the process of sealing his suit, suddenly struck by a new thought. What if Teilani existed in this universe? If so, what had she become? Whom had she found? What if, somehow, his actions so long ago had made her life unbearable, or worse, doomed her here?

The moment of reflection ended quickly in Kirk. He and his abductors were still the targets of a chase. He sealed his suit components, snapped on his helmet, and glanced down at the control displays built in at chin level. Immediately, the suit's systems powered up. Kirk felt a soft rush of air move over his face and welcome heat began to build around him as he realized there must be a sensor system in his helmet that tracked where he was looking, so he could activate controls with a glance.

Janeway tapped Kirk's helmet with her fingers. She pointed to the left and he looked across the controls to see an icon for communications. Testing his conclusions, Kirk stared at the small symbol. At once, his helmet speakers clicked on.

"Can you hear me now?" Janeway asked.

Kirk said he could, saw that she could hear him, too. Then he asked, "Why did you bring me here?"

"The Alliance doesn't know about our transporter network on the moon in our universe," Janeway said.

"At least, not yet," T'Val amended. She was using the tricorder built into the sleeve of her suit to check Intendant Spock's status. He had stopped shivering as the suit's heating system shielded him from the cold, but he looked pale, almost gray behind his suit's clear visor. Exhaustion, Kirk knew, from long experience with someone almost just like him.

T'Val steadied her superior by holding his arm. "We're almost there, Intendant. A few more minutes."

Janeway scanned the chamber with her larger tricorder, then told everyone to return to the platform.

"These are like underground tunnels, then," Kirk said as he moved as directed. "You disappear from my universe, go to a different location in your own, then reappear back in mine."

"Exactly." Janeway checked to make certain everyone was in place, then tapped commands into her tricorder. "But each time we use this network, we risk the Alliance discovering what we're doing."

The chamber around them began to dissolve again, and since Kirk knew they all could have survived the time they had spent here without suits, he also knew what their next destination must be—

—the magnificent desolation of the lunar surface itself.

A gently rolling gray plain of scattered rock and smooth dust took form around Kirk.

For an instant, he allowed a smile of pleasure to play across his face. He had walked on thousands of alien worlds in his career, but he found it ironic that he had never actually set foot on the uncovered lunar surface—the one alien world closest to his home.

He had visited the moon many times, of course. As a child, he had gone on school-organized day trips to Tranquility Park to see the first landing site, carefully preserved in vacuum fifty meters away from the tourist viewing dome. He had enjoyed the occasional weekend of shore leave in the infamous low-gravity hotels of the Lunar Appenines. But somehow, he had never quite found the time to rent a suit and venture out

128

beyond the airlocks, to experience the moon as the first explorers and colonists had.

For all the years he had lived, for all the light-years he had traveled, even close to home there had always been still more to do, to see, to experience. He could almost hear Teilani add, *And for you, James, there always will be.*

How is it she knows me better than I know myself? Kirk asked himself.

But Janeway didn't leave him any time to consider the answer.

"This way," she commanded, pointing toward a deep shadow at the edge of a small rift fracture, about a hundred meters away. It formed a protected wall of sorts, one that snaked off toward the deceptively near lunar horizon. "Follow the trail."

Kirk looked ahead and saw the path where the dust had been disturbed by the passage of others. But whether they had come this way a few minutes ago, or in centuries past, there was no way to be certain.

Kirk fell into a slow, bouncing gait with Janeway and the rest. In the long seconds before each landing and push-off, he checked the angle of the shadows, glanced up to catch a flare of sunlight, and realized that the Earth should be visible. As he traveled closer to the fracture zone, he angled his head in his helmet to find the planet of his birth. At least, this universe's version of it.

And seeing it, he tripped.

Tumbling forward in the dust, sending up a slow-motion billow, arms spread wide, skidding to a soft landing, overwhelmed.

Janeway and T'Val were at his side at once. Kirk felt them pull him quickly to his feet. T'Val was already scanning him, checking his suit's integrity.

"Are you all right?" Janeway asked.

Kirk couldn't answer.

For the same reason he had tripped.

He twisted out of the women's grip to look again at Earth. And what he saw made his throat tighten.

Earth was dying.

On the sunlit half, it was as if a colony of virulent mold had spread across a sample dish in some abandoned lab. The seas, once blue, once laced with delicate swirls and arcs of brilliant white clouds, were now vast tracts of brown and black and purple.

The land, once wreathed in green, wrapped by soft bands of desert brown and the dramatic gray-black of mountains, capped north and south by gleaming fields of pristine ice, was now a single smear of gray, broken only by obscuring blots and whorls of ink-black cloud.

And on the nightside, it was as if civilization had been wiped from the planet. All Kirk could see was a handful of glowing red dots—volcanoes or fires burning out of control, he couldn't be sure—and, over what used to be the Midwest region of North America, the flickering dance of lightning from a major storm.

He looked where Montreal should have been—he himself had just been there moments ago, it seemed. But where the sparkling spiderwebs of light from a city and cultural center of eight million souls should have appeared, there was nothing.

"What . . . happened?" Kirk asked, knowing no answer could be satisfactory.

"We already told you," Janeway said coldly.

"You happened," T'Val added, as if she enjoyed his distress.

Kirk stared at his desecrated world. He had heard the mirror Spock's description of this Earth, but the words had only been an abstraction. To actually *see* it was . . . to think that he was in some way responsible . . .

"We have to hurry," Janeway said.

Kirk felt the women grab his arms again, pull him ahead.

He stumbled forward, but his instinctive training soon

pulled his faltering steps into smooth rhythm with his abductors', even while his mind struggled with its shock.

Just before he passed into the shadow of the rift, he looked to his side and saw the mirror Spock staring at him from his own visor.

The counterpart of his closest friend said nothing, but in his eyes were the accusations that raced through Kirk's own mind.

Murderer. Maniac. Monster.

"Spock, I didn't know," Kirk said as he passed into the shadow.

The mirror Spock's voice crackled through the darkness. "Now you do."

Kirk remembered little of the long traverse along the fracture zone. In less than a minute, his eyes had adjusted to the shadow and the reflected sunlight was enough to see the way.

All he heard was the steady breathing of his companions. The mirror Spock's was weak. T'Val's was like a metronome. And Janeway's deep and rhythmic like an athlete's.

Kirk did his best to keep up, aided most of all by the physical labor he had undertaken in the past year. But he realized that if Janeway and T'Val had not reduced their pace in deference to the mirror Spock, they eventually would have had to reduce the pace for him.

Just about the time Kirk was thinking he would have to request a rest break, the party came to a stop. Again T'Val scanned the area; then Janeway pushed at a rock near the base of the fracture wall, and a moment later, a narrow hatch silently swung up from the base to reveal an opening about the size of a Jefferies tube. The outside surface of the hatch was studded with small rocks and sections of dust which didn't move—permanently affixed camouflage. The inside surface was ribbed metal, the same vintage as the ice-mine chamber Kirk had been beamed into after his abduction from Earth.

Kirk could feel vibrations through his boots, and guessed that the upper section of the hatch was an airlock, and what he felt was the machinery that pumped air in and out.

Janeway had T'Val enter first. When Kirk's turn came, he found himself standing in the narrow tube just below the hatch, which, Janeway confirmed for him, was an old miners' escape route. Silent vibrations traveled through his suit and blended with a growing rumble of audible sound. As the vibrations and noise stopped, a display inside his helmet revealed that the exterior atmospheric pressure was 250 torr, about one-third Earth normal, which he recognized as the common, low-pressure standard for spacecraft and habitat structures in the early days of space travel, when the threat of explosive decompression was an ever-present possibility.

A few moments later, a muffled hiss accompanied the opening of a second hatch in the lower half of the tube and Kirk used the handrails to swing through it, feet first.

The new chamber he dropped into was again metal-walled, with each surface coated once more in frost. A small fusion globe, weakly flickering, was the only source of light.

Kirk saw T'Val already wriggling out of her suit, and he stepped away from the interior hatch as it began its cycle again. As he heard the air pumps begin their labor, he unsealed his helmet.

The cold in this chamber was even more biting than the last, and Kirk knew they would have to beam out quickly, especially given the mirror Spock's condition.

In less than five minutes, all four of them were in the chamber, their environmental suits safely stowed in a sealed crate for whoever would next come this way. Kirk and the others waited on a transporter platform. Janeway and T'Val now wore loose tunics and leggings over their combat suits, and T'Val carefully adjusted her intendant's cloak so that it covered the mirror Spock's head like a shawl.

"I'm almost afraid to ask where we're going next," Kirk said. He was shivering as violently as the mirror Spock had in the last chamber. His ears felt numb. His hands ached.

"Last stop," Janeway told him, trembling less than he did, as if she were somehow used to experiencing these extreme conditions.

"Really?" Kirk asked.

"Let me put it this way," Janeway said. "Where we go after our next beam-in will be up to you."

As Kirk puzzled over any hidden meaning, or threat, in what Janeway had told him, the surrounding ice-mine chamber dematerialized, then re-formed into—

—a riot of color and sound, movement and confusion, so explosive Kirk found it almost overpowering.

"Welcome to Lunar Station New Berlin," a pleasant voice announced. "Please step from the platform as a courtesy for the next passenger."

Kirk's leg muscles tensed as an artificial field of Earth-normal gravity tugged on him, and as he stepped from the glowing circular disk beneath him, he looked around to see that he was in the downtown square of one of the oldest and largest cities on the moon. Janeway had returned them to *his* universe.

Quaintly retro shops and restaurants, built in the hopelessly naive technological style of the late twenty-first century, ringed the square before him with its open fountains and eucalyptus trees aromatic in the warm lunar air.

Kirk heard music playing, laughter, the excited cries of happy children playing. Relieved, he moved forward, following the flashing lights in the floor that guided him to the nearest passenger exit.

Then he quickly ran down the few stairs to an open pedestrian walkway, and looked up past the sloping roof of the transporter station.

Exactly where he had seen the Earth less than an hour ago, he saw it again, though now against a background of the terraformed moon's summer blue sky, and not the black of space.

But this time, on the nightside, Montreal shone like a jewel, filled with light and with life. North and South America were clearly delineated by their cities and the transportation corridors that wove them together. And on Earth's dayside, the seas were blue, the clouds a filigree of lace, the vast nature parks of Western Europe and Africa vibrantly green and alive.

Kirk felt as if he had returned from the underworld. Each color was purer than before. Each sound clearer. Each breath more precious.

"Now you know why it is so difficult for us," Spock said beside him.

Kirk spun around, but it wasn't his Spock who addressed him. It was the other. Kirk's strange encounter was clearly not over.

"Your Earth, your universe, is a paradise beyond our understanding," the mirror Spock continued. Janeway and T'Val moved up to flank the mirror Spock. In their loose civilian clothing, they did not stand out among the crowd.

"Are we safe from the Alliance here?" Kirk asked, unable to shake the feeling that the Alliance's presence here meant that he was somehow a threat to his own universe now.

"They can detect our transporters when we beam from place to place, but not when we cross over," Janeway said. "We're safe. Until you turn us in."

"Do you actually think I'd do that?" Kirk asked.

"The other Kirk would," Janeway answered.

Kirk looked back up at the blue sky of the moon, at his Earth. Maybe not a paradise to him. But he knew better than ever why the people of the mirror universe would think so.

He closed his eyes for an instant, and saw their Earth again, decaying, decimated. Because of him.

He looked back at his three would-be kidnappers, and suddenly he wondered if they had wanted to kidnap him at all.

"You never intended to hold me captive," Kirk said. "You just wanted me to return to your universe and see your Earth. See what I'd done."

The two Vulcans gave nothing away by their expressions. Even Janeway might as well have been Vulcan by the way she so thoroughly hid whatever she might be thinking and feeling.

But Kirk had worked with Vulcans, at least, one in particular, long enough that he felt confident about reading their moods and intent. He saw before him three beleaguered soldiers, fighting a losing war, looking to him to provide new hope and the chance for victory they could no longer provide themselves.

He looked at them and knew that he could walk away now, and they would not follow. It was not in them to harm an innocent civilian. The choice to help them was truly up to him.

Kirk couldn't help the grin that could only confuse his serious-faced audience. His days of adventure might be over, but he'd just thought of a way he could still make a difference—put right the past, change the future. By making a gift of his guidance and whatever wisdom he had achieved to these soldiers in such desperate straits.

"I know exactly what to do," Kirk said decisively, "to give you the power to resist, and to defeat the Alliance."

The mirror Spock, as literal as the one Kirk knew, asked the obvious question. "And are you prepared to share that knowledge with us?"

"I am." Kirk offered his hand, knowing the Vulcans would not accept it, but that Janeway would.

But it was T'Val who surprised him by stepping close to him and reaching around to his back and sliding her hand inside the waist of his trousers.

Kirk looked at her, startled by the sudden intimate gesture, until he realized she was detaching something from his waistband.

T'Val stepped back, holding up a thin wafer, no more than

three centimeters in diameter, no thicker than a few pieces of paper stacked together. A small red light glowed on one side of it. "You may deactivate it, Intendant."

The mirror Spock removed a small padd from his cloak, entered a code sequence.

The light on the wafer changed from red to green.

"Contact explosive," T'Val said. She put the disk beneath her tunic. "I installed it when I used the tissue regenerator on your back."

"If you had refused us," Janeway added, "Intendant Spock would have triggered it, and the shaped explosion would have cut you in half."

"But that is in the past," the mirror Spock said. "For now, we are at your disposal."

Kirk looked at the three soldiers before him and was shaken by how completely he had misread them.

They're aliens, Kirk thought, trying to hide his own reaction to the knowledge of how close to death he had been. *Not just to my world, but to my universe.*

In that telling moment, Kirk realized that he was now involved in something that no longer made sense to handle on his own.

And, fortunately, even in the twenty-fourth century, he knew exactly to whom he could turn for help.

TWELVE

☆

"Fascinating," Spock said.

"Indeed," the mirror Spock replied.

As the two Vulcans in the opulent hotel suite studied each other with intense curiosity, Kirk looked from one to the other, assessing their intriguing differences as much as their eerie similarities.

The Spock he had met at the beginning of his career, whom he had last seen a year ago on Vulcan, stood with shoulders straight and square beneath his jeweled ambassadorial robe. Kirk recalled having seen Spock's father, Sarek, wearing almost exactly the same formal dress.

But the mirror Spock showed the stress and privations of a lifetime as a fugitive. He was stooped a few centimeters shorter, his shoulders rounded, his hair streaked with more white. And his voice was just a touch weaker, less assured, as if he had more cause to doubt his logic.

Through the window, beyond the open balcony, the lights of Montreal spread out like a galaxy of stars. The faint hum of antigrav cars and transports was carried on the soft evening breeze. Like every other city on this planet, this Earth, it was a city at peace. In the past, Kirk had grown impatient with the perfection of this world: its boringly scheduled weather; its annoyingly free-of-conflict world government; its all-pervasive lack of excitement and challenge. But whether it was a sign of all his years of struggle, or a result of the single year he had just spent in a simple cabin on Chal, Kirk was surprised by how much he had enjoyed the week he had spent in this city, waiting for Spock to arrive. Perhaps perfection was not as bad as he had once thought. At least, in moderation.

Both Spock and his mirror counterpart continued staring at each other, as if caught up in a mind-meld at a distance, if such a thing were possible. Certainly, a physical mind-meld was not in their plans. It had been one of the first things Kirk had suggested to them, a way to have all their questions answered before they even knew the questions existed. But both Spocks, for a reason they would not state, refused to consider it. Now, in the meantime, their silence fueled the mood of quiet expectation in the suite. Janeway and T'Val were on either side of their intendant. Montgomery Scott stood next to Kirk, not attempting to hide his surprise at seeing both Spocks, but not inclined to break the mood of their dramatic meeting.

Finally, though, Kirk had had enough. "I think this calls for a drink," he announced. Without waiting for anyone's reaction, he walked over to the antique wet bar at the side of the suite's sitting room. There was a collection of fine crystal bottles on top of the bar, their fiery reflections doubled by the mirrors behind them. And beneath the bar counter, hidden behind a panel of carved oak, was a replicator alcove, though Kirk hadn't bothered to access it since Captain Bateson had arranged the suite, courtesy of Starfleet.

Since Earth's twenty-fourth-century economy no longer operated with money—something that Kirk still didn't comprehend, no matter how many times Scott explained it to him—Kirk wasn't quite certain how, exactly, Starfleet was responsible for providing the suite when theoretically it was available to anyone on the planet. At least in Kirk's day, during the unsettling time when physical money was being phased out on Earth, a different system of exchange had replaced it. Even then, solid, easily transportable credits remained in circulation on the frontier, just as in this era a bewildering variety of currency was still in constant use beyond the Federation's borders. But however Bateson had managed it, Kirk was grateful for his kindness. After his lunar escapade, the large antigrav mattress in his bedroom had been a blessing for his back.

Kirk peeled back the top of a container of iced tea for himself, smiled at his guests. "What can I get you?"

"We've wasted too much time already," Janeway said firmly, her face registering displeasure with the tempting softness of Kirk's world. "We need computer access now."

Kirk poured the iced tea into a crystal tumbler. "Kate, Ambassador Spock has just this minute stepped through the door. It has taken him a week to come here from . . ." Kirk hesitated. Bateson had reminded Kirk that Spock's ongoing mission to Romulus was still unofficial and still off-the-record. ". . . from his last posting," Kirk continued. "Some refreshment while we talk is not going to delay anything." He held up his tumbler. "Iced tea?"

"I also believe we should commence right away," Spock said.

Kirk sighed. So much for easing into the critical planning that had to be done.

Kirk remained at the bar as Spock sat down in an uphol-stered chair—an antique from the twenty-second century, the automated porter had explained—and placed a small padd on the low table before him.

Intendant Spock took a seat at the opposite end of the table. Janeway and T'Val sat down beside one another on a couch to Spock's left. Scott dragged a hard-back chair from a dining table and sat to Spock's left.

Janeway pulled out a padd, switched it on, and held it out

to Spock. "We've prepared a list of the files we want, and a series of technical topics for which we need further information before determining what other files we'll add."

But Spock made no effort to take the padd. "I have not come here to reveal the secrets of Starfleet technology," he said calmly.

Kirk saw the angry look that flashed between Janeway and T'Val.

Instantly he stepped forward. "Spock—I don't think you received my report about what these people—"

Spock cut Kirk short. "I received the complete file. I know what these people want. I have no intention of giving it to them."

Janeway shifted in her seat as if she were about to pull a phaser from a leg holster.

"Kate," Kirk said quickly. "Why don't you give us a moment to straighten out the . . . uh . . . miscommunication?" He stepped up to Spock and Scott. "Ambassador, Scotty, will you join me on the balcony?"

"Certainly," Spock said as he rose to his feet. "But I assure you, I am aware of no miscommunication."

Kirk refrained from arguing in front of Janeway and T'Val. He ushered his two friends through the sliding glass doors, then turned back to the mirror Spock. "This'll just take a minute."

As Janeway and T'Val glared at him, Kirk slid the doors shut.

Spock and Scott stood at the stone balcony railing. Above, only the brightest stars could be seen against the glow of Montreal's lights. Below, those lights traced the streets that made up the regular grids of the city's newer sections, and the meandering, narrower roads that remained of the old town. Montreal had escaped major damage during the Third World War, and much of what lay below was original, not reconstructed.

"Spock," Kirk said, "I don't think you realize how serious my guests are."

"On the contrary," Spock replied. "I do not believe you realize what a critical question their presence raises, especially in regard to the Prime Directive."

Kirk sighed again. If there were two words he didn't want to hear again as long as he lived, they were "Prime Directive." With "time travel" coming in a close second.

"Spock, the Prime Directive has no bearing on this. Number one, they aren't from our universe. Number two . . ." Kirk took a deep breath. This wasn't going to be easy. ". . . I've already interfered in their natural development. I have to set it straight."

Spock regarded Kirk with a skeptical expression Kirk knew well. "Jim, can you honestly believe that a handful of words you exchanged with my counterpart can have led to such far-reaching consequences in the mirror universe?"

"It's not a question of belief. Scotty got me Starfleet's classified reports on the mirror universe. The ones coming out of *Deep Space Nine.* Everything Janeway, and T'Val, and your counterpart have said is backed up in those reports." Kirk looked at Scott. "Scotty, you've read them. You've talked with Janeway. Tell him."

Scott nodded. "I have t' say Jim's right, Ambassador. The Deep Space Nine logs do confirm that 'Kirk' is one of the most famous, not t'mention 'infamous,' names in the history of the mirror universe."

"Why would it not be?" Spock asked. "Their Kirk was the despot whose reign led to the worst excesses of the Terran Empire."

"Spock, 'Kirk' refers to *me. I'm* the starship captain who 'crossed over more than a century ago.' Their Kirk is known as Tiberius."

"At this point, there is no way to be certain if that interpretation is correct."

Kirk struggled to understand why Spock was being so stubborn. "We *can* be certain. Go back in there and ask . . . yourself."

Spock folded his hands behind his back and looked out at the city lights beyond. "Jim, by your own analysis, the Janeway, T'Val, and Spock of the mirror universe are losing a desperate battle. Were you or I in such a situation, would we not say or do anything in an attempt to reclaim victory?"

Kirk knew better than to argue with a Vulcan. Outmaneuvering them was a far better strategy. "All right, Spock. What's going on?"

The picture of Vulcan innocence, Spock turned to Kirk. "I merely came in response to an urgent communiqué from Starfleet Command, asking me to meet you here on Earth. While I was in transit from Romulus, your preliminary report arrived by subspace. Had I read it before I had left Romulus, I would not have left Romulus. But as I was almost here, I decided to continue my trip. That is the extent of what is 'going on.'"

Ha! Evasion, Kirk thought. He had long ago learned that the longer one of Spock's answers was, the more likely it was he was hiding the truth.

"I don't understand, Spock. Why don't you want to give your counterpart the technical secrets that could help free billions of humans and Vulcans from lives of slavery and despair?"

"They are not humans and Vulcans," Spock said. "I will concede that they are analogous to both species, but—"

"Spock!"

Spock widened his eyes at Kirk's outburst.

"They're *Vulcans* and *humans.* No equivocation is possible. What is wrong with you?" Kirk looked at Scott. "Scotty? Do you know what he's up to?"

Scott stared at Spock. "Ye dinna seem to be yourself, sir. That's for certain."

Spock looked mildly insulted. "In what way, Captain Scott?"

"You're like Jim, here. Ye never let the Prime Directive stand in your way before if you thought justice was not being served. I mean, it's a fine principle and all, but life is never as black or white as the lawmakers think it's going to be. There're always exceptions to every rule, and you and Jim used to be able to recognize those exceptions with the best of them."

As unused to hearing praise from Scott as he was, Kirk was nevertheless appreciative of the engineer's support. Though it was still odd to hear Scott call him by his first name. "Scotty, are you agreeing with me . . . again?"

Scott seemed as unused to the idea as was Kirk, but he didn't argue the point. "Appears so. I must be mellowing in my old age."

Kirk leaned on the balcony railing beside Spock. "I still say there's something you're not telling me."

Again, Spock looked away from Kirk, his gaze following the lazy flight of a distant orbital shuttle as it took off from Earth Station Dorval.

Now Kirk was intrigued by Spock's silence. Despite the popular belief to the contrary, Vulcans could lie whenever they chose to, and Spock had certainly proved no exception to that rule over the years. He would not do so to profit himself, but in the past he'd had no compunction about misleading enemies or serving a greater good. Most important, though, Kirk knew, Spock would never lie to him. So his friend's silence now distinctly implied that there was an unspoken truth that might answer Kirk's suspicions. Yet, for whatever reason, Spock was restrained from talking about it.

But why? Kirk asked himself. *What could Spock have learned about the mirror universe in the time it took him to reach the hotel from the transport station?*

Then Kirk realized the obvious. Whatever Spock knew,

whatever he was hiding, he had known it before setting out for Earth.

Spock looked at Kirk. "Is there something more *you* wished to say?"

But Kirk remained silent as he completed his reasoning. Spock said he had received Starfleet's urgent request to meet Kirk on Earth. While in transit he had read Kirk's report. But he was so far along in his journey that rather than turn back, he had continued to Earth. Kirk had it.

"Spock, it's not logical."

Spock raised an eyebrow.

"As soon as I came back from the moon, I asked Bateson to locate you on Romulus. Less than a day later, I gave him my encrypted report to be transmitted to you. If you read it in transit, you'd only be a day away from Romulus. Why not turn back?"

Spock started to say something, then stopped.

Kirk held up a finger, making his point. "You were about to say there was a delay in your receiving the report, weren't you?"

Now Spock remained silent.

"But that would be a lie, wouldn't it?" Kirk asked.

Silence.

"The truth," Kirk said, "is that you were *already* on your way to Earth when I asked Bateson to find you. And the reason you were coming to Earth has something to do with the mirror universe."

Spock looked away again. "Jim, I truly regret these present circumstances. But all I am at liberty to say to you is . . . go back to Chal."

"Chal?"

Spock touched Kirk's shoulder, and Kirk knew the level of concern Spock must feel for him to express himself in such human terms. "Go home. You are no longer part of Starfleet. I know you no longer want to be involved in . . . in Starfleet activities. You should not think about returning to the mirror universe and trying to right ancient wrongs."

Kirk felt the satisfaction of knowing he had been correct. He also understood the reason why Spock was worried about him, even though there was no need for it. "Spock, believe me. There's nothing more I want to do than get on the next liner back to Chal. I plan to . . ." He smiled as he realized he was about to say aloud what he had been thinking for months. "I'm going to ask Teilani to marry me. I intend to spend the rest of my life tending my garden. Chal is world enough for me, now.

"And the last thing I want to do is go back to the mirror universe. But I feel responsible for what happened there. I have to do something to help. Besides, what harm is there in telling these people what they want to know? I won't be fighting their battles for them. Those days are over for me. But if I can give them the tools they need to do their own fighting, I owe them that much. And that's why I asked you to come here and help."

Spock looked up at the handful of stars above. "I cannot help you. And I am sorry."

Kirk felt anger well up in him, but he knew it was just a visceral response to frustration. If he thought Spock was open to logic, he'd spend the rest of the week debating the situation if he had to, until Spock was forced to agree. But there was some other factor at work here, and it was unlikely Spock would reveal enough to let Kirk know what the rules of the game were. And in that type of situation, Kirk knew, the best strategy was to write his own rules.

"Then I am sorry if I have interfered with something more important you're involved in," Kirk said, almost formally. "And I appreciate your taking the time to come to see me. But, for now, it seems there's nothing more to be said."

Spock turned away from the railing as if Kirk had spoken a spell which had broken through some enchantment. "Starfleet Command would like to offer you transportation home by starship. The *Sovereign* is departing Spacedock tomorrow morning at—"

"I have no intention of going home, Spock. I made a promise to those people. I'm going to keep it."

Kirk could see Spock respond to the challenge in his voice. "You no longer have the security clearance to obtain the information they request. And Captain Scott would be facing grave consequences if he attempted to use his position to do so for you."

Scott fairly blustered at Spock's threat. "Now, see here, Spock."

"It's all right, Scotty," Kirk interrupted. "What I'm going to do won't involve you. I have other friends in this century. And I'm sure Captain Picard has more than enough authority, and more than enough compassion, to try to help billions of innocent beings regain their freedom."

Kirk nodded to Scott. "Good night, Scotty. Thanks for coming." He looked at Spock. "Ambassador." He started toward the sliding doors.

But Spock didn't let him take more than three steps. "Jim, wait."

Kirk stopped, but did not turn back. There was nothing like forcing the other player to make his move first.

"You won't be able to find Captain Picard."

Kirk slowly turned back to Spock. "I'm waiting."

Spock looked troubled. "I am under . . . strict Starfleet orders . . ."

Kirk understood the dilemma. Starfleet duty versus a lifetime of friendship and trust. But Kirk knew a way around that. "Spock . . . if we follow the logic of the situation, strictly speaking, I'm a civilian and you're part of the Vulcan diplomatic corps. I can understand how Starfleet might strongly *insist* on certain types of behavior and nondisclosure, but neither you nor I are truly subject to *orders* anymore. Are we?"

The night wind was picking up, and it blew at Spock's robe, as if even nature—or the dull bureaucrats at the Department of Weather—were attempting to steer him on a new course. Kirk could almost see Spock thinking, calculating all possible actions and results, as if they were facing each other across a three-dimensional chessboard. "What you are proposing," Spock finally said, "is, I believe, what is commonly called a slippery slope."

Scott snorted with laughter. "Och. As if you two haven't careened down a few of those in your day. C'mon, Spock, ye know what ye have to do."

"Tell me what I need to know, Spock," Kirk urged. "Then, if I can help you, I will. If I can't, I'll go back to Chal and . . . build myself a rocking chair."

The offer to take himself out of the game seemed to be the condition that finally convinced Spock to bend the rules. Kirk and Scott drew closer to Spock as he prepared to tell them what he had been holding back.

"Eight days ago, Starbase 310 received an automated EFA alert, requesting authorization for a change in command. The starship was identified as the *U.S.S. Voyager.* The new commander, as Captain Jean-Luc Picard."

Scott's eyes flashed with genuine excitement. "The *Voyager*'s back?"

But Spock shook his head. "No, Mr. Scott. The real *Voyager,* it seems, remains in the Delta Quadrant. Starfleet Intelligence believes the EFA alert came from a duplicate *Voyager.*"

But that made no sense to Kirk. "Spock, the *Voyager* is one of the latest Starfleet designs. There hasn't been a Starfleet in the mirror universe for almost a century. How could it be duplicated when the two histories have diverged so completely?"

"In short, stolen plans. According to the *Deep Space Nine* logs, the Terran resistance successfully stole and used the plans for the *Defiant.* Since that time, Starfleet Intelligence has become aware of an increase in the number of attempts to access the classified specification files for a variety of Starfleet vessels, including several at Earth Station McKinley, where *Voyager* was constructed. Break-in attempts at McKinley ended almost two years ago, which might logically imply that the last attempt was undetected, and successful. Starfleet Intelligence believes the Terran resistance is responsible for those attempts, and has succeeded in creating a mirror-universe *Voyager*."

"That cannae be right," Scotty protested. "If those lasses and your counterpart already have that kind of access to Fleet computers, then why go to all the trouble of coming after Jim to have him do the same?"

"You have answered your own question, Captain Scott. To cover up the fact that they already have been successful."

"But, Spock, if Jim hadna decided to help them, they were going to *kill* him."

Spock was undeterred. "Or so they say."

"Gentlemen, this is . . . fascinating," Kirk said, "but there's a more important matter at hand. What happened to Jean-Luc?"

"That is unknown. Starfleet dispatched a high-speed fighter wing to the *Voyager*'s coordinates, which were within a light-year of the *Enterprise*'s last reported position. Both the *Voyager* and the *Enterprise* were gone. However, residual warp trails indicated they had both been in formation at that location only hours earlier. The quantum signature of the warp particles left in the *Voyager*'s wake confirms that it is from another quantum reality."

"Could the warp trails nae be traced?" Scott asked.

"No, Captain Scott. Either both ships employed a warp-particle containment field to mask their trails, or . . ."

Kirk didn't wait for Spock to finish. "Or both ships are now in the mirror universe."

"You see my dilemma, Jim. The three people who abducted

you could very well be involved in the hijacking of Starfleet's most powerful and—in the wrong hands—deadliest starship."

Kirk stared down at the tiles of the balcony. As if he were about to face combat, his mind became focused and totally aware at the same time. He sensed the cool temperature of the night air, the growing gusts of wind, the distinct sounds of traffic moving above the roads below and through the sky above. But there was no rage in his heart, no sudden adrenaline call to action.

Only disappointment. Sharp and overwhelming.

Because he had just realized why Spock had not been forthcoming.

"Spock, I want to ask, Why didn't you tell me all that at the beginning? But I know the answer."

Hidden by years of Vulcan training, that same disappointment could still be seen in Spock's eyes. Not a reflection of Kirk's, but Spock's own.

"You think I might be involved," Kirk said, each word a knife to stab the cooling air between the two friends. "Involved with the Resistance, the hijacking . . . all of it. The truth you were trying so hard to keep to yourself, is . . . you don't trust me."

Spock chose his words carefully, as if this moment of revelation was as difficult for him as for Kirk. "Starfleet feels . . . it is not prudent to accept your involvement with the resistance members at face value. Whether you are truly driven to correct an imagined wrong you might have done a century ago, or whether any guilt you might feel over such an action might leave you open to manipulation without realizing you were being used, Starfleet feels that, at best, you are . . . compromised in this matter."

Now Kirk felt true anger begin to crawl up from some deep inner cave within him. And this time, it would not be denied. "Spare me the speeches, Ambassador. The plain and simple truth of it is you don't trust me. Starfleet doesn't trust me. After all I've done for them, for the Federation, for *you* . . . to be treated like this is . . . is unacceptable."

"Jim, I remind you that you are no longer part of Starfleet. Since your return to this time and this region of space, you have shown little interest in the Federation."

Kirk threw his hands in the air. "What about the virogen? The Federation was facing collapse. And I was there to stop that from happening."

Spock was unperturbed. "The virogen threatened Chal. Your efforts to save the Federation are seen, in some quarters, as a mere offshoot of your efforts to save your new home."

Kirk was more than insulted. He was outraged. But Spock kept speaking.

"And, in this past year, when the Federation faced its greatest threat from the war with the Dominion, when virtually every retired member of Starfleet voluntarily returned to active duty, you remained on Chal."

Kirk was so appalled by these accusations, he was almost incapable of speech. "Is this what the Federation has become in this century? Sparta? If I'm not a soldier, I'm not a citizen?"

Kirk couldn't believe it, but Scott looked as if he was being swayed by Spock's argument. "The war with the Dominion, that was—that *is*—still serious business."

"The Dominion was able to threaten us because of *one* passageway," Kirk insisted. "The Bajoran wormhole. Close the wormhole, the Dominion is no more dangerous than Cardassia. The Federation has fought worse enemies, stronger enemies, and won. The Federation doesn't need me to survive. Especially when Starfleet's got people like Ben Sisko."

Scott seemed surprised by the familiar tone Kirk had used. "Do ye know Captain Sisko?" he asked.

"We've met," Kirk said. "A long time ago." But he didn't elaborate. It was enough that when he had first seen an image of Captain Sisko in an update on the Dominion War he had finally realized the answer to the puzzling mystery of the disappearing lieutenant who had caused a brief flurry of excitement on his *Enterprise* a century ago. Kirk looked forward to someday comparing notes on time travel with the ubiquitous Captain Sisko.

"They're not going to respond well to being refused," Kirk said to Spock, making it clear he referred to Janeway and her companions. "We could be in danger." Kirk looked over his shoulder at the sliding glass doors. They were covered by sheer curtains that glowed with the light of the suite. Kirk was a bit surprised that Janeway hadn't come marching through those doors by now, demanding to know what the delay was. In his brief experience of her, she was always in a hurry.

"We never have been," Spock said. He removed a Starfleet comm badge from his robes. "The moment we stepped onto this balcony, Janeway, T'Val, and my counterpart were beamed to detention cells on Spacedock."

Kirk felt the bitter shock of betrayal. "Why didn't you beam me up, too?"

Spock fixed Kirk with an unblinking gaze. "Starfleet wanted to. I convinced them otherwise. You are free to go. Provided you go to Chal."

"You'll forgive me if I don't sound properly grateful," Kirk said angrily. If it had been anyone else but Spock, Kirk would never consider leaving this balcony without satisfaction of some kind. But he, at least, believed friendship and loyalty must stand for something.

He spun around before Spock could say anything more. He ignored Scott's plea to return. He strode to the doors, slid them open, and stepped through the suddenly billowing white curtains.

The chairs were empty. Spock had meant what he'd said. Starfleet had struck.

And then he realized that one person still remained in the suite. A slightly built man at the bar, in Starfleet's latest uniform, his back to the balcony as he appeared to be mixing a drink.

"Did you change your mind?" Kirk asked in challenge. "Are you going to beam me to detention, too?"

The thin man turned slowly, and Kirk felt a shock of surprise as he suddenly recognized him.

"Bones?"

At 148 years old, hand trembling slightly, Dr. Leonard McCoy held up what could only be a mint julep. "Hi there, Jim. I was beginning to wonder if Spock was going to be keeping you out there all night."

"Bones!"

McCoy ignored Kirk's reaction and carefully placed the mint julep on the bar beside a second one. "When your vocabulary recovers from whatever Spock has done to it, maybe we could have a talk."

Kirk crossed the suite and held back from hugging McCoy, only because he looked so frail that Kirk was afraid he might injure him. "I . . . I can't believe . . ."

"That I'm still alive?" McCoy completed helpfully.

"Nooo," Kirk said, though he had to admit to himself that that was part of it. A healthy Vulcan could live more than two hundred years. Kirk and Scott had reached the twenty-fourth century by the intervention of science and inexplicable temporal effects. But McCoy had arrived in the future as most humans do—one long, hard day at a time. Even given the medical breakthroughs of the age, McCoy was among a handful of humans breaking the records of human longevity. And Kirk believed few people deserved it more.

"I can't believe you look so good." Kirk stepped back to take in the sight of his old friend. McCoy was dapper in the new uniform—it was the best word to use; his white hair almost glowed against the dark gray and black. "The last time I saw you, you had the . . ." Kirk gestured at McCoy's legs.

"Exoskeleton," McCoy said. "Implants now. Artificial muscles grafted over my own. My fifth set of hips—they tell me these ones are going to last. And a new pair of cloned lungs. I'm not a doctor anymore, I'm a medical experiment."

Kirk was overcome. But he was also suspicious. "So, are you in on this, too?"

"On what?" McCoy asked.

Kirk looked toward the balcony as Spock and Scott reentered the room, and reacted to McCoy's presence with as much surprise as Kirk had displayed.

"All right," Kirk said after the highly charged greetings were exchanged, "now I am confused. Bones, you knew . . . the ambassador and Scotty were here, but they didn't know you were going to join them."

" 'The ambassador'?" McCoy repeated. "Do I detect a chill in the environmental system?"

"Somebody better tell me what's going on," Kirk said.

McCoy sighed, steadied himself against the bar, then handed Kirk one of the mint juleps. "Drink this," he said.

Kirk took the drink, sniffed it. Real bourbon. "I . . . gave it up."

McCoy gave him an inquiring look. "Any particular reason?"

Kirk shrugged. He gave up alcohol at the same time he removed tissue regenerators, computers, replicators, and communicators from his life. "Simpler," he said. "And healthier."

"Well, I'm your doctor," McCoy told him. "And I say, drink it."

Kirk had to admit it did smell good, and the mint was fresh. After a year on Chal, he knew the difference between plants just picked and those a day or more older. One was a sensory experience, the other was just food.

He sipped the drink. Sweet and cool, the flavor and delicate chill released a flood of memories from the first *Enterprise,* the long nights in his cabin, talking through to ship's dawn with Bones and Spock, as if no other life would ever be possible.

"What are you, a cadet?" McCoy said. He downed half his own drink, then blinked in surprise as if he hadn't intended to swallow so much.

Kirk decided his long fast was over. He took a long swallow too, amazed at the forgotten but pleasurable sensation of the liquid burning down his throat and into his stomach.

Then he exhaled slowly and placed the glass on the bar. The sugar and alcohol were hitting him that quickly.

"You all right?" McCoy asked.

"You're my doctor," Kirk told him. "What are you doing here?"

McCoy put his glass down beside Kirk's. "Bad news, I'm afraid, Jim. From Chal."

The effects of alcohol and sugar left Kirk at once. "Teilani . . ."

McCoy nodded. "Someone . . . took her."

Kirk felt his heart start beating again. McCoy said "took," only "took," nothing worse.

"Who? Took her where?"

"No one knows. There was a message left, telling you that if you helped the intendant, Teilani would be . . . well . . ." McCoy hesitated, but Kirk left McCoy no room for doubt that he wanted to hear it all. "If you helped the intendant, they'd kill Teilani."

Kirk could tell that wasn't all of it, either. "What else, Bones? What else?"

McCoy looked all of his near century and a half in age. "If you want Teilani back, they will trade."

"The intendant?"

McCoy nodded. "And his lieutenants."

"Janeway and T'Val."

"They weren't named, but . . . Starfleet Intelligence agrees that's who the message refers to."

Kirk turned accusingly to Spock. "Did you know any of this?"

"No. Nothing."

"Scotty?"

"Nae, laddie. I've no truck with none but Engineering at Command."

"Starfleet wants to talk with you, Jim."

"I don't care what Starfleet wants, Bones. Two hours ago, Starfleet was ready to beam me into detention."

"When haven't they wanted to do that?" McCoy asked with a wry grimace. He took another sip from his drink.

"This isn't the time, Bones."

"At my age, it doesn't make sense to put anything off."

"And I'm not going to. Two hours ago, Spock, I was ready to turn the intendant and his lieutenants over to you and Starfleet, wish everyone good luck, and go back to Chal. Two minutes ago, after what you told me, I was still going back to Chal. But not now."

"I think that's what Starfleet wants to talk to you about," McCoy said again.

"Bones, *you're* dealing with Starfleet Intelligence. Spock's dealing with Starfleet Intelligence. But whoever you're talking to there aren't talking to each other. I'm not getting caught up in that. I've had it with Starfleet's bureaucracy and channels. Someone has Teilani. I'm going to get her back. It's as simple as that."

Scott looked from McCoy to Spock and back again, then stepped forward. "Well, you'll nae be goin' alone."

"Hell," McCoy said, "I haven't done anything exciting in . . . I can't count that high. I'm in." He put his drink down on the bar.

Kirk looked at his friend, said kindly, "Bones, no. At your age—"

"At my age I've got so many damn artificial body parts that if someone cut off my head the only difference'd be that my bedside manner would show a remarkable improvement.

155

Besides, at *your* age, how many friends do you have left stupid enough to go off on one of your harebrained adventures?"

Kirk forced a smile. "Thank you for that vote of confidence."

"May I inject a note of reason into these ill-considered proceedings?" Spock asked.

But Kirk had no more time to waste. And he certainly had no time for those who would try to waste it for him. "No, Mr. Spock, you may not. I've had it with reason. This time, I'm just going to get the job done."

Kirk started for the door, aware that McCoy and Scott were following close behind.

Hand on the doorknob, Kirk looked back at Spock. "What about it? Are you coming with me?"

"I believe the question is: Are *you* coming with *me?*"

"And why would I do that?" Kirk asked.

Spock pulled out his comm badge. "Because you have a firm grasp of logic, for a human. And I, whatever your feelings toward me are right now, have a ship."

Kirk hesitated, tempted. Getting a ship had become his first priority, though how one went about doing that, in an economy that used no form of currency or system of economic exchange, remained a mystery.

"What kind of ship?" Kirk asked.

"You may inspect it yourself," Spock answered. He squeezed the comm badge so it gave out its familiar chirp.

"Spock to *Sovereign,*" he said. "Four to beam up."

THIRTEEN

☆

There were conditions for saving Teilani, of course. With Starfleet, Kirk knew, there were always conditions. And the worst of them was the uniform.

He stood in front of the holographic mirror projected from the bulkhead in his quarters on the *Sovereign,* adjusting the jacket for the tenth time, at last understanding why Picard kept tugging on his. Kirk had worn one of these new ones before. It had been part of his disguise when the Vulcans had arrested him during the virogen crisis. But last year, it had simply been a costume.

Today, it was an actual uniform, a sign of his reenlistment in an organization he once had been glad to leave. Where Starfleet had been eager for James T. Kirk, civilian, to return to his backwater retirement home on Chal, it now was even more willing to put its resources at the disposal of James T. Kirk, Starfleet officer.

On the bridge of the *Sovereign,* Fleet Admiral Alynna Nechayev had, with an insincere smile, given Kirk exactly thirty seconds to make his decision. The admiral had left him no choice, and she had known it.

Kirk fingered the four pips on the right side of his collar. At least there he had managed to draw the line. He'd rejoin, he had told her, but not as an admiral. That would only guarantee him another instructor's post at the Academy. So he had held out for captain, the only rank that had ever suited him. The rank that had once given him a starship, and might again.

Nechayev had agreed as if that had been her plan all along, told *Captain* Kirk to report to the observation lounge in one hour, and then had spun around in her chair to grill two technicians on the half-percent deviation in warp efficiency she had noticed at factor seven point six.

Spock, who knew his way around the impressive ship, the first of her class, had wasted no time escorting Kirk, Scott, and McCoy from the bridge. Kirk interpreted Spock's prompt action as confirmation of his own suspicions that Nechayev was one of those officers of whom it was unwise to remain in her sights any longer than necessary.

Now, in his quarters, Kirk heard a chime that to him could only mean someone was at his door—though he was still not entirely familiar with all the technology of this latest of Starfleet's vessels.

"Computer, mirror off," he said, and the virtual reflective surface before him vanished. Its absence revealed a pale wall decorated by an art screen. The screen, which could display any one of hundreds of thousands of different images stored in the ship's computer, had been set to show a fancifully colored painting of an old Constitution-class starship, which might even have been of the first *Enterprise*. Kirk had checked the artist's signature and was pleased to see the work was a Jefferies. It was good to know that one of Starfleet's greatest shipwrights had not been forgotten in this age.

Kirk walked over to the door—his quarters were that large—stood before it, and said, "Come."

The door slid open. Spock and McCoy waited outside, and for a moment it was as if all three had suddenly been thrown back a century.

Kirk took in the sight of Spock in one of the new uniforms,

and read the insignia at his collar. *"Admiral* Spock? Were the robes getting drafty?"

"As I mentioned, the war with the Dominion has brought many of Starfleet's retired officers back to the service."

McCoy stepped through the doorway, surefooted, no sign of age or hesitation, his implants and artificial muscles working perfectly. "Have you seen yourself in that new getup?" he asked.

Kirk shook his head, admitting to nothing. "It's just a uniform. They'll have another one in a few more years. They always do."

"The Hawthorne effect," Spock said, stepping through the doorway after McCoy. "A twentieth-century insight in Earth sociology. Inconsequential, though regular modifications in the workplace lead to employees feeling that their management is concerned about their well-being. Consequently, they exhibit greater job satisfaction, and thus function with greater productivity."

Kirk stared at Spock. "Spock, if no one in Starfleet is getting paid anymore, how can we be employees?"

"Admittedly, the economics of the twenty-fourth century do appear complex on the surface, but a system devoid of any instrument of exchange is inherently logical and deceptively simple."

"If it's so simple, explain it to me in twenty-five words or less," Kirk said.

Spock's face remained blank for several seconds, then he admitted, "I cannot."

"That makes me feel much better." Then Kirk noticed his missing shipmate. "Where's Scotty?"

"Mr. Scott is on duty and will join us in the lounge," Spock said.

"On duty? On this ship?"

"The *Sovereign* is Captain Scott's current assignment. He adapted a great many of her engineering breakthroughs for use in his designs for the *Enterprise*-E, and is now working on further refinements for the new *Constellation.*"

Kirk took a moment to absorb that revelation. "Scotty . . . *designed* the new *Enterprise?*"

"Portions," Spock said.

"They don't design themselves, you know, not even these days," McCoy added.

Kirk decided not to be surprised. He had always known Scott's talents were considerable, though he probably didn't tell him that as often as he should. "Impressive, as always." Kirk tugged down on his jacket, then started forward. "Shall we join the admiral?" But he stopped as he saw McCoy grinning at him. "Yes, Doctor?"

"I saw that tug. You've been standing in front of a holographic mirror admiring yourself in that uniform, haven't you?"

"A what kind of mirror?"

"You can't fool me, Jim. You're glad to be back in the Fleet."

First Teilani. Now McCoy. Why does everyone insist on believing they know what I'm feeling better than I do? Kirk thought.

"I was blackmailed, Bones. All I care about is getting Teilani back. And then I'm going to burn this uniform on Chal."

"That is not the arrangement you agreed to with the admiral," Spock pointed out. "You have rejoined Starfleet for the duration of the war, plus one year."

"Don't you start," Kirk said. "I'm going to the bridge."

Kirk walked out of his quarters and . . . and . . . he refused to look back.

"The nearest turbolift is to the right," Spock said from behind him.

Kirk turned to the right, into the corridor leading to the turbolift alcove. But by the time the lift arrived, Spock and McCoy were at his side again.

McCoy patted Kirk's shoulder as the lift doors slipped open. "Don't worry, Jim. We'll get her back."

"I know we will," Kirk said. "With or without Starfleet." The doors closed. The bridge, and Fleet Admiral Nechayev, awaited.

"Not another word, Captain Kirk."

Kirk opened his mouth to protest, read Nechayev's mood, then decided instead on silence, folding his hands on the glowing surface of the conference table in the *Sovereign*'s observation lounge. This was not the time to question Starfleet's strategy for dealing with Teilani's kidnappers.

He was aware of Nechayev watching him, waiting for him to dare to interrupt her opening statement again.

But Kirk looked off to the side of the room where a large glass case contained an elaborate terrarium in which a dozen or so small lizards, most from Earth, remained motionless beneath warming lights.

"That's better," the admiral said. "Anyone else have something to add?"

Kirk didn't risk looking at Spock, McCoy, Scott, or Nechayev's executive officer, Commander Tan Kral, a serene-looking Trill whose spots merged on his bald head, creating the impression of a covering of extremely short and splotchy hair. Commander Kral had had nothing to say beyond greeting Kirk and the others when they had entered. Kirk doubted he would speak now.

"Good," the admiral said. She brushed her pale blond hair from her forehead as if she had just completed a physically demanding task. "As I was saying, this is how the mission will proceed.

"We are en route to the mirror *Voyager*'s last known position near the Goldin Discontinuity, and will arrive in three days. We will then track the *Enterprise* and the mirror *Voyager* to locate the mechanism, artificial or natural, which serves as the link between our universe and—" The admiral snapped her head toward Kirk with no attempt to hide her anger. *"What is it, Captain Kirk?!"*

Kirk forced himself not to respond to the admiral's painfully obvious dislike of him. True, he had tensed as she had spoken, shifted in his chair, all minor and unavoidable responses to the . . . the stupidity of her plan. Apparently, though, just his presence in this room was enough to annoy her.

"I believe we're forgetting there is a woman's life at risk," Kirk said, struggling to remain calm for Teilani's sake.

"There are potentially billions of lives at risk, Captain."

"But Teilani is the key!" Kirk could no longer stand the confinement of remaining seated at the table, as if he were a willing member of her crew. He jumped to his feet. "Why waste time searching for ships that have hidden their warp trails and might already be in the other universe? Whoever took Teilani wants to conduct a trade. Intendant Spock, Janeway, T'Val, they're on this ship. Let's make that trade."

Nechayev rocked back in her chair. "The famous Captain Kirk, hero of his century, wants to give up so quickly? Give in to blackmail like a . . . a Ferengi?"

Kirk looked out the observation windows to see the stars slipping away at high warp. He tried to draw strength from them. "Admiral, of course we will not give in to blackmail. But we can use the trade to set a trap. Whoever has Teilani is from the mirror universe. If you want to know how they got their *Voyager* into this universe, how they plan on taking the *Enterprise* back, they'll have those answers. Do it my way and Teilani's safe, and you have a prisoner or two who can tell you what you need to know, instead of wasting a year scanning space for something you might never find."

Nechayev looked at Kirk with contempt. "The best minds in Starfleet Intelligence have spent decades developing the proper response to the demands of kidnappers and terrorists.

If we find the crossover mechanism and either destroy it or take control of it while the kidnappers are in our universe, they will be cut off from escape, and more willing to deal."

Kirk pounded his fist on the table. "They'll be cut off and desperate and more willing to kill their hostage!"

Nechayev jumped to her feet, as well, and leaned over the table to face Kirk eye to eye. "No! Once the mechanism is shut down, Teilani is the only thing that gives the kidnappers a way to get back home. They won't harm her!"

"She is not a thing! And you are putting her in harm's way!"

"You are out of line, Captain!"

"You are!" Kirk shouted. "You made me an offer so I would help you. I accepted. But now you're not listening to anything I say."

Nechayev's pale complexion was becoming flushed. "These are not the old days of the final frontier, Captain. Starfleet no longer straps on its laser pistols and warps off to blow up strange new life-forms first and ask questions later."

"We didn't do it that way in my time, if that's what you're implying."

"Excuse me?" the admiral said in mock confusion. "I *know* that's how you did things. I've read the history books."

"I *lived* that history. I made some of it."

"And that's what makes you think you're better than the top people at Starfleet Intelligence?"

"Listen to what you're saying, Admiral. You're provoking a confrontation. Always trying to make everything into a good or bad situation. Am I *better* than Starfleet's experts? That's not a question that should be asked. Who are those experts? What's their experience? It's all twenty-fourth century, isn't it? So *that's* what they're good for. If a band of present-day Orion pirates had kidnapped Teilani, or a renegade Klingon crew, then Starfleet's experts would know exactly what to do and I'd stand back and let them do it.

"But we're dealing with people your Starfleet knows nothing about. They're ruthless. Unswayed by logic. Driven by generations of frustration, hatred, and the need, the desire, for revenge. And forgive me for saying so, but in this perfect Federation you've inherited, I don't think the Starfleet of this day understands that kind of passion. And the proof of it is that useless plan you just laid out."

Kirk and the admiral remained standing, watching each other like wary knife fighters about to do battle, each waiting for the other to make the first move.

"Admiral Spock," Nechayev said, "before I have Kirk escorted from my bridge, explain to him that Starfleet's plan is logical."

"The plan is quite logical," Spock said. "But, the beings who captured Teilani are not. Thus, I must agree with Captain Kirk that the plan stands little chance of success."

The admiral broke her gaze from Kirk and looked at Spock as if she'd been betrayed. "How can you say that?"

"Because it is true."

Nechayev narrowed her eyes in thought. Then she smiled. The effect was not pleasant. "I see. You're in this together. Of course, Kirk and Spock. And let's not forget Dr. McCoy. All three of you. Caught up in some . . . pitifully transparent attempt to recapture the glory of your youth."

The insults Kirk could ignore, because they weren't true. He couldn't be responsible for what people who didn't know him thought of him. But given Nechayev's sudden resistance to his presence, why had she offered him a berth on the *Sovereign* in the first place?

He looked at McCoy. The elderly doctor rubbed the fingers of one hand together, a nervous gesture exposing the tension he felt.

Spock, of course, remained placid, though Kirk had no doubt that he was feeling the same outrage at being so wrongfully judged.

But then Spock surprised everyone by also getting to his feet. "Fleet Admiral Nechayev, by refusing to consider Captain Kirk's advice, I believe you are sidestepping the orders you were given by Command at the outset of this mission."

Nechayev looked momentarily confused, then laughed scornfully. "What? You're going to have McCoy declare me unfit for duty so Kirk can take command?" She shot a glance at Kirk. "As I said, I've read *all* the history books. I know how you think." Then she looked at her Number One. "Commander Kral, how do you respond to Admiral Spock's charge? Am I disobeying my orders?"

The Trill shook his head slowly. "No, ma'am. You are required only to ask for Kirk's assistance in those matters you feel are appropriate."

"And since it's clear you find me completely inappropriate," Kirk said, "why am I here?"

McCoy answered the question, and Kirk could hear the bitterness he felt. "It's obvious, Jim. Starfleet was so eager to stop you from being involved in any of this, they asked you on board to keep you out of the way and under their control."

Kirk stared at Nechayev in dawning comprehension. "You have no intention of helping me save Teilani."

Nechayev shook her head at him. "No matter what you think of us in this century, we're not monsters. We will do all we can to save Teilani, *after* the security of the Federation has been assured."

Kirk felt sick. Starfleet had lied to him. And he had no recourse. He was trapped—on one of the most advanced starships in the Fleet, the prototype from which Jean-Luc's own new *Enterprise* had been developed. And it was hurtling at maximum speed to a region of space hundreds of light-years from Chal, and from any chance of rescuing the woman he loved more than life itself.

He could see that the admiral sensed his sudden feeling of defeat.

She sat down, gestured for him to do the same.

But Kirk couldn't see the point. "It seems we're finished here."

Nechayev shrugged. "As you wish."

Kirk started for the door. Spock pulled out McCoy's chair, helped him stand.

"Captain," the admiral said before Kirk could leave. "Starfleet did invite you on this mission for a reason other than the one you imagine."

Kirk looked over his shoulder. Somehow, he doubted that.

"You seem to have developed some sort of relationship with the three intruders from the mirror universe," Nechayev continued.

"Because they trusted me, Admiral. But that was before you ambushed them in my suite. I doubt any relationship exists by now."

"If it did," Nechayev said, not letting him go yet, "Starfleet would be most appreciative if during the next few days, you could speak with them, to help develop our understanding of their universe. Their ancient history, the events of the last century, the struggles they face today. It would be most helpful."

"If I refuse?" Kirk asked. "Do you have a plank on this ship I could walk?"

Nechayev did not respond to his sarcasm. "The choice is yours, Captain Kirk. Remember that. The choice Starfleet offers has always been yours."

"I make my own choices," Kirk said. Then he walked out, not waiting to be dismissed.

He knew what he had to do, now.

And to save Teilani, he had only three days in which to do it.

FOURTEEN

★

"I could kill you," Janeway said.

Kirk kept his back to her, gazing out at the magnificent vista of Yosemite National Park as it could only be seen at sunset from the summit of El Capitan. "You could try," he said, "but—"

Janeway's hands struck Kirk's shoulders with the force of a charging targ, knocking him into a fatal one-kilometer fall which lasted just long enough for him to feel an overwhelming sensation of déjà vu, and then—

"Warning," said the computer voice, "physical risk parameters exceeded. Safety overrides engaged."

Kirk felt solid ground beneath his feet. When he looked down, there was still nothing to see below his feet except air. But he could walk on it.

He turned around to look at Janeway, still standing at the edge of the summit, hands on her hips, distinctly disappointed that he was not plunging to his death.

"As I was saying," Kirk continued. "You could try, but the holodeck won't let you."

Kirk walked through the air to return to the simulated granite—a perfect illusion created by shifting holographic projections and transporter-based replicated rock and stone.

"That's what I thought," Janeway said.

"But you had to be sure."

"I had to be sure." Her quick smile surprised Kirk. It seemed genuine. "You'd have done the same."

Kirk didn't answer. Better to keep her guessing. But she was right. He was beginning to see the starship captain at her core.

Janeway broke the sudden moment of silence between them by looking around, breathing deeply, eyes shut. "Even with my eyes closed, the illusion is perfect. The wind, the heat rising from the rock, the smell of the pine trees . . ." Her eyes fluttered open and she looked away, as if stricken with a sudden wave of unbearable sorrow.

"What is it?" Kirk asked. He was genuinely concerned. In the past three days, he had come to see Janeway as more than an enemy to be manipulated as he worked to achieve his own goals. There were layers of intrigue within this woman, concealed beneath a deceptively brittle shell of indifference, as if at her core she carried a burden so great, she was afraid to reveal it even to herself.

Janeway ran her hand across her short auburn hair. She had removed the harsh red dye since being beamed to the *Sovereign*. An attractive change, Kirk felt. "I was just thinking . . . trying to think of the technology that goes into something like this. The thousands, the *millions* of hours of design, testing, programming. . . . Do you know what that says about a culture if it can afford to expend all those resources on entertainment?"

"They use it for training simulations, as well," Kirk said.

But Janeway ignored him, continuing with her point. "It means all the other problems are solved. No hunger. No disease. No war. . . ."

"That's one way to look at it. But it could also mean that this culture is trying to distract itself from the challenges it still faces. Time spent in entertainment can be a respite from ongoing struggles, not just a reward for having completed them."

Janeway held the palm of her hand up, turning to face the holographic sun as the simulated star reached the horizon, swollen, red, coloring slender trails of clouds salmon pink against the deep indigo of darkening sky. Then she angled her hand as if judging the falloff in heat. Kirk had noticed that Janeway never stopped measuring and testing her environment. She definitely had the soul of a scientist in her.

"Do you always look at everything from both points of view?" she asked.

"Occupational hazard," Kirk said. "I'm a starship captain—*was* a starship captain. Diplomacy is the best policy. Do you always ask important questions while you're pretending to be involved in something else?"

Janeway lowered her hand and gave Kirk her full attention. In the flattering glow of sunset, she had lost her pallor. She now seemed rested, renewed. "Occupational hazard. I'm a soldier. And I'm in enemy hands. Deception is the best policy."

Janeway was now clad in the civilian clothes the replicators had provided for her. They were similar in cut to Starfleet's shirt, jacket, and slacks, but made from a softly textured, dark green fabric that clung to her with a subtlety missing from the more utilitarian uniform. She no longer reminded Kirk of the grim-faced soldier in a combat suit who had kidnapped him more than a week ago.

Kirk looked back over the magnificent expanse of the pine-filled valley floor. The distant trees were different in number and size from what he remembered. The three-dimensional images that had been used to make this amazing reconstruction must have been recorded recently, and the vegetation no longer corresponded to his century-old memories. "Starfleet's not the enemy," he said.

With Kirk, Janeway watched the shadows move across the valley floor. "You've told me that before," she said. In a scattering of small clearings, the flickering dance of pinpoint campfires could be seen, as if here in Yosemite the stars had found a home on Earth. "But I don't believe you," she continued. "Because I think *you* think Starfleet is your enemy as much as it's mine."

I'm surrounded by mind readers, Kirk thought.

"Kate," he said firmly, "I don't make any apologies that I've disagreed with Command from time to time . . . all right, a lot of the . . . most of the time, especially recently. But in its own, plodding, earnest way, I believe Starfleet is simply trying to discover the truth behind your presence here, and the disappearance of the *Enterprise.*"

Janeway looked directly into Kirk's eyes, as if to convince him that each word she spoke was the truth. "I told you why we were here. I told you we know nothing about the *Enterprise* or the mirror *Voyager.*"

"Admiral Nechayev is reluctant to accept that both incursions from your universe happened at the same time by coincidence."

The sun was more than halfway gone, and the fading sky and deepening shadows brought a new intensity to Janeway's features. "What do you think?"

Kirk let her see the truth that was in him, as well. "I don't care. Only one thing matters to me—Teilani's safety."

Janeway studied him carefully. "Is that so?"

Not for the first time Kirk wished that he could read minds.

Then Janeway reached out, took his face in her hands, and forcefully kissed him, her body pressed close against his. One of her hands moved to the back of his neck so the pressure of their joining became unrelenting.

For an instant, Kirk's body responded, and he pulled her even closer. There was a quixotic fire in this woman of the kind that always drew him, a fire fueled by willfulness, by independence, by a shared inability to accept defeat, that would always make him consider her an equal.

But as quickly as that wellspring of passion rose within him to meet her advance, his heart rebelled.

He pushed Janeway away, breathless in the sudden, unbid-

170

den rush of physical desire, stared at her face in the fading crimson light of the sun and knew that his was as flushed as hers.

"No," he said.

She drew the fingers of one hand across his face, across his lips. Her touch was insistent, not gentle. "Now *I* don't believe *you.*"

At another time in his life, Kirk knew, his heart *and* his mind wouldn't enter into this equation. Beneath these stars he and this woman would exhaust their passion without regret, for their past or for their future, exulting in an eternal present of sheer experience.

At another time in his life.

But not this time.

He caught her hand and cut himself off from her touch. "Believe me," he said.

Nothing would happen between them. He wouldn't allow it.

"You really do love her," Janeway said.

"Love" seemed such a small word for what he felt, but even a book full of words could not express what he had found with Teilani, and what still remained for the two of them to discover, together. "I really do," Kirk said.

Janeway stepped back. The limits of her environment had been tested again, and now she processed her observations.

"Help me get her back," Kirk said.

Janeway didn't play any games. "Help me get the intendant and T'Val back to where we belong, with the information we need." There was a directness to her style of negotiation that Kirk admired.

Kirk held out his hand to accept her challenge and seal the bargain.

But then Janeway hesitated. "What about Starfleet?"

The blunt, archaic term Kirk chose to describe what he thought Starfleet could do to itself made Janeway laugh.

"Such language to be coming from a starship captain," she chided him. "What happened to diplomacy?"

"Diplomacy is born of patience," Kirk said. "At this point in my life, I'm all out."

Overhead, the simulated stars of a simulated world shone in breathtaking spectacle.

Beneath them, Kirk and Janeway were exactly where they belonged.

They shook hands.

Not as man and woman, but as soldiers, allies.

And now that their own alliance had been forged, the war for each of their worlds' survival could begin.

FIFTEEN

☆

I'll be home soon, he had told her.

Teilani repeated those words, softly, a whisper, as she rubbed her thumbnail back and forth against the leather strap that bound her hands, crossed at the wrists.

I'll be home soon.

James had told her that. She closed her eyes, closing off the ominously stained and tattered fabric-padded walls of her four-meter-wide, spherical cell, and saw James once again. Smiling at her from the communications screen on Chal.

His trip to Earth had gone well, he had told her. Spock was coming to see him. He was going to help an old friend, and then—

Home soon.

At the time, days ago, weeks ago, she couldn't be sure with all that had happened since, Teilani had rejoiced at that message from her James. There was a lightness to him, a familiar sparkle to his smile, a new energy and purpose to his mood.

And she could see that he had made his decision.

He *would* return to Chal.

And to her.

As she slowly floated in zero gravity, legs curled, arms

folded close, in the center of her cell, Teilani once again wished that she had been at City's central comm station to receive that message, to talk with James herself. But what she saw and what he said in the recording more than made up for any disappointment she might have felt.

Because when James had left Chal, Teilani truly had not known if he would return. All she had known was that he would follow his heart, and that there was nothing she, nor anyone else, could do to influence that journey.

The stars James Kirk steered by were his own. And she treasured each moment that their paths remained the same.

Then Teilani heard the distant creaking of a pressure door and quickly opened her eyes, ending her escape into memory.

Whenever she had heard that door in the past few days, since her abductors had taken her to this place, it meant one of them would be coming soon.

But it was too early for her daily meal. Which meant something had changed. Something new was going to happen.

Teilani uncurled her legs and swung her hands up over her head, still rubbing her thumbnail furiously against the strap. Her change in configuration stopped the slow spin she had fallen into as her angular momentum was conserved.

In another few seconds, she saw that her hands would brush against the curved wall of the cell, and she would be able to cling to it by grabbing on to the ribbons of torn fabric that swayed like fronds of seaweed.

She had no idea what this cell had been intended for originally, but judging from the rips in the padded wall and the dark splotches of dried liquid that stained it, the previous occupant had not enjoyed his incarceration here any more than she did.

She heard a thrumming noise in the air—the sound of some mechanism or device she still hadn't identified—and, as they had all the times before, the six round light panels arranged equidistantly around the cell dimmed. However the sound and the dimming lights were related, their presence meant that the hatch to her cell would open in only a few more seconds.

Teilani's thumb burned from the friction of her constant rubbing. Another day, she estimated, and she would wear through the leather strap completely. One more day, and she would finally be able to fight back. But not now. Escape would have to wait.

Then there was a rush of air and the circular hatch of the cell popped open and swung away. In the sudden breeze, all the tendrils of shredded fabric in the cell waved toward the dark hatchway as if pointing the way out.

Teilani ceased her rubbing. She risked a quick assessment of the strap. The crease she had worn through the leather was noticeable, deep. Perhaps even less than a day's effort would be required to slice all the way through.

Then, one of her captors appeared in the hatch. Looking around, cautiously.

And Teilani was surprised.

It wasn't one of those who had abducted her on Chal, taking her so simply and efficiently from her bed with a single transporter beam that had given her nothing to fight against.

Those responsible had been Cardassians. They had not spoken to her at first, only stared at her in the small cell she had been beamed to in what she had guessed was a commercial freighter in orbit of Chal.

It was only after the third time she had thrown herself at the security screen that sealed the cell, and had almost succeeded in grabbing the throat of the spindly Cardassian who seemed to be the one in charge, that her abductors had finally broken their silence.

When she had awakened from the neural shock of the forcefield, the thin Cardassian had informed her that the screen was now set to lethal intensity. If she tried to push her way through it again, she would not wake up.

But other than that, her abductors had refused to answer any of her questions or respond to her threats.

A few days after that, she was again transported as she slept, reappearing inside this cell, wherever it was. Even with the presence of zero gravity, she couldn't be certain if she were actually in space—antigravs might be used specifically to mislead her, or to make any escape attempt more difficult. About all Teilani could be sure of was that she was no longer on Chal. There, her absence would have been noticed within hours, and given Chal's limited island landmass and population of under one million, local Federation authorities could have conducted a search of the entire planet within an hour.

That Cardassians were involved in kidnapping her was not surprising. The war with the Dominion still continued, and not for a second did she doubt that what had happened was in some way connected to James.

But the sight of the stranger in the hatchway caused her to reconsider every other reasonable conclusion she had drawn.

This captor was not Cardassian. She was human. A young woman with a strong square face and short blond hair. She caught sight of Teilani at the side of the cell and called out, "Stay there."

Teilani chose to do so anyway, watching carefully as the young woman pushed herself through the hatch and floated across to her. The stranger wore a dull gray jumpsuit with a stylized image of Earth on the left shoulder. It was not a uniform Teilani recognized.

Expertly, the young human landed on the curved wall beside Teilani. Teilani saw that the woman wore snug foot coverings that let her toes move freely, as if they were fingers in a glove, allowing her to grasp the fabric of the wall and hold herself in place while still leaving her hands free.

"Where am I?" Teilani asked.

There was an air of flattened resignation to the young human. Teilani recognized it. It reminded her of the people of Chal during the virogen crisis, before James had returned, and there had been no hope.

"I can't tell you," the human said. She had an equipment

176

pouch clipped to the belt of her uniform. From it, she now withdrew what seemed to be a medical tricorder, though it was twice as large as the ones Starfleet used.

"Can't, or won't?" Teilani tried again.

The young human said nothing. She seemed to be having trouble getting the tricorder to switch on.

"What's your name?" Teilani tried.

"Tasha," the human said. She hit the flat of her hand against the side of the tricorder and its status lights at last flickered on.

"What's that for?"

Tasha disconnected the remote scanner from the tricorder and held it at the appropriate distance to ensure a deep three-dimensional scan from two point sources. "To make sure you're all right."

Teilani found that unusual. Her Cardassian captors on the freighter had been prepared to have her kill herself against the security screen. *Unless,* Teilani thought, *they lied to me.*

"Is that important?" Teilani asked. "That I'm all right?"

Tasha ignored her.

Teilani sighed. "All right. Can you tell me about this . . . room?"

Tasha frowned as if the tricorder still wasn't functioning properly. "What about it?"

"What's it for?"

"Medusan feeding chamber."

"Oh."

Medusans were noncorporeal life-forms so hideous in appearance that most humanoids were driven mad just by glimpsing them. Teilani had heard stories of what Medusan ships were like, and she realized that if she was on such a craft now, no escape would be possible. One look at the ship's crew would be enough to—

She was beginning to think like James—she saw the flaw in the argument.

"Where's your visor?" she asked Tasha.

For those humanoids who had to interact with Medusans, a protective visor had been developed. If Tasha didn't have one, it could mean that there were no Medusans on board.

But Tasha didn't bother answering that question either. All she said was, "You can't escape."

"How do you know?"

For the first time since she had entered the feeding chamber, the young human looked Teilani directly in the eye. "Because I've tried."

Teilani studied Tasha's jumpsuit again. "Is that a prison uniform?"

"It might as well be." Tasha frowned at the tricorder.

"Is there something wrong with that?"

Tasha made an adjustment, turned the tricorder around and held it so Teilani could see it. "Did you know about that?"

It took only a moment for Teilani to see what Tasha meant. The look of surprise on her face must have been obvious.

"I guess you didn't," Tasha said. She slipped the remote scanner back into place, then snapped the tricorder closed. "That might make a difference when you get to the labor camp and—"

Using her joined hands as a club, Teilani swung her fists against the tricorder to drive it into Tasha's forehead. The zero-gravity reaction slammed Tasha against the wall, made Teilani bounce away from it, and launched the tricorder into a spinning straight-line trajectory across the spherical cell.

Even as Teilani spun in midair, she drew her knees up to force her feet between her wrists, then pushed with all her strength.

The leather strap keeping her hands together dug into her wrists. But she kept pushing, as if her feet were a wedge and her wrists were a single piece of stone with a crack running through it.

Finally, just as the pain threatened to become more than

even she could withstand, she heard the weakened strap rip along the line she had gouged through it, and her legs snapped out as her hands burst free.

Teilani didn't care what waited for her outside the hatch—Cardassians, Medusans, or even the Dominion's own Jem'Hadar. Escape was no longer something that was just for herself, or for James.

There was something more to fight for now.

Teilani slammed into the padded wall, clutched at it to absorb the momentum of her flight, sighted on the hatchway across the chamber, then pushed off like a swimmer plunging through frictionless water.

A meter from the hatch, Tasha rose in front of her, blood bubbling from the gash on her forehead, hands driving for Teilani's throat.

The two women spiraled around so that Teilani hit the wall to the side of the open hatch, her legs swinging through the opening while her head and shoulders remained inside, Tasha still firmly attached.

"There's no place to run!" Tasha shouted.

Teilani slapped her hands together against Tasha's ears. The blow made Tasha release her grip. Braced against the chamber wall, Teilani pushed out and Tasha spun away, sputtering.

Teilani flexed her legs against the edge of the hatchway and curled forward to pull herself through it and into the corridor beyond.

At once she was stricken by vertigo. This *was* a Medusan ship, and the topography of its twisting corridor followed an understanding of three-dimensional space that made no sense to a humanoid brain.

Keeping her eyes tightly closed, Teilani braced herself on a handhold attached to the corridor surface beside the hatch. She told herself that if she just kept her eyes shut, propelled herself by her sense of touch alone, she would be all right.

"I'll be home soon," she whispered as she opened her eyes for just an instant, chose a direction, and pushed herself along, holding her hands out in front of her, "I'll be home soon."

Somewhere on a ship like this, she knew, there would have to be a shuttlebay. Or an escape pod. Or even an emergency transmitter. All she would have to do is find one or the other, and somehow James would come for her. Come for them both.

Suddenly her hands hit bare metal. She had reached a turn in the corridor.

She steadied herself, turned her head, and prepared to gaze again on the unsettling alien architecture of the Medusan ship.

But just as she opened her eyes, a voice called out to her.

Not Tasha's. But a Cardassian's.

"Chal!"

Startled, Teilani turned her head reflexively to look up—down—across—through the corridor she had just traversed, feeling her head spin and her stomach rebel as she fought the disorientation to make sense of directions that seemed to advance and recede at the same time, like an optical illusion.

But in the midst of the visual confusion, two figures were clear.

A Cardassian.

And Tasha.

The Cardassian, wearing thick goggles that presumably enabled him to function within the Medusan ship's geometry, held a disruptor to Tasha.

"This is why there's no escape," the Cardassian said.

Then he pushed Tasha into the corridor ahead of him. For a moment, Teilani saw the young woman's eyes, saw the despair in them.

And then the corridor flickered and buzzed with the disruptor's discharge and Tasha was consumed by fire and became . . . nothing.

"There are fifteen more Thetas on this vessel," the Cardassian hissed. "All human or Vulcan. Each minute you remain out of your holding cell, we will kill another of them."

If Teilani had thought there was the slightest chance she could overpower the Cardassian, or reach a shuttle, she would have risked everything to do so—everything except the lives of innocent people.

Steeling herself, she pushed herself back along the corridor to the hatch. She passed through a cloud of scorched air—the scent of Tasha's death.

At the hatchway, she paused.

The Cardassian had backed down the corridor, remaining out of reach.

"Why kill them and not me?" she demanded.

"The Thetas belong to me," the Cardassian said. *"You* belong to the Regent."

Teilani was ready to launch herself at him. "No one owns me!"

The Cardassian leveled his disruptor at her, and though she knew it would be set only to stun, she suddenly feared risking even that level of neural shock. Not after what Tasha had shown her on the tricorder.

Without another word, Teilani swung through the hatch and returned to the spherical chamber.

"How disappointing of you," the Cardassian sneered as he began to swing the hatch closed. "The Regent prefers his playthings to show more spirit."

"Tell the Regent he's a dead man," Teilani said.

The Cardassian leered. "Much better."

Then he shut the hatch and, with a rush of air, it sealed itself.

Teilani floated in the chamber, without even a leather strap to focus her concentration on.

"I'll be home soon," she whispered to herself.

Against all reason, she wondered if James might hear her.

SIXTEEN

Kirk and Janeway made their way through the thick trunks of the pine trees, guided by the heady scent of the nearby campfire, protected from bumping into serious harm by the light of a full moon Kirk estimated to be about twenty percent brighter than it really should be. The holodeck was still taking care of them, managing to add a slightly annoying layer of twenty-fourth-century moderation even to the wild grandeur of Yosemite.

Then they stepped into a clearing, pine needles and small twigs crackling under their boots, to join the others as they had planned: Spock, McCoy, and Scott all sitting uncomfortably on fallen logs; T'Val standing by the hoverchair which placed the mirror Spock as close as possible to the rock-ringed fire.

Scott immediately got to his feet. "Where have ye been, Captain? I'm on duty in twenty minutes."

McCoy tossed a small piece of kindling into the banked fire. "Do you have to ask?" he muttered to the engineer.

Kirk was insulted. "Bones, it's not like that at all."

McCoy shrugged. "Just promise you won't make us sing again."

"I like singing around a campfire," Kirk said. "It's part of the whole experience of—"

But T'Val, as angry as a Vulcan could appear to be in public, stepped forward to confront him. "As impressive as this holographic technology is, recreation is inappropriate at this time."

Janeway intervened, to calm her fellow rebel. "It's all right, T'Val. Kirk and I were . . . establishing some ground rules."

McCoy snorted. "Oh, is that what they're calling it these days."

Kirk frowned at McCoy. "Bones, behave yourself."

"Have you been behaving yourself?"

"Yes," Kirk said with measured indignation.

"Well, that's a first."

Kirk let McCoy's comment pass. In most cases, he had learned it did no good to struggle to correct false impressions of his personal life, even when they were held by his closest friends. Such protestations only served to draw the attention of others and help give new impetus to the same false impressions he would prefer go unnoticed. Instead, he simply concentrated on the fire and its welcome warmth. He began to remember the fires he had shared with Teilani in their clearing on Chal. Making love beneath the stars. Waking to the sound of—

"Dr. McCoy has informed me that I am dying of Bendii syndrome," the mirror Spock suddenly announced.

The intendant's revelation had the no doubt intended effect of focusing everyone's attention on the immediacy of the moment.

But Kirk didn't understand the diagnosis. He had learned a great deal about Bendii during the virogen crisis. "Intendant Spock, from what I know of Bendii, you're far too young to exhibit signs of the disease, let alone to be dying of it."

"That's in our universe, Jim." McCoy held out his hand as if it were his regal right to be helped to his feet. Scott did the honors. "A healthy Vulcan today would have to be over two

183

hundred years old before the disease would manifest. But the intendant, he's had a different life from most Vulcans we know. Incredible stress. War wounds. Poor nutrition. All of those can speed up the appearance of the disease. And in his case, they have."

"Are you sure?" Kirk asked, knowing how foolish that question was the instant he said it.

As McCoy rolled his eyes to the holographic heavens, Spock rose to his feet. "I remind you, Captain, that my father also contracted Bendii, so a family history of the syndrome is established."

"Is it the same in your universe?" Kirk asked the mirror Spock.

The intendant's hands played with the edge of the plaid blanket that was folded over his legs, adding to the fire's warmth. He stared into the flames as if seeing another world.

"I have learned from my counterpart that in this reality, Sarek, husband to Amanda, son of Skon, grandson of Solkar, was a respected ambassador for your Federation. In my reality, my father, whose genealogy is the same, was Arbiter of the Vulcan Mineral Syndicate, perhaps one of the most powerful business lords on my world. I do not know if he would have developed Bendii, because he died at the age of one hundred and two." The mirror Spock's face betrayed a fleeting moment of sorrow as the flames sought out the deep shadows of his features. Loss of emotional control was one of Bendii's symptoms. "He was assassinated by Orion spies disguised as Andorians, during the military action to annex Coridan."

Kirk understood the loss the mirror Spock felt. In this universe, he felt Sarek had been as much a father to him as to Spock. "Here, Sarek brought Coridan into the Federation by the use of exquisite diplomacy."

"In my universe, Coridan is a lifeless world." The mirror Spock looked across the fire to Kirk, and it was as if he stared out from the fires of hell. "Punishment for those citizens of

Coridan who conspired with the Orions. An unasked-for gesture of good faith from my Captain Kirk, to show how he valued my alliance with him. It was many years before I could control his precipitous inclination to act on instinct, rather than careful thought."

"He destroyed a world . . ." Kirk said.

"It was not the first," the mirror Spock said. "Nor the last."

"What I don't understand, Intendant Spock," Scott interrupted, "is how so many things could be the same in the two universes—your father, your grandfather, even Amanda, a fine lass. And yet, everything is still so . . . so different. If ye see what I'm saying."

Spock had obviously given the question much thought and answered for his counterpart. "There is ample evidence, Mr. Scott, to suggest that there are an infinite number of universes existing in parallel with one another. Presumably, all these universes share a common moment of origin as a single reality. But then, for each event which follows, for which there might be multiple outcomes, those universes branch off from one another. Each possible outcome thus produces its own divergent reality. Those universes which diverged billions of years ago might no longer resemble each other in any way. While those that diverged only minutes ago, might be so similar that the only difference we might notice is that Dr. McCoy chose to remain seated rather than stand as he just did."

"But, Spock," Kirk said, "if there are an infinite number of universes constantly branching off from one another, what is it that links us with the mirror universe so that people in both can keep slipping back and forth between just these two, and no others?"

"Clearly," the mirror Spock said, suddenly emerging from his own contemplation of the campfire flames, "our two universes are linked in a manner different from most other quantum realities."

"Indeed," Spock added as he walked over to stand by his

mirror double. "My counterpart and I have discussed in great depth the history of both our realities, and until relatively modern times, those histories are virtually identical."

"Virtually," Kirk said, "but not absolutely?" He was trying to hold his own in this discussion, but keeping up with *two* Spocks was taking its toll on him. He looked at McCoy and Scott, who both just shrugged.

"What differences exist," the mirror Spock explained, "seem to arise from the different interpretation that has been placed on historical events and personalities by contemporary researchers. In my reality, Vulcans admire the early Romulans for the way in which they courageously resisted the overwhelming might of those who followed Surak's teachings of logic, until they heroically set off to carve their own destiny on other worlds."

"While in our universe," Spock continued smoothly, "contemporary Vulcans tend to look back on the early Romulans as lost and misguided people, tragically blinded by emotion, who chose to run from Surak's truth."

"Thus, any apparent historical differences between our universes may only appear—" the mirror Spock began.

"—as differences of interpretation, and not differences of fact," Spock concluded.

"My Lord," McCoy grumbled, finally voicing Kirk's own unexpressed thought, "and I thought it was bad when there was just one of you."

But now Kirk ignored him. It was just possible that two Spocks were what it took to make sense of the intersection of two universes.

"But all that's in the past," Kirk said, walking around the fire to join the Vulcans. "What about *now*, the present?"

"Today, our two universes are quite different," the mirror Spock said, "primarily because of the radically different actions undertaken by your Federation and our Empire and Alliance."

"However, since these differences were not as profound at

the time of the first crossover," Spock added, "that suggests that by continuing to trace the divergent world lines back through time, we might reach a point somewhere in the recent past, perhaps no more than two or three centuries, when both universes were, in fact, absolutely identical."

The mirror Spock nodded thoughtfully. "A point when one singular, pivotal event took place that had at least two probable outcomes. One of which led to the development of a benign and democratic Federation. The other to a militaristic and repressive Empire."

"And something about that event involved . . ." Kirk searched for the word or concept he needed. ". . . a disturbance . . . in the nature of quantum reality, which led to the two universes diverging, yet somehow remaining linked."

The two Spocks looked at each other.

"Quite logical. He is most unlike my Captain Kirk," the mirror Spock said.

"I can understand why you would think so," Spock replied.

Kirk had the feeling he had just been insulted, but this was not the time to explore the possibility. "As fascinating as I'm sure this philosophical debate could become, we do have more pressing matters to consider."

"Thank you," T'Val said sarcastically.

Janeway held up her hand to ask her friend to refrain from interrupting. "Captain Kirk has suggested we work together."

"To what end?" Spock asked.

Janeway picked up a twig to stoke the fire. Revitalized, the flames threw her moving shadow up against the tall, surrounding pine trees, as if a dark giant were trapped among them, struggling to break free.

"We want to go home," she said. "Back to our universe with the technical files we need to fight the Alliance. Kirk wants to rescue Teilani. If we help him, he'll help us."

Kirk watched Spock carefully. This was where his plan could break down before it had even begun. Spock met his eyes. It was clear to Kirk that the Vulcan ambassador disapproved, but he said nothing. Whatever misgivings Spock might have, his old friend was giving him the benefit of the doubt. For now.

But T'Val had no reservations about voicing her disapproval. "He betrayed us once. How can you know he will not do so again?"

"I didn't betray you," Kirk said heatedly. "Starfleet beamed you from that hotel suite, took action without telling me. This time, *we'll* take action without telling *them.*"

"Now, wait here just a minute," McCoy said. "I am not prepared to act against Starfleet. Well, not without a good reason."

"Bones, I'm not suggesting we act against Starfleet. Command wants to recover the *Enterprise.* Kate, and T'Val, and the intendant can help us do just that."

McCoy folded his arms. "Then let Command make that decision to help them."

"Command thinks they might be involved in the *Enterprise*'s disappearance. But they're not."

McCoy was unconvinced. "Who died and made you a Betazoid?"

"A what?" Kirk asked.

Scott exhaled in noisy frustration at the two of them. "Captain Kirk, perhaps it would help if you tell us how you *can* prove they're not involved with the hijacking."

"I can't do that, Scotty," Kirk said. "But Spock can."

Kirk looked to his friend.

"You are suggesting a mind-meld again," Spock said, apparently still not in favor of the idea.

"We have discussed it, Captain," the mirror Spock added. "But we have concluded our initial concerns are well-founded. Our minds are so similar, even to a molecular level, that there is the danger we would become locked in a recursive neural iteration. Irreparably confused memories, or even the loss of our separate identities, might result when the meld is broken."

Kirk shrugged. "T'Val, then. Vulcan mind to Vulcan mind. No secrets."

But Spock shook his head. "I do not know T'Val, nor am I aware of the training she has undertaken in mental discipline. It could be possible that she is far more adept than I, in which case I would emerge from the meld saying that they are innocent of any attempt on the *Enterprise*. Which would be exactly what I would say if they were innocent. Since you would not be able to ascertain if I were under her control or not, you would still have no proof of what you have concluded."

"Then do it to me," Janeway volunteered. "I'm only human. No Vulcan mind tricks."

"You are not the leader," Spock said.

"Are you sure? Rebel cells are compartmentalized to protect against Alliance infiltration. I could be the leader of the entire Vulcan resistance movement, but I'd still move around like a foot soldier to protect my identity and disguise my importance." She planted her feet firmly in front of Spock and tilted her head up to him. "There's only one way to be sure."

Kirk could see Spock considering all his options, finally using logic to arrive at the same conclusion Janeway had presented to him by instinct.

"Very well," Spock said. "Are you ready?"

"Try me."

Spock raised his hands to Janeway's face, the tips of his long fingers searching out then finding her *katra* points. "My mind to your mind," he intoned. "Our thoughts are one. . . ."

Kirk motioned to the others to move away, to leave Spock and Janeway undisturbed. T'Val helped guide the mirror Spock's quietly humming hoverchair to join Kirk and the others well to the side of the clearing, where the light from the campfire was little more than a pale wash of soft amber.

As Kirk looked back to where Spock and Janeway were locked in a communion more intimate than anything physical could be, Scott stepped up to him, speaking in a loud, stage whisper. "Captain, I'll not be the one to interfere with whatever plans you're making, but you seem to be missing the point of what really has Starfleet concerned about all these mirror-universe goings-on."

Kirk turned to the engineer and spoke normally. "There's no time like the present, Mr. Scott."

"Well, the first time the four of us crossed over, it was a transporter accident."

"I remember it well."

"And now, with all those incursions on *Deep Space Nine,* they're coming through on specially rigged transporters."

"That's right. That's how I shifted to the mirror universe and back again on the moon. What's your point?"

"Don't ye see? It's all transporters, sir. And ye cannae transport a starship."

Kirk resisted the impulse to smile, because he was worried that Scott might misinterpret his reaction. But though Kirk understood the seriousness of the engineer's concern, what struck him first was how his friends had each reacted to the current situation in their own unique manner. Spock had immediately been drawn to the larger, almost metaphysical mystery of the mirror universe's origin. McCoy had focused on the health of the visitors from that reality. And Scott, by his nature, was drawn to the physical mechanics of moving from one universe to another.

Somehow, Kirk knew, if he could find a way to harness all those different approaches and viewpoints, to unite them into a single, concentrated strategy, everyone's questions would be answered, and he would hold Teilani in his arms once again.

However, Scott had missed one telling detail. "There is another method, Mr. Scott. When the first two people from *Deep Space Nine* crossed over—"

But, by the way Scott jumped right in, Kirk realized that the engineer hadn't missed anything at all. "Aye, they brought a whole runabout with them. But that was because of something they did within the Bajoran wormhole—the only stable one known to exist, as I'm sure ye know. In fact, to tell ye the truth, Captain, I have my doubts as to whether or not it really is a wormhole, what with aliens living within it and all those . . . mystical doings surrounding it." Like any true engineer, Scott said the word "mystical" as if it left a sour taste in his mouth. "So the fact of the matter is, since that mirror *Voyager* didn't pop out of the Bajoran wormhole, there's a chance that it's not from the mirror universe at all. That this is all . . . some kind of hoax."

Kirk thought that the question Scott was raising had already been answered. "But what about the warp particles Starfleet detected? Their quantum signatures prove they're from another quantum reality."

"Aye, but strictly speaking, all that tells us is that the *warp particles* come from the mirror universe, not the *Voyager* herself." Scott dropped his voice even lower. "One of this lot could easily have brought through a couple of kilos of antimatter from their universe and used it to create a false trail of warp particles. 'Twould be a simple matter."

"Have you raised this possibility with the admiral?" Kirk asked.

Scott frowned. "Aye. But she's convinced that once we reach the Goldin Discontinuity, we should be looking for some kind of wormhole phenomenon to explain how the ships might pass between the universes."

"And I take it you disagree with her assessment."

Scott looked as if anyone with a mind larger than three neurons would have to disagree with the admiral. "Captain, we're smack dab in the middle of Federation space, so any kind of wormhole phenomenon that could possibly exist here would have been noted years and years ago."

"What about a stable wormhole? Couldn't the people from the mirror universe have built something like that here?"

Scott's eyes widened as if Kirk should feel embarrassed for asking such a ludicrous question. "Captain Kirk, if these people know how to build stable wormholes, then they dinnae need the *Enterprise* nor any other paltry technology we might have. If Starfleet had such a thing, believe me when I tell ye that we could end the war with the Dominion in a week with . . . with just the original *Enterprise*. That's the tactical advantage a wormhole will give ye."

"So what you're saying is that there is no possible way for the *Voyager* to have come to this universe from the other, and no way the *Enterprise* can be taken back."

"No way that I know of or can imagine."

"And the admiral's not listening to you."

"She's being a . . . typical officer."

Since Kirk had no doubt that Scott included him among the company of typical officers, he let the matter rest there. "Have you explained any of this to Spock's counterpart?"

Scott looked alarmed. "If it's a hoax, he might be in on it."

"In which case, Mr. Scott, you won't be telling him anything he doesn't already know."

Kirk ushered Scott across the floor of pine needles to the mirror Spock in his hoverchair. "Intendant, T'Val, I'd like you to listen to Captain Scott's . . . thoughts concerning the mirror *Voyager*. Scotty?"

With clear misgivings, Scott told the mirror Spock, T'Val, and McCoy why he thought the mirror *Voyager*'s presence and the *Enterprise*'s absence might be part of a hoax.

When he had finished, the mirror Spock was the first to speak. "We have faced the same technological difficulty on our side, Captain Scott. That is why we seek computer data which we can take with us to our universe. Taking anything larger than could be dematerialized by a personnel transporter is . . . beyond our ability."

"Is it beyond the Alliance's ability?" Kirk asked.

"I do not have that information. I believe Captain Scott is correct when he states that if the Alliance could construct a stable, artificial wormhole, they would have no need of your technology. However, I find it interesting that no one has commented on what is clearly an anomalous situation in your own universe."

"And that would be . . . ?" Kirk prompted.

"The chain of command in your Starfleet is extremely informal. The sharing of ideas and strategies between the ranks seems . . . almost mandatory."

"Welcome to the twenty-fourth century," Kirk said.

"Therefore," the mirror Spock continued, "I am at a loss to understand why it is that Admiral Nechayev will not at least admit the possibility that Captain Scott has raised legitimate concerns."

"I'm not," Scott said. "She's a strong-willed lass—officer—used to getting her own way. And she's a fleet admiral, so she must be doing something right."

But Kirk wasn't so quick to dismiss the mirror Spock's assessment. He was too like Spock for Kirk to take anything he said lightly.

But before he could ask the intendant for more details of his insight, Kirk heard footsteps behind him.

He turned to see Spock and Janeway approaching.

Janeway moved slowly, as if recovering from some overwhelming physical exertion. And Kirk knew Spock well enough to detect the same, almost stunned hesitancy hidden beneath his placid exterior.

Spock wasted no time. "Your conclusions were correct, Captain. Kathryn Janeway is not connected to the arrival of the mirror *Voyager* nor to the disappearance of the *Enterprise*. There is no room for deception within her."

Janeway caught Kirk looking at her, then glanced down as if she had been caught in an embarrassing position. Kirk wondered what secrets she had revealed in response to Spock's probing.

McCoy had no fear of being blunt. "What about the other two, Spock? Any chance they've been lying to her?"

"I detected no pattern of falsehood. Janeway has melded with my counterpart in the past." Then Spock looked over to T'Val, as if seeing her for the first time.

Kirk watched T'Val draw herself up in defiance, as if for a moment she had abandoned a lifetime of Vulcan training and conditioning.

"And," Spock continued, "through that link, I am also aware that my counterpart has melded with T'Val . . . his daughter with the counterpart of Saavik."

Now everyone looked at T'Val, and suddenly Kirk understood the hundred small gestures of caring and protection T'Val had offered the mirror Spock. Not just as someone respecting her superior officer, but as a daughter caring for her sick father.

And Kirk also understood the unsettled emotions he had sensed in his friend.

The path not taken.

Genetically, T'Val could be Spock's daughter as well. Certainly, Spock and Saavik in this universe had been close enough that a second T'Val had not been an unlikelihood. And through Spock's meld with Janeway, Kirk was certain his friend knew very well what his mirror daughter had become in that other reality.

And more, he would know, or be cursed with wondering, what she might have become in this reality.

Kirk went to Spock, and had no need to ask how he was. The bond between them was strong enough for Spock to understand his concern. And for Kirk to know that Spock was touched by it.

They would talk about this moment, Kirk knew. But only when the mission had been completed.

All that passed between them in a look, a moment of connection.

But, Kirk saw, there was something else there that troubled his friend.

Something unconnected to whatever sorrows he held within his heart as he contemplated a child he never had.

"What else, Spock?" Kirk asked.

Spock looked at Janeway as if asking permission to proceed. Kirk saw the slight nod she gave him.

"Kathryn was once held in an Alliance prison camp." Something dark moved behind Spock's eyes at that, and Kirk did not want to think what degradations Janeway might have endured, degradations that were now part of Spock's memories as well. "A special camp for . . . those humans who had counterparts in this universe."

Kirk looked questioningly at Janeway.

"I didn't know who the Janeway of this universe was," she explained. "All I knew was that . . . somewhere, there was another me."

Kirk turned his attention back to Spock. "What was the purpose of the camp?"

"Kathryn was never told, but from the conditions she remembers, it appears obvious. Infiltration."

"Good Lord," McCoy said. "Duplicates so exact they'd pass voice analysis, brain scans, even DNA testing."

"Precisely," Spock agreed.

"About a year and a half ago, they came for me," Janeway said. "They told me I wasn't needed anymore."

"The timing corresponds to the final conclusion of the board of inquiry investigation into *Voyager*'s disappearance in our universe," Spock said. "At that time, the ship was officially declared lost with all hands. With her counterpart, Captain Janeway, presumed dead, the mirror Janeway was slated to be reassigned to a labor camp."

"I got away during the transfer," Janeway said. "I had to . . ." But she stopped there, as if the memory of how she had managed to escape her guards was too disturbing to recount.

But to Kirk, there was even more to Spock's revelations than explaining Janeway's past. "Spock, if the Alliance knew exactly when Starfleet ruled on *Voyager*'s loss, if they knew who among their Terran slaves had counterparts here . . ."

Spock nodded. "It does suggest that they maintain close watch on developments in our universe, most likely through a sophisticated network of counterparts who have taken the places of their duplicates."

Scott muttered in shocked disbelief. McCoy nervously rubbed his thumb over his folded fingers.

And Kirk saw the unexpected solution to what had been a frustrating mystery.

"I have a theory," Kirk said.

Spock knew him too well. "And I concur."

Kirk turned to the mystified faces of McCoy and Scott, and the three rebels from the mirror universe.

"The *Sovereign* may already be under enemy control," he said.

And if it was true, then Kirk knew his war might already have been lost before it had even begun.

SEVENTEEN

☆

Kirk watched as McCoy moved efficiently around the *Sovereign*'s spacious sickbay. But the veteran physician's ease in these surroundings came as no surprise. Kirk knew McCoy had made his career that of being a perpetual thorn in the sides of Starfleet's medical planners. He doubted there was a single component of current starship health-care facilities that had not been influenced in some way by McCoy's vast experience and unwavering dedication to his patients.

Unlike many others in Starfleet, McCoy had never been driven by the desire for bigger postings, or notoriety, or even fame. In fact, he was one of the few survivors of Starfleet's heroic age of exploration never to have written his memoirs. All McCoy cared about was the chance to serve to the best of his abilities. Beyond that, he was content to live his life simply, devoting himself to those people he loved.

Kirk admired him for that, more than he had ever said.

And it was with that same admiration that Kirk now watched as McCoy brought all his skill and experience to bear on the terrible disease that ravaged Spock's counterpart.

"I thought there was no cure for Bendii," Admiral Nechayev said.

Kirk had invited her here to speak with Intendant Spock before McCoy began his treatment. Kirk had told Nechayev there was a chance the intendant would be unconscious for days, but that he was willing to answer any questions she might have about the mirror universe, to put her at her ease.

For now, the intendant lay on the main diagnostic and treatment bed, his eyes closed in meditation. A small, neuro-cortical monitor was affixed to his forehead, silently pulsing with a constellation of colored lights. McCoy, wearing a long, rumpled lab coat over his vest, worked at a medical replicator station, preparing the first stage of his assault.

"True," Kirk said, "but it's been centuries since the last case of it in a Vulcan so young. Dr. McCoy is convinced that means he can induce a remission by treating some of the intendant's other infirmities."

Nechayev seemed unconcerned. "So what am I here for? A deathbed confession in case it doesn't work?"

Kirk held his temper with difficulty. He reminded himself there were other things at stake here. Most important, Tei-lani's life. The admiral had yet to share with Kirk any of Starfleet's progress in responding to her abductors' demands. All she had permitted herself to say was that Starfleet had communicated over a long-range subspace channel, specified by the abductors, that Kirk was in no position to aid the intendant because he was being held in custody by Starfleet Intelligence. According to Nechayev, no reply had been forthcoming. Teilani's fate was unknown. And it took all of Kirk's self-control not to explode in rage at the admiral's frustrating obstinacy. But Kirk knew Nechayev would be within her rights to return him to Earth, an action that would add immeasurably to the obstacles he already faced in saving the woman he loved.

"I don't believe he has anything to confess to," Kirk said, hiding his anguish as expertly as any Vulcan. "I spoke to him about Starfleet's desire to know more about the history of the mirror universe, and he volunteered to speak with you. I think he hopes that if Starfleet learns the truth about conditions in his universe, they will offer aid."

"He can hope all he wants."

"I wouldn't discourage him at the outset. You know how Vulcans are when they decide to . . . keep a secret."

Nechayev nodded distractedly, as if she had fifty other things she'd rather be doing. She looked over at McCoy. "Is it all right with him?"

"Dr. McCoy says a few minutes' delay won't affect the treatment."

Nechayev rolled her neck as if it were stiff, or as if she were bored. "We'll be arriving at the search coordinates within the hour, so let's get this over with." She strode over to the mirror Spock's bedside. "Are you awake?"

The intendant's eyes fluttered open. "Greetings, Admiral."

"Kirk says you have something to tell me."

"The captain informed me that you had many questions about my reality. I offered to answer them to the best of my ability."

"Why?"

The mirror Spock shifted in his bed to look at the admiral more directly. "Your Starfleet has, in effect, abducted me, and my companions. You are preventing us from completing our mission here."

"You mean, stealing Starfleet secrets."

"Nothing so drastic. We only wish to copy computer files to obtain information that will have no effect on your universe. Nothing would be taken from you. Nothing here would change."

"But your universe would change."

"That is my intention."

Nechayev seemed to be losing patience. "Did you ever have a Prime Directive in your Starfleet?"

"Of course. Starfleet General Order Number One. Authorizing all personnel and spacecraft to use whatever means necessary to persuade the inhabitants of a planet, no matter what their level of development, to join the Empire." Before Nechayev could respond, the mirror Spock added, "I understand it is somewhat different in this universe."

Kirk could detect the deliberate, though extremely understated wryness of what the mirror Spock had said.

Evidently, so could the admiral. She wasn't impressed. "Never mind. Let's start at the beginning. What is the composition of the Terran resistance?"

The mirror Spock raised both eyebrows and shook his head, and if not for the beard, Kirk could believe he was looking at his own Spock. "I do not know."

"I thought you were its leader."

"Not of the *Terran* resistance. I serve as . . . a figurehead for the Vulcan resistance. The two groups, for our own protection, do not meet, except circumspectly, cell to cell."

"Yet you know about the Terran resistance members who built a duplicate of the *Defiant* in your universe."

The mirror Spock nodded as if he were enjoying a fascinating conversation about any other subject. "Certainly. Their success has revitalized all the resistance groups actively engaged against the Alliance. It is what inspired us to come to this universe ourselves to obtain similar information."

Nechayev waved her hand as if discounting everything the intendant had said. "Yet you still claim you're not in contact with them."

"I, personally? No. Neither have I knowledge of anyone in my cell having direct contact with them. Which *is* as it should be, as I am sure you will agree."

Nechayev chewed her lip in thought. She glanced at Kirk but he shrugged, said nothing.

"All right," she finally continued. "Tell me about the Vulcan resistance."

"It formed at the time of the Vulcan Capitulation, when it became clear the Alliance would not live up to its promise of—"

But Nechayev wouldn't let him finish. "I'm not interested

in ancient history." She looked sharply at Kirk again, as if suddenly remembering his presence. "Starfleet wants to know about *current* conditions first. We can work backward from there."

The mirror Spock settled back on the small pillow on his bed and gazed up at the medical sensor array suspended above him. "Very well. Today, the Vulcan resistance comprises sixty-four cells of which I am aware, each with eight operatives."

As if she had just thought of the question, Nechayev asked, "How do you communicate?"

"Each member of a single cell has knowledge of only one other cell. Messages are passed blindly in that manner."

"No, no. That's not what I meant. I presume you engage in acts of . . . sabotage? Terrorism?"

The mirror Spock kept his eyes carefully focused on the sensor array. "We prefer to think of our activities as military actions intended to regain our independence."

"Your kind always do," Nechayev said. "Look, I'm trying to get an understanding of your level of technology."

The mirror Spock shifted his gaze to look at her. "Why?"

The admiral didn't look away. "To understand what might happen to the status quo in your universe if certain . . . components of Starfleet technology were . . . to be released to you."

"You would do that?"

Nechayev started to reach out to place her hand on the mirror Spock's shoulder, then reconsidered and simply laid her hand, palm flat, on the side of his bed. "It's not up to me. But there is a small group within Starfleet who believe—" She glanced at Kirk. "—as does the captain, that the natural development of your civilization has been so hopelessly compromised by contact with us that further intervention is not prohibited under the Prime Directive."

She lifted her hand, raising a cautionary finger. "I am not one of those people. But it is my duty as a Starfleet officer to

201

provide a complete, unbiased report to the committee members who will eventually rule on this matter. What you say to me will be relayed to them. So whatever happens is up to you."

Kirk was surprised by the admiral's sudden candor. He was even more surprised as the mirror Spock began to detail the organization and technological capabilities of the Vulcan resistance. Spock's counterpart named the top seven leaders whom he had met personally. He explained how their training camp on Mars was disguised by a cloaking device salvaged from a damaged Romulan vessel. And he detailed the encryption techniques Vulcan operatives used as they communicated over randomly shifting subspace radio frequencies, so that anyone inadvertently hearing a few seconds of conversation would assume that only static had been picked up.

By the time the mirror Spock was finishing his dissertation, McCoy had returned to his patient's bedside with a tray of hyposprays. He carried a flashing medical tricorder and kept using it to check readings on the intendant, first from one side, then from the other. Unlike Kirk, the doctor could allow his impatience to show.

When he had finished speaking, the mirror Spock licked his dry lips. He seemed older than McCoy. "Is that helpful, Admiral?"

Nechayev's remote mood had lessened, Kirk saw, as if by lowering his defenses the mirror Spock had made it possible for her to lower her own. "It's what the committee will need to know. And I know they will be impressed by the thoroughness of your report."

"You will remember it in enough detail?" the mirror Spock asked.

Nechayev looked up. "Computer, replay the intendant's previous statement, beginning with his description of the Mars training camp."

With no appreciable delay, the intendant's voice spoke from the communications speakers in sickbay.

"End playback," the admiral said. "The committee members will hear everything you told me, word for word."

McCoy snapped shut his tricorder. "Why don't we end it there?"

Nechayev didn't seem to have any objection. "If Starfleet has further questions . . . ?"

"The intendant might be able to answer them tomorrow," McCoy said. "And definitely will be able to answer them within three days."

Nechayev patted the side of the mirror Spock's bed. "Then I wish you good luck with your treatment."

"It is not logical, but thank you."

The admiral motioned to Kirk to accompany her to the doors. He fell into step beside her.

"I don't know if *you* think anything was accomplished," Nechayev said, "but *I* think that was a very valuable session. So . . . thank you, Captain." The doors slid open before her and she paused at the threshold. "I wasn't sure if we'd be able to have a working relationship."

Kirk didn't know what was behind her abrupt change of attitude, but he played along. "Just trying to do my part."

"Good. Carry on."

The admiral left.

As soon as the sickbay doors slipped shut, the mirror Spock pushed himself up to sit on the side of the bed and peeled the neurocortical monitor from his forehead. McCoy was about to speak, but Kirk held up his hand in warning.

"Computer," Kirk said, "disengage record mode."

"Record mode disengaged," the computer confirmed.

"Now, Doctor," Kirk said.

McCoy flipped open his tricorder with a practiced flick of his wrist. "Her quantum signature matches the intendant's. She's not the real admiral."

Kirk helped the mirror Spock to his feet. "Tell me you didn't reveal actual information about the Vulcan resistance."

The mirror Spock raised an eyebrow. "Why would the Vulcan resistance maintain a training camp on Mars?"

"My thought, exactly," Kirk said, hoping he was convincing. He hadn't thought about that, at all.

McCoy held up a hypospray with an ampule filled with dark blue liquid. "One shot of this and she'll sleep for a week. I say we get her on the bridge."

"What about the others?" Kirk asked.

McCoy didn't know what he meant.

"There're more than a thousand crew members on this ship," Kirk said. "Some of them are bound to be counterparts and we don't have time to scan them all."

"We're just supposed to leave her in command?"

"She's Starfleet's problem. Not mine."

But McCoy didn't agree. "Jim, maybe you better take another look in the holographic mirror and see whose uniform you're wearing."

Without thought, Kirk felt his hands become fists, as if a fight were only seconds away. "I'd wear a Cardassian uniform if I thought it would help me get Teilani back."

McCoy was growing more agitated with each moment. "For God's sake, Jim, the admiral's been standing in the way of everything you've tried to do to find out what's happened to Teilani. Don't you think Starfleet will take that into consideration when you've exposed her as a mirror-universe spy?"

Kirk threw up his hands, as upset as the doctor. "Eventually. After fifteen boards of inquiry, twenty-two reports, and six months' worth of investigations into what I had for breakfast. There's no time, Bones. I am *not* going through channels on this one. I'm sick of it."

McCoy gave up. He looked at the mirror Spock. "So, is this

what your Kirk was like? A stubborn, pigheaded megalomaniac with a piece of inert matter for a brain?"

The mirror Spock seemed unperturbed by the argument that raged before him. "My Kirk would have assassinated the admiral the instant she was revealed as a spy. And then he would have killed you, slowly and painfully, for insulting him."

McCoy rolled his eyes. "So, what's the captain's pleasure? Assuming you're not going to assassinate her."

Kirk had already given that careful thought. "The *Sovereign*'s carrying runabouts. They're for Starbase 250, but they're fully operational."

"Piracy, hijacking . . . sounds like you're off to a fine start," McCoy said. "These are special runabouts, I take it. Ones that can outrun the *Sovereign?*"

"All we have to do is make it to the Goldin Discontinuity. Even the *Sovereign* can't find us in there."

McCoy stared hard at Kirk. " 'We'?"

Kirk was surprised. "Bones, back on Earth you were all set to help me, even when Spock was following Starfleet orders not to."

"That was before I found out one of Starfleet's most important fleet admirals was a spy, and in command of one of its most powerful ships. That's a dangerous situation and I have to do something about it, even if you don't."

Kirk looked to the mirror Spock. "For what it's worth, this is usually when our Spock suggests some completely different approach to the problem."

"Any ideas?" McCoy asked hopefully.

"It is not wise to leave the Nechayev from my universe in command of this ship. However, to wrest command from her will undoubtedly entail identifying all the other counterpart spies who have infiltrated the crew. And, I estimate that within four point two six hours, Nechayev will have learned from other Alliance operatives that the information I gave her concerning the Vulcan resistance was false. At which point, our lives are forfeit. Including yours, Doctor.

"Thus, logic dictates we do as Captain Kirk suggests—get off this ship in the most expedient manner possible."

"Well, you're no improvement, that's for sure," McCoy said. To Kirk, he added, "And how does stealing a runabout and disappearing into the Discontinuity help Teilani?"

"We can go to Chal, Bones. I can get that message from whoever kidnapped her. I can respond to it myself, track them down, set a trap . . . *anything* is better than being a prisoner on this ship and doing *nothing.*"

"You really think you can get away with it?"

Kirk put aside all pretense. "Honestly? I don't know. But I do know that I have to try. Now, are you going with me?"

McCoy looked at the mirror Spock again. "If he gets away with this, how long am I going to last on this ship when Nechayev figures out what happened?"

The intendant considered the question for several moments. Then, "Assuming she follows standard Alliance protocol, you would be in her custody in approximately twenty-two minutes. Your time of death then would be determined by your resistance to torture, and I do not have enough data to calculate that time period with any confidence."

McCoy sighed and started taking off his lab coat. "Have you ever heard of a press-gang?" he asked Kirk.

"We'll make it," Kirk said. "Everything's arranged."

"Now you tell me." McCoy pulled on his jacket, then opened a storage locker to take out a medkit.

"I had to know if you were staying or going. Intendant?"

"I am ready."

Kirk, McCoy, and the mirror Spock started for the sickbay doors. But McCoy balked before reaching them. "Is it such a good idea to just walk through the corridors? Shouldn't·we be crawling through the Jefferies tubes?"

"Scotty said the engineering controls would report unauthorized access to the tubes," Kirk explained.

"Scotty's in on this?"

"Everyone is," Kirk said. And the fact that he had such a strong team gave him the confidence he needed to face what he knew was going to be a risky operation. He wasn't familiar with all the capabilities of this new starship, and he suspected that attempting to evade her in a runabout would be the equivalent of taking on the old *Enterprise* with a shuttlecraft. Alone, he wouldn't think of attempting it. But with his friends, he knew he would at least have a chance.

"We're going to make it," Kirk said as he approached the doors and they began to slide open. "This is going to work."

And then he stepped into the corridor to face five phaser rifles held by an equal number of serious-faced security officers.

Admiral Nechayev stepped forward and took McCoy's medkit. "Your use of the tricorder was very clumsy, Doctor. Especially with the intendant's neurocortical monitor already in place."

Kirk said nothing, at last understanding the reason why the admiral had left sickbay in such a nonconfrontational manner.

She had misled him. Perfectly.

And he had let her.

"Don't look so surprised, Kirk," she said. "Where I come from, so many studies were written about Tiberius, analyzing him, deconstructing him, trying to understand why he became what he became . . . I almost feel as if I know you. And I certainly can predict every move you make."

She waved her hand at her security team, and Kirk knew without question that they were all counterparts, just like the admiral.

"Take the intendant and McCoy to the brig." The admiral walked closer to Kirk, and her features were transformed into a mask of unrestrained, primal hatred. "But Captain Kirk I will personally escort to the agony booth."

EIGHTEEN

☆

In that instant, total awareness came to Kirk.

The flow of air in the corridor, empty of all personnel except for his companions, the security team, and the admiral.

He could smell the slight antiseptic tang that had spilled through the doors from sickbay.

He could see the flutter of Nechayev's pulse in the hollow of her neck, the stubble on the chin of the lead rifleman, the texture of the traction carpet beneath his feet.

In that instant, he closed his eyes, and saw the clearing in Chal that would become his home.

Would become his home.

That knowledge became his dream. His mantra. His goal.

Kirk felt the heat of Chal's twin suns on his back. He inhaled slowly, finding his center, filling his senses with the memory of Chal's burgeoning vegetation, its promise of life.

And at the core of everything he experienced, at the core of everything he had become, there was Teilani.

Nothing in this universe, or the other, would ever keep him from her.

There was no chance of failure.

No possibility for error.

And as surely as he drew that single, centering, focusing breath, he knew that was a truth beyond all others.

He opened his eyes again, looked directly into the cold stare of Alynna Nechayev, a human collaborator from some other reality, and knew she could no more stand before him than she could withstand the fury of a supernova.

It was apparent that she mistook his silence for surrender.

"Fear looks good on you, Tiberius."

Kirk still didn't respond. His mind raced with all the possibilities before him.

The agony booth did not concern him.

What was pain compared to the loss of Teilani's life and love?

But this starship was the unknown factor in the equation of his escape.

It would have security forcefields at every intersection. Anesthezine gas. More than a thousand crew members who would follow their commander's orders to stop Kirk without question.

Once captured, he conceded it might be possible that escape would no longer be an option.

Thus his strategy chose itself.

He must not be captured.

Therefore, he *would* not be captured.

All this, in less than a second.

The action that followed was even more quickly determined.

He drove his open hand into Nechayev's jaw, hearing the satisfying splinter of her teeth as she was knocked back into the corridor bulkhead.

And before he had even finished following through on that sudden blow, he spun to kick away the closest phaser rifle.

It was not a kick of his youth. It did not have the height or the power of what he had once commanded.

But its aim was perfect.

He heard the crack of the rifleman's thumb breaking and

his cry of pain, even as the muzzle of his phaser rifle snapped through the air to hit the face of the next rifleman in line.

By then, in just that split second, the mirror Spock had joined Kirk's attack. Again, he was not as fast as the Spock of old, not even as fast as the Spock of today, but his hand found the shoulder of the middle rifleman and dropped him with a nerve pitch perfected over twice a human lifetime.

By then, however, the element of surprise was gone.

Kirk and the mirror Spock faced two riflemen. Even as a cadet, Kirk could never have reached them before they could fire.

Which meant, they could not be allowed to fire.

Slowly, one rifleman raised his hand to his comm badge.

Kirk beat him to it.

"Computer—security alert! Suppress weapons fire in corridor B, deck eight. Authorization: Kirk!"

The riflemen fired.

Too late.

Their weapons had been suppressed.

Kirk and the mirror Spock were on them in moments.

But these were young men, and they were ready for the assault.

The first blow from his attacker, Kirk deflected. But the second came too quickly after the first, and struck him in the solar plexus.

Kirk felt his breath explode from him, even as the shock of the impact traveled through to his back.

He stumbled to one side, in danger of losing his footing.

But in the face of victory, the young man made a mistake born of enthusiasm and inexperience. He threw a kick at Kirk's face when it wasn't needed.

Kirk only had to move his head a few centimeters to avoid the blow, then grabbed the young man's boot, simultaneously steadying himself, then rotating the captured foot until a resounding crack exploded in the corridor.

The hapless security officer screamed and Kirk released his foot.

Enraged, the young man instinctively, foolishly, inadvertently, shifted his weight to his fractured ankle as he swung his leg down.

He was on the corridor deck a second later, writhing in torment.

The mirror Spock's attacker, though, had made no mistakes. He held the intendant in a head lock and was pressing his body forward to cut off the elder Vulcan's blood flow to his brain.

At the same time, he was backing away with his captive.

Kirk picked up a useless phaser rifle, caught up with the last officer, and started to swing the rifle butt toward his head.

The officer went into a crouch, pushing the mirror Spock into the path of the rifle.

But Kirk had never intended to follow through and so stopping his swing was simple.

Instead, as he had planned, Kirk had forced the officer to loosen his chokehold and the mirror Spock exploited the moment by driving a precisely placed elbow into the man's groin.

The security officer instantly lost all strength, and the mirror Spock spun around to pinch his shoulder, ending his distress and his consciousness at the same time.

Kirk turned to check on the status of the first combatants. McCoy was already dispensing the blue liquid from his hypospray.

"Help me get them into sickbay," McCoy said.

"I didn't hit them that hard."

"You want to leave them here for someone else to find?"

Kirk and the mirror Spock began dragging their defeated attackers, and their weapons, into sickbay, placing the unconscious security officers and the admiral on treatment beds at McCoy's instructions.

Then McCoy said, "Computer: Activate the EMH."

A holographic doctor rippled into view in the center of the sickbay. Kirk was surprised to see it was not the familiar, acerbic-looking version he had encountered before, but a thinner, younger model, with a shock of blond hair.

"Please state the nature of the medical emergency."

"These people are spies," McCoy said quickly, "who intend to take over the *Sovereign* and deliver her into enemy hands."

"My goodness," the hologram said. Kirk thought it was an unusual reaction for a computer construct. Perhaps its programming was still being adjusted.

McCoy gave the doctor his instructions. "Treat them as necessary for minor injuries, but keep them unconscious until new personnel arrive from Starfleet Command. Under no circumstances are you to allow them to be revived on the instructions of anyone currently onboard this vessel. That is a direct order."

But the hologram seemed taken aback at the sight of one of his patients. "That's not a spy, that's Admiral Nechayev!"

"Check her quantum signature," McCoy said.

"I'm a doctor, not a quantum mechanic."

"She's not from this universe," McCoy insisted.

The EMH looked pained. "How can someone not be from this *universe?* By definition, that's all there is. I'm so confused."

Kirk wasn't willing to accept any more delays. "Bones, what's wrong with this thing?"

At that, the hologram actually appeared insulted. "I'll have you know I am not a *thing.* I am an Emergency Medical Hologram, Mark Two."

"You're a doctor and a Starfleet officer," McCoy growled. "Get to work and follow orders."

The hologram drew himself up in a huff. "Very well, but I don't have to be happy about it."

212

"You're a program," Kirk said. "You're not supposed to be happy about anything. C'mon, Bones, Intendant, let's move it." Kirk picked up one of the phaser rifles, checked its charge readout. Full. It could be useful in other areas of the ship where the suppression system had not been activated.

"Now, I'm feeling depressed," the hologram said.

But by then, Kirk, McCoy, and the mirror Spock were already stepping through the sickbay doors.

"And *alone*," the hologram called after them.

As they walked quickly along the corridor, the mirror Spock seemed troubled by what they had just seen.

"Was that program functioning properly?"

"None of them do," McCoy said. "But Starfleet insists on field-testing them anyway. I think they do it to make doctors feel needed."

They came to a turbolift alcove.

The mirror Spock seemed unsure about continuing. "Such a confined space. Is this wise?"

"We're on borrowed time as it is," Kirk said. He forced his thumbnail into a narrow gap at the side of the rifle he carried, then flicked open the cover of the weapon's internal control panel. As he waited for the lift to arrive, he quickly input his security code, to allow him to reset the rifle's computer ID. If another security team tried to suppress this weapon in a different location on the ship by specifying its original ID, Kirk knew he might gain a few extra seconds of phaser firepower before anyone realized he had changed the code. "The turbolift will at least be faster."

"Good idea," McCoy said as the lift doors puffed open. "After all, it's not as if we want to stop and take some time to think about what we're doing."

Kirk smiled as he waved his phaser rifle toward the empty lift car. "You go first, Bones. Just in case it's a trap."

Grumbling, McCoy entered the lift with the mirror Spock. Kirk checked up and down the corridor one last time, then followed them. "Main shuttlebay," he said.

The turbolift slipped sideways as it began its run through the upper hull section of the ship.

"Is that where we're going to meet Scott?" McCoy asked.

Kirk nodded. "And Janeway and T'Val. And Spock."

McCoy frowned. "You've been busy."

"I do my best."

Only ten meters of corridor separated the nearest turbolift alcove from the large doors leading to the main shuttlebay. Kick stepped out into that stretch first, the mirror Spock hanging back with McCoy and the phaser rifle.

There was no one in the corridor.

And that was immediately suspicious.

Kirk knew the shuttlebays were among the busiest areas of a starship. There were always engineers, shuttle pilots, cargo handlers, and maintenance specialists coming and going. The fact that none appeared to be doing so now suggested that the corridor had been purposely cleared, just as the corridor outside sickbay had been. He wasn't willing to accept that for some reason, all shuttlebay activity had been suddenly consigned to the aft bay on deck fourteen.

Kirk walked cautiously along the long curve of the bulkhead, past the large cargo doors. The corridor here was high-ceilinged, intended to accommodate oversized crates and machinery being transferred from the bay to storage areas elsewhere on the ship. Sound traveled well here, but Kirk heard nothing except the muffled rumble of the ship's environmental systems.

He jogged past the alcove in the opposite direction.

Still no sign of anyone.

At the very least, he, McCoy, and the mirror Spock would be able to reach the shuttlebay doors before anyone else could come after them.

He waved the others forward.

"Run!" he said.

Even McCoy moved quickly, aided by his implants.

They were five meters from the shuttlebay doors when Kirk thought they were going to make it.

That was when the first forcefield went up.

Kirk and the mirror Spock managed to stop in time, but McCoy slammed into it, possibly because his artificial leg muscles were slower to respond to stimuli than his natural ones.

Kirk picked his friend up, wheeling in time to see a second forcefield shimmer into view just before the lift alcove.

They were trapped in a five-meter section of corridor, only a few steps from freedom.

Without waiting to see who was responsible for this trap, Kirk took the phaser rifle from the mirror Spock and flipped it to its sixteenth and most destructive setting. He aimed it at the ceiling, just in front of the forcefield's origination point, and fired. As he had planned, the new code he had entered into the rifle allowed it to operate despite any suppression field that might currently be active here.

Instantly, smoke billowed and sparks exploded from the ceiling panels. Kirk swept the high-power beam to create a line of fire, probing for any field emitter that might not be properly shielded.

As the panels sputtered and the line of fire began to crackle, the computer announced a fire warning and containment forcefields suddenly materialized around the flames.

Kirk sliced the beam down the right-hand bulkhead, hit an ODN cable behind a panel that geysered with sparks, and kept going.

But just as he reached the floor, the phaser beam winked out.

The ship's weapon-suppression system had finally reached the part of its programming that prompted it to activate a full-suppression field, instead of searching for weapons by ID numbers.

McCoy coughed as smoke swirled around them. "At least we get to die of smoke inhalation before we can be tortured."

"Bones, were you always this negative?"

"Not when you weren't around."

The mirror Spock studied the bulkheads. "Do the force-fields extend behind the walls as well?"

"They'd be useless if they didn't," Kirk said. He hefted the rifle in his hand, getting ready to swing it as a club if given the opportunity. "Why don't they show themselves?"

A harsh voice answered from his comm badge. "Because we're trying to wake the admiral. So she can take charge of you personally." It was not a human voice.

Then McCoy pointed past the shuttlebay doors. From that direction along the corridor, three figures were approaching. "Good Lord," the doctor said.

Kirk felt a knot of anger grow in his stomach.

There were Cardassians on board the *Sovereign*.

He was certain they were not Cardassians from his universe.

That certainty was confirmed when the largest Cardassian stepped up to the forcefield and smiled coldly at the mirror Spock. His lustrous black hair was almost blue in the corridor lights, his skin the dull gray of a long-dead human corpse.

"Greetings, Intendant. I always told you we would meet again."

"I never doubted you," the mirror Spock replied. "And as I always told you, that meeting would occur on the day you would die."

The Cardassian was amused. "Brave words from a dying, senile old man."

"Say that to my face."

"Oh, I intend to. Just before I apply the agonizer myself." The Cardassian withdrew a small, cylindrical communicator, one that would bypass the *Sovereign*'s own internal comm system, Kirk knew. He pushed his thumb against it and an amber light glowed on its tip. "This is Arkat. I have found the prisoners on deck seven, outside the main shuttlebay. Scan the bay for the others."

Kirk knew the Cardassians had three options. Kill them here, either by keeping the forcefields in place until the oxygen was exhausted, or by flooding the contained area with a fatal gas. Beam them to detention. Or march them there physically.

The first option held no promise of escape, but given the apparent personal animosity between the intendant and Arkat, Kirk didn't think it was likely. And either of the two other options would result in the forcefields being dropped. Either to permit a transporter beam to lock on to them, or to allow them to be led away at phaserpoint.

Kirk readied himself for one option or the other. He would not make it easy for the Cardassians and, he was sure, neither would the mirror Spock.

Another voice, also Cardassian, replied over the communicator. "Scan complete. No life signs detected in main shuttlebay."

"Where are your accomplices?" Arkat asked.

"What accomplices?" Kirk answered.

Arkat smiled broadly. "So like Tiberius."

"You'd be surprised."

"My people were spared the enjoyment of seeing that monster destroyed before their eyes. I think you might provide a worthy substitute."

Kirk was ready for him. "As my friend said, Say that to my face."

But Arkat shook his head. "For now, you belong to the admiral. Though perhaps I could ask to have whatever's left when she's finished with you. Not that I think there'll be much to go around." He raised the communicator again. "What is the status of the admiral?"

"The EMH will not allow us into sickbay. He claims he must wait for authorization from Starfleet Command."

That did not seem to be an insurmountable problem for Arkat. "Delete his program from the computer."

"At once."

Kirk refused to feel sorry for a program, though by having so many odd quirks, it had seemed to him to be one of the more human artificial beings he had encountered.

"How long do you think you can keep the corridors cleared?" Kirk asked. The Cardassians must be remaining hidden on board this ship. Any crew member who saw one would take action first and question any order to release them.

"We're in no rush," Arkat said. "As long as Commander Kral orders all crew confined to quarters and their duty stations while the environmental system is searched for the source of a potentially dangerous tetralubisol vapor leak, we have the ship to ourselves."

"The Trill is one of you?"

Arkat shrugged elaborately, enjoying the game. "You tell me."

The Cardassian's communicator clicked back into life. "Glinn Arkat. The EMH has linked his program to the life-support subsystems keeping the admiral and five security officers in medical stasis. If I delete the program, the admiral will die."

Kirk recognized the look of sudden anger that came to Arkat's eyes. And Kirk knew that anger was the enemy of reason. He had no idea how a mere computer program could be so creative, but he decided to increase the stakes.

"Don't look so surprised, Arkat. You're dealing with superior technology. The Cardassia of your universe is a third-rate power. It doesn't even compare to the real Cardassians in this universe. And none of you compare to the Federation."

Arkat clenched his fist around his communicator as the two Cardassians with him drew their disruptors. "You *will* die, Tiberius."

"It's Kirk, you primitive, low-tech savage. James Kirk. Even your Tiberius was a failure. He couldn't stand up to you. But, in this universe, even though the Cardassian Union is a hundred years more advanced than you, the only way it could threaten the Federation was with the help of the Dominion. And now that the Dominion is cut off from this region of space, Cardassians are being defeated like the rock-throwing barbarians they are."

Arkat lunged forward. "Drop the shields!" But his soldiers stopped him, pulled him back.

"No, Glinn," one of them said, and Kirk could sense that one's reluctance to criticize his superior officer. "They are to remain within the forcefield at all time. Gul Rutal's orders."

Kirk made a note of that new information. Gul Rutal must be the Cardassian in charge.

"I don't care about orders," Glinn Arkat snarled. He shrugged off the soldiers' grip on his arm, drew his disruptor, and fired.

The ship's weapon-suppression field had obviously been adjusted to ignore Cardassian weapons. The disruptor beam hit the security screen full force, sending out ripples of dissipative energy across a vertical plane. If Kirk had not already tested the forcefield with his phaser rifle, he would have tried to dodge, just in case the field was weak.

But it was so much better to fight his instincts and stand his ground calmly, mocking the Cardassian's impotent attempt to harm him.

"Is that how backward your scientists are?" Kirk sneered. "They can't even design a simple polyphasic disruptor to penetrate a pitifully weak *security* screen?" Kirk had no idea what a polyphasic disruptor was, but it sounded good, and he looked at McCoy and laughed. Loudly.

The doctor didn't seem convinced by Kirk's tactics, but joined in halfheartedly.

Arkat's face was twisted with rage.

That's it, Kirk thought. *Now do something foolish.*

He tightened his grip on his phaser rifle, preparing for the shields to drop.

But Arkat surprised him.

"Transporter control, this is Glinn Arkat. Lock on to James

T. Kirk, one meter in front of me. He's the human with the phaser rifle."

A human voice answered. A counterpart, Kirk knew.

"Preliminary lock established. I will have to drop the shields to engage a full lock and transport."

Arkat did not take his hate-filled gaze from Kirk. "Do so on my command."

"Destination?" the transporter technician asked.

"Space," Arkat said slowly. "And keep the beam focused. I want him alive when he materializes. So he knows what's happening."

Instantly, McCoy grabbed Kirk's arm. "If you send him, you send me."

A moment later, the mirror Spock did the same. "And me."

But before Arkat could respond, Kirk pushed McCoy and the intendant away. "Keep fighting," he told them, mind racing for another option, another chance to rescue victory from the absolute certainty of defeat.

"Drop shields," Arkat said in triumph, "and *energize.*"

The second the forcefield sparkled away, Kirk lunged forward.

But before his hands could reach Arkat's throat, the Cardassian and the corridor began to break apart in shimmers of golden energy.

Kirk knew it was not the first time he had miscalculated the intentions of an enemy.

But he was sorry that this appeared to be the last time he would ever do so.

As the glow of the transporter effect washed away the protective cocoon of the *Sovereign,* Kirk braced himself for the bite of vacuum, the cold of space.

And for the final darkness of death.

NINETEEN

☆

As the transporter effect faded, Kirk was surprised by the brightness of the stars in this area of space. *Must be the Goldin Discontinuity,* he thought. If it was to be his last sight before dying, at least he had heard it was supposed to be spectacular.

And then the bite of vacuum became the impact of a duranium deck as he fell head-first against it, transported in mid-lunge.

For a moment, Kirk lay flat on his face, arms outstretched, wondering why he wasn't gasping soundlessly for air. And why he could feel gravity.

Then he rolled over and looked up at Scott and Spock.

"You've been takin' your own sweet time," Scott said.

Spock held out his hand and helped Kirk to his feet.

They were in the *Sovereign*'s shuttlebay. It was a deep and wide facility at the aft of the primary hull, but low-ceilinged and compact compared with the overall volume of the ship. Most of the maintenance work, Kirk knew, took place on the next deck down, served by elevator platforms set into the shuttlebay deck. But among the stacked cargo crates and palletized equipment on this level, Kirk saw three of Starfleet's newest sleek shuttlecraft—including one with the name *Galileo* written boldly on its side—and the two runabouts destined for Starbase 250.

Kirk dusted off his trousers. Not that the starships of the twenty-fourth century allowed dust to accumulate on any surface. "How'd you manage that little trick?"

"Why, Captain, how many times have ye told me yourself: I'm a miracle worker."

Kirk wouldn't let it go at that.

Scott gave him the answer. "All right. A transporter override. I *am* the chief engineer on this ship, after all. And I've still got a few tricks up my sleeve."

"Janeway and T'Val?" Kirk asked.

"In the runabout," Spock said. He looked down at the tricorder he held. "Dr. McCoy and my counterpart are still confined within the security fields in the corridor outside."

"When will the Cardassians know they didn't beam me off the ship?" Kirk asked.

Suddenly, the broad shuttlebay filled with flashing red lights and a blaring alarm—intruder alert.

"Right about now," Scott said. He glanced over at Spock's tricorder. "How're they doing with those forcefields?"

"They are . . . down," Spock said.

Scott hit his comm badge. "Scott to Janeway, energize!"

A few moments later, Kirk heard Janeway's reply. "We have them, Captain Scott. Standing by."

Spock started for the runabouts with Scott. Close behind them, Kirk raced for the closer of the two large craft, the one whose running lights and glowing impulse conduits were already operational.

"No, Captain," Scott called to him. "Not the *Coprates,* the *St. Lawrence.*"

Kirk changed course for the second runabout as he heard the electric hum of a security field crackle into place. Still running, he looked over his shoulder to see the shuttlebay doors leading to the corridor begin to glow with disruptor fire.

At least, if the doors failed, the forcefield would buy them extra time.

As soon as they reached the second runabout, Kirk turned to Scott. "Why'd they think there was no one in here?"

Scott shook his head in disbelief. "Captain, how many times do I have to tell ye? I'm the chief engineer. Give me some credit for knowing how this ship works."

Kirk leaped up the small set of fold-out steps that led into the *St. Lawrence.* A quick glance around showed Janeway and T'Val already in the starboard passenger seats, both wearing Starfleet uniforms. The newly rescued McCoy and the intendant were strapping themselves into the passenger seats that ran along the port side bulkhead. Kirk realized that McCoy and the intendant must have been beamed to safety by the runabout's own emergency-escape transporter.

Behind him, Scott punched the door control and the steps folded up as the pressure door sealed.

Kirk slipped into the pilot's seat and heard Spock take his position in the jumpseat behind him. A moment later, Scott was in the copilot's chair.

Kirk ran his eyes over the runabout's flight controls, comparing all settings to the ones he had memorized during his recent practice runs on the holodeck. "How long is the security field over the corridor doors going to hold?"

Scott gave him a sidelong glance. "How long will it take you to get this crate into space?"

"Is the second runabout programmed?"

Scott looked exasperated. "Captain, I don't know what retirement's done to ye, but ye have to stop asking me the obvious."

"My apologies, Mr. Scott. Please . . . proceed."

"Aye, don't mind if I do."

Scott's fingers played over the control surfaces as if he had never trained on any other system. Kirk felt a slight vibration as the *Coprates,* a runabout named for one of the first of the new Martian rivers to flow across a terraformed landscape, lifted on her antigrav propulsors and rotated into position for takeoff.

Kirk activated the *St. Lawrence*'s launching preparation system and his runabout lifted and rotated, as well.

Then Kirk heard an insistent chime. "Warning," the computer voice announced. "The shuttlebay door is closing. All craft must return to their landing areas."

"Don't bet on it, darlin'," Scott muttered.

Kirk looked through the forward viewports. Past the reflections of the runabout's control consoles, the low, wide door of the *Sovereign*'s main shuttlebay was beginning to close against the backdrop of stars and space. This wasn't part of his plan.

"Uh, Mr. Scott, not to belabor the obvious . . . but are we going to be able to squeeze both runabouts under that door before it closes?"

Scott didn't take his eyes off his controls. "I took the liberty of making a few refinements to your plan. From an engineering viewpoint, getting through a shuttlebay atmospheric forcefield is difficult. But getting through a shuttlebay *door,* as my grandmother would say, that's a piece o' haggis."

Kirk had had haggis. The experience forced him to ask, "Is that a good thing?"

"Ye just watch," Scott said.

The thump and pressure lock of the now-closed bay door trembled through the shuttlebay and into the runabout. They were now sealed into the bay with no possible way out, except, of course, by transporter. But as long as the runabout's shields were up, that wasn't an option to worry about.

Kirk saw an alert light flash on the communications board. That would be Arkat, he knew. Best to ignore him. Kirk doubted that many things could be worse for the Cardassian's ego than to be treated as inconsequential. And the angrier Arkat became, the easier he would be to deal with.

"All right, Mr. Scott, surprise me," Kirk said.

"Hold on to your thrusters," Scott said with a gleeful tone. "Stand by to fire quantum torpedoes."

Kirk looked over at the engineer. "Runabouts have quantum torpedoes?"

"They do now, laddie."

Scott punched a finger onto his control board and instantly the *St. Lawrence* echoed with the twang of a torpedo's induction launch.

Before the sound had faded, the shuttlebay door vanished in a wall of escaping zero-point energy, released not from the torpedo, but from the underlying quantum structure of space-time itself.

"Launching *Coprates!*" Scott said, and punched a fist down on the control board.

To Kirk's explosion-dazzled eyes, one instant the *Coprates* was to his starboard, the next instant she was a blur of motion, disappearing into the writhing fireball that still occupied the space where the bay door once stood.

"Atmospheric forcefield coming online," Spock announced.

"Not for long, it isn't," Scott said. "Fire two!"

Again the *St. Lawrence* thrummed with the launch of a quantum torpedo and an instant later the stars filled the viewports as the runabout emerged in open space.

"I thought I was the pilot," Kirk said.

"Nothin' human could have reacted fast enough to find the hole in a quantum explosion," Scott said, "but she's all yours now."

Kirk began piloting as he had practiced.

On his forward sensor screen, he saw the rapid course of the *Coprates* as she sped away from the *Sovereign,* came about, and went to warp speed. As soon as he was certain the decoy runabout was clear, Kirk shut down his own runabout's warp core and impulse drive, then activated full maneuvering thrusters. Even as the *Coprates* sped away at warp four, with luck Kirk would be only able to manage a few meters per second in the *St. Lawrence*.

But if his plan was going to work, that was all the velocity he would need.

Flying strictly by eye, Kirk brought the *St. Lawrence* around so the runabout's prow matched the orientation of the *Sovereign*. Next, he slipped the small craft backward and down along the *Sovereign*'s dorsal spine, no more than two meters above her gleaming duranium-composite hull, until he had reached a point approximately two deck levels below the main shuttlebay's exterior flight deck—a blind spot that, Spock had precisely calculated, put the runabout safely out of visual observation range of any of the starship's viewports.

Then Kirk programmed the autopilot to hold this exact, relative position, and trusted in Starfleet technology to do the rest.

He didn't have to wait long.

With a gentle lag of the inertial dampers, he felt the *St. Lawrence* bank to port, matching each movement of the starship only two meters below.

A second later, Kirk's runabout lurched slightly as the *Sovereign* went to warp and began to accelerate within the faster-than-light realm.

No runabout could match the *Sovereign*'s speed, of course, but the *St. Lawrence* was safely contained with the starship's warp bubble, as if she were still parked in the shuttlebay. Wherever the *Sovereign* went, the *St. Lawrence* would go, and at whatever speed as well.

If Kirk had attempted this maneuver with any craft other than one which had come from the starship, the carefully calibrated engineering systems of the *Sovereign* would have at once detected the extra mass of Kirk's ship. But the beauty of this plan was that since the *St. Lawrence* was already included in the *Sovereign*'s cargo manifest, the fact that her mass was also being carried into warp by the ship wouldn't register as an anomaly.

Kirk looked back at his passengers. "So far, so good. Mr. Scott, what's the estimated time until the *Sovereign* comes within weapons range of the *Coprates?*"

"A little over two minutes, sir, depending on rate of acceleration."

Kirk waited patiently. The time frame was close to what he had anticipated.

When he had begun to develop his plan for getting off the *Sovereign,* he had known from the start that there was no possible way he could outrace the starship to the Goldin Discontinuity. Thus, he had concluded that the only way to reach that sensor-disabling region of space was by inducing the starship to take him there herself. Thus far, the plan was working perfectly.

"When will they be able to tell there's no one on board the *Coprates?*" Kirk asked.

"Hard to say," Scott admitted. "I've rigged seven tricorders to transmit life signs consistent to all of us, one each. The autopilot is set for evasive maneuvers, and she'll even launch two quantum torpedoes of her own—which should be a fair surprise for whoever's in the center chair of this scow. But once they lock tractor beams on to her, the jig'll be up. And then, no doubt, someone will start wondering what happened to the *St. Lawrence.*"

Kirk checked the time readout on his controls. Another minute to reach the *Coprates.* Perhaps another two minutes' delay bought by the torpedoes. Then another minute to lock tractor beams and discover the ruse. And after all that, four minutes from now, the *St. Lawrence* would still be three minutes away from the protective cover of the Goldin Discontinuity.

If it took the *Sovereign* two minutes to catch her, that was a minute too long.

"We're not going to make it," Kirk said aloud. But by the very act of stating that dilemma aloud, his mind went to work on the solution.

Kirk pictured the small craft he was in, perched on the back of the mighty, 700-meter-long starship like a remora on a shark. Even at this point-blank range, the runabout's phasers weren't powerful enough to disrupt the ship's warp engines. The single quantum torpedo still remaining on the runabout, however Scotty had managed it, would definitely penetrate the hull of the *Sovereign* and slow her down, but any rupture of the outer hull would also cost the lives of innocent crew.

Was Kirk willing to pay that price, even for Teilani?

Afraid of what his answer would be, Kirk refused to consider that question.

At least, not yet.

There *had* to be another way to buy that minute. A way that did not involve weapons and death and—

"Scotty—what would happen if I took the runabout to warp while we were still inside the *Sovereign*'s warp bubble?"

Scott frowned. "Before or after we both were torn t' pieces by the stress of the collapsing field?"

Kirk sat back in the pilot's chair, stretching his back, that question answered. He checked the time readout. They would be coming up on the *Coprates* any second.

But Spock leaned forward. "I believe the captain has hit upon a worthwhile strategy."

"Blowin' both ships out of space?" Scott asked.

"No. Disabling the *Sovereign*'s warp drive by inducing a harmonic overload."

Scott's scowl indicated he was unimpressed. The runabout began to sway back and forth, duplicating the maneuvers of the *Sovereign* as she matched the *Coprates*'s automated evasive course changes. *Three minutes,* Kirk thought, *and then I'll have to choose—Teilani's life or those of a dozen . . . or a hundred Starfleet crew I've never met, never known.*

"Admiral Spock," Scott said, "the *Sovereign* is a robust ship. Any harmonic overload this wee runabout could induce wouldna interfere with her warp capabilities for more than a minute."

"Which is precisely the length of time we need," Spock said. Gratified, Kirk knew Spock's observation meant that his friend had worked out the math of the chase and had arrived at the same conclusion.

The runabout rocked forward along with the starship. A quantum torpedo must have hit her shields. That bought a few more seconds' delay.

"What about it, Scotty?"

Now the chief engineer looked worried. "Captain, the timing would have to be so exact, it'd be almost impossible."

"I can live with 'almost.'"

"And it won't get ye as much time as ye need. I mean, for this t' work, you're going to have to do it *before* the *Sovereign* drops from warp. And that'll happen as soon as they lock their tractors on to the *Coprates.*"

Kirk put his hands on the control surfaces. "Then let's not waste any more time. Tell me what to do, Scotty."

The engineer shook his head in dismay, but punched in a set of coordinates. "On my mark, rise to this exact point midway between the *Sovereign*'s nacelles, then go to warp, bearing two seven zero, mark zero."

"Straight up," Kirk confirmed.

The runabout lurched and Kirk looked out to the side, past the starship's white expanse, to see the movement of the stars begin to diminish, indicating the *Sovereign*'s drop in velocity. Then another shudder shook the craft as the second and last of the *Coprates*'s automatic quantum torpedoes detonated. For a fleeting moment, Kirk saw the vast curve of the *Sovereign*'s shields light up as she absorbed the impact.

"We're almost out of warp, Captain," Scott said. "Get ready, on my mark. . . ."

But Kirk knew that even after he broke away from the ship, they would still need more time. Another few seconds at the very least.

"Scotty, wait!" Kirk spoke his thoughts aloud, rapidly. "Can we leave a quantum torpedo here, holding position the way we've been doing?"

"The torpedoes have maneuvering thrusters, but why on Earth would ye want to do that?"

"To set it off on a delayed fuse, after we take off."

"Ye'd be killing a lot of innocent crew."

"No! I don't need it to penetrate the hull, just . . . explode. Can we have it hold position far enough away it won't cause damage?"

"Aye. But again, what's the point?"

To Kirk, it was the perfect solution. "No matter how fast we go, the *Sovereign* is faster. But what if just as she's closing on us, she takes a quantum torpedo hit from the aft? From a torpedo that didn't even show a trace on her sensors?"

Scott looked over at him, nodding agreement. "Aye, whoever's in command would have no choice but to think he'd been attacked by a cloaked vessel, coming to our rescue."

"And you can bet he'll think twice about any action he takes next."

Scotty sighed. "That's worth a few seconds, at least. Releasing torpedo."

There was a clunk as the magnetic clamps unfastened their deadly cargo beneath the runabout's deck. Then Scott entered the command codes that would set it for delayed detonation and shouted, "Mark!"

Kirk activated the sequence he had programmed and the *Sovereign* appeared to drop away from the runabout. Her saucer hull, no longer a true circle as in the early days of starship design, seemed to grow longer as Kirk's viewing angle changed. Then the glowing red emitters of the Bussard collectors on the forward ends of the ship's enormous nacelles moved into view at either side. Just by themselves, the *Sovereign*'s nacelles were longer than Kirk's own *Enterprise,* the whole ship, more than twice the length.

But Kirk ignored the view and watched his board, counting off each meter until the runabout was just in the exact middle of the overlap coordinates of the twin warp fields, each generated by one of the nacelles.

At the proper coordinates, Kirk touched the activate control, and the stars streaked downward as the *Sovereign* disappeared below.

"Clear!" Scott shouted and Kirk immediately put the *St. Lawrence* into a corkscrew maneuver that brought her into a straight-line course for the Goldin Discontinuity.

As the stars spiraled in the main viewports, and the multicolored mass of writhing plasma grew before them, Scott brought up on the console viewscreen an aft sensor image.

The *Sovereign* was tumbling like a toy boat on a windswept sea, overbalanced by the sudden disruption and collapse of her warp drive, tipping over her center of gravity as her inertial dampers fought to restore dynamic equilibrium.

But those systems were not fast enough and Kirk saw the immense ship's prow bear down on the decoy runabout.

The *Coprates* blossomed into a blue fireball of plasma as the *Sovereign*'s shields smashed against her, crushing the smaller craft's hull and triggering a warp-core breach in her miniaturized generator.

"Did they know we weren't on board?" Kirk asked no one in particular. He didn't expect an answer. How could anyone know? But if the commander of the *Sovereign* thought Kirk and his companions were dead, it might give the *St. Lawrence* an even longer head start.

"Och, she's going to warp," Scott said in disgust. "Comin' straight for us."

Kirk read the forward scanners: two minutes and thirty

seconds to the Goldin Discontinuity. Once inside, the only way they could be detected would be by visual observation. The runabout was too small to even provide a shadowy sensor return.

But to wrap themselves in that impenetrable cloak of safety, they had to reach the plasma storms before the *Sovereign* reached them.

"In range in forty seconds," Scott said.

One minute, fifty seconds, Kirk thought. That was the difference between success and failure. In all this vast immensity of space and time, Teilani's existence had come to one minute fifty seconds.

"Evasive maneuvers?" Spock asked.

But Kirk knew they would be useless. Any deviation from the course he had plotted would simply delay their arrival within the protective interference of the discontinuity.

"Let me know when their tractors power up," Kirk said. He'd try evading the starship then, but not an instant before.

Suddenly, the runabout rocked violently.

"Phasers!" Scott shouted. "Direct hit. Shields at seventy percent!"

Almost simultaneously, Kirk increased the matter-antimatter mix to five percent higher than the runabout's maximum rated power.

"Warning," the computer said. "Magnetic containment field failure in sixty seconds."

"Captain," Scott said. "Ye cannae be serious."

But Kirk had never been more serious in his life. "I will not be captured."

The runabout shook again. Sparks flew from an overhead ODN bus.

"Shields at fifty-two percent. She cannae take much more o' this!"

"When's that torpedo set to go off, Mr. Scott?"

"I didn't think they'd be catching up to us so quickly."

"When?"

Scott checked his controls. "Three . . . two . . . they're powering up their phasers and . . . *now.*"

On the console viewscreen, Kirk saw the *Sovereign*'s shields appear in a scintillating ovoid of blue fire. The quantum torpedo he had left behind had just detonated over her engineering hull.

"Ye did it!" Scotty shouted as the *Sovereign* suddenly banked and swung about to face in the opposite direction.

Strands of blue fire streaked away from her, heading back in the direction she had come.

"Ten quantum torpedoes away," Scott said. "They think they were hit from behind!"

"Fifty seconds," Kirk whispered as he willed the timer to move faster.

The console viewer shimmered with blue light as the quantum torpedoes, now hundreds of thousands of kilometers distant, exploded in a deadly spread.

Deadly, that is, if there had been any ship there to be caught by their destructive force.

"She's coming about again," Scott said.

"Forty seconds to the discontinuity," Kirk announced.

"Fifty seconds to contact," Scott read out. "They're too far behind. We're going to make it."

But the computer had another opinion. "Warning, ten seconds to magnetic containment field failure. Nine . . . eight . . ."

Kirk held his fist above the console—

". . . six . . . five . . . four . . ."

—and hit the intermix control to bring it back within nominal range.

No longer overpowered, the runabout dropped in speed by five percent.

Scotty pushed back in his chair as if giving up. "They're going to have us in range the moment we reach the plasma storms." He looked at Kirk. "It's no good, sir, they've got us."

"Never," Kirk said. "Hold on."

He could feel Scott and McCoy staring at him, neither willing to break his concentration by asking what he was thinking—but neither able to conceive of a way out.

But Kirk knew what to do.

This had been a race to reach the discontinuity.

Despite every effort, he was going to lose.

Which meant that once again, it was time to change the rules.

TWENTY

☆

The *St. Lawrence* was so close to safety that the flashing colors of the Goldin Discontinuity filled the viewports. Already the subspace compression waves emanating from the twisted region of space made the runabout quake. But they were still not close enough.

"Ten seconds to contact," Scott said. "Maybe if they miss, we'll have a chance."

"They're not going to miss," Kirk said, filled with white-hot conviction. "They're not even going to have a chance to fire."

He ignored the puzzled look from Scott, braced himself against the console.

"They've locked phasers," the engineer said. "Five seconds till they fire . . . shields at forty-eight percent . . . WHOOF!"

Scott's cry came just as Kirk drove his hands onto the console and shut down the warp drive. In less than half a second the *St. Lawrence* hung at relative rest in normal space, so abruptly that the dampers had strained to keep everyone from flying forward from their seats.

But without the relatively sluggish dampers, Kirk knew, everyone in the runabout would now be a one-molecule-thick layer of protein on the forward viewport, and the runabout would have torn itself into a billion spinning shards of debris. Even so, power couplings overloaded, the gravity generators whined under the strain, and all the lights and control consoles flickered, cut out, and only slowly regained their brightness.

But, even before the runabout's systems could fully recover, the *Sovereign* streaked past as a radiant, color-smeared starbow traveling at speeds human senses could not react to except through sophisticated computer systems as it disappeared deep into the boundary of the Goldin Discontinuity. Even if her commander took all of two seconds to react to Kirk's sudden maneuver, at warp six, those two seconds would carry the *Sovereign* almost a quarter-billion kilometers away.

Kirk swiftly reestablished the runabout's warp drive, and by the time he had accelerated to warp factor one, the *St. Lawrence,* at last, was safe, protected like an ancient merchant-marine freighter crossing the Atlantic, by an impenetrable shroud of thick fog.

Within that obscuring blanket of plasma storms, the *St. Lawrence* would be able to detect the *Sovereign*'s approaching mass long before the starship could detect the minuscule runabout. To all intents and purposes, Kirk and his team had vanished.

Seconds from defeat, they were safe.

Kirk could not deny the rush of excitement that still reverberated in him. As if he had enjoyed the chase. As if he had relished the victory over death.

As if he had not spent a year on Chal, focusing all his efforts and all his life on one simple field, searching for peace. Searching for his place within the universe.

But Kirk thrust those personal thoughts aside. He spun around in his pilot's chair, ignoring the openmouthed stare Scott directed his way. "Is everyone all right?"

Janeway had removed a small medical-waste container

from the compartment under her seat and was in the process of recycling her last meal.

T'Val had her arm around the mirror Spock, her father, who appeared ashen in color. McCoy was busy checking his patient's vital signs. Even her Vulcan discipline did little to hide T'Val's outrage. "You are *insane!*" she said hoarsely. McCoy touched his temple in a small salute of agreement.

"And *you* are alive," Kirk said. "How about you, Spock?"

"I am . . ." He looked up at the ceiling as if searching there for the proper word. "Impressed," he said at last. "Though, like T'Val, I am also concerned about your intellectual well-being. To face down a Sovereign-class vessel in a runabout requires extraordinarily large—"

"Motivation," Kirk said. There was no need to get personal. He spun his chair back to Scott, aware that he was suddenly ravenous, as he had never been on Chal. Facing death did that to him. Awakened all his senses, his appreciation of life. "All right, Mr. Scott. Lay in a course for Chal."

"I . . . might have another suggestion, Captain."

But Kirk wasn't interested. "We're going after whoever has Teilani. Lay in that course."

But Scott kept his hands off the controls. "If ye'd listen to me for a moment, I might have something interesting to tell ye."

Kirk leaned back in his chair, impatient, but trying not to let ego rule him in the the way it had affected the Cardassian's judgment. "All right, I'm listening." He looked at the time readout. "For one minute."

"The *Sovereign* was under orders to search for the warp trail of the *Enterprise* and the mirror *Voyager.*"

"Warp trails that had been cloaked somehow," Kirk said. "Which makes me think it was an order from a counterpart spy in Starfleet to engage the *Sovereign* in a useless assignment, and deny her to the rest of the Fleet."

"Then again, p'raps not. Ye see, to prepare for that search, all the sensors on all the ship's shuttles and even the runabouts were recalibrated to look for the quantum signature of the *Voyager*'s warp particles. And look—" Scott tapped on a sensor display screen. "—here they are."

Kirk read the display. "That's hardly surprising, Mr. Scott. The *Enterprise* was on patrol in the discontinuity when it found the mirror *Voyager*. It follows that the *Voyager*'s warp trail would be detected in here as well."

"No, no, *look*," Scott insisted. He adjusted some controls and the image on the sensor screen expanded until, Kirk saw, the graphic representation of the warp particles' trail split in two.

"Two trails?" Kirk asked. "Is there another mirror-universe ship in here?"

Scott gave him a measuring look. "Captain, a warp particle is a wee beastie, and under normal conditions, it decays fairly quickly. So in another day or two, they'll nae be here to see. And under the conditions within this region, we really shouldna be picking them up at all."

"But we are."

"Aye, because their quantum signature is different, they don't decay as rapidly in our space-time, so they stick out like a sore antenna on an Andorian. We'd never find a trail of the *Enterprise*'s warp particles in here. The quantum signature from those would be smeared all to Edinburgh and back. But the particles from the *Voyager* . . . well, sir, that ship might just as well be leaving a trail of breadcrumbs."

Kirk braced himself for the inevitable, looked back at Spock.

But Spock reassured him. "I am familiar with the legend of Hansel and Gretel, Captain. However, I do confess I also do not understand the significance of a double trail."

"Och, will ye two look at the orientation of the particles' spin," Scott said. "It's obvious. One trail was created as the mirror *Voyager* came *out* of the plasma storms. And the other trail—"

Kirk saw it in a flash. "Was left behind when the *Voyager* returned!"

Scott nodded. "Ye did it yourself when ye settled the runabout down on the *Sovereign*'s spine. Hiding in plain sight."

Kirk immediately understood the implications of Scott's discovery. "Spock, if the *Voyager* exited the Goldin Discontinuity at any other point along its boundary, could it be detected?"

"Without question. We are deep within Federation space. The mirror *Voyager* would show up on any number of deep-space tracking networks, especially now that a concerted search is in progress."

"So," Kirk said, "at least ten days after the *Enterprise* found her, we can be certain she *hasn't* come out. And while half of Starfleet is scouring the rest of space, trying to find out where the *Voyager* went, probably taking the *Enterprise* with it, we're the only ones who know she came back *here.*"

Scott raised a cautionary finger. "Aye, but if anyone on the *Sovereign* runs a sensor sweep in here and picks up the double trail, they're going to know it, too, as quickly as we did."

"The *Sovereign*'s under enemy control," Kirk said. "I have no doubt Admiral Nechayev and Glinn Arkat already know exactly what happened to *Voyager.*"

Then Kirk checked the main sensor display. Nothing but static. He noted that Scott had set the mass detector to maximum sensitivity. The *Sovereign* would trigger it the moment she closed within fifty thousand kilometers—more than enough of a safety zone to allow escape.

He turned back to the two Spocks and McCoy, to T'Val and Janeway. The idea he was considering was unlikely, but served to coalesce all that happened into one underlying, connected whole. Five minutes ago, he would never have considered the possibility of delaying his departure to Chal. But if the idea he had just had turned out to be possible . . .

"Let's say I'm Jean-Luc Picard," Kirk began.

"That is not as unlikely a supposition to make as you may think," Spock observed. "Indeed, you share many similarities, including—"

"I'm trying to form a hypothesis, Spock."

Spock stopped talking. "Please, continue."

"I'm Jean-Luc Picard. I'm on patrol in the Goldin Discontinuity and . . ." Kirk stopped as he noticed the stares of Janeway and T'Val. "What is it?"

"Is it true Jean-Luc Picard is a starship captain in this universe?" Janeway asked.

"He's the captain of the *Enterprise*," Kirk said. "And a friend."

Janeway and T'Val exchanged a look of shocked amazement. Kirk could guess why.

"I take it there's a Picard in your universe, as well."

"You would not consider him a friend," the mirror Spock said. "Please, continue with your hypothesis."

Kirk tabled his curiosity about the mirror Picard. Once again, Janeway and T'Val reacted to the name with almost the same reaction as they had shown to the name Tiberius.

"Suddenly," Kirk went on, "I find the *Voyager*. A missing starship. Back home at last. Probably, I make contact with someone on board who's known to be a *Voyager* crew member. They're in trouble. Need help at once. I waive security procedures, beam them all over at once. These are colleagues in trouble. Heroes for having survived all they've been through." Pausing, Kirk considered the emotion of that moment, the thrill of discovery, the relief of knowing that no matter the odds, sometimes space could give up her dead. "I would have done the same thing," he said truthfully.

"But, of course," Spock said, "it was not the real *Voyager*. The crew members, at least those who made contact, were counterparts. . . ."

"And," Kirk continued, "I would have beamed a boarding party of Klingons and Cardassians onto my ship."

"Captain, I can't believe that a ship as sophisticated as the new *Enterprise* could be taken over by anything as simple as a boarding party. The new computer lockout systems are designed to take weeks to work around."

"Maybe the boarding party was led by *your* counterpart, Scotty."

The engineer nodded thoughtfully, as if he agreed that the best security systems of Starfleet would, in the end, offer no challenge to him, or anyone like him. "Ah, I see your point."

Kirk hid his smile, went on with his scenario. "So, Picard's neutralized. Now, let's look at it from the other side. I'm the leader of an Alliance commando team—and I have two starships. What do I want with them?"

"The same thing we do," Janeway said. "Take them back home. To win the war. Or, to defeat the resistance."

"But *you* just want the building plans," Kirk said. "You can take those home with a transporter and build your own ships, the way the Terran resistance built a duplicate of the *Defiant*. But for me to take the *ships* back, and save all that time and effort, I need a wormhole."

Spock looked perplexed. "Why?"

Kirk remembered that Spock had been otherwise engaged when he and Scott had discussed the various methods of crossing between the universes. "Only two ways to cross over, Spock. Small masses can be transported with specially modified equipment. Large objects, like this runabout, require a wormhole."

Spock looked troubled. "I suspect there is a flaw in that logic."

"Let me know when you find it," Kirk said. He turned his attention back to the others. "So, the questions remains. If everything I've said is true, or close to the truth, why here? Why did the mirror *Voyager* appear in the Goldin Discontinuity? And why did she return here?"

T'Val stated the obvious, logical conclusion. "Because the wormhole is here."

"Och, no, lassie. I've been having this argument with

Starfleet for years, now. Ye cannae have a stable wormhole in such an unstable region of space. Nearby, perhaps, the way the Bajoran wormhole is near to the Badlands. But not in the Badlands themselves."

"Then what brings them here?" Kirk asked. If he was going to have any chance at all of defeating the Alliance agents in this universe, he had to understand their strategy.

The mirror Spock seemed to make a difficult decision. "Captain Kirk, in sickbay, when I appeared to answer Admiral Nechayev's questions about the Vulcan resistance, everything I said was a deliberate misstatement. Except for my role as figurehead."

"No," T'Val said emphatically. "You *are* our leader."

The mirror Spock did not acknowledge his daughter. "But what I am going to tell you now is true, and potentially dangerous to our ongoing efforts to overthrow the Alliance. Should we be captured . . ."

"Understood," Kirk said. Whatever secret he was about to learn would die with him.

"The Terran resistance cell operating near Bajor has its base in the Badlands."

"In our universe," Spock said, "the rebels known as the Maquis did the same. The masking effects of the plasma storms make the region impenetrable to sensors, thus an eminently logical place to hide."

"So," Kirk said, "we can assume that the Alliance faction we're facing has chosen this region for their secret base for the same reason—assuming the Goldin Discontinuity exists in your universe."

The mirror Spock nodded. "It does, by the same name, as well."

Kirk turned to look out the forward viewports. The view reminded him of low-orbital passes over Jupiter—colorful swirls and whorls beyond any identifiable scale, churning in constant motion, lit from within by unceasing discharges of energy.

Yet, for all its violent beauty, this place was a sanctuary.

A place for the Alliance to transfer ships.

To hide.

To plot their strategy against their enemies at home.

And if it was all those things, then what if it was one other?

"Kate?" Kirk said, without taking his eyes off the shifting grandeur before him. "When you were in the Alliance prison camp, where was it?"

"Alpha Centauri IV," Janeway said. "New Montana. It used to be a big Earth colony. The Alliance left most of it intact. They were always digging through the facilities. I never knew what they were looking for, though."

Kirk frowned. He had been hoping to hear of a prison camp where the sky was on fire with twisting sheets of incandescent plasma.

"But the labor camp . . ." Janeway said softly, as if she had suddenly realized what Kirk was after. "Where they were going to send me after your Kathryn Janeway was declared lost . . ."

Kirk looked back at her, waiting for the words that could determine what he would do next. That could determine if they would live or die.

"They gave me a discharge suit," she said. "Made me put it on." She closed her eyes briefly as she relived the moment.

"You're sure that's what they called it?" Kirk asked. Discharge suits had been around for centuries, and he could think of no reason why the mirror universe wouldn't share the technology. Early in the history of warp flight, it was discovered that spacecraft moving through clouds of interstellar dust could pick up powerful electrostatic charges impossible to dissipate in ordinary vacuum. On stations without force-field technology to bleed off those charges, maintenance workers had to wear insulating suits that would protect them from powerful electrical discharges should they touch conductive parts of the craft.

Janeway nodded. "They told me I had to wear it for the labor camp. Otherwise, I could die."

For Kirk, the final piece of the puzzle slipped into place. "You were coming here," he said.

"I can't be sure," Janeway told him. "I escaped at the transfer station at Lake Riker."

"Where's that?" Kirk asked.

"Outside New Montana. Where the spaceport is."

Kirk knew the main spaceport on Alpha Centauri IV. "In our universe, it's called Lake Sloane."

Kirk saw Spock react with interest, but let it pass.

He was convinced he had uncovered the one fact that made sense of all the other questions.

Why the *Voyager* had appeared here.

Why the *Enterprise* had disappeared here.

And why Admiral Nechayev's *Sovereign* had been assigned to conduct the search for the *Enterprise* in every region of space *except* for here.

"There's a labor camp in the discontinuity," he told the others. "Probably two—one in each universe."

"For what purpose?" Spock asked.

Kirk turned back to his console and called up the main sensor configuration controls. "We're going to find transporters, Spock—hundreds of pads, maybe thousands. And the prisoners, they take apart the starships and they transfer them through, piece by piece."

Kirk was prepared for Scott's hoot of disbelief. "Captain, that'd take years, even if ye could cut up hull metal in such small pieces and have a hope of rejoining them all later."

"You said it yourself, Scotty. If there can't be a stable wormhole in here, transporters are the only way to go. And since the mirror *Voyager* made it into our universe, we know whatever system they're using works."

Scotty looked dismayed. "Aye, ye've got me there."

Kirk finished setting all sensors to maximum sensitivity for quantum-signature detection. "Follow that trail, Scotty. Wherever the mirror *Voyager* went, that's where we're going."

McCoy was completely lost. "But Jim, what about Chal? What about Teilani?"

Kirk stared into the writhing madness of the tortured plasma. Whatever forces of nature were at work there remained beyond his understanding, and that of the best minds of Starfleet.

But he was ready to risk them to do what his heart demanded.

"If I'm right, Bones, Teilani is a lot closer than we think."

"What happens if you're wrong?"

As the *St. Lawrence* plunged deeper into the storm, Kirk didn't answer.

Because if he was wrong, then Teilani would die.

And nothing would ever matter again.

TWENTY-ONE

Picard awoke in a cloud of pain.

Every muscle, every nerve, every memory protested the agony that engulfed him.

But he forced himself up from the cot.

This *was* the day.

The day he would live. Or he would die.

He would not turn away from his duty, his responsibility.

Beverly Crusher was beside him, kneeling in the narrow walkway, cradling his head, speaking softly to him as she held a weak brew of something that passed for nutrient soup in this dark and humid hellhole.

"Drink this, Jean-Luc," she said. Then she looked around furtively.

Picard followed her gaze, even as the putrid fluid scalded his tongue and his throat.

There were at least one hundred other cots in the dismal, filth-strewn barracks. Half were filled with fitfully sleeping gamma-shift workers. Most were human. A handful were alien. And some were from the *Enterprise*.

The miserable occupants of the other half of the cots, other workers, the delta shift, were sitting up groggily, all, without exception, shifting uncomfortably in the constricting pressure of the discharge suits they wore, the suits they could not remove without facing death.

Picard, like everyone else, despised his.

It was sickly green-black in color, rubbery in texture, thick and impervious to sweat, except through a number of small fabric-covered slits cut into the sides of the chest piece, back, and upper leg segments. The hateful garment stretched from his neck down over his entire body, leaving only his head and face and hands uncovered. Picard had already learned that a mere half-hour of heavy labor in the suit was enough to make its inner surface slip and chafe against his skin as the fabric lining became sodden with sweat. The insufferable heat dizzied him.

He had seen more than one fully-suited wretch succumb to that heat by passing out in the middle of the shift.

Some were so far gone that even the excruciating assault of the overseers' agonizers would not be enough to shock them back to consciousness.

Picard, like the others, had heard, among the rumors that swept through this camp, that the overseers allowed each new prisoner three bouts of fainting in the first month—what they considered to be a period of acclimatization. This rumor, however, appeared to be fact. After a month, or after the fourth collapse, offending workers disappeared.

Rumor also had it they were recycled into the nutrient broth which was all there was to eat or drink.

But to refuse the salty broth was to guarantee collapse, and Picard had let his captured crew know that it was his order that they all drink it, whenever it was offered. And he did so now, without protest.

They all needed to be strong for the escape attempt.

And that attempt was to be today.

"How are the others?" Picard whispered, as he took the nutrient cup from Beverly and dutifully swallowed the disgusting brew.

"Will has the alpha shift ready to move at shift break. Geordi has briefed the beta shift."

Beverly pulled out her medical tricorder—one of the few implements the captured crew of the *Enterprise* had been allowed to keep. She scanned Picard with it.

Picard looked at the flickering lights on the tricorder. "You're certain that's functioning properly?"

The tricorder was their only hope in launching an operation to reclaim their ship. The *Enterprise*'s own computer identification systems had been fooled by up to five counterparts. Picard had seen his own counterpart face-to-face. He guessed that dozens, if not hundreds, of other *Enterprise* crew had counterparts from the mirror universe, as well. All it would take was one of them infiltrating a shift team, and Picard's careful plan would be exposed.

But thus far, Beverly Crusher had been able to guarantee the real identity of all senior staff involved in the impending attempt.

Over the past week, ever since the *Enterprise* had been brought here, she had scanned each crew member, ostensibly to check health—an activity the overseers did not object to, as it also served their purpose. Then, with a sharp sliver of composite she had snapped from the tricorder's shell, Beverly had surreptitiously given each crew member she had scanned and confirmed as being from this universe a small, triangular wound.

Those whose last names fell within the last half of the standard alphabet had a small tear on their left hands. Those whose names fell within the first half of the alphabet were similarly marked on the right hand. Names beginning with vowels brought the wound to the palm, close to the fleshy base of the thumb. Initial consonants meant the wound was made near the knuckle of the little finger.

At the beginning of the identification procedure, if the overseers, for whatever reason, had asked to check the hands of the *Enterprise* crew members, there would be no one distinctive mark that might give the scheme away. By now, only days later, those identifying wounds were hidden among the other abrasions and tears that had come from seven days of intense physical labor.

So far, eight crew members had disappeared after collapsing for the fourth and final time. And Beverly had identified six counterparts who had been switched for their duplicates. For Picard, that meant twenty-one crew had been lost so far, and he felt each death or disappearance as a personal attack.

Beset by pain, mouth sour with the ghastly broth, Picard faced this day knowing that Gul Rutal would pay for what she had done to his crew. And the Cardassian's accomplices would share her fate.

A jarring blast of noise rent the air, making Picard jerk in response. It was time for the next shift. His shift.

The last shift, he thought as he stood up, willing himself to dismiss the stiffness of his legs.

He noted and set aside the concern Beverly wore. "Are you sure you're up to this, Jean-Luc? You haven't missed a shift yet. I could have you relieved."

Picard took her hand, thinking of all the other times he had done so, when other matters had been on both their minds. "They have my ship, Beverly. I am going to get it back."

That, Picard knew, was the end of it,

He turned to face the narrow passageway between the cots, waiting for the next blast of sound that would signal it was time to march.

Beverly stood aside.

The scream of the shift-commencement signal echoed in the confined barracks. Picard's ear canals throbbed and popped as the pressure seal on the barracks airlock was unsealed. He heard the metallic rumble as the large disks of metal that were the inner and outer doors of the Cardassian-style airlock rolled to the side, opening the barracks to what lay outside. He could smell the hot, sulfurous blast of outside air as it rolled in, potent enough to eclipse the ever-present stench of stale sweat and human waste.

"Any word of Deanna or Data?" Picard asked quickly.

He saw Beverly shake her head.

Picard could understand why the overseers had removed Deanna from the main population of prisoners. With her Betazoid ability to detect falsehood in most beings, she could easily have identified those counterparts who had infiltrated Picard's crew. But he had no idea why Data had been taken, unless it was to examine the technology that had given birth to him.

The barracks filled with lines of workers, the prisoners marching rhythmically in file along the paths between the cots, between the waste buckets left at each corner, continuing on to the outside and the new day's labor.

Picard squinted as he stepped outside. But not because the sun was bright.

There was no sun in the sky.

The sky itself was on fire, glaringly incandescent with the plasma storms of the Goldin Discontinuity.

To the left, Picard perceived that a new ion formation had filled the horizon—an enormous blue billow of swirling light, embedded with hidden points of light, like spotlights seen through heavy rainfall.

Ahead, and to the right, past the low structures of the other barracks, warring clouds of red and blue still collided like monstrous stormfronts. The other barracks, if that was the function that all the other buildings shared, were all the same in appearance—low, circular structures of rough-finished, rust-colored metal, arranged in a large circle with a single, double-height building at the center. That structure was the overseers' command station, bristling with sensor dishes and antenna masts, and linked with all the other buildings by a network of raised plasteel walkways and platforms intended to keep the prisoners and guards from ever having to risk making contact with the asteroid's metal surface. Even with the discharge suits, the likelihood of plasma induction was appreciable.

Picard had no doubt that the vista he saw was millions of kilometers distant on all sides. And under any other conditions, he would find the vividly colored, almost blinding sight wondrous, exactly the reason he had first ventured into space to see, record, and understand.

But he had no use for wonder here.

Not when the view directly overhead was so abysmal, so soul-crushing, so inescapable.

There was no doubt in Picard that the site of the prison camp he and his crew had been brought to was an asteroid that had never known life. The slick surface was of nickel-iron. Hard and unyielding. Uneven except where plasteel walkways had been laid between the barracks and the work staging areas.

From the distinctive curve of the horizon, La Forge had calculated the asteroid's diameter as no more than fifteen kilometers. Somewhere beneath them in the mines, he'd reasoned, an artificial-gravity generator must be keeping all the workers in place, and maintaining their atmosphere.

La Forge had also pointed out that a certain percentage of asteroids did not exist as single bodies. And this asteroid was obviously among them.

Because, no more than two kilometers straight overhead, a second asteroid of equal size hung in chilling counterbalance. Its natural gravity would not affect the body on which the prison camp existed, though the feeling of inescapable pressure from its presence was so powerful that its effect was enervating on the spirits of those who toiled below.

To look up to what should have been open sky—where, evolution and experience had ingrained in the mind of every member of Picard's crew, unbounded freedom would be found—there was only a flying mountain of rock, impossibly poised, as if mere seconds from completing its deadly descent.

Day after day it had weighed upon the prisoners from the *Enterprise*, until even Picard acknowledged it was one of the most depressing sights he had ever encountered.

He had not been alone in his response.

Riker, too, had said he felt he was no more than a bug beneath a boot, the remainder of his life inconsequential, measured in seconds.

Beverly had refused to look up, believing it was a psychological ploy on the part of their captors—a ploy with which she would not cooperate.

And La Forge, whose ocular implants had replaced his VISOR, and who now could see even farther into realms beyond the sensitivities of ordinary human vision, had detected and reported on the rivers of shifting energy that stretched between the bleak landscape of the prison asteroid, and the overbearing mass that hung above their heads.

He had identified the energy wavelengths as a forcefield—something of such power that it kept the asteroids linked in tandem, as well as maintaining a column of breathable atmosphere from one asteroid to the next. Why an atmosphere was necessary for the second asteroid was still a question to be answered. A large grid of sensor dishes and thick cables could be seen on its surface, directly overhead, but no prisoners were ever sent there for maintenance or construction work. Riker had assumed it was either a power-generating facility, or the artificial-gravity facility that kept the two asteroids connected.

La Forge had told Picard that he viewed the invisible field as a glass column linking the two chunks of lifeless metal and stone.

And, more significant to Picard, La Forge had recognized at once the safeguards that had been built in.

Should any prisoner, or group of prisoners, ever decide to attack their overseers by disabling the power generators that kept them imprisoned, the end result would be an explosive loss of atmosphere, coupled with the slow but inevitable drawing together of the two asteroids, until everything between them—prison camp included—was crushed.

The forcefield La Forge saw was not keeping the two rocks together; it was keeping them apart.

The ultimate deterrent to escape.

After two days of carefully considered study and analysis, Picard chose to ignore the threat of the second asteroid. Instead, he focused all his efforts on the even more unusual body which hung halfway between the two asteroids.

A kilometer above the prison-camp asteroid, sparkling with the actinic flicker of fusion torches used in its construction, was a device as large as any spacedock, though of a completely different, even alien configuration. It seemed to be composed of rectangular panels of dull copper metal— ten meters by fifteen meters on a side, La Forge had confirmed. Each panel was suspended within a weblike framework of fine cables and metal rods, making the device seem almost transparent, as if it had been built as a child's construction toy.

But the structure, no matter what the style of its construction, was clearly a device.

Because beside it, in stationkeeping alignment, hung the *Enterprise.*

Which meant the device's purpose was not difficult to divine.

When Picard had first seen it, the fragile-appearing framework of metal panels and delicate cables was easily large enough to contain the *Voyager.* And he knew at once it was the means by which the duplicate *Voyager* had crossed to this universe.

Since Picard's arrival, evidence of construction on the crossover device was undeniable. By holding his fingers up at arm's length, and sighting through one eye, he had been able to see that where once the structure had been as long as three fingers were wide, it was now as long as five. In a day or two, its length would have almost doubled beyond its original dimensions, and the *Enterprise* was almost twice as long as the *Voyager*.

Picard had no doubt that when the crossover device was doubled, when it was long enough to contain his ship, then his ship would be stolen from this universe, and used in the other.

That was why today was *the* day.

He would not, could not, allow that to happen.

Not to his ship.

"Delta shift! Form work details!"

The guttural command issued forth from a delta-shift overseer. Krawl. A Klingon, young, with a flat look of total disinterest behind his eyes.

Picard had seen Krawl slap an agonizer against the neck of a woman who had dared to stop to catch her breath, with as much emotion as he might expend to brush an insect from his shoulder.

Picard kept his head down as he shuffled to the platform with the other twenty-three workers who made up his detail. If today was like every other, he would be sent down into the mines to physically transfer ore from an antigrav conveyor to a hopper bin.

From what he had been able to piece together from Riker and the others during shift changes—the only time the scattered crew of the *Enterprise* could find a few moments to talk—the hopper was routed to a fusion kiln. Like the mines, the hopper was also underground, where, under conditions of nightmarish heat, the nickel-iron ore was transmuted by a crude replication technology and extruded into the panels and support trusses used in the crossover device overhead. There were other assembly facilities elsewhere, Picard knew, perhaps even on the other asteroid, where circuitry and power couplings were assembled. But thus far, no one from the *Enterprise* had been assigned to those crucial jobs.

From this asteroid, a gravity-tether elevator lifted the

construction materials to the crossover device. And it was on the tether platforms that Picard and his gold team would reach the *Enterprise,* while the red and blue teams, respectively, neutralized the guards and took over the power-generation facilities.

If not for the prospect of failure, Picard would have looked forward to the challenge before him.

His team would be launching cables from the crossover device to the hull of the *Enterprise*—essentially, affixing grappling lines as if they were a seventeenth-century boarding party.

Provided his team could cross the lines quickly enough and reach the *Enterprise*'s outer hull, the entry codes for the airlocks were all mechanically set, specifically to guard against a computer failure making it possible to lock crew in environmental suits outside the ship.

Five minutes, Picard told himself as he stood with the others of his detail. *Five minutes and the ship would be his again, or she would be cycling toward an unstoppable warp-core breach.*

One way or another, the *Enterprise* would be his.

Or it would be no one's.

"Prisoner Delta 06-13-40, step away from the platform. *Now!*"

Only when a nearby fellow prisoner pushed Picard forward did he realize, startled, that the serial-number designation was his own.

The delta-shift overseer stood before Picard, his own discharge suit covered by nonconductive armor. Krawl whacked an agonizer probe against one massive thigh as if the probe were a riding crop.

Picard remained motionless, head down, seething with anger, yet unwilling to provoke any escalation of response from the Klingon.

"Hard of hearing, Delta 06-13-40?"

Picard did not raise his head, aware that eye contact between prisoner and overseer was considered provocation. "No, Overseer."

Then Picard gasped as the agonizer probe bit into his neck, making his vision explode with red bursts of light. He dropped to his knees, fiercely suppressing his impulse to shove the probe down Krawl's throat.

"Look at me when I speak to you," the overseer said. "Is your hearing damaged?"

Picard raised his head. His neck throbbed with pain, but he managed to look into the overseer's large dark eyes. "No, Overseer," he rasped.

And then he barely had time to close his eyes in a reflexive act of self-preservation as Krawl's probe slashed across his face, knocking him off the plasteel platform to the hard metal of the asteroid's surface.

"How *dare* you look me in the eye," the overseer roared.

Picard pictured his hands closing around Krawl's neck. He pictured his thumbs ensuring that the Klingon would never see anything again.

But for the sake of his crew, for his ship, Picard did nothing.

Someone else did.

Who it was, Picard wasn't certain. An ensign from below-decks, he knew. Someone in astrometrics. A young man with a full life before him.

But who didn't know how to follow orders.

"No!" the ensign shouted as he launched himself from the platform in defense of his captain.

"Ensign, stop!" Picard commanded.

But the young ensign collided with the overseer, forcing the Klingon back with a flurry of useless punches directed against his armored stomach.

Picard saw what was to happen and was powerless to stop it—there was just no time.

As if wielding a *bat'leth,* Krawl swiftly flipped his agonizer probe into the air above the ensign, then drove it down with unerring accuracy into the unprotected back of his neck.

The ensign's scream was immediate.

His arms and legs shook uncontrollably and he collapsed face-first on the plasteel platform.

Picard was on his feet at once, and lunged for the ensign. The plan meant nothing, now. The safety of his crew, everything.

"Leave him alone!" Picard ordered the Klingon. He used his own body to shield the half-conscious ensign. "He's young. He didn't know what he was—"

Krawl's boot caught Picard in the face, sent him sprawling.

But only death could keep a starship captain from his mission.

Picard rolled to his feet, crouched to attack Krawl even as the Klingon grabbed the back of the ensign's discharge suit and effortlessly hauled the young man to his feet.

"Don't harm him," Picard warned.

Krawl looked amused. *"I* won't do anything," he said. Then he jerked his powerful forearm so rapidly that the series of suit connectors running along the ensign's back split open like a chain stitch unraveling.

Picard blanched in horror, knowing what the overseer was planning. He started forward again.

But the Klingon raised his agonizer probe toward Picard, and the inducer tips on it sparked with blue energy.

"Don't be a hero, Terran. It's set to kill."

The ensign was on his feet, dazed, barely able to stand as Krawl held Picard at bay with his agonizer and ripped off the rest of the discharge suit.

"Don't do this," Picard said. "He'll learn his lesson." The words caught in his throat even as he said them. "He'll be a good worker."

Krawl snarled at Picard as the last of the ensign's discharge suit fell away, leaving him in Starfleet-issue shorts and

257

undershirt. "Trust me, Terran, he'll make an even better *example."*

Then the Klingon kicked the ensign savagely, sending him flying from the walkway to the asteroid's surface.

The asteroid's conductive surface.

Picard had had enough. He threw himself forward.

But four hands grabbed him from behind and he twisted to see that two other overseers—one Klingon, one Cardassian—had him in their grip.

"No . . ." Picard protested.

But in his heart he knew he was too late.

The ensign, alone on the asteroid's surface, pushed himself up to his feet, looked at his arms, realized his suit was gone.

He staggered from side to side, looked up at all the other prisoners, all the other overseers watching him.

His hair began to bristle as the charges built up in him. Charges that the suit would no longer bleed harmlessly away.

His gaze found Picard.

His hand reached out.

"Captain . . . I'm sorry. . . . I'm—"

And then, as if he were a lightning rod, the first and last tendril of antiproton energy blazed from the plasma-filled sky and hit the youth, and engulfed him.

The image of the impact etched itself forever into Picard's memory, but he did not turn away.

The ensign's hair was on fire. Flares of light burst forth from his eyes and mouth, and crackles of energy shot out from his rigid, outstretched fingers.

The overseers held Picard so he would have no choice but to see what was happening, but Picard did not struggle. A starship captain always faced the consequences of his actions.

Finally, the ensign was gone. Replaced by a crumpled, blackened body, bearing no resemblance to the life that had once been there. The promise.

The overseers pushed Picard to his knees. He felt blood

trickle from the bridge of his nose, dripping onto the walk-way's smooth surface, but he did not move. Even when the side of Krawl's boots shoved against his cheek, close enough that Picard knew he could twist the monster onto his back and break his neck with one deadly blow.

But what of the rest of his crew?

"This was your fault, Terran. Remember that."

Picard felt the agonizer probe tap his shoulder. But it wasn't turned on.

And for all the rage that burned within him, Picard knew Krawl was right.

Among his crew, each death *was* his fault.

They trusted him. They put their lives in his hands. Willingly.

And as Picard got slowly to his feet, he made a silent promise to the ensign that that trust had not been misplaced.

Each death might be his fault. But he would see to it that those who were responsible would pay the full price.

Personally.

He raised his head to look at Krawl's obscenely grinning mouth, but no higher, not yet.

The overseer would die.

Picard was as certain of that as he was that he would once again take the center chair of the *Enterprise.*

"Better," Krawl said. "You have a special assignment today."

Picard did not react. For his plan to work, he *had* to be with his gold team at the end of the shift. It was absolutely necessary to take control of the antigrav platform that took them down into the mines. Only that platform could take his team up to the crossover device and the *Enterprise.*

But though he gave no outward sign of his concern, Krawl seemed to sense something. Like a hunter scenting the instinct for escape in his prey.

"Have I interfered with something?" the Klingon asked with mock concern.

"Just don't send me down into the mine," Picard said in a low voice. "I . . . I can't stand that anymore."

Krawl had obviously never heard of the ancient Terran folktale of Brer Rabbit. His momentary suspicion was deflected, as Picard had hoped, and he shoved Picard forward, force-marching him across the walkway to an off-limits barracks.

The ominous symbol of the Alliance—the Cardassian raptor whose wings embraced the Klingon triskelion—was emblazoned on the wall of the facility, though in all other respects, the structure was identical in size and shape to every other building but the double-height command center.

In the past week, three *Enterprise* crew had been taken here.

None had returned.

Picard hoped that at least one member of his gold team would learn of this, so they would not wait for him at the end of the shift. The escape had to be attempted today; otherwise, the *Enterprise* would be lost.

Krawl pushed Picard toward an airlock platform to one side of the barracks.

All the life-support facilities on the asteroid's surface were pressurized, Picard had noted. That made sense to him.

In the case of insurrection, the forcefield could be dropped long enough to kill the prisoners by suffocation, while the overseers remained safe within their sealed barracks.

Picard had allowed for that capability in his plan.

Now Krawl pushed Picard's head down so he could see nothing, and Picard heard the delta-shift overseer enter a security code into the airlock panel.

The thick circular Cardassian door rolled open.

Krawl kicked Picard to make him move forward, then left him in the transfer chamber.

"Good-bye, Terran," the Klingon said with a scornful laugh. "Each ensign I kill today, I dedicate to you."

Picard wheeled around but only in time to see the door roll shut, and Krawl grinning at him through the small viewport.

Then there was a rush of air as the pressure equalized, and the interior door rolled open.

Picard knew the drill, knew the tests the overseers set up for prisoners.

He stood his ground.

Then a familiar voice said, "Very good, Jean-Luc. You *have* learned your lessons."

The voice was familiar because it was Picard's own.

"Please, enter. My home is your home, in more ways than you can imagine."

So Picard walked forward, stepping from the airlock into a large area that reminded him in design of the patterned wall panels of *Deep Space Nine.* It was utilitarian in finish, yet in one corner, a section was furnished almost like a private apartment.

In the midst of that unlikely setting stood Picard's counterpart, resplendent in the battle armor of a Klingon regent. Yet this man's existence and appearance were no longer a surprise to Picard. By now, he had grown used to seeing this unsettling duplicate of himself.

But Picard was not prepared for the woman who stood beside the regent. A woman he knew.

She was draped in the sheerest of Argelian silks, no more substantial than a veil. Her long hair was drawn back in the Klingon style, intricately braided with glittering Klingon bloodstones—the gift of a warrior. But even the heavy makeup she wore, as if there had been some attempt to have her resemble an Orion slave girl, could not disguise the distinctive pattern of her subtle head ridges, nor the points of her ears, nor the distinctive scar that marred her singular beauty.

The regent saw the flicker of recognition in Picard's eyes.

"You know this prisoner?"

Picard shook his head. Too many lives were at stake in the planned escape to allow him the satisfaction of facing down his doppelgänger. Any action Picard took here today would have to be swift, and deadly. "I was mistaken. She looked familiar, but . . . I was wrong."

The mirror Picard looked upon his captive in feigned shock. "A mistake? Jean-Luc Picard—captain of the *Enterprise*—admits a mistake?" He held a hand to his heart. "And here I thought I knew you so well. You must admit, I played you like a Centauri salmon, getting you to voluntarily reestablish the command codes for your ship. Or, should I say, *my* ship."

Picard glared at his counterpart, but still refused to escalate their confrontation. He had come to realize that no matter what he felt about his duplicate, it was more than matched by the overwhelming contempt his counterpart felt for him.

The regent looked back at the woman in silk. "For myself, I'm not often wrong. And when I am . . . I hate to be reminded of it. Are you like that, too, Jean-Luc?"

Picard said nothing.

His counterpart accepted that silence as agreement. "I think you are like me. I think you're embarrassed by mistakes. So, the best way to forget those mistakes, *mon cher ami,* is to erase them, *n'est-ce pas?"*

Picard stared straight ahead, giving his counterpart nothing to react to.

"You forget, Jean-Luc," the regent said, as if deeply amused by Picard's lack of response, "I might as well be reading your mind."

Then, with a loud and startling slap, the mirror Picard drew his disruptor, thumbed it to full power so its capacitor hum filled the air, and aimed it directly at the woman.

"And since you don't know this unfortunate, since her continued existence can have no meaning to you other than to remind you of your failings, I'm sure you won't mind if I erase her from existence. Will you?"

The woman looked up, no fear in her eyes.

Only courage.

But then, Picard knew, that was the only reaction to expect from the remarkable woman so loved by James T. Kirk.

TWENTY-TWO

━━━━━━━━━━━━━ ☆ ━━━━━━━━━━━━━

The tossing of the runabout reminded Kirk of old sailing vessels. There was a rhythm to the motion, a pattern to anticipate, accept, and direct.

Flying in these conditions required that he keep his hands on the controls at all time, but he found the activity almost enjoyable.

Doing something—anything—was preferable to waiting. Especially because all that had happened since he had decided on this course of action was the passage of time.

"You like piloting, don't you?" Janeway asked.

She was in the copilot's chair now, spelling Scott. Runabouts were designed for longer journeys than shuttlecraft, and there were bunks in the back, and a small galley. Scott, T'Val, and McCoy were presumably sound asleep, secure in their privacy screens and antigrav bunks.

But Spock and his counterpart seemed to have little use for rest. They remained in the passenger area, engaged in earnest conversation. Kirk had smelled tea an hour ago, and for their sake, he hoped it contained a stimulant. The conversation had been going on for close to thirty hours.

Then again, if, like Intendant Spock, he knew he was facing

264

an irreversible slide into an incurable disease, he supposed he wouldn't have much use for sleep, either.

"Piloting's a lost art," Kirk said. He kept his eyes moving from the sensor screens to the incredible panorama of the plasma storms they flew through. The mirror *Voyager*'s warp-particle trail set the runabout's course, directly into unknown, and unknowable, territory.

It wasn't the first time Kirk had made such a journey. From time to time, when he let his concentration drift, he found himself admitting that sometimes it was the best kind of journey of all.

"You seem to be doing well enough at it," Janeway told him. "Piloting, I mean."

"I've spent my time at the helm." Kirk braced himself as a small shudder made the craft tremble. He compensated before the dampers could, rolling the runabout gently, riding the compression wave out.

"Was that part of your training?" Janeway asked. "To be a starship captain?"

"Part of it. Theoretically, we were trained to be able to do everything that needed to be done on board a starship." He smiled, remembered how full of confidence and bravado he had been at the beginning of his career, certain he could handle a Constitution-class vessel on his own. Who needed a crew? "None of it well, though. Thinking back, the whole point was to learn integration. To know what everyone else's duties were, so we could see how they worked together."

"And did you?"

"Not at first." Kirk watched his hands move across the controls as if they belonged to someone else. Like so many aspects of his training, his piloting skills had returned without conscious thought. A year on Chal and all his best intentions had not been enough to drive the starship captain from the man. He didn't want to think what that might mean.

It was a conversation he would have with Teilani when they reunited.

And they would reunite.

He refused to consider any other eventuality.

"I was thirty-one when I earned my first ship." Even as Kirk said the words, he didn't know how such a thing could ever have been possible. Had he ever really been that young? That naive? That full of wide-eyed innocence? "And back then, I thought I could do everything."

He remembered meeting Chris Pike on the day Pike had been promoted to Fleet captain, and Kirk had been given the *Enterprise*. Kirk had known the ship would be available. After two five-year missions, Pike wanted a change and Kirk wanted that ship. For years he had played the political games behind the scenes at Command. Gone to the right parties, volunteered for the right committees, directed all his duty assignments to that one, inescapable destiny he knew was his.

But the day that long-sought goal had finally been achieved, Kirk had felt anything but prepared. When he had first taken the center chair, with the *Enterprise* in spacedock, with the mysterious Vulcan who would come to be his friend looking menacing at his science station, and the unflappable and soon-to-retire Dr. Piper at his side, Kirk had felt more like an understudy called to the stage without knowing his lines than the captain of a starship.

But somehow, he and his ship and his crew had survived that first shakedown cruise. When the orders had come through for a five-year mission—again, something he had worked toward since graduating the Academy—he had once again felt the faint misgivings of doubt infect him.

But the mission had been completed—the *Enterprise* returning more or less intact; his crew lessened by death, strengthened by experience, united by triumph and sorrow.

Kirk had always taken it as one of the supreme ironies of life that only when he had completed his mission and left the *Enterprise* to become a deskbound admiral had he finally understood what it meant to be a starship captain.

"You can't do it all yourself," Kirk now said, merging their course with the currents of plasma as if the runabout were an extension of his body. "All through the Academy, they burn it into your brain—it's all up to *you*. Everyone's depending on *you*. The captain's got to be the one in front, taking the first shot, firing the first torpedo, being responsible."

"But that's not it?" Janeway asked.

"Being responsible, yes. That's the most important part. But everything else, it's just Starfleet laying down the party line." He glanced at Janeway beside him, and despite the fact that she was an adult, that she had lived and trained and fought as a soldier in a war few people in the Federation would ever have the strength and determination to face, he saw in her eyes that familiar cadet gleam.

For a moment he thought of that child in the field of Chal.

He surprised himself by remembering the child's name.

Memlon.

Eyes wide, curiosity still unbound.

He remembered Teilani asking him what he thought of the child.

Kirk had said the boy needed someone to explain things to him.

You'd be good at that, Teilani had said.

Kirk wondered if that was true. He wondered if he could live up to the quest for knowledge that burned in Janeway.

Because he saw that same hunger for knowledge in her.

She wanted to *know*.

So she could *become* something more.

And there was no question in Kirk's mind what that goal was.

"At the Academy, I struggled with almost all my science classes," Kirk said. "Then they put me on a ship with Spock, and all those science classes amounted to was that for the first few months I had the vocabulary to ask a few questions now and then. If he hadn't been a Vulcan, he probably would have laughed at me for most of them.

"In engineering classes, they taught me how to build a

starship, if I had to, with my own two hands. And then they gave me Scotty. He could build the same starship in his sleep, with *one* hand, in a third the time, with fifty percent fewer pieces, and it would run more efficiently, too."

"So what you're saying is, it all comes down to your crew."

Kirk looked out at the rolling clouds of the storm and thought of his crew. His first crew. His best crew. He saw their faces, heard their names as if a roll call were under way on the hangar deck and a dangerous mission still lay ahead. A mission that only the *Enterprise* could take on.

Spock and McCoy and Scotty were still with him, here in this craft. But Sulu and Chekov and Uhura, wherever the worlds and time had taken them since their missions together, they would always be with him, too, always a part of whatever success the universe had conspired to give him.

It all came down to one simple truth. One simple statement. "You can't be a captain of an empty starship," Kirk said. In life, he knew, there were other truths more important. But in his work, in his career, that was the one above all others.

Then he realized he had been concentrating too much on himself—a tendency of which Teilani had laughingly reminded him, more than once. From his solitary audience's expression, Kirk could see that his insights regarding his Starfleet career were not exactly what she had had in mind as a subject of conversation.

"Do you know the Janeway of this universe?" she asked.

Kirk knew it wasn't the change of subject the question might seem to be. He saw where the question was heading and he left it in Janeway's hands.

"No," he said. "She was after my time. But from everything I've heard about her, I know she's one of the best."

After a moment's silence, Janeway asked, "Is she like me?"

Kirk hoped this Janeway wouldn't hold it against him, but even here, even now, he felt there was no time to waste.

So he gave her the answer he knew she was working toward.

"Kate, there's no doubt in my mind you could be a starship captain. Whatever it is a person needs for that job, in your heart, your mind, your spirit, it's in you, too. Don't forget that."

Janeway rode in silence for many minutes after that. Like Kirk, she watched the ever-changing vista of the plasma fields.

The region they were in now was dominated by waves of deep amber and red.

Kirk remembered the sunset on the holodeck, in the re-creation of Yosemite, when Janeway had tested her environment by kissing him.

He wondered if she was thinking of the same, sharing the memory.

"I hated you, you know," she said out of nowhere.

But again, Kirk looked beneath the words to find their meaning.

"You hated Tiberius."

She threw his own words back at him. "If I'm in any way like your Janeway, then you're the same as Tiberius."

Kirk was silent. She'd voiced something he had not fully grappled with himself. Nor was he ready to yet.

"When T'Val gave me this assignment, I wanted to kill you. Even if you cooperated with us."

Kirk saw a sudden billow of plasma compression heading directly for the runabout, and brought the craft up to skim over top of it. "Since you're telling me all this, I have to assume you've changed your mind."

"If we live through what you're planning, ask me again."

Kirk couldn't look away from the controls, so he couldn't be sure if Janeway was trying to make a joke.

He decided it was time he changed the subject.

"What's Jean-Luc Picard like in your universe?"

Even without seeing her, he could sense the way she tightened at the mention of that name.

"What makes you think he has a counterpart?"

"The way you and T'Val recognized his name. Hold on!"
The runabout seemed to rise up, hang motionless, then drop precipitously. It was all an illusion in the directionless void of space, Kirk knew, brought on by the complex interplay of the artificial gravity and inertial dampers. But it felt as if they were in a small craft in heavy seas, nonetheless.

"Picard's like you," Janeway said, taking Kirk by surprise. "If there were still a Terran Empire, he'd be running it the way you did."

"*Tiberius* was your emperor," Kirk said firmly. "Not me."
He felt Janeway's eyes on him. "You were born in Iowa, weren't you?"

Kirk confirmed it.

"When you were thirteen, you were living in the colony on Tarsus IV."

"It was supposed to be a summer trip," Kirk said, suddenly uncomfortable with her questioning, wondering what any of this had to do with anything. "But there was trouble in the Neutral Zone. I ended up being caught there when the food shipments stopped."

"So you formed a gang. Took over the warehouses. Killed Governor Kodos."

"Not in my reality," Kirk said. "Kodos killed half the colonists to try to make the food last until relief could arrive."

"That's what you told the authorities in my reality, too," Janeway said. "Kodos did it. But it was really you and your gang."

Kirk felt his discomfort begin to turn to anger, and he knew there was no reason for it. "You know the histories of our two universes are different," he told her. "So why are you doing this?"

"Because you're not being truthful," Janeway persisted. "You feed me this great philosophy about trusting in your crew, being part of a team, deferring to the better skills of others, and you say that's what it takes to be a starship captain.

"But I've seen you in action, Kirk. You're not just the person you describe. You're Tiberius, too. Whatever's in you that was in your counterpart, that drove him to be the most corrupt—and the most powerful—emperor of human history, is in you, too. It's only because your historical context was different that you became a starship captain, not a tyrant.

"At your core, you and Tiberius are the same. And you don't have the honesty to admit it."

Shaking off the unwelcome implications of Janeway's argument, Kirk took his eyes off his console and glared at her. "I'm getting tired of people telling me what I really think and who I really am. Don't you think I know myself?"

"No. I don't think you have a clue about who you really are. I think you're closer to Tiberius than you want to believe. And by denying that, you're denying yourself, and any chance you might be someone different."

Kirk felt his pulse begin to race, knew his face was flushing. How dare this woman, this refugee from a war zone with no personal skills that were remotely apparent, attack him in this way?

"You don't know what you're saying," Kirk told her, jaw clenched, holding his temper in check only by a force of will.

"I studied you in school, you know," Janeway told him, as if her buried anger were the equal of his own. "And you can't hide behind platitudes of being part of . . . of one big happy Fleet."

If not for Teilani, Kirk would have left his controls to finish this unsettling confrontation with Janeway. And as if sensing the tension that had developed on the flight deck, Spock was suddenly behind Kirk, one hand on the back of his pilot's chair, looking ahead through the viewports.

"My counterpart and I could not help but notice the rather intense conversation you appear to be having," Spock said calmly.

"It isn't a conversation," Kirk told him. "It's a series of groundless accusations."

"It's a series of truthful observations," Janeway insisted.

"In any event," Spock said, and Kirk sensed the Vulcan's desire to change the subject if only to maintain proper piloting efficiency, "in our conversations, my counterpart and I appear to have identified the period of history in which our two universes may have diverged. It is a fascinating prospect."

Kirk instantly abandoned his growing resentment of Janeway's probing, and, just as quickly, she appeared to set her argument aside.

"Well, what is it, Spock? Where does the branching point lie?"

"As best as we can determine," Spock said, "approximately three hundred years ago, when—"

And then alarms blared and the runabout shuddered as the first torpedo hit, and the *Starship Voyager* rose up in the forward viewports, phasers already firing.

TWENTY-THREE

───────────── ☆ ─────────────

"Don't kill her," Picard said.

In the bleak interior of the overseers' barracks, his mirror counterpart kept his disruptor pointed at the woman in silk. But he looked back with interest at Picard. "Is that a general plea for mercy, symptomatic of the invertebrate worms you Terrans have become in this reality? Or do I detect a *soupçon* of recognition in your tone?"

Picard steeled himself. He was prepared to play his counterpart's game, no matter how demeaning, if he could save this woman's life.

"Her name is Teilani," he said.

His counterpart twirled his disruptor around his finger, then dropped it, grip facing backward, into a low-slung holster. Picard noticed a second disruptor in a matching holster on his counterpart's other leg.

"So," the regent said, "I was right again." He stared critically at Teilani as if the silks she wore were nonexistent, making no attempt to disguise the fact that he regarded her as little more than property. "You do know her."

"We've met," Picard clarified.

His counterpart shook his head. "Such concern with the preciseness of words. Are you all lawyers in your universe?"

Picard decided it was time to address another subject. "Why am I here?"

"Why do you think you're here?"

"So you can gloat."

The regent shrugged. "I can do that anyway. Try again."

Picard looked around the open space of the barracks. Though, to be accurate, it wasn't really a barracks. There were no cots, no facilities for food or waste. Just a bare metal floor and metal walls stamped with Cardassian-designed structural supports. And the one corner furnished with a couch, table, chairs, and cabinets, all of Klingon manufacture. Tall candlesticks of burnished metal stood on the table, caked with melted wax.

"I said, try again," his counterpart repeated.

"You want to question me again."

The regent folded his gloved hands behind his back and walked slowly toward Teilani. "Jean-Luc, I'm so disappointed in you. I have your ship. It does whatever I ask it to. Did you know the quality of our voices is that exact? The degree of correspondence so identical that not even the *Enterprise* computer can tell the difference. I find that fascinating, don't you?"

He bent forward, a finger extended as if to trace Teilani's scar. Her hands came up in what Picard recognized as a Klingon defense posture. It was only then that he saw that her wrists were bound with ODN cable.

The regent leaned away from Teilani as if he had come too close to a flame. Teilani looked beyond him, silent, as if refusing to acknowledge his right to confine her.

"Women don't behave this way in my reality . . . for long," he said lightly, wandering back to Picard as if he had nothing more important to do than engage in idle conversation. "We're much more effective in breaking their spirits. That's why I had to tie her up. Did you know she's tried to kill me seven times since she was brought here. *Seven* times. Your friend, Tiberius, is fortunate to have such a spirited captain's woman. And that scar. The stories it tells . . ."

"Tiberius?" Picard asked.

The regent leaned close, pronouncing the name with sarcastic care. "Kirk. James T. I believe he's a friend of yours."

Picard couldn't waste such a perfect opportunity. He swung his right hand toward the regent's temple, thumb folded so his knuckle would crush the side of the regent's skull.

But the regent's hand was there to grab Picard's in midswing.

"Don't you understand?" the regent said. "There is nothing you can plan, nothing you can even imagine, that I cannot anticipate."

The regent pushed Picard's hand away. "You're a disappointingly pale reflection at best, Jean-Luc. I've skimmed through your tediously pure service record, struggling to keep myself from dozing off at the sterility of it all, and . . . frankly, I'm quite let down that you're my counterpart."

"I am appalled that you are mine."

But the regent went on as if he hadn't heard Picard. "Now, Teilani. She has no counterpart in the *real* universe. I suppose she did at one point. But when the Romulans were in retreat, and tried to activate the Children of Heaven on Chal as part of a most ineffectual last stand . . . well, what could the Alliance do but wipe out her planet? The planetary sea boiled for weeks, I'm told. It took a month for everyone to perish from the heat." He looked at her again, this time making no effort to disguise his desire for her. "A shame to have lost another one such as her. A few years in a Theta camp, and *she* would have been much more . . . compliant. As this one shall discover, with my help." He smiled at Teilani.

Teilani spit in the regent's eye.

Unconcerned, Picard's counterpart removed a folded cloth

from the cuff of his glove and wiped his face clean, as if he were dabbing at sweat and Teilani no longer existed.

"Is there some reason for my being here?" Picard asked, hoping to distract the regent's attention.

The regent studied Picard, and Picard wasn't sure if it was a prelude to his being beaten, or if there was indeed something important on his counterpart's mind, which he had yet to reveal.

"What was it like for you to have a brother?" the regent asked.

Though nonplussed by the question, Picard saw no need to evade it. Every moment's delay was a moment closer to his crew's attempt to retake the *Enterprise.*

"Fulfilling," Picard said, thinking of Robert. "Sometimes exasperating. But . . . it serves to bind a family. A united front against the progression of time."

"And what would your brother have thought of me, the real Picard?"

"I wouldn't know," Picard said coldly. "Robert is dead."

Clearly, the regent was prepared for that revelation. "You assassinated him?"

"He died in a fire," Picard said.

"Which you set, of course?"

Picard's jaw tightened. He still saw no point to these questions. "It was an accident."

The regent nodded sagely. "Clever. That's what I said when I killed my Robert. An accident. It was simpler that way. And his daughter? Your niece. What happened to her?"

Picard's hands became fists as he fought to remain unreactive in the face of this sadism. "Robert had a son. René. He died in the same fire."

The regent rubbed thoughtfully at the back of his head, making his long queue of hair sway back and forth. He appeared puzzled. "A son . . . a son . . . that's different. Your Robert, he married Louise?"

"His wife's name is . . . was Marie."

The regent gestured with empty hands. "Well, then, there you go. The universes continue to diverge. I can't be certain, but I would guess that whoever this . . . this Marie is, or was, in your universe, she doesn't exist in mine. So your brother's history is different here. Different children, different fates. Another few generations, and I doubt there will be any counterparts left. At least, among Terrans. Do you agree that's a likely progression?"

"Why am I—"

Picard never got a chance to finish the question, because the back of his counterpart's gloved hand smashed across his face.

"I did not give you permission to question me, Jean-Luc. Now answer *my* question. In three generations, will there or will there not be any counterparts left among the Terran race?"

As the pain faded from Picard's face, and he saw the spittle spray from his counterpart's lips, he realized in one chilling moment that he was no longer dealing with a sadistic soldier. He was facing someone who was truly insane—one whose next move even he might not be able to predict. No matter how much he and this creature outwardly resembled one another.

Carefully, Picard chose his words. "If the conditions you've described exist throughout your universe, I would say you were correct."

"Good! Good! You don't know how long I've been trying to make this point to the Alliance. If we want to invade this alternate reality, enslave its population, employ its technology, then we must act now!" The regent abruptly stepped closer to Picard to stroke his cheek with compassion. "Did I injure you? I could call a doctor."

"I'm fine." Picard kept his tone unemotional, but within he recoiled from his counterpart's touch. *Invade. Enslave.* Whoever these people were, they weren't the self-absorbed Alliance described in the *Deep Space Nine* logs. These vandals wanted nothing more to do with their universe—and everything to do with his.

"That's the spirit," the regent said. He began to wander away again and as he turned his back, Picard risked meeting Teilani's gaze.

And in her dark eyes he saw the same terrible knowledge.

Their lives were in the hands of a madman.

"So . . . to continue, you killed your brother to gain control of the family shipping line," the regent said.

"With your permission, Regent," Picard said politely, "in my reality, the Picard family business is a vineyard."

"Really? How very interesting. In France, I take it?"

"That's right."

"Well, if there were still a France on Earth, no doubt that would have been my family business as well." He scratched at his chin, then stared at his right-hand glove as if seeing it for the first time. "Here, look at this. I know you'll appreciate it."

Picard watched in confusion as his counterpart peeled off his heavy Klingon glove, then held up the back of his right hand for Picard to examine.

There were three red scars there, as if something sharp had tried to rake the skin from the back of his counterpart's hand.

"It looks as if it was painful," Picard said noncommittally.

"Oh, it was, it was. She did the same to my face." He leaned forward to point to his lower left eyelid. "Nearly tore this off. I had a Vulcan healer restore it, though. Odd, those Vulcans. We destroyed their world and their culture, but if one of them is a doctor, they'll cure anyone."

Picard's counterpart shook his head at the absurdity of the universe, both of them. Then continued.

"But I had him leave the scars on the back of my hand. A souvenir of sorts." He looked directly at Picard. "From Beverly Crusher."

Picard stiffened. He had just seen Beverly a few minutes ago. She had seemed fine. But could it be possible that—

The regent waved his hand dismissively. "Not *your* Beverly Crusher. The *real* one. Honestly, Jean-Luc, you flatter yourself."

The regent moved back to Teilani, walked around her, hands behind his back. "My Beverly, ahh, there was a woman. Trained as an apprentice to a Vulcan healer. There were always suspicions about her, though. Was she working for the Terran resistance? Was she working for the Vulcan resistance? The smart Terrans always face that kind of innuendo.

"But I took a fancy to her. Saw there was something there. Unawakened passion. Fires only my love could provoke and quench. Like you and your Beverly, don't you think?"

Picard refused to give this monster any power over him. "I have no such relationship with Dr. Crusher."

The regent smiled archly. "That's what you say now. But if I brought her here, draped her in Argelian silks, held a disruptor to her head . . . I wonder what you'd say then, hmm?"

The regent moved as if to touch Teilani's scar again, but quickly withdrew his hand as she shifted stance to strike him. He smiled as if he enjoyed the game.

"Getting back to my Beverly. The moment I saw her in the camp, I had no doubt. She *was* going to be mine."

Picard felt momentarily sickened. Hadn't there been a time in his past when he had thought exactly that of Beverly? That they would be together no matter what?

"So, I did what any young swain in love would do. I set out to win her. And, at first, it went well. I challenged Jack Crusher to a duel. Fought him to the death, and won, of course. All his possessions, including Beverly, then became mine. But . . . you know Beverly, single-minded to a fault, her pretty head full of her own ideas. She actually took some exceptions to the Alliance's property laws as they applied to Terrans."

The regent made a fist of his right hand, studied his own

scars there. "I don't want to bore you, but I had to dispense with her, as well. On our wedding night, no less. At least, when it was over. I regretted it. I had been so certain I could win her over in time. But . . . you of all people will understand this, Jean-Luc, my honor was at stake, and I am a regent of the Klingon Dependencies. There're not a lot of Terrans who have risen to that station. I'm under a great deal of pressure."

Picard had had enough of this monster's rantings. He wanted no more knowledge of the hideously distorted reflection the mirror universe had become.

In his mind, he paced off the distance between himself and his counterpart. Three quick steps, a running leap, and then all he would have to do was unholster one disruptor before his counterpart could draw the other.

But without even looking at him, his counterpart said, "You'll never make it, Jean-Luc. And all that will happen is you'll get to watch me punish Teilani for your transgression. Very slowly and very thoroughly."

"Punish me?" Teilani said proudly. "You haven't even been able to put a hand on me since I came here. You're a coward, Regent. A pathetic Terran puppet whose masters only let him dress up in the uniform of a real warrior."

Picard saw the dark red blotches that rose to stain his counterpart's face as he drew a disruptor.

"Teilani," Picard cautioned.

But the regent faced Picard instead of the woman. "Oh, don't worry, Jean-Luc. She still has her uses, alive. The Alliance has something quite special planned for the consort of Tiberius."

Then he swung his disruptor around to aim at Picard. "You, on the other hand, have no purpose to serve other than to amuse me. But you don't amuse me, anymore. You *repel* me."

"How can I," Picard asked, knowing his life was in the balance, "when I *am* you?"

The regent paused. *"You* are actually comparing yourself to *me?"*

"Whatever we are, somewhere inside each of us is the kernel of the other."

Picard was relieved to see that he seemed to have captured his counterpart's interest.

"You mean to say, you are willing to admit that somewhere deep in the darkest recesses of your heart, you could be a killer? Captain Jean-Luc Picard of Starfleet, a merciless Klingon warrior regent?"

"If conditions were right," Picard said. And to his dismay, he believed that to be true. *"And,* by the same regard, somewhere in you is the capacity to be a peaceful scientist, an explorer. A diplomat."

The regent remained motionless, as if somehow those words had struck a chord in him.

"You mean to say, if conditions were right, I might also have become a starship captain, as you did?"

Picard tried to reel his counterpart in, to build a connection. "That's right. I believe that is so."

The regent hung his head in deep thought. "Just . . . one small matter, though."

Picard could feel the rapport growing stronger. He *knew* he could win this man to his side.

But then his counterpart looked up, his eyes a dark window into fathomless chaos. "Thanks to you, I already *am* a starship captain." Then he laughed, and Picard felt a chill even through the stifling heat of his heavy discharge suit.

"Ah, Jean-Luc," the regent said when he had wiped the last tear of mirth from his eyes with his free hand. "You're so transparent to me. Allow me to give you another example of how ineffectual you are. Screen on."

At the far end of the chamber, a virtual viewscreen flickered into life. Picard recognized the technology. It had first been used in *Deep Space Nine,* and now was a standard feature of the newest starships, including the *Enterprise.*

"You recognize what you're seeing?" the regent asked.

The most recognizable parts of the image were the color-streaked ripples of the plasma storms surrounding the twin asteroids. At the bottom of the screen, Picard could also see an expanse of bare asteroid. But he couldn't tell what scale the image was on. He might be looking at a few square meters, or an expanse kilometers wide.

"It's the edge of the asteroid," Picard said.

The regent clapped his hands. "Very *good,* Jean-Luc. I knew you'd be paying attention." He beamed at his prisoner. "That is why you're here, you know. I mean, in this facility, at this time."

Picard didn't understand.

The regent was only too happy to explain.

"You see, when we took over the *Enterprise* that first time, we knew we wouldn't get to you fast enough to maintain command and control of the vessel. So we set up a game. And we know how I—you—love games. Dixon Hill, for you, isn't it? Holodeck mysteries. Such a demeaning waste of time for someone of our—your—abilities.

"So we led you through a scenario as clever as anything *Monsieur* 'Dix' might have encountered, and you gave us the *Enterprise* on a dilithium platter."

Picard couldn't help himself. "You won't keep it."

The regent was gleeful. "Careful. You're almost giving away your secret plans. And you do have secret plans, don't you? For escape, I mean. Escape and the recapture of the *Enterprise.*"

Picard looked away.

"Look at that," the regent said with real joy. "You can't even meet my eyes. That's because I knew what you would be thinking. One or two days to get the measure of the camp. Another day for your Beverly to work out some way of identifying which members of your crew were from your reality, and which were counterparts, and then a plan.

"It's breathtaking, I'm sure. Dynamic. Exciting. And prob-

282

ably a very good one. In fact, if it were up to me—and in a way, you know, it *is* up to me—today would be the day I would put that plan into action."

The regent stood close to Picard, stared at him intently even though Picard continued to look away. "You can't lie to me, Jean-Luc. Even if you say nothing. Because I know you the way . . ." He held out his scarred hand. ". . . the way Beverly knew the back of my hand."

The regent put his glove back on, hiding his wounds. "Your plans were for today, and you can't deny it. And regardless, the plans won't work, because we've captured your co-conspirators." He held his hand to his mouth as if whispering an aside. "I'd really watch the screen if I were you. It's your last chance to say good-bye. . . ."

Picard looked at the screen and recoiled.

It was as if he were twenty meters away from the events unfolding on the asteroid's surface.

Riker, La Forge, Beverly, Deanna, even Data wrapped in glowing induction coils to sap his android strength—each member of his senior staff stood in a line on the asteroid's surface. A few meters behind them, a firing squad of Cardassians in formation, disruptor rifles held at ease.

"Do I have your attention?" the regent asked.

Picard knew there was no more time for posturing or game-playing. If he was going to be able to outmaneuver his counterpart, he would have to do it quickly, without pretense.

"Let them go. They had nothing to do with it."

"Correction," his counterpart said. "They *will* have nothing to do with it."

"You accomplish nothing by killing them!"

"An interesting idea, but, on the contrary, they could serve as a lesson for the rest of your crew. I mean, I don't know exactly how many of them we ended up with here, but it's more than a thousand. So we execute a few dozen here and there—your senior staff, a few others just at random to keep everyone guessing—and experience tells us that eventually we'll end up with three or four hundred loyal workers who won't dream of risking their lives to escape.

"That's what I'd do, Jean-Luc. Tell yourself that what you're about to witness isn't really punishment. It's the beginning of a long process of conditioning for those who survive."

Picard heard the click of a communicator, and the regent slipped a small, cylindrical object from his belt. An amber light glowed atop it as he spoke into it.

"Picard here, go ahead."

The voice that answered was Cardassian, broken up by subspace static—the effect of this region of space.

"The prisoners have been assembled at the edge of the atmospheric screen," the voice reported. "We await your orders."

The regent stared at Picard. "Fear me," he said, "and you might live."

Picard leapt at him.

The regent drew his disruptor as swiftly as if he had anticipated Picard's move by seconds.

But before the regent could fire, his aim was deflected by an expertly thrown candlestick.

Teilani.

She had been ready for Picard to make his move.

Picard slammed into his counterpart's chest, head driving into the man's stomach, forcing him backward.

They rolled across the floor and Picard heard the welcome clatter of the regent's communicator cylinder hitting the floor and bouncing away.

Picard locked his hands around his counterpart's neck.

"You're not a killer," the regent said.

Picard squeezed.

". . . never . . . do it . . ." his counterpart croaked.

But Picard wouldn't relinquish his grip. Even more, he raised the regent's head and smashed it against the floor, again and again until the regent's eyes rolled up and showed only their bloodshot whites.

Then Picard felt a hand on his shoulder.

He twisted around, ready to continue the fight.

But saw only Teilani.

For an instant, her exotic beauty was unnerving. She did not belong in this place of death.

The regent moaned and Picard felt his counterpart's body slump beneath him. He looked up at Teilani, trying not to be distracted by the thin silks that passed as her clothing.

"Teilani, why did they bring *you* here?"

"I don't know," she said as she looked around the chamber. "I think I'm an insurance policy. They wanted to keep James from becoming involved."

"Jim? He's here?" Picard got to his feet.

"If I know him, he will be." Then Teilani's eyes made contact with something across the floor.

Teilani moved swiftly to retrieve the regent's communicator. The amber light was flashing. Its tiny speaker kept clicking in the equivalent of a comm badge's chirp.

Teilani returned with the small device, then handed it to Picard. "If the *Enterprise* thinks that maniac is you, why not see if those Cardassians think you're him?"

Picard checked the communicator, found the activate switch, tapped it on. He looked at Teilani as he spoke into the communicator. "Picard here. The prisoners are not to be killed. I need them for further interrogation. Return them to me." As he waited for a reply, his eyes asked Teilani for her reaction to his effort.

"You sounded like him to me," she whispered. "Good to see you again, by the way. Did James ever thank you for that horse?"

Picard was struck by the surrealness of the moment, until the communicator clicked again.

"Regent Picard," a Cardassian voice said, "I remind you that the prisoners were brought to the forcefield perimeter not to be killed, only tortured. Thus, according to your instructions, I must assume you have fallen victim to a Terran escape attempt. Unless you provide the authentication code in seven seconds, the prisoners will be killed."

Picard tapped the communicator again, responded as if he shared his counterpart's fury. "Those orders were rescinded, you fool. Return the prisoners for further interrogation or *you* will be killed."

"You gave me those orders yourself," the Cardassian replied. "Five seconds."

Picard thrust the communicator into Teilani's hands, leaned down and grabbed his counterpart by the neck and snapped his head up.

"Wake up," Picard growled as he slapped the regent, hard. "I need the authentication codes."

But as the regent's eyes flickered open and Picard saw the dawning of awareness in him, all he did was look to the side. To the screen.

"Time is up," the Cardassian announced.

On the screen, one of the Cardassians to the side of those with the rifles made an adjustment to a control padd.

Picard straightened up as he saw a wall of sparkling blue energy form before his senior staff.

It was the atmospheric forcefield, he knew. The equivalent of the low-power energy screen that covered the open door of a shuttlebay, to keep atmosphere in while allowing shuttles to come and go freely.

Picard saw his people react to the screen's sudden appearance before them.

And then he saw them draw back as the screen moved toward them, skimming over the smooth metal ground until, with a series of sparks and flashes, it had passed over them.

"No . . ." Picard said as he saw his senior staff, save for Data, reach for their throats, grimacing as the sudden vacuum of space sucked their last breaths from their bodies.

Riker staggered. La Forge dropped to the ground.

"Save them!" Picard shouted at his counterpart who lay grinning up at him.

The regent's voice was weak but triumphant. "They're already dead, Jean-Luc. And this time, *you* are the one who killed them."

TWENTY-FOUR

☆

Kirk pushed the *St. Lawrence* to maximum warp, and the *Voyager* slipped to the side faster than the human eye could follow.

But the starship's phasers tore at the runabout's shields and a warp-powered torpedo burst aft, sending the small craft spinning into a violent plasma field that picked her up and tossed her aside like flotsam on a storm-driven sea.

Kirk fought the controls as he brought the *St. Lawrence* into trim. Nothing mattered except stabilizing the craft—without a steady orientation, none of her weapons could find their targets.

Kirk corrected himself.

There were no more weapons.

The *St. Lawrence* was out of torpedoes. Only phasers remained.

And what good were a runabout's phasers against the state of Starfleet's art?

As the chase began, everything in the runabout's cabin seemed to happen at once, but Kirk focused only on the flight controls.

"She's in pursuit!" Janeway said. Kirk could hear the

urgency in her, but was pleased that he could detect no sense of panic.

"Shields at twenty-three percent," the computer stated. "Warp-core imbalance in progress."

Then a loud rush of compressed gas exploded in Kirk's ear. An automatic fire-control system came online to extinguish a sudden eruption of flames. Thankfully, the intervention cut off the shrill blare of the fire alarm, though smoke still swirled through the small cabin, as if the plasma storms had penetrated the viewports.

"What the blue blazes is goin' on?" Scott shouted from the aft.

It seemed the sleeping passengers had finally awakened.

"Warp-core imbalance!" Kirk answered. "We've got to keep the generator online and stable! Do it, Scotty!"

Kirk heard the crash of the engine compartment panel being thrown to the side behind him and knew Starfleet's best engineer was on the job.

"Who the hell's after us *this* time?" McCoy asked, stumbling forward from the far aft where the bunks were.

"Voyager," Kirk and Janeway said at the same time.

"Isn't she on our side?"

"The mirror *Voyager,* Bones," Kirk explained.

Then the runabout swung port as another eruption of phased energy blasted at her shields. The *Voyager* was closing and her aim had been perfect.

Kirk saw the power display graph on the console instantly drop to zero, even as the computer reported, "Shields have failed."

"We can't take another hit," Janeway said through clenched teeth.

"Then we better not let them hit us," Kirk told her.

"They're powering up . . ." Janeway warned.

With a slap of his hand, Kirk took the acceleration safeguards offline and threw the runabout into a ninety-degree turn as a streak of phaser fire blazed past her, a clean miss.

The structural-integrity alarms roared like a foghorn. Kirk knew he was forcing the runabout to perform well past her design limitations and, as he had expected it might, the computer took exception to his maneuver. "Warning! Hull buckling in starboard storage chamber."

Kirk tracked the *Voyager* on his sensor screen. The big ship didn't have the maneuvering capabilities the runabout had and needed more space to complete a turn. It was the only thing that was giving him an edge.

"Spock! Seal off that storage chamber! Scotty, I need maximum warp!"

"And I need a vacation!" Scott yelled back.

Janeway kept Kirk apprised of the *Voyager*'s status. "Phasers powering up again . . . two torpedoes launched!"

Kirk didn't stop to think. The torpedoes couldn't hit. The phasers couldn't hit. He had to offer them another target.

He flipped open the safety cover in the center of the console and punched the first antimatter-pod jettison control.

Behind him, Scott cried out in surprise as the warp core suddenly lost half its fuel and the imbalance went critical without warning.

The runabout lurched forward as one of her antimatter pods sped back into her wake.

Then the craft shuddered and creaked as Janeway shouted: "Impact!"

Kirk checked the screen. Both torpedoes had locked on to the nearest target—the antimatter pod—and both had detonated, creating an energy screen that shielded the runabout from the phaser fire.

Janeway stared at Kirk in awe. "Where did you learn that trick?"

"It wasn't a trick until it worked. Scotty? How's that warp balance?"

"That all depends," Scott yelled back over the incessant alarms. "D'ye intend t' leave me any antimatter to keep us in warp?"

"We've got one pod left, Scotty. Use it or lose it."

A hum of power thrummed through the craft.

"Warp is back online!" Scott called out.

But was it enough?

Janeway started another countdown. *"Voyager* is powering up!"

So Kirk forced the runabout to maximum warp without a run-up—just as the *Voyager's* phasers hit.

He rocked back in his seat as his controls overloaded and sparked, then caught fire with a power surge.

But through the heat and the flames he kept his hands pressed against the acceleration controls, holding his breath against the billowing smoke, crying out to distract himself from the startling pain that seared his hands, his forearms, crackling up his arms like lightning.

"Distance!" he shouted, fearing his request was little more than a guttural snarl.

"Forty thousand . . ." Janeway read out. *"Fifty thousand kilometers! We're clear! We're clear!"*

But Kirk was unable to disengage his hands from the controls, as if they had been fused there.

He felt others grab him, by his shoulders and his arms, pulling him back. He was yanked off his chair, into T'Val's firm grasp.

Both Spocks were beside her, looking down at Kirk in disbelief for what he had done.

The *St. Lawrence* had survived. Against impossible odds.

But at what cost?

McCoy already had his tricorder out.

Shuddering, Kirk held up his hands.

Saw the white of bone. Fine threads of red blood. Charred flesh. His ruined hands and forearms had the texture of a deeply fissured dry lake bed. One thumb was unmarked. He stared at its unchanged familiarity.

Mercifully, McCoy sprayed his wounds with something cool and his pain diminished, at least on the surface.

"Oh, shit," Janeway said.

Kirk looked forward in time to see the monstrous mass of an almost spherical asteroid rise up from within the plasma clouds.

"Warning! Collision alert. Collision alert. Contact in eight seconds . . . seven . . . six . . ."

And then Kirk was thrown from T'Val's grip as the runabout dropped wrenchingly to impulse and pulled up savagely, knocking both Spocks back into the passenger compartment.

Scott's voice rose in complaint about the unexpected company but Kirk pulled himself up to look past Janeway, lifting his weight by pressing his elbows against the empty pilot's chair.

Janeway had transferred flight control to her own, undamaged console and was handling the runabout like a born pilot.

The crater-strewn surface of the asteroid raced ahead and below them. Kirk read from the sensors that they were at ten meters' altitude.

At this velocity, that altitude was insane.

"Bring us up," he instructed her.

But she refused his order. "This is where the *Voyager*'s warp trail was taking us," she said. "If we move too far away from the asteroid's surface and they're out there, we're target practice."

The runabout swayed as Janeway forced it into a tight curve around a sudden uprising from the asteroid.

"This is where that labor camp has to be," she said. "You were right."

Kirk ached to get back on the runabout's controls. But both his hands were numb. Useless. For an instant, all he saw before him was the crude, biomechanical hand that T'Val wore. Is that what his fate would be? What if he were never able again to truly feel the satin smoothness of Teilani's skin, to . . . He refused to dwell on what might wait for him. To reach that future, he would first have to survive this nightmarish present.

"Drop back on your speed," he told Janeway. "If there's a labor camp on this asteroid, they'll have defenses. Go to forward scanning."

The runabout crested a curve on the asteroid and the computer alerted them again.

"Warning: Impact with atmospheric forcefield in fifteen seconds."

Kirk blinked as the life-sign display in the sensor screen went off the scale. "What the hell is down there?"

The life-sign mass index showed a conglomerate of more than two thousand individuals, so closely packed together that individual resolution was impossible at this speed and range.

Suddenly, Kirk felt elation. His hypothesis had been born out. They had found it—the labor camp where the Alliance kept their Terran prisoners to disassemble starships. The camp where Janeway had been destined to work.

Provided, Kirk knew, those life signs were for humans and Vulcans, and not Klingons and Cardassians. He didn't want to think what might happen if instead of a prison camp they had discovered a bivouac area for Alliance warriors.

With his one uninjured thumb, Kirk reached forward and readjusted the sensor selectivity. "We have to find out who those people are."

"Warning: Impact with atmospheric forcefield in ten seconds."

The life-sign sensors recalibrated themselves.

An alert window flashed red.

"What's that?" Janeway asked.

"Dying," Kirk said as he read the sensor return. "We've got four humanoids . . . at the edge of the forcefield. . . ."

"Too late," Janeway said. "I've got to change course."

"No! Hold position!" Kirk looked into the aft compartment. "Scotty! I need you on the emergency transporter!"

"I've only got two hands and this warp core isn't going to stay together much longer!"

"Spock—four humanoids! Just outside the forcefield. We have to get them aboard!"

"I'm picking up the *Voyager!*" Janeway announced. "She's going to have us in range in less than two minutes if I stop for a beam-up!"

"I don't care!" Kirk said. "We'll beam them up and be gone before—"

Another alarm screamed. How could such a small craft have so many alarms?

"What the hell is *that* one?" Kirk demanded.

"That's the mass detector you set!" Janeway told him. "The *Sovereign*'s coming around from the other side of the asteroid!" She took her eyes off the controls just long enough to look challengingly at Kirk. "They've got us in a pincer!"

But Kirk would not be deflected. He needed to be sure about that camp and it was certain he wasn't going to be taking up a standard orbit to scan it at his leisure.

"Beam them up, Spock!"

Spock stood at a wall panel, pushed his fingers up a familiar control surface. "Energizing."

"We have sensor lock!" Janeway shouted. "The *Sovereign* is closing."

Kirk looked back to see two huddled forms resolve from the transporter effect. For a moment, he felt relief. They were in Starfleet uniforms, human, still moving. They were gasping for breath but alive.

And then he was startled as he recognized them.

"Commander Riker? Dr. Crusher?"

But whatever surprise Kirk felt, it was only a fraction of the shock he saw in the eyes of Picard's crew.

Riker spoke first, not even bothering to acknowledge Kirk. And Kirk knew why when he heard what Riker said.

"Geordi and Deanna are down there! And Data!"

"Kirk!" Janeway cried out. "Both ships are coming in range."

But Kirk wasn't going anywhere. "Spock! The next two! Save Data for last! He doesn't need air."

Two more columns of golden energy formed between the runabout's emergency transporter panels. Riker stepped forward to catch Deanna as she materialized and fell, semiconscious. Geordi La Forge was curled on the floor, clutching at his throat, but a quick hypospray of tri-ox from McCoy eased his symptoms at once.

"They're locking phasers . . ." Janeway warned. "The *Voyager* and the *Sovereign*. . . ."

A final column of transporter energy formed.

Data took shape, saw Kirk, and in a most un-android fashion, his mouth dropped open in utter surprise.

"Captain Kirk . . . ?" Janeway said, almost pleading.

Kirk looked to Riker. "Commander—is there any place to hide around here?"

Riker didn't have to think about his answer. "Full impulse—straight through the atmospheric screen, keep an altitude of one kilometer."

Kirk knew Riker well enough not to question his unusual instructions. "Do it!" he said to Janeway.

The runabout's impulse engines began to hum as the craft spun about to face the energy screen.

"What's in there?" Kirk asked.

"I'm not sure exactly what it is," Riker confessed. "But the Alliance isn't going to want to shoot at it, that I guarantee you."

"This is going to get bumpy," Janeway called out. Then, with a rumble and flash of light, the *St. Lawrence* punched through a forcefield never intended to hold back anything but atmosphere, and was suddenly reverberating with the scream of air rushing past her.

Kirk stared ahead, along with everyone else in the crowded runabout.

"Och, that's the *Enterprise,*" Scott said.

"But look what's with it," Riker added. "Can you get a full sensor scan of it?"

Kirk leaned forward and pressed his thumb against the targeting control to focus the main sensors on the strange construction hanging in midair a half-kilometer from the *Enterprise.* At first glance, it seemed to be an open-lattice spacedock. But the equipment panels sent back sensor returns that indicated the panels had functions other than providing light, antigrav manipulation, and communication relays.

And then the *St. Lawrence* whipped past the two enormous structures, starship and unknown device, heading for the other side of the cylindrical forcescreen.

"Any sign of weapons lock?" Kirk asked.

"Nothing," Janeway said. "We're clean. But the *Voyager* and the *Sovereign,* they're circling the forcefield, coming to meet us on the other side."

"Go to warp," Kirk said.

Janeway stared back at him. "I know we're not in a gravity well. But we *are* in an atmosphere. And we don't have shields."

"Trust me," Kirk said. "The runabout's hull is tough enough to take the friction for all the time we'll be cutting through air. But if you wait till we come out of that forcefield, those two starships won't give you the chance to press the warp control."

Janeway turned back even farther, until she saw Scott.

The engineer shrugged. "Ye better not quote me on it, lass. But I'd do what the captain says. It's not as if we'll be around to complain if it doesn't work."

Janeway turned back to her controls. "What factor?"

"The faster we go, the less time we'll spend in the atmosphere," Kirk said.

Janeway cracked her neck, programmed maximum warp. "Engage," she said.

For a split second, everyone but Data grabbed their ears as a deafening shriek blasted through the cabin, but as quickly as that, the noise vanished.

Instead, the runabout rocked gently with the usual buffeting of the plasma storms.

All aboard the *St. Lawrence* sighed with profound relief.

"Are we in any additional danger?" Data asked. Those were the first words he had spoken since beaming aboard.

Janeway checked her controls. "In all this interference, we're out of their sensor range," she said. "The only way the *Voyager* or the *Sovereign* will find us is by luck."

"Good," Data said. "Then I believe I speak for everyone when I say: Will someone please tell me what the hell is going on?"

Kirk grinned at the android. Offered him his hand, then thought better of it. At least until McCoy had had a chance to work on it.

But that didn't stop him from speaking. "Mr. Data, I believe it has fallen upon us to save the universe."

The android took on a bemused expression. "Captain Kirk, coming from you, I would expect no less."

But Geordi La Forge wasn't one to go along with the sudden bout of raised spirits that was shared by everyone else. He looked around the runabout's cabin, fore and aft—panels hanging free, ODN cables dangling, smoke and fire damage visible in almost every square meter. "I just wish we had a bigger ship," he said.

"Don't worry, Commander," Kirk told him. "I have an idea."

"I was afraid you were going to say that," McCoy complained.

But Kirk ignored him.

He and his team had just had their first, full-scale encounter with the Alliance, and had survived.

But the next time, Kirk knew, he had to do more than survive. He had to *win*.

TWENTY-FIVE

Picard drew back his fist to drive it into his counterpart's face hard enough to reach the floor beneath him.

He was going to tear this murderer apart.

But Teilani stopped him.

"Jean-Luc, look!"

Picard forced himself to look back to the virtual viewscreen in the overseers' chamber. He tried unsuccessfully to prepare himself for the horror he knew he would see there.

Riker, La Forge, Beverly, and Deanna, in the vacuum of space, dead of suffocation at Data's feet.

But instead he saw a miracle.

Riker and Beverly were no longer there.

Deanna and La Forge were in the process of disappearing.

Not within disruptor fire, but within the welcome familiar glow of a transporter.

And not just any transporter effect—a *Starfleet* transporter.

"There's another ship . . ." Picard murmured in wonder.

He grabbed the regent, savoring the startled expression his duplicate wore. "There's another Starfleet vessel out there and it just saved my people!"

"Impossible," the regent said.

Picard laughed exultantly, drew out one of his counterpart's two disruptors, flipped it through the air so Teilani could catch it with both, tied-together hands. Then Picard aimed the second disruptor at his duplicate.

"To your feet," he said. "Slowly."

"This signifies nothing, you understand," the mirror Picard told him. "Whatever's happening, it's too late."

"Not while the *Enterprise* is still in this universe," Picard said.

Teilani came to stand beside him. She held out her wrists so Picard could untie them, while at the same time she kept her disruptor trained on the regent.

"That ship won't be here for long," the regent said. "And you know it. I mean, look at yourself, Jean-Luc. Listen to your reaction. You didn't know that other ship was out there. It's all some fluke. Some cosmic accident. Whoever flew by and rescued your people, they don't know what to expect here."

"They will when Riker's finished briefing them." Picard gave a final tug and Teilani's hands came free. She rubbed her wrists.

"Do you have him?" she asked before turning her weapon away from the regent.

Picard centered his disruptor unwaveringly on his duplicate's head. "I just hope he tries to get away."

Then Teilani returned to the oddly furnished section of the chamber—as if this facility were nothing more than an afterthought, a playroom to keep a psychotic human amused.

That probably isn't that far from the truth, Picard thought.

Thrown across one long couch was a length of fabric marked with a monochromatic Klingon design. Teilani pulled the fabric loose, began to fold it into a more demure covering than the silks she wore.

"Keep your eyes on me," Picard said to his counterpart whose gaze had followed Teilani. To underscore his command, he fired a disruptor blast into the floor beside the man.

The mirror Picard locked his eyes on the disruptor's emitter and didn't look away again. Teilani changed in privacy, wiped the garish makeup from her face, and took the Klingon stones from her hair.

But the mirror Picard did not await his fate in silence. "You know, Jean-Luc, each second you keep me here is another hour I'll keep you alive in the agony booth."

"Then I'll be sure to kill you before I go."

Recovered from his initial surprise, the regent once again looked amused. "Go where? Don't you realize you're trapped here? In this chamber. Pay attention, Jean-Luc. Some passing Federation science vessel full of useless Vulcans just transported away five prisoners in full view of their guards. Remember the Cardassians who were out there? They've reported in by now. The overseers already know what's happened. They know that whoever pretended to be me didn't know the authentication codes. If this building isn't surrounded now, it will be within ten seconds."

Also fully recovered from Picard's earlier attack, the regent now got easily to his feet and held out his hand. "Give me the disruptors, Jean-Luc. In return, I'll put in a good word, use my influence. Kirk's woman will die cleanly, and you . . . well, I'll make it as fast as I can. A few hours at most."

That's when Teilani shot him.

The disruptor blast hit the regent square in the chest, flashed red, then drove him halfway across the chamber, where he finally came to a stop in a crumpled heap, like a discarded toy.

Teilani squinted at the side of the disruptor, frowned, then held it up to Picard. "Was this set for stun?"

Picard read the tiny Klingon inscriptions beside the power display. "It appears so."

"Too bad," Teilani said coolly.

She shoved the disruptor into the makeshift belt she had fashioned from a strip of cloth, draped elegantly across her hips. Though the new apparel she had created from the cloth on the furniture was less revealing than what she had worn before, Picard was beginning to understand why no one had heard anything from Kirk once he had returned to Chal. If Picard were in Kirk's position, he would want to do nothing except keep this woman close, protect her, ensure her—

"Is there a problem?" Teilani asked.

The question served to pull Picard back from his disconcerting reverie.

For a moment, Picard was troubled by what had happened. Usually he was easily able to put issues of male and female attraction aside. Those matters did not belong in Starfleet. At least, not during missions. But in Teilani's alluring presence, he found himself forced to focus on everything but Teilani.

"I'm afraid he's right," Picard said.

"We're surrounded?"

"And they have a deadly effective defense against prison breaks."

Teilani waited for him to explain.

"The atmosphere for the camp is held in place by a forcefield that extends between the asteroids. If the overseers shut off that field, everyone outside dies."

But Teilani reacted to his explanation with suspicion, not horror.

"They marched me across the camp when I arrived," she said. "It was before the *Enterprise* was brought here, but I saw the other workers. I saw the guards. And the guards weren't wearing environmental suits."

Right away, Picard understood the importance of her observation. "If the overseers shut off the forcefield, they have to get word to their guards."

"And that gives us time." Teilani crossed over to the unconscious regent, prodded him, ungently, with her foot. He moaned, but didn't stir. "Was he right about you having an escape plan?"

And at that seemingly innocent question, Picard froze. His counterpart had said Teilani had no counterpart of her own in the mirror universe. But how could he be sure that was true? That she was who she said she was?

Teilani seemed to understand his dilemma. "Before you turn paranoid, I asked about the horse you gave James, didn't I?"

"Idaho Dream?" Picard asked.

"Iowa," Teilani corrected.

Picard moved closer to her, disruptor held loosely, but ready. "You could have tortured the real Teilani to obtain that information."

Teilani looked at him with almost pitying compassion. "The Alliance has your ship, Jean-Luc. What more do they need from you?"

"I don't know."

"Do you know why I would have shot your counterpart instead of you?"

"I don't know that, either."

Teilani crouched down by the regent's still form and pulled his *d'k tahg* knife from its scabbard. "Well, I do." She pressed the hilt release and the outrider blades snicked into position, guaranteeing that any deep-enough wound the knife made could not be closed before the victim bled to death. "The regent was wrong." She gripped the regent's body by the shoulder, and with a surprising display of strength, threw him over on his stomach. "Your people weren't saved by some random Starfleet vessel flying by. No cosmic fluke." She took firm hold of the regent's Klingon-style queue and pulled on it as if she were about to slice his scalp from his skull. "That ship came here for a reason."

"And that would be?" Picard asked, having no idea what she was planning.

"To find me."

She brought the knife down and with a sudden flick, cut off the regent's white queue. Had the mirror Picard been a real Klingon, what Teilani had just done would be a mortal insult, forgivable only by death.

For a moment, Teilani looked at the limp braid as if it were something more intimate she had sliced from the regent's body, then dropped it to the floor.

Picard suddenly realized what she was saying.

"Kirk."

"You know him," Teilani said as she began slicing again at the regent's fringe of white hair, taking it off close to his scalp, but not scraping it away completely. "He went looking for me the moment they told him they had me—as if he'd agree to anything a blackmailer told him. And if anyone was going to find his way through all these plasma storms . . ."

Picard nodded. He had no doubt. "It would be Jim Kirk."

"So he's out there right now, hiding in all the plasma-storm interference, talking to the people he rescued, trying to figure out a way to get down here and save the rest of you. And you—at least according to your counterpart—have figured out a way to get back on board your ship."

She flipped the regent over again, and used the knife to attack the wavy white hair at his temples. Except for its length, Picard saw that his duplicate's hair grew in the same scalp pattern his own hair did. A legacy from his father, he knew. Their fathers. A pattern encoded in his genes in both universes.

Picard decided he had nothing left to lose. If this remarkable consort of Kirk's had been a mirror-universe counterpart, then she was right—she could have killed him at any time.

Thus, he accepted her as the Teilani he had known in his universe. And tried not to think how much he wanted to protect her—almost a compulsion. It was a reaction to the tension of the moment, he decided. Of the whole situation.

"My counterpart was right," Picard admitted. "My people are ready to retake the ship at the end of this shift."

"Is there something special about that timing? He seemed to think so."

"Whatever device they're building up there, I'm convinced

it's what they're going to use to transfer the *Enterprise* to the mirror universe. When we were brought here, the crossover device was long enough to accommodate the *Voyager*. By the end of the next shift, it will be long enough for the *Enterprise*."

Teilani held the regent's head up to admire her tonsorial efforts. With his duplicate's fringe of white hair now close-cropped to the sides and the back of his head, Picard saw that the degree of resemblance between himself and his counterpart was even more pronounced.

"You'll have to get your people to move faster than you planned," Teilani said. "Before the guards can drop the atmosphere."

She was right, Picard knew. And fortunately, from the beginning of his planning, he had already devised a contingency signal in case something like this happened and everyone had to move ahead of schedule.

"I need to reach the overseers' command post," Picard said. Once there, he could send the coded signal that would let his people know that time was of the essence.

"And once James sees your escape attempt in progress, he'll come in to help everyone get away."

Picard knew she was right about that, too. Between the two of them, Kirk in space and Picard on the ground, both working together, the Alliance didn't have a chance.

"So," Picard said, "it seems the only thing left to do is figure a way past the guards undoubtedly surrounding this building, so I can reach the command post." He looked around the chamber, checking for any sign of secret passages or weapons storage lockers.

Teilani let go of the regent and his head dropped back to thud against the floor. "I've already got a way," she said, moving closer to Picard.

"Let's hear it."

"Good," Teilani said. "First thing you have to do—take off your discharge suit."

Picard stared at her, certain he had misheard.

But Teilani folded her arms impatiently. "You know, James told me you could be like this, but believe me, this isn't the time to get all proper. I want that suit and all your clothes off, *now,* Jean-Luc. And I don't like to be kept waiting."

Picard reached for the suit seals at his neck. He had no idea what was going to happen next, but he did as he was told.

TWENTY-SIX

───────────── ☆ ─────────────

There were eleven passengers on the crowded runabout, and Kirk was fully aware that ten of them—nine plus an android—were staring at him in utter incomprehension.

So he went back to the beginning and said it again.

"I need a starship. It's the only way we can make this work."

"Captain," Scotty finally said. *"Jim,* there's only one word for it. Ye're *daft."*

"It does appear to be a more descriptive term for your strategy than 'illogical,'" Spock said.

The mirror Spock regarded his counterpart with equanimity. "Though 'illogical' certainly obtains in this instance."

"Indeed," Spock agreed.

McCoy was next to hold forth. "And your hands, Jim. So you get on board, and then what? It's going to take months to get your fingers working again."

"Weeks, at least," Dr. Crusher amended.

"And what if the programming isn't in place?" La Forge said, adding his voice to those against. "You'll be standing there with your . . . your gel packs in your hands while the Cardassians blow disruptor holes in you."

But Kirk wasn't swayed. He looked from one to the other of

those who stood before him. His gaze stopped on Deanna Troi. Her lustrous dark eyes held his, as if trying to communicate some secret fact known only to the two of them.

"You have something to say, Deanna?" Kirk prompted.

Deanna addressed herself to the others. "Only that I feel immense confidence in the captain. No matter what our objections, he is certain he can make his plan work."

"Taking a starship with only a broken-down runabout. It's suicide," McCoy said. "Plain and simple."

Kirk waited to see if anyone else had something to add. No one did. He spoke again.

"Computer, given the passenger load of this craft, and the damage she has sustained in recent action, how long will her life-support system continue to function?"

"Total life-support failure will occur in seventeen hours, fifteen minutes."

"The nearest starbase is weeks away at the top speed we can manage," Kirk said. "And I guarantee any distress call we put out once we're clear of the plasma storms will bring the *Sovereign*—before any other vessel gets a chance to hear it. So the way I see it, it's suicide if we *don't* do anything."

Exasperated, Scott ran a hand through his hair, succeeding only in making it stand on end. His good-natured face was streaked with soot and he looked exhausted from all his efforts to make the *St. Lawrence* last even this long. "Captain, even if everything ye hope for is true, it's the gettin' aboard that's . . . that's impossible. I mean, the maneuvers you're talking about, even Sulu couldna have handled them in his heyday. No human could."

Kirk had no argument with that. "I agree, Mr. Scott. No human could possibly do what I'm suggesting. But in case you haven't noticed, Starfleet is not restricted to humans." He held out his hand to Commander Data.

Scott looked pained. He stared at the android. "When ye start the run to warp factor one, we'll be traveling almost at light speed, ye understand."

Data appeared to be caught off guard. "My positronic net *is* capable of operating within a relativistically accelerated frame of reference for short periods of time. And I have no doubt as to my ability to perform the maneuvers the captain has described. My concern, however, is that this runabout has experienced considerable damage, and may not operate according to manufacturer's specifications."

Scott reacted as if Data had slapped a glove across his face. "Just ignore the dents and the smoke damage, lad, and I guarantee ye she'll outperform her specs any day of the week, and twice on shore leave."

Data shrugged, resigned. "Then, since I have no desire to watch the rest of you succumb to life-support failure, I suggest we do as Captain Kirk has suggested."

McCoy moaned in dismay. The others still looked unconvinced.

So Kirk tried again, knowing that he would soon have to take his strategy out of the realm of suggestion and into the context of a direct order. On this runabout, only Spock outranked him, but Kirk hoped his friend would comprehend that a chance for survival—no matter how slim—was preferable to certain death in just over seventeen hours. He was betting that Spock would support him, logic be damned.

"You heard what Commander Riker said," Kirk told the group. "The guards in the prison camp can shut off the forcefields and the atmosphere will dissipate in less than a minute. So it's not just our lives we're dealing with, here. It's Captain Picard's. It's all your shipmates'. It's the lives of all the other prisoners in the camp."

Kirk paused then, letting that brutal reality sink in, even as he thought of the one life that meant more to him than all the others.

Somewhere within himself, he knew he didn't care about the odds or the chances or the noble admonition to save as many lives as possible.

Once, long ago in his youth, he might have embraced that selfless aspect of his plan.

But not now. Not today.

Because, at this point in his life, after all the incomprehensible horrors he had seen, all the injustices he had watched go unpunished, he had no more stomach for righting the ills of the galaxy.

He had tired of that game, and all he wanted now to do was to go home.

With Teilani.

That was the sum total of what had brought him out to this region of space.

The sum total of why he had dared suggest such a reckless plan.

All he wanted was Teilani.

All he was prepared to do was for Teilani.

If others were saved as a result of those efforts, then he would be the first to be pleased.

But one irreplaceable life had become infinitely precious to him. And he could no longer deny it.

Not here. Not now. Not anymore.

He had to save Teilani and nothing, no one, could stand in his way.

Not even the ten on this dying spacecraft who stared at him in disbelief. Not even his dearest and his oldest friends.

"And the guards," Kirk said, playing his part to perfection, "don't forget the guards *saw* you people from the *Enterprise* being rescued by our transporter." He looked to the mirror Spock. "Intendant, how long do you think it will be before the Alliance guards take measures to prevent a further rescue attempt?"

The mirror Spock considered his shaking hands. The battle endured in the *St. Lawrence* had affected him more than he had revealed, and now the strain of that desperate attempt at self-control was exacting its price from him. "If they have not done so already, then they will take action within the hour. The logic of their rule is overreaction—to make any potential enemy realize that either they must wipe out the Alliance to the last soldier, or be prepared to pay a price beyond all reasonable expectation.

"A world destroyed in retaliation for a ship attacked. A prison camp wiped out in retaliation for five prisoners escaping." The mirror Spock looked up at Kirk. "It is a strategy they learned from you—forgive me—from your counterpart, Tiberius." The Vulcan sighed and Kirk saw Spock regarding his counterpart with grave concern. "Because of what has happened, the people in that camp are already dead. That is the logic of the Alliance."

But Kirk disagreed. "I refuse to accept that. From everything Commander Riker and the others have said, the only purpose that camp has is to allow the *Enterprise* to cross into the mirror universe. The prisoners won't be killed until that happens."

"You're arguing over nothing," Riker said. "The crossover's going to happen today. Captain Picard was convinced of it."

Kirk swept one hand to the side as if to push aside any and all objections to what he had to convince them of. Once again the sight of his hands shocked even him, wrapped as they were in glittering antiseptic bandages that made them look like twisted clubs. "I know this is how you do things in your Starfleet," he continued without a pause, "but we're not debating the best way to study a supernova. I *want* to do this. We *can* do this. We *have* to do this."

He looked each of them in the eye.

"And we have to do it *now.*"

Surprisingly, it was Riker who became the one to turn the tide. He looked at Kirk, then nodded and turned to address his fellow crew members. "Today might not be a good day to die, people, but I for one can't think of another way to save our crew, and our captain. And I know that time is running out."

Kirk acted before anyone else had a chance for second thoughts. He stood up, Janeway following suit beside him, as if knowing exactly what would be required of her.

"Strap yourself in," Kirk advised them all, the debate at an end. "Like Kate said, it's going to be a bumpy ride."

In the first stage of Kirk's plan, everything hinged on the runabout's sensors.

La Forge programmed two levels of sensitivity into their mass-detector subroutines.

One for the mirror *Voyager*. One for the *Sovereign*.

One starship would mean Kirk had a chance at winning. The other would mean a quick and relatively painful death for them all as the *St. Lawrence* was blown out of space.

La Forge told Kirk he had worked under conditions of greater pressure, but didn't elaborate.

After the programming was completed, there would only be the waiting. Kirk was certain their limbo wouldn't last long, not since they were heading back to the twin asteroids at full impulse—a trip that would take less than twenty minutes.

Except for the hum of her generators, and the wheezing of her malfunctioning air recyclers, the *St. Lawrence* ran silent.

Data was in the copilot's chair. None of the flight controls in front of the pilot's chair were operational. But Riker sat there anyway. Kirk knew why. Picard's senior officer had the need to be at the cutting edge of action. And Kirk understood that compulsion. Shared it.

Kirk and Janeway were the only members of the runabout's crew not to be strapped in someplace. They stood together on the flush-mounted platform of the emergency transporter. Janeway had linked her arm through Kirk's.

Scott was positioned just ahead of them, a strap he had jury-rigged from an away pack looped tightly around one hand. The strap was wedged between two wall panels, so that no matter what happened, even if the gravity failed, Scott would still be within reach of the transporter controls.

Spock and T'Val had taken the jump seats behind Data and Riker, for no reason other than as Vulcans, they wouldn't admit to preferring not to sit up front, where they might see their fate unfolding seconds before the end. The mirror Spock was flanked by McCoy and Beverly Crusher in the starboard passenger seats, unable to see much of anything. Both doctors were ready to sedate the frail intendant, or otherwise care for him if the ride became too rough.

La Forge, with Deanna Troi, who had been enlisted as the engineering assistant to both La Forge and Scott, had, like Scott, made handhold straps to anchor themselves to the runabout's deck near the engineering access panels. If they had to, the engineers and the counselor had told Kirk they would keep the warp core together with their bare hands.

So the ten flew on, each at their own station, each with their own thoughts. After ten minutes of silence, interrupted only by the creaking caused by the slow rise and fall of the plasma displacement swells, a sensor alarm finally chimed. But as quickly as everyone automatically tensed in expectation, Riker announced it was coolant temperature warning.

La Forge reached over to a small access panel, opened it, and made an adjustment. The alarm stopped.

More silence.

Then a second alarm sounded.

"That's a mass alert," Riker said.

"Which one?" McCoy asked.

The delay as Riker checked his readings was unbearable.

But the answer was worth waiting for.

"It's the *Voyager.*"

Kirk and Janeway exchanged a look of relief, and of nervous expectation. Kirk had guessed from the attack formation the two starships had taken up when they had tried to snare the *St. Lawrence* in a pincer that the *Voyager* would cover the asteroids to the relative starboard.

His guess had been right.

Now, if this was going to work, they would have their answer in only minutes.

Or they would never know anything again.

Data began a running commentary. Now that contact had been made, everything was dependent on proper timing. "I am setting course toward the *Voyager,* one-quarter impulse."

The low speed had been part of Kirk's plan. It would give the commander of the *Voyager* ample time to change course and bear down on the small runabout, prow first.

Kirk was counting on that.

When the *Voyager* opened fire, he needed its torpedoes to approach in a clean, direct, straight-ahead trajectory.

"The *Voyager* is changing course to meet us. Holding at one-quarter impulse," Data said.

Riker leaned over to operate the sensor controls at the top of Data's board. *"Voyager*'s phasers are online, but are not powering up," he said. "Quantum torpedo tubes are loaded."

Another good sign, Kirk thought. "How are those shields, Commander?"

"Forward shields at ninety-eight percent," Riker said as he read the console.

Ninety-eight percent was an impressive figure, and Kirk knew by the time the *Voyager* might possibly fly by the runabout, and notice that she had no side or aft shields—all power being forced to the forward screens—it would be too late for her to do anything about it.

"We're receiving a transmission," Data announced.

"Refuse it," Kirk said quickly. "Let's get them worried. Commander Riker, if you please . . ."

Riker cleared his throat, then opened a channel to the mirror *Voyager* and, in his most guttural Klingon, snarled, "Today is a good day to die!"

"That got their attention," Data said. "Their shields are up to full power, phasers coming online, and—"

The first phaser blast made the runabout yaw, but Data expertly corrected for unwanted movement.

"Shields holding at eighty-one percent. Accelerating to half-impulse," he said, each measured response according to the script Kirk had set out.

Now, Kirk hoped, whoever was commanding the *Voyager* would believe the *St. Lawrence* was on a suicide mission, intending only to collide head-on with the starship.

In a sense, that was right.

But not completely.

"Phasers firing again," Data warned.

This time, at closer range, the effect was more violent.

But still Data held the runabout to her course and her proper orientation.

"Shields at seventy-two percent. They must be wondering what we've done to this ship," Data said. Though in truth, to maintain high shield figures, Scott and La Forge had stolen power from almost every other system in the runabout, including life-support.

"What's the status of their torpedo tubes?" Kirk asked. That was the key. The only way this plan would work.

"Still powered up, but no sign of launching."

"Go to three-quarters impulse," Kirk said.

The whine of the runabout's engine began to rise in volume.

"They're bringing their warp engines online," Data said.

"That means they're getting ready to run," Kirk told him, and the rest of the unknown commander's strategy was suddenly clear. "They're taking their phasers offline, aren't they?"

"Phasers *are* offline," Data confirmed.

Kirk pressed Janeway's arm closer to his side. There were only seconds remaining. "Watch those torpedo tubes, Mr.

Data. They're getting ready to fire and warp to a safe distance."

There was a rising tone of excitement in Data's voice. "Torpedo tubes are powering up!"

"Stand by for warp!" Kirk said. "Scotty—*energize!*"

And then, just before the transporter effect drowned out all other sound, Kirk heard Data call out, "Torpedoes launching!" and Kirk knew the next three seconds would bring victory or oblivion.

Whatever happened, though, it would occur too fast for him to be aware of it. Which was why only Data could pilot this craft now. Because only the android had the speed and precision to do what had to be done in those few moments of transport, in the culmination of Kirk's daring plan.

The first step of that plan *required* that the *Voyager* be enticed into launching quantum torpedoes.

And that was because whenever a torpedo was launched, a momentary hole had to open up in a starship's forward shields; otherwise the torpedo would hit the forcefield and explode only a few hundred meters from the ship that fired it.

But, since torpedoes had warp capability, that opening would exist only for hundredths of a second.

Yet it was through that opening that Data now aimed the runabout, because to an android, those few hundredths of a second were like an eternity.

Thus, even as Kirk and Janeway dissolved into the transporter beam, Data pushed the runabout to warp, aiming directly along the firing line of the *Voyager*'s torpedoes to the opening in the shields.

It was a given that such a course would bring the runabout into a collision course with the torpedo whose path it traced. But torpedoes were set not to arm themselves until they were a safe distance from their ships.

The forward screens of the runabout hit the selected torpedo. Well within that safety zone. Instead of exploding,

315

as Kirk had anticipated the torpedo simply bounced off to one side.

And then, just as Kirk and Janeway had vanished from the transport platform, Data found the gap in the shields, and the *St. Lawrence* was traveling *within* the *Voyager*'s protective energy screen.

The final stage of Kirk's and Janeway's transport was preprogrammed and almost instantaneous.

As Data piloted the runabout up the slope of the *Voyager*'s primary hull, now shedding speed as quickly as possible, Kirk and Janeway were beamed directly to the starship's bridge.

And even as Kirk and Janeway were thrown forward, stumbling across the bridge's carpet, their trajectory halted only by the bridge's metallic guardrails, Data had already found the weak points in the starship's aft shields where the exhaust products of the warp and impulse drives were allowed to escape.

Operating at a speed that would cause human observers to simply see his hands as a blur, Data fired full phasers at those attenuated sections, knowing full well that shields were designed to give way in response to pressure from within. Otherwise, a small explosive device could be set off within a starship's shields, with the full force of its blast reflected back toward the ship by an impenetrable shell of energy.

But all these technical details—faced, dealt with, and exploited in less than a second—existed only in Kirk's mind. Because, by the time Kirk had fully materialized on the bridge of the starship, Data was long gone with the *St. Lawrence,* having found both his entry and his exit from the *Voyager*'s shields.

On the bridge of the duplicate *Voyager,* broad and sweeping, metallic in finish, and accented by dark gray covering on the chairs and protective pads, Kirk whirled around to see a bridge crew of Cardassians leap to their feet, startled beyond belief at the sight of two humans who had apparently done the impossible and beamed through shields.

Kirk's bandaged hands throbbed with pain, because he had used them to stop his forward momentum from the transport. He doubted he would be able to get in more than one or two good punches before the Cardassians overpowered him.

But with luck, if Janeway remembered what she was supposed to do next, fighting Cardassians would not be among the things Kirk would have to deal with.

He looked past the gathering Cardassians to see Janeway standing in the center of the bridge as if she belonged there.

A large Cardassian female rose from the command chair to face Janeway. Kirk assumed that she was the *Voyager*'s commander. And it was apparent she didn't recognize Janeway or understand what she might be able to do.

"Are you this eager to die, Terran?" the Cardassian commander said.

Kirk put up no struggle as other Cardassian crew members grabbed him and held him painfully in place against the bridge's guardrails.

It's all up to you, Kate, Kirk thought.

Janeway didn't disappoint him.

Before the Cardassian commander could reach her, Janeway lifted her head and said, "Computer: Captain Kathryn Janeway reporting for command duty as ordered. Emergency condition red. Transport control to the brig: Clear bridge of unauthorized Cardassians. Disperse anesthezine gas in all other Cardassian-occupied areas."

Before the startled Cardassian commander could shout out her countermanding order, the unflappable voice of the ship's computer said, "Janeway, Kathryn, voiceprint confirmed." Then one by one, in rapid succession, each Cardassian on the bridge vanished in a column of light.

Less than fifteen seconds had passed since Kirk had said "energize." And in that brief moment, James T. Kirk had gone from passenger on a doomed runabout to commander of a starship.

Then he caught the look of wonder growing on Janeway's face.

He understood why it was there.

And suddenly knew he couldn't deny her.

Standing alone in the middle of the bridge, Janeway turned to Kirk.

"What . . . what do I do now?"

Kirk made his decision. Unlike most other starships, the Intrepid class, to which *Voyager* belonged, had no center chair. Instead, it had *two* chairs set back from the helm consoles, one for the commander, and one for the first officer.

"The chair on the right," Kirk said. "That's the one you want."

Janeway approached it, slowly, ran her hand along its arm.

Through her, Kirk relived his own moment of so long ago—on his first tour on the *Enterprise*. And even in the midst of all that was happening, he felt honored to offer a similar moment to the next in line.

"Take it," he said. "You belong there."

And so, fulfilling a dream so powerful it had crossed from one universe to the next, once again, a Kathryn Janeway took command of a *Starship Voyager*.

Kirk saw the expression of awe on the young woman's face as she contemplated the possibilities before her. Kirk knew as she did not that what she had just done was only the beginning.

Kathryn Janeway had been given a starship. Now, like all starship captains throughout time and both universes, Kirk knew she would have to earn it.

And he'd just bet Teilani's life that she would.

TWENTY-SEVEN

☆

Picard thought of Worf, pictured Worf, became Worf.

Then, like Worf, but wearing the regent's armor over a lightweight discharge suit, he swaggered through the airlock of his personal quarters in the midst of the labor camp, and from its entry platform, called out for the nearest guards.

At the same time, Picard hoped his ridiculous disguise would work. Except for Teilani's insistence, he would never even have thought that such an impersonation would be possible, let alone have attempted it. Looking the same was one thing. But there were so many subtleties of identity, so many facts that his duplicate would know by second nature, but that he would not. Picard feared he would be exposed in the first, inconsequential conversation he was forced to engage in. And even if he didn't have to speak, he felt the makeup Teilani had spread over the cut on his nose marked him as an impostor at twenty paces. She claimed it would not be noticeable in the shifting, plasma-storm light of the camp. He could only hope that would be true.

Surprising him with the speed of their response, two Klingons ran to him along the plasteel walkway leading to his building. Their heavy boots pounded like thunder. One of the Klingons was Krawl, killer of ensigns.

They saluted Picard and he returned it without conviction or interest, as he had seen the senior overseers express disdain for those who served them.

"Yes, Regent?" Krawl said eagerly.

"These Terrans are weak," Picard said, staring directly at Krawl until the Klingon had to look away. It gave Picard confidence that Krawl hadn't recognized him from their earlier encounter just that morning.

"A touch of the agonizer," Picard complained, trying to capture the character of his counterpart, "and they fold like children." He waved both Klingons through the circular airlock and into the building. As the Klingons entered, they stared salaciously at Teilani. But Picard directed their attention to the body on the floor, dressed in the discharge suit of a prisoner.

"Captain Jean-Luc Picard of Starfleet," Picard said contemptuously. "Counterpart to a vole, not an intelligent being."

The Klingons laughed.

"Well, pick him up," Picard said, as if in a hurry to rid his home of dead vermin.

Krawl threw the real regent's body over his shoulder, and expressed surprise that this Picard was still alive. "Shall we recycle him, Regent?"

Picard allowed himself to look tempted, but reluctantly decided against it. "That wouldn't be wise. Not till we're finished with the *Enterprise.* There might be other secrets about it we need to explore."

The Klingon guards dipped their heads in obedient agreement. "As you command, Regent." Then one looked back to Teilani. The fabric she wore had enticingly worked its way farther up her legs. Teilani had arranged it so, deliberately. Her hands were tied tightly together at the wrists, the better for her to appear helpless.

"What about the woman?" Krawl asked.

"She's coming with us."

Krawl seemed confused. "Where?" The delta-shift overseer shifted Picard's duplicate to his other shoulder with a grunt.

"To the command building," Picard said. "I'll take her. You take Captain Picard. Perhaps seeing what happened to him will inspire her to be more . . . cooperative."

The Klingon guards bowed low, not bothering to hide their leers. "As you command." Picard marveled that a mere human, albeit his counterpart, had earned such obsequiousness from Klingon warriors.

Not that he was about to complain.

"And one last thing," Picard called after them. "If my counterpart starts to regain consciousness . . ."

"I understand," Krawl said, turning back to look at Picard. "The agonizer."

"As long as he lives to scream another day," Picard cautioned Krawl and the guard with a smirk.

The Klingons laughed again and exited through the airlock with their burden.

Picard turned to Teilani and exhaled. "Do you think they bought it?"

"As long as they don't look at your hair too closely, you'll be fine."

Picard nodded, rubbing lightly at the back of his head. Teilani had pinned to his short hair the long braid she had cut from the Regent Picard. In the regent's discharge suit and armor, the long, Klingon-style queue was the last telling detail that had transformed Picard into his mirror duplicate. At least, physically.

He tugged down on his chest armor, then started for the airlock himself. "I'll be back as soon as I can."

But Teilani followed after him. "You're not leaving me here. Especially after you told the guards I was going with you."

Picard looked at her, uncertain as to what he should do. His inexplicable need to take care of her could compromise his effectiveness if they left together.

"I'm half Klingon," Teilani reminded him, "so I know what the guards here are like. And I'm half Romulan, so I know what they think of me. Either give me both disruptors for protection, or take me with you as your prisoner."

Picard had a strange feeling of apprehension as he drew one of his backward-facing disruptors in her presence and held it on her. But the charade of making her his prisoner was the better of the two options. Left on her own, she was right— there was no way to be certain what fate might befall her. "Then walk before me," he said. "And remember, keep your hands together so they appear tied."

Teilani nodded and started through the airlock. Picard stepped through after her, disruptor high, trying to be like every Klingon he had ever met—with the possible exception of Worf's son, Alexander. That boy was far too gentle-mannered for a Klingon.

As they marched along the plasteel walkways that ran anywhere from two to five meters above the asteroid's surface, Picard searched for any sign that the guards were being called back to put on pressure suits, in preparation of releasing the atmosphere.

"There doesn't seem to be anything different going on," he murmured to Teilani. "It's as if no one is aware of the escape."

"Or else, they've already dealt with it."

Picard winced at the thought. He refused to accept the possibility that any or all of his senior staff were lost to him, beyond help. "No," he said, as much for himself as for Teilani. "They got away. I know it."

Teilani kept her head down like a well-trained prisoner, watching the walkway, speaking softly so that only Picard could hear her. "Then perhaps the Cardassians who were with them were the regent's personal guard, and they haven't reported back to the overseers."

"Then why haven't they reported back to me?"

Teilani didn't have an answer for that. She just kept walking.

As they reached a long stretch of walkway without intersections, Picard took a moment to look up at the sky.

And, as always, seeing his ship filled him with an inexpressible longing.

It wasn't so much the fact that the magnificent vessel poised above him was the *Enterprise*. On her own, that name belonged to the ages, and he was just one of a chain of her masters, from April, Pike, and Kirk, to Harriman and Garrett, and who knew how many others there would be to take his place in the years and the adventures to come.

But more than just that name and that history, it had been the very *idea* of a starship that had compelled him to go into space. To take up the mission of Starfleet.

For a moment, as he gazed up at his ship, he recalled pacing her bridge, no more than two weeks ago, anxious for some other mission, some other challenge.

Something worthy of a starship.

And what was happening here was not worthy of anything or anyone. This travesty had to end. Here and now.

"Eyes front, Jean-Luc."

The whispered warning had come from Teilani, who had caught him continuing to stare up at the *Enterprise* so close to the bizarre construction Picard's crew had labeled the crossover device. Picard looked ahead, beyond Teilani, and saw that they were coming to a plasteel platform that served as an intersection among the walkways—the final one before they would reach the main control building where the shift alarm controls were located. All Picard had to do was get to that building and activate the alarm, not with one long blast, but three short ones.

That was the signal that would begin the escape attempt before the shift was over. That was the moment his people were waiting for.

Provided nothing went wrong.

But as he saw the delta-shift overseer and one of the Klingon guards standing on that final platform, supporting

Picard's counterpart, Picard had the sudden feeling that something had already gone terribly wrong.

He shoved Teilani ahead to quicken their pace as if he really were her keeper, then made no effort to hide his displeasure with both Klingons. "How dare you stop without orders!"

But Krawl was looking at Picard with equal displeasure—and given that Krawl was an overseer and Picard a regent, that look was almost an act of insubordination.

"Picard woke up," Krawl said.

"And what were your orders if that happened?" Picard demanded.

Krawl did not respond with any sense of deference. "I take orders from the regent."

Picard looked at his counterpart. The regent was disoriented, barely able to stand without the help of both Klingons. A long thread of spittle hung from his mouth. Picard felt relieved that nothing of import would be coming from his duplicate for hours to come. He gathered his energy and seized the initiative. He only hoped he was not too late.

"Were my orders to put that Terran back to sleep too complex for your feeble minds?" Picard shrieked.

Krawl grabbed the true regent by the front of his discharge suit. The man's head lolled to one side. "I had an altercation with *Captain* Picard at the beginning of the delta shift," Krawl said. "A violent altercation."

"That's all these Terran scum understand," Picard said.

Krawl shook the regent. "But it has become apparent that this one *isn't* Terran."

Picard made no move to draw his twin disruptors, but he drew strength from knowing both were there. "Explain yourself, or get back to your duties."

"I used my agonizer probe on Picard," Krawl said. "I hit him across the face. *Slashed* him across the face. *But his wound has already healed!*"

If that's the best you have, Picard thought with sudden, deep hope, *you don't have anything.*

"The electrostatic field in these asteroids," Picard bluffed. "It affects the healing process, especially in Terrans."

But Krawl pushed forward until he was almost nose to nose with Picard. "If that's the case, *Regent,* then why is that cut on *your* nose not yet healed? Could the makeup you've used to disguise it be slowing the healing process?"

Picard knew there was no time to check the area, to see who else might be watching this confrontation on the platform. He knew that the instant he turned his attention from Krawl and the guard was the instant the overseer would attack.

Which meant he had only one option.

Picard brought his gloved fist up into the overseer's nose, doing no useful damage, but causing considerable pain.

Krawl's head snapped back, and after only a split second's hesitation as he grabbed his nose, the Klingon overseer whipped his agonizer probe from his belt and spun it around so its crackling induction tips faced Picard.

Beside Krawl, the Klingon guard did the same.

But both of them had taken too long.

Because as they faced Picard with their agonizer probes, Picard faced them with both disruptors drawn.

"Drop them," Picard said.

Krawl answered by slashing his probe toward Teilani.

She ducked back, flipping over the platform railing like a gymnast so the probe swept by her without connecting.

"Wrong move," Picard said.

"Then shoot me, and attract the attention of all the guards." Krawl feinted with the probe and Picard stepped back, knowing that if he fired the disruptor even once, he would have to be prepared to fire it until it was exhausted.

And then, as if fireworks were suddenly going off, flashes of red and blue light played over the platform.

Teilani was quickly pulling herself up from the asteroid's metal ground. She wasn't wearing a discharge suit, so she had only seconds to reach the insulated safety of the plasteel platform before she would begin to draw tendrils of charged plasma.

"Jean-Luc," she said breathlessly, gazing straight up. "Look up!"

But Picard kept his eyes locked on Krawl's.

"The *Enterprise*," Teilani insisted. "It's moving!"

Only by force of will did Picard refrain from looking up. Only by intense concentration did he not look at Teilani as she finished climbing back to the platform.

But Krawl looked up, and Picard felt sick as he saw the overseer's face contort into a hideous grin of black and broken teeth. "You lose, Terran. She's ours."

It was too much for Picard.

He had to look up.

And the *Enterprise* was alive above him.

Her nacelles, dark only moments ago, were now glowing red and blue with the power of antimatter annihilation. With the power that was needed to fly among the stars themselves.

But she was flying alone now, without him, sliding forward toward the gaping monstrosity that was the crossover device, leaving her captain behind, forever.

"No . . ." Picard said. She couldn't go yet. He had made his plans. He was going to get her back.

"Jean-Luc!" Teilani shouted in warning.

Picard dropped his gaze just in time to see Krawl lunge for him, agonizer probe leading the way, one hand curled into a savage claw to tear at his eyes so he would never see anything again.

Picard had no choice, no time for thought.

And he fired both disruptors from the hip.

Two incandescent shafts of twisted golden energy writhed forward, catching the Klingon overseer in mid-leap, splashing, flashing across his body like a ravenous liquid, engulfing

326

him even as that light burrowed deep within, to bring hellfire to his eyes, his mouth, a dozen random places on his body, so that light streamed from him, dissolving him, changing him, if just for an instant, into a luminous being.

Krawl was gone before he could fall to the ground.

The only sound of his destruction was the thud of his agonizer probe hitting, then rolling along the platform until it dropped off the side and clattered onto the asteroid's metallic surface.

The disruptors were warm in Picard's hands, and he realized with a fierce sense of satisfaction that he did not regret what he had done. He only wished it had lasted longer.

The delta-shift overseer had deserved to die more slowly. More painfully. Picard owed that to his young ensign. And to all others whom Krawl had tortured before that.

And then he heard the sound of one man applauding. Hollow, mocking.

"You liked that, didn't you?"

It was his counterpart. Recovered. Still dazed, but now fully upright on the platform, with the Klingon guard beside him.

"You proved my point," the regent said. "We are exactly the same, deep inside."

Picard trembled with an emotion he could not name. But it left him feeling naked and exposed.

His counterpart pushed the Klingon guard forward. "Go ahead. Do it *again*. Feel the power, Jean-Luc. The control."

Picard longed to throw the disruptors away. But he couldn't. He needed them. Not to kill. But to—

He looked up to see his ship sliding forward, into the maw of the device.

That's why he needed the weapons. To stop that from happening. To stop the loss of everything he cared for. Everything he had left.

Beside him, Teilani urged him to act. "Just shoot them, Jean-Luc. Both of them. We have to go."

But the mirror Picard mocked him. "That's a good excuse,

327

Jean-Luc. Shoot them. Shoot me. Kill me the way you killed your brother and his nephew."

Picard held the disruptors to his ears to shut out the awful things his counterpart was saying. "I didn't kill them! I wasn't there! I couldn't know!"

His counterpart started forward. "Liar," he taunted Picard. "You can't fool me. I can read your mind, Jean-Luc."

Picard shoved one disruptor under his arm, fumbled with the setting of the other.

And for that moment he was defenseless.

"Take him!" his counterpart shouted at the Klingon guard.

The guard leapt forward.

Picard swung out the disruptor.

Teilani's elbow found the Klingon's temple and crushed it with a single blow.

The guard hit the platform without even a whimper or the sigh of death.

Picard held the disruptor on his counterpart.

His duplicate self looked up. To the ship. *The* ship.

"You're losing her, Jean-Luc. You'd better run."

Picard could not fire, not certain what setting he had made in all the confusion.

He could not look up because he couldn't bear to lose his ship.

So he reached out for Teilani's hand and, pulling her along with him, began to run toward the command center.

His boots struck the walkway like claps of thunder. His breath came in lung-searing gasps.

But all he could hear was his counterpart's scornful laughter as its echo pursued him.

And far away, the cries of Robert and René and everyone else he had lost and abandoned in his life.

Jean-Luc Picard raced to save the *Enterprise.*

But he ran to redeem his life.

TWENTY-EIGHT

☆

"Is there something I can help you with?" Deanna Troi asked.

Thirty minutes after he and Janeway had surprised and rounded up the mirror *Voyager*'s twenty-two-member skeleton crew of Cardassians, courtesy of automated transporter control, Janeway was in the command chair. Spock was seated beside her, as acting first officer. T'Val was across the bridge, alone at the conn. And the others from the *St. Lawrence* were scattered throughout the ship—Scott and La Forge in engineering; McCoy and Beverly Crusher in sickbay with the mirror Spock, and the few Cardassians who had not responded well to the anesthezine; and Riker and Data on security detail, monitoring the dazed prisoners now waking up in the brig.

Those prisoners who were conscious were still not too sure what had happened to them. Riker reported to the bridge that he was taking delight in giving the captive Cardassians a two-word answer: Captain Kirk.

Kirk had taken up position at the security/tactical station on the starship's bridge. If he had been in a mood to consider such things, he would have had to admit he liked this new design, with duty stations set up so they faced the forward viewscreen. Though the rest of his team was actually running

329

the ship, Kirk found that even looking up at that main screen was giving him the feeling that he, too, could be involved in their mission.

Even though he wasn't.

Even though he no longer cared that he wasn't.

Kirk held up his bandaged hands to Deanna, nodded to the sensor display. "I can't figure out the voice command for getting the main sensors to recalibrate the resolution settings for plasma-storm interference. If you could . . . just run your finger along that green band . . ."

Deanna reached past him, recalibrated the sensor resolution as he instructed. "Like this?"

At least a thousand data points suddenly sprayed across Kirk's graph. He began to study them intently.

Deanna smiled at him. "From the relief I'm picking up from you, I guess so."

"Thank you," Kirk said without looking at her. He knew the smile he gave her was perfunctory, but the sensor board was all that was important now. That's where the truly relevant information would be displayed. Where he would find the data that would restore him to life.

Because, right now, he was only a shell. Empty of everything vital.

Despite the slowness of the data updates on his sensor board, Kirk had no interest in the bridge's main screen. All it now showed was a visual image, distorted by plasma interference. When Kirk had squinted at it through half-closed eyes, he had almost been able to believe he could see an extremely crude rendition of the twin asteroids, so close together it was as if there were no separation between them at all.

The mirror *Voyager* was less than 100,000 kilometers away from those asteroids, yet the resolution of the main-screen image made it seem as if the asteroids were millions of kilometers more distant.

At least the same interference that degraded the visual sensors was keeping the *Voyager* safe from the *Sovereign*. That renegade ship, which might or might not be under the command of the revived mirror-universe counterpart of Fleet Admiral Nechayev, still patrolled the region around the asteroids. But because of the *Sovereign*'s size, nearly twice that of *Voyager,* the smaller starship would easily detect the *Sovereign* before the larger ship could detect her.

Still, none of this had any real meaning for Kirk. Since beaming aboard and ensuring that the bridge was secure, he had delegated the remaining actions of the boarding party to Janeway and Spock. Then he turned his full attention to adjusting the nonvisual life-sign subroutines in the main sensor array. In just a half hour, he had been able to improve the resolution of that data band to pick out individuals among the asteroid's prisoners and guards—not by visual image, but by life-sign signature.

This was the reason he had come this far. The only reason.

But he had not found what he had been so desperate to find.

"You musn't feel so frustrated about your hands," Deanna said to him.

Startled by her pronouncement, Kirk looked down at them now. They were little more than thickly bandaged claws, his flame-ravaged fingers only abstractions within their wrappings, newly numbed by whatever McCoy had injected into them. "Why shouldn't I be upset?" he asked without urgency, not referring to his hands at all.

"Because they'll get better."

Kirk knew that, of course. McCoy had enough artificial body parts in him to set up a used-organ store. These weren't the days of Chris Pike. He had no doubt that he could have his hands repaired, or even grow a new pair, if that's what it took. Eventually. His physical self was not beyond restoration.

But whatever it was that dwelled within the flesh, be that flesh old or new, real or artificial, that was a mystery that not even the science of the twenty-fourth century had begun to address.

What good was a hand without another to hold?

What good was a heart, without love to quicken its beat?

Without such things, Kirk cared for nothing anymore.

He felt his world, his will to continue, collapsing, and he couldn't even lean forward and rest his head on his hands. How could he finish clearing his lot on Chal with hands like these? How could he dare take on the challenge of removing that last, remaining, insufferably stubborn stump?

And what could any of that mean without Teilani?

The overwhelming emotion of loss that dear, sweet, wide-eyed Deanna Troi was responding to in him had nothing to do with any deficiency in his physical self.

But everything to do with the loss of his soul.

"Irony?" Deanna asked. "It's coming off you in waves."

Kirk held up his hands, as if in losing them, he had lost the ability to hold on to life, to hold on to the woman he loved. "All I ever wanted was to be able to touch life, build something, create something with these."

Deanna was unconvinced. "That's not *all* you ever wanted. Not really." She scanned Kirk's sensor board with all its individual life-form traces, filtered by age, sex, and species. Watching her, Kirk realized that the technological display, at least, could make obvious what his emotional state could not, so he was not surprised at her next question.

"Who are you looking for?"

Kirk hesitated, wondering if he could ever explain to anyone else what Teilani had become to him. How could that simple question be answered in mere words?

Quietly waiting for his answer, it seemed to Kirk that Deanna had no interest in going elsewhere on the bridge or in the ship until he responded, as if she had somehow chosen the well-being of James T. Kirk as her own personal mission.

Kirk studied her face, noting the dark alien heritage of her empathetic eyes, as distinctive as Spock's ears. "You're the ship's counselor, aren't you."

"On the *Enterprise* at least."

"We didn't have one of those on my *Enterprise.*"

Deanna smiled at him, she was always smiling, and somewhere in the back of his mind, in whatever subroutines of his own that were still running, Kirk recognized it as a comforting smile. "Of course you had a counselor," she said. "Except on your *Enterprise,* he was probably called the ship's doctor. And he most likely concentrated on keeping the command staff stable."

Kirk frowned. He wondered if the counselor had ever loved as he had loved Teilani. He wondered if she had ever lost that love, lost all meaning to her life, been caught in a despair so dark and deep that not even the fiery birth of a sun could illuminate its depths.

But she was looking at him now as if she did know, as if every terrible thought that had tormented him in this past half hour were laid bare before her. He felt exposed, dissected, like a sample on display in some ancient naturalist's study.

Kirk was suddenly grateful that he hadn't had a counselor as advanced as this one on his ship.

But Deanna didn't appear to care what he thought. Only what he felt. "Who are you looking for?" she asked again. Her smile was gone.

Kirk hesitated only a moment, then used his elbow to activate Teilani's personnel screen—one he had created himself. *Let's see if this charming, persistent expert can sense* real *loss,* he thought bitterly. He believed she wouldn't have a chance.

Kirk stared down at the picture of Teilani that accompanied the sensor board's personnel display. The image had been recorded only a few months ago, in Chal's blissful summer. She had been outside their cabin, currying Iowa Dream, emphatically warning Kirk that he absolutely, *positively,* must not take her picture while her hair was a mess and she was all sweaty.

But Kirk had taken it anyway.

Teilani had retaliated by attacking him with a bucket of water, and he had laughed so hard she had pinned him easily, demanding the sensor camera, insisting that she would erase that image.

But the day had been warm, the weather clear. And very quickly they had surrendered to the magic of being in each other's arms.

Much later, when they had stirred themselves from the blanket they had spread upon the ground, and made their way to the clear and rushing stream to swim, Teilani had forgotten all about the sensor camera and the picture.

But neither one of them had forgotten that day.

Neither one ever forgot those timeless gifts that came to them so easily.

That image had become Kirk's favorite picture of her. A perfect moment in a perfect day.

The counselor surprised him. "Oh my," Deanna said softly, her cheeks red. Kirk had no doubt what Deanna was reacting to. He would never forget those moments, those eternities, in Teilani's embrace. Never. "Teilani, of course. We met during the virogen crisis. And you believed she would be in the camp."

Of course that's what I believed, Kirk thought in sudden despair. *Why else would I come here, have risked what I have risked?* "It was the only place that made any sense," he told her. Then he found himself, under the counselor's compassionate gaze, outlining all the reasoning, all the details he had learned from the mirror-universe rebels, that had led him to conclude that the prison camp would be the one and only place where Teilani would be taken.

Deanna continued to watch him intently all through his explanations, and the comprehension in her eyes was so absolute that Kirk was forced to wonder if she had learned how to actually read minds.

"You're certain she's not in the camp?" Deanna asked.

Kirk tapped another control with his elbow, read out the figures that were displayed. "Three thousand, two hundred, and fifty-two individuals are in that camp. Two thousand and twenty-two are human. Fifteen are Bolian. A handful of humanoids are so close to human it doesn't matter. And the rest, the guards, are Klingons, Cardassians, and thirty-five Bajorans."

"And you couldn't have missed her among all of those?"

"I programmed the computer myself," Kirk said, making no attempt to hide his desolation. He wanted there to be some way it would be caught up by Deanna's empathic ability and taken from him forever, so he would never feel anything again. "Teilani's parents were Klingon and Romulan. A distinctive mix. But the computer can't find anyone who matches her criteria." He took a deep breath, felt the tremor that passed through him. A tremor he did not want to acknowledge.

A tremor Deanna Troi understood. Felt. Shared with him.

"Captain Kirk . . ." she said in a low voice, as if somewhere a child were sleeping. "Why do you think she's dead?"

Deanna might as well have torn out his heart for asking that question.

"Because she was kidnapped," he said, and if there was any emotion left in him, it was nothing he felt. "Because she was taken by people who told me not to interfere in the politics of the mirror universe." He closed his eyes as if that act might banish existence itself. "Politics I helped create." But existence continued and he opened his eyes and looked at Deanna. "And I did interfere. By going with the *Sovereign*. By fighting Nechayev. By stealing the *St. Lawrence* and taking this ship." Kirk's hands would have become fists, but his hands were useless. *He* was useless. "Because I thought I could beat them the way I've always beaten everyone who's ever stood in my way."

Kirk drove his elbow down on the console and that perfect image of Teilani, taken on that perfect day on that perfect world, vanished from the screen.

From his life.

From his future.

"Not every possibility has been explored," Deanna said.

"By the time we're finished here, it won't matter. Wherever they have her, she is dead."

Deanna stood by his side for several more minutes, studying the individual sensor returns from the prisoners and the guards in the camp hundreds of thousands of kilometers away. But she said nothing more, and Kirk could guess why.

There was nothing she could say that could bring Kirk back from the hell he had created.

Nothing, and she knew it.

"I'm . . . so sorry," she said, placing a hand lightly on his shoulder. And then she moved away, to the forward station beside T'Val at the conn.

Kirk spent the next moments counting Klingons and Cardassians. Wondering what it would be like to kill each one of them. Personally.

Then Scott and La Forge reported in over the comm channels from the lower sensor platform behind the main array.

"Go ahead, Mr. Scott," Kirk heard Janeway acknowledge. In less than an hour in that chair, his erstwhile kidnapper had fallen into the ease of command.

"Geordi and I have taken the liberty of narrowing the bandwidth of what the sensor dish can pick up," Scott explained. "I mean, there's precious little that gets through the plasma storms as it is."

Kirk looked up from his sensor screen. Trust Scotty. That sounded like a worthwhile modification. He was glad that some people still had purpose in their lives.

"Understood, Mr. Scott," Janeway said. "You're giving us the capability to see in greater detail but over a smaller range of wavelengths."

"Right ye are," Scott said. "So, since we seem to be getting all the right readings down where we are now, we thought we'd throw the big picture up on the main screen."

"It's not as if we'd be missing anything," Janeway said. "What we've got up here now is like looking through mud."

"Well, lass, let's just see if we can do somethin' about that. . . ."

The main screen flickered—nothing new about that in the Goldin Discontinuity. Then a new image appeared and remained.

Kirk glanced up at it, only because it was new. A distraction.

The image was monochromatic—a wash of blue gray.

But it was clear. And compared with what they'd been receiving, it was crisp.

It was also chilling.

Quite clearly, this new image showed the *Enterprise,* floating between the asteroids, undoubtedly held in place by some complex arrangement of tractor beams and antigravs.

And just as clearly, the image showed that the *Enterprise* was moving, very slowly, into the device that not even the close sensor scan from the *St. Lawrence* had been able to identify.

Kirk saw Spock stand up and walk closer to the screen. "They are about to achieve their goal," he stated matter-of-factly. "If, indeed, that device can be used to transfer ships between the universes, at the rate the *Enterprise* is moving into it, in less than an hour she will be gone."

Janeway stood up and joined Spock. Still seated at the security/tactical station, out of the real arena of action, Kirk shifted restlessly, remembering when he would have been the one standing with Spock like that, gazing into the mysteries of the universe, determining how to control them.

"The *Enterprise,*" Janeway said in reverence, in fear. "No resistance group in my universe can stand up to her."

T'Val was also riveted by the image on the screen, and by all it meant to her universe and her struggle. "They've won, Kate. And there's nothing we can do."

Kirk stood up. He could no longer hold back while the future unfolded. The wrong way. Without his involvement.

"Of course there's something you can do." Kirk's voice was decisive.

Janeway, Spock, and T'Val turned to him.

"Destroy them," he said, his voice firm, steady, filled with experience. "Crush their camp, their device, and if you have to, the *Enterprise* herself. But how dare you stand there and *give up!*"

Only Spock stepped away from the others to face him.

"Captain, I have studied the sensor scan we made of their camp during our flyby in the runabout. Any attack on the generators that power that device, whatever its purpose, will collapse the atmospheric forcefield."

"So?" Kirk asked.

"The prisoners will die."

Kirk moved down the steps, onto the main level with the others, leaving behind the sensor board and its empty displays of damning data.

"Not all of them. Riker and the others, they said the barracks were pressurized."

"The majority of the prisoners are civilians, Jim," Spock said. "To lose one civilian's life is unacceptable."

"What is it to lose a *billion* civilian lives?" Kirk asked. His gaze measured the Vulcan who had been his friend for longer than he could remember, and the woman who had been given the greatest opportunity fate could bestow and yet did not know how to use it. "Because that's what they'll do with the *Enterprise* and you know it. The Alliance won't be using her to seek out new life, new civilizations. They'll use her to hunt down the resistance and end it. They'll take her into the Badlands and destroy the mirror *Defiant*. They'll track down the headquarters of the Vulcan resistance and obliterate it.

"They'll use that ship for every purpose Starfleet turns a blind eye toward. To change the orbits of worlds. To stop the fusion of suns. To wipe even the slightest memory of Terrans and Vulcans from the history of the galaxy."

Kirk gestured angrily with his useless hands, not caring if their trailing bandages made him seem as if he were some decaying corpse from an earlier time best forgotten.

He measured the two before him, and saw himself in the middle, between them—James T. Kirk, finally defeated by the loss of the one thing that could never be explained, never be replaced.

After a century and a half of fighting his war with the universe, Kirk had no doubt that the universe had won.

Yet there was something in him still that refused to allow those around him to be defeated as well. Not while he could still make a difference. If not for himself and Teilani, then at least for others.

"I know how offensive it sounds," Kirk said to Spock. "I know how wrong you think it is to put the blood of innocent people on your hands. But you don't know the Alliance." He felt his body shudder involuntarily with the intensity of the words he spoke. "You don't know what it means to *hate.*"

Now he spoke not to his friends, his allies, but to the stars that had always waited for him, to claim the dust of his life, his dreams, his bones, and hold them all in their uncaring, disinterested embrace.

"But after all this time," Kirk said, "I do."

TWENTY-NINE

Picard hit the pressure door hard, with his shoulder. Forced the door open, jumped inside, then raced through the airlock's transfer chamber to leap into the wedge-shaped room beyond—a cluttered storage area with rows of spacesuits hung along two of its walls.

Three Cardassians seated at flashing consoles to one side of the doorway spun round to face him, their hands already reaching for the disruptors at their sides.

But Picard drew both his own weapons and fired first, energy beams lancing through the air, dissolving the enemy even as their flailing limbs reached out for life.

Picard granted them none.

Then Teilani was at his side.

"What is this building?" he asked her, eyes never resting as he scanned the storage area and its haphazard stacks of equipment, each panel of its monitoring equipment ablaze with flashing displays and status lights.

"It's camp headquarters," Teilani said. The area they were in, she explained, the area they had just taken, was one of seven wedges sliced out of the outer rim of the circular building. "And behind one of those doors is the main control room."

340

Picard fixed his gaze on the storage area's third wall and the three small pressure doors set into it. At least three-quarters of the building's volume was hidden behind them. And he knew there was another full level above. The enemy could be anywhere.

He started forward through the disorderly rows of equipment, a disruptor in each hand, looking for anyone who might be hiding behind a crate. The Cardassians he'd killed near the doorway had been busy at small workstations, a tray of food scattered to one side, a stack of isolinear chips sprayed across the floor to another.

But he had no sense of what they had been doing here. No idea if their work had involved what was happening to his ship, only a kilometer overhead.

Picard made his choice. "Right door," he said. The floor in front of it seemed to be the most distressed, as if it had seen the highest traffic. Perhaps the controls he needed would be behind it.

He was just about to fire at that right-hand door when he heard running feet behind him, approaching the open airlock.

Not the soft pad of a prisoner's discharge suit, but the heavy clang of metal-shod boots.

"Get down!" he shouted to Teilani, then ran out of the storage area, back to the transfer chamber, where he dropped to one knee to brace a disruptor across his forearm as he drew a bead and—

Three Klingons flew up into the air, blown off the plasteel walkway outside the airlock as Picard's withering fusillade of disruptor fire struck them.

Picard saw other guards on the run across the walkways, all heading toward their camp's headquarters.

He stood up in the open airlock to give himself a better angle and fired both disruptors again, slicing the walkway directly in front of him in half, cutting through it so the far side collapsed onto the asteroid's metal ground.

He stepped back into the airlock entrance and fired straight down again to blast the plasteel platform.

Now the command building was isolated from all the others. Alone in the center of the camp.

He glanced up, saw the *Enterprise* being pulled into the crossover device like an insect being devoured by a carnivorous plant.

Then he backed up, retracing his steps to Teilani, methodically closing each mammoth rolling door behind him, and fusing their controls so whoever came after him into the building would have to carve through its metal walls, or wait until he had used the emergency levers to open the doors from the inside.

When he entered the storage area, he reached behind his head and ripped off the hateful braid of his counterpart's white hair.

Teilani looked at him questioningly.

But Picard knew there was no time to discuss the situation. The rest of his disguise—his Klingon armor—was lightweight, and would provide some protection against disruptor fire. And the regent's discharge suit he wore beneath it was sleeker and lighter than the first one he had been forced to wear as a prisoner. He might be facing impossible odds, but he was well equipped. And it was time to use that equipment.

Picard focused his attention on the third door on the storage area's back wall. He needed to start the escape attempt, if only to add to the guards' confusion.

He raised his disruptors.

"After what's gone on out here, they'll be ready for us," Teilani said. Her voice was even, without fear.

Picard looked at her, and remembered who she really was. Not a frail prisoner to be rescued. But a warrior to be reckoned with.

He flipped a disruptor around, caught it by its barrel, then tossed it to Teilani.

She plucked it easily from the air, spun it again, and

expertly rolled her thumb over its power gauge, setting it to FULL.

"They won't be expecting both of us," Picard said.

Then he sprinted toward a crate, leapt over it, and took up a firing position to the left of the target door.

On the other side of the door, Teilani rolled over another crate to the floor and crouched behind it with both hands on her own weapon, ready to create a deadly crossfire.

Impressed again by her attitude, Picard targeted the door controls.

Got ready to fire.

And then, very slowly, creaking only slightly, the target door sighed open, and Picard's aim wavered as he heard a voice from the room speak to him.

"Come in, Captain. I've been expecting you. And you're late."

Picard recognized that voice and lowered his disruptor.

He abandoned his cover and stood slightly to one side of the open doorway, preparing himself to meet Gul Rutal.

One last time.

They were all on the bridge now. All yelling at each other in a way that would be unthinkable for starship crews, even in Kirk's time.

"And what if we meet up with the *Sovereign?*" Scott demanded.

"She'll be just as disadvantaged as we are," Kirk said. "And at least we'll have taken the first shots."

"Our captain is down there," Data argued. "This attack could kill him along with the rest."

"Look," Kirk said to the android, "I'm five seconds from getting into a shuttlecraft and doing this myself. Picard's already dead. All those prisoners on that asteroid, the moment the *Enterprise* has crossed over, they've served their purpose. Accept it. They're already dead. But at least my way, some of them might make it through the attack. And the Alliance won't have the *Enterprise.*" Kirk looked at Janeway. "We've got the coordinates of their generators from that flyby we did. We'll shoot at the backups first. Get their attention. Let them start whatever evacuation procedures they have so as many prisoners as possible can get back to their barracks in safety."

McCoy pounded his fist on the railing he stood beside. "Dammit, Jim. Listen to yourself. 'Some' of the prisoners? Do you know how many people could die down there if we attack?"

Kirk glared at McCoy. "Do you know how many will die if we *don't* attack?"

"You can't know that."

"Yes, I can." He turned to Janeway. "You've fought the Alliance. You know what they're like. And whether you want it or not, this is your ship. Start the attack, Kate. Start the attack or your resistance movement is finished and your universe is lost!"

Kirk looked her in the eyes and knew this was her moment. Everything she would become in her new life would flow from this next second.

The bridge was silent.

No one dared speak.

Until the commander of the *Voyager* had made her decision.

And she made it.

"Battle stations," she said. "They're not getting the *Enterprise.*"

Janeway turned to her chair as T'Val ran for the conn.

Beverly Crusher reached out to take Janeway's shoulder, forced her to turn and look at her. "You're going to kill all those people. . . ."

Janeway pushed Crusher's hand away. "I didn't start this war."

Everyone on the bridge looked at Kirk.

Everyone knew whose war it was.

Picard kept his disruptor pointing down though he could hear scuffling in the control room beyond. He was careful not to betray Teilani's presence as he heard her take up a new position behind him.

"I won't let you take my ship," he said.

"We've had this conversation," Rutal said from somewhere deep within the control room.

Picard chanced a glance through the open door. Saw a circular control area ringed by display screens.

On them, he could see guards and prisoners caught up in a mad melee. This was the room he had been looking for. Somewhere inside, on one of its consoles, would be the control he needed to signal for the escape to begin.

"Why don't you come in? So we can talk about something new?" Rutal said.

"Long enough to let your guards cut through the doors outside?" Picard asked.

"I don't need my guards to deal with you."

"Then why don't you come out here?"

"Captain Picard, really. You have a disruptor."

"And you don't?"

A shadow moved by the consoles in the room. Picard resisted the impulse to fire at it.

"Mine isn't as big as yours," the Cardassian Gul said. Her voice now seemed to be coming from farther away, another location.

Picard didn't know why the enemy was moving, what her plan was. Perhaps there was another exit from the control room. But he had to do something to take the initiative.

"You have five seconds to leave the control room," Picard said. "Then I am going to throw in a particle grenade." He had seen some of the camp guards carrying the small but deadly devices, designed to kill organic beings with a minimum of explosive damage. He trusted the Gul might believe he had managed to obtain one.

But her reply suggested she had another strategy in mind. *"You* have five seconds to drop your weapon, or I will kill you."

The five seconds passed.

"It seems both our bluffs have been called," Picard said. He needed to hear Rutal speak again, so he would know where to fire when he ran into the room.

"But one of us wasn't bluffing," the Gul answered.

To the left, Picard thought.

He began to picture himself rolling in through the door, coming up on his feet, firing to the left at whatever moved.

He got ready to spring forward.

"Jean-Luc!" Teilani cried. "Get down!"

Picard dropped to the floor as a blaze of disruptor energy tore through the air above him and struck a figure who had appeared in the center door of the storage area's back wall.

Of course, he thought angrily as he ducked and ran toward the center door. He had been blinded by the obvious trap— three doors usually meant three rooms.

But here, all *three* opened onto *one* room—the control room.

Picard didn't know who it was that Teilani had just shot, but he pushed his way through the first door on the left, into the control room, and swept his weapon back and forth, ready to shoot Rutal if she was still present.

And she was. Alone. Her arrogance assuming she could dispatch a mere Terran like Picard by herself. Starship captain or not.

The armor in the Gul's chest piece still glowed from Teilani's beam. But her armor had held and now Rutal raised her disruptor at Picard. "A pity you won't live to see me in command of your ship," she said.

Picard fired.

A golden halo of energy flared around her.

But didn't stop her.

Picard's disruptor cut out, recycling.

"My turn," Rutal said with a terrible smile. She raised her weapon.

Picard lurched to the side as he heard the air crackle beside him.

"You're merely delaying the inevitable," Rutal said.

Picard knelt behind a small console, hearing her footsteps clump nearer.

The console creaked as Rutal fired directly into it. Picard leapt up and fired back.

Again the Gul was enveloped by energy. Again her armor protected her.

But then the glow around Rutal suddenly increased as a second beam hit her from behind.

Teilani.

Rutal's eyes widened in surprise and she whirled around to see Teilani in the middle doorway, firing point-blank.

Quickly, Picard seized his chance to set his disruptor to full discharge.

As Rutal raised her weapon against Teilani, Picard moved forward.

No matter how effective Rutal's armor was against disruption, it would not be able to dissipate the heat generated from two full-power beams.

The Gul dropped to her knees, mouth open, gasping for air.

But Picard and Teilani kept up their joint barrage.

Rutal's armor failed.

For a brief, shining moment, the Gul was replaced by a glowing sculpture of herself, a final echo of the energy that consumed her.

Then she was gone.

Picard didn't even waste time staring at the empty space she had occupied. He moved swiftly to the closest console, sounded out the Cardassian script on it, selected WORK OPERATIONS from the menu it described.

He punched in the commands that would accelerate the shift change.

Even in the control room, insulated within the camp's command building, Picard heard the three loud bellows of the shift alert.

It was one of the signals his crew had been instructed to respond to.

He watched the console displays as sudden images of insurrection appeared.

Two prisoners suddenly turned on a guard. Another guard was jumped before he could draw his weapon.

More prisoners scattered across the asteroid's surface, heading for the gravity tether that led to the *Enterprise.*

"It's working," Teilani said beside him.

"Best crew in the Fleet," Picard said with proud satisfaction.

Then the control-room floor shook with the sound of a distant explosion.

Picard beamed. He and Data had assumed it would take at least twenty minutes for the prisoners to be able to sabotage the camp's main generators powering the tractor beams that held the *Enterprise* in place. "They're well ahead of schedule." The backup generators would be more than enough to contain the atmosphere.

And then another explosion, closer, more powerful, shook not only the floor, but the whole control room.

"That wasn't part of the plan," Picard said to himself.

"Look," Teilani said. "On that screen. . . ."

Picard saw where she was pointing, saw the display there.

And seeing it, realized that his and Teilani's actions, his team's brave efforts, all had been for naught.

In helpless rage, Picard could only watch as his careful plan was destroyed, as the mirror *Voyager* descended, phaser banks afire.

Ruining everything.

Kirk withdrew to the back of the bridge. He had set this in motion but he was no longer part of it. The people of this era had to learn for themselves. They had to experience for themselves the true price of existence.

The *Voyager* echoed with the constant discharge of her phasers.

Once they were through the atmospheric forcefield, no other energy screens protected the ground installations. The backup generators were all easy targets.

The main sensor screen was not distorted at this close range, as the small starship slipped over the camp, targeting all energy systems. Kirk saw the camp's prisoners scattering as explosions erupted around them. He saw the camp guards attempting to fire up at the ship or down on their escaping charges. He saw people begin to die.

"Jim!"

Kirk looked over at McCoy, now seated at the operations station.

"Look at this!"

But Kirk shook his head. He knew what was happening, who was dying. Starfleet officers. Mirror-universe counter-parts. Klingons. Guards who would argue they were simply doing their jobs. Some who deserved to die. Some who didn't. It didn't matter. He didn't want to know. Their deaths were all part of the price that had to be paid to prevent an even worse horror.

Death for life. The real currency of the twenty-fourth century. A basic fact of human history that never seemed to change. Despite any and all individual efforts to make that change.

"Get over here, man!" McCoy insisted. "It's Teilani!"

Kirk braced himself against the safety railing as T'Val's maneuvers made the starship groan. Then, in a heartbeat, he crossed the bridge, looked down at McCoy's screen.

"That's . . . that's impossible. I scanned for her. I scanned *everyone* down there."

"You're not a doctor, you idiot," McCoy said as his hands moved quickly over the controls. "You're not a programmer or a sensor specialist. But you tried to do everything yourself anyway, just as you always have . . . and you did it wrong!"

"Bones, I made the computer compare *every* individual— *everyone*—with Teilani's life-sign signature. *There . . . was . . . no . . . match.*"

"Not with her *old* signature," McCoy agreed. "But you were too strict with your parameters. You didn't allow any room for change. That's why the computer didn't find anything."

Kirk felt his legs weaken. "What change, Bones? How is she different?"

McCoy placed a finger on a life-sign profile labeled with Teilani's name. The readings on it were confused, as if a second signal were mixed with the first and—

"She's pregnant, Jim," McCoy said quietly.

Shocked to his depths, Kirk stared past McCoy to the main screen, where a fireball roiled up from a blazing generator station. Where Teilani now was. With their unborn child. Because of him.

There was no time for thought. No time for anguish. No time for anything but action.

He turned his back on the bridge as if turning his back on his past life.

I have a plan, he heard Teilani whisper in his ear as they stood together in the clearing. *You might be leaving Chal, but you will always be here with me.*

Only now did Kirk understand what she had meant.

Only now did Kirk understand that hell had many levels.

350

He headed for the transporter room, pursued by the screams of the dying that echoed in his mind.

The price of existence had just been raised.

Picard and Teilani froze as a new alarm blared in the control room. Red lights spun and flashed.

Picard read the warning that flashed on every screen.

Atmosphere failure.

"Can you find out what's happened?" Teilani asked.

Picard put his weapon aside. He called up the unfamiliar Cardassian screens, read the reports.

"My people were to hit the main generators, to force the camp to go to backups, and give us time to retreat to the barracks and get up to the *Enterprise.*" He called up a second screen. "But the *Voyager!* . . . She attacked the *backup* generators first. The whole camp's lost its power supply. The forcefield's down and—"

He was cut off by a rising whistle of wind.

"We're losing atmosphere," Teilani said, understanding their situation at once.

The command building had just lost pressure integrity.

If they stayed here, they would suffocate.

"We're also losing whatever was keeping the *Enterprise* in place above us."

Picard and Teilani looked at each other, knowing they had only minutes to act. Only seconds.

Then the control room lost all power and the screens went dark.

The whistle of the escaping air had become the shriek of a storm.

"I have to get you to a barracks for shelter," Picard said.

Teilani disagreed. "You have to get to the *Enterprise.*"

Together, they ran for the airlock.

Kirk materialized in fire.

He had set the transporter to beam him through a standard

351

shield cycle as the *Voyager* had fired her phasers. But to achieve the precision of timing necessary to punch through that momentary gap in the shields, he had surrendered any chance of accuracy in selecting his beam-down position.

And he appeared in the midst of a fireball.

But as quickly as he became solid, the fireball passed before it could consume him.

He looked around, coughing, getting his bearings.

And this time, when he heard screaming, it was not just in his mind.

Fires blazed everywhere.

Hundreds of people fled across the metallic surface of the asteroid.

From portions of elevated walkways, guards fired down at those who tried to escape them.

The *Voyager* roared by overhead. Tendrils of plasma stretched out from the surrounding storms of the discontinuity, erupting around her shields as if she, too, were on fire.

And everywhere, in every direction, a terrible wind blew.

Kirk held his bandaged hands close against his chest, struggling to breathe, struggling to understand.

This is necessary, he told himself. *This attack is all that will save the billions of the mirror universe.*

That was the cold hard logic of survival.

But now that he was in the middle of the storm—now that the woman he loved beyond all else, now that the child they had created as the promise of a future he had not understood was what he truly wanted—now that both of these pieces of his heart faced that same hard logic, everything was different.

Everything.

Kirk called out for Teilani. Called out for that lost future, swallowed by this mad and deadly present he had brought into being.

He looked around wildly, ash and debris whipping around him in the howling wind. He *had* to be within a few hundred

meters of Teilani. He knew he had locked on to her life sign—
her life *signs*—as his target.

There! To his left!

Two people stumbled toward a circular building.

One a Klingon male, though a rather slightly built one.

The other a female.

Teilani.

The child.

"Jean-Luc! Hold me!"

Picard turned to Teilani, shocked as he saw her long hair
begin to rise from her scalp.

She wasn't wearing a discharge suit.

A deadly charge was already building within her.

They were a hundred meters from the barracks that was
their destination, and without breaking pace, Picard swept
her up into his arms to break her contact with the metal
asteroid. He ducked reflexively as the *Voyager* roared past
overhead. His stride did not falter as Teilani's hair began to
fall back around her shoulders as the charge diminished in
the rapidly thinning air.

"I'm all right, Jean-Luc," Teilani said. "It's passed. Put me
down."

Unwilling, but aware she was right, Picard let her slide to
the ground, but then he took her hand before she could
protest. With Teilani beside him, Picard charged onward,
faster now that he was freed of her extra weight. Both gasping
desperately for oxygen that was rapidly disappearing into
space.

Picard risked a fast look upward at his ship.

The *Enterprise* was now half within the crossover device
and both were spinning in a slow downward spiral, both
bodies larger than they had appeared before as they fell ever
closer to the prison-camp asteroid.

And beyond them, the second asteroid was also getting larger, moving closer.

Even if he got Teilani to a barracks, Picard knew it would shield her for an hour at most.

And then—

—impact.

The asteroids would meet. The *Enterprise* would be crushed. And everyone in this cursed camp would die. Horribly.

But he had to get Teilani to shelter. He couldn't stop trying.

Until he felt the hand strike his shoulder to make him release his hold on her.

Picard looked down.

It wasn't a hand. It was a filthy bundle of blood-crusted rags and as it spun him around, he raised his arm to block the blow he knew was coming even as he raised his disruptor to—

Kirk blinked in surprise as he realized why the male Klingon with Teilani was not Klingon in size.

"Jean-Luc?"

"Jim?"

Then Teilani pulled at them both. *"We can't stop!"*

"She's right," Picard said, and he again began to run.

"She usually is," Kirk said, as he kept pace beside them.

But Kirk's eyes were on Teilani, almost unable to believe that she lived, that he had found her, that she was here, so close beside him.

"I love you," he shouted at her as wind roared around them and the *Voyager* screamed and generators exploded and disruptors fired and guards and prisoners shrieked in bloody battle.

And even as they rushed onward, on their hopeless mission, Teilani turned her glorious face to him.

In it was answer enough for them both.

As if new life had suddenly burst within him as well, Kirk pushed ahead, leading the way.

THIRTY

☆

Kirk, Picard, and Teilani gasped for breath as the circular airlock door of the barracks building rolled open. They squeezed through as soon as the space was wide enough, and Picard ran for the controls to start the next step of the airlock sequence.

As the door began rolling shut, Kirk heard the sounds of the explosions and the rumble of the *Voyager* diminishing. Here, too, the air was almost gone.

But then he felt the solid vibration of the door sealing and heard the rush of new air being pumped in.

He squeezed his arm around Teilani's as he drew in great lungfuls of air, of life.

Kirk found Picard staring at him. "You know, Jim, the worst part about us meeting again like this, is that I can't say I'm surprised."

"Did I ever thank you for the horse?" Kirk asked.

Picard held up his hand. The pressurization sequence had ended. The inner door was about to open.

Kirk knew what Picard's concern was.

They had seen dozens of people running into this barracks before them. But neither Kirk nor Picard had any way of knowing how many of them had been prisoners or guards.

When the airlock's inner door opened, they could be facing friends or enemies.

Picard held his disruptor ready.

Kirk stood in front of Teilani to shield her.

She gave him a look of annoyance and moved forward to shield him.

The door began rolling open and beyond—

—there was no one.

Picard edged forward, disruptor pointed straight up. He stepped into the barracks.

Then he waved Kirk and Teilani in.

The one-room building was empty, except for long lines of cots and a terrible smell.

"They've been transported," Kirk said. It was the only answer.

"Yes," Picard agreed. "But by whom?"

Then Kirk heard the phased harmonic of a transporter beam begin. "We're about to find out," he said.

"Mr. Scott!" Picard said as he jumped down from the transporter platform. "A pleasure to meet you again." Picard looked around the transporter chamber, recognized it. "I take it we're back on the duplicate *Voyager?*"

"Aye," Scott said. Then he looked startled and pushed past Picard to help Kirk help Teilani down from the platform.

Picard suddenly did the same.

But Teilani pulled back from the three men, shaking their arms free from hers. "I am quite capable of getting off a transporter platform by myself," she said.

Picard was intrigued by the look of real concern on Kirk. "But . . . you're pregnant."

"You are?" Picard said.

Scott made another effort to take her arm. "Then ye really should be sitting down, lass."

But Teilani held her hands up and retreated. "It's pheromones, gentlemen. A little bit of genetic baggage from my

Romulan half. They had such a violent early history that pregnant females began producing pheromones that inspire males of any age to protect them at any cost. An advantage in the past, perhaps. But certainly not now."

"Pheromones," Picard said with huge relief. "Then that explains . . ." He stopped as he saw that Kirk was looking at him intently.

"Explains what?" Kirk asked.

"Absolutely nothing," Picard said, clearing his throat. There was no need to discuss how compelling Teilani had appeared to him. Not if he wanted his friendship with Kirk to continue. He looked at Scott. "How many did you manage to transport to safety?"

Scott frowned. "Maybe half. There're a lot still in the pressurized buildings. More than we can handle on this ship."

"The asteroids are moving together," Kirk said. "We've got an hour to get those people out of there."

"Tell me how, and I'll do it," Scott said. "But not even the *Enterprise* could stop the asteroids from colliding, not when they're this close."

"What is the *Enterprise*'s condition?" Picard asked. There was so much else he wanted to know, but that was the question to be answered before all others.

Scott sighed. "It's almost totally within that thing they've built. Mr. Spock is picking up power readings from it and he thinks it's getting ready to . . . to do whatever it's supposed to do."

"Scotty, we can't let them have that ship," Kirk said.

But Scott shook his head in defeat. "Captain Kirk, I don't think we have a choice in the matter."

Kirk burst onto the bridge of the *Voyager* to see the *Enterprise* in the center of the screen.

The inner panels of the crossover device were glowing, casting eerie green light on the great ship.

"Do we have *any* idea what that is?" Kirk asked.

He heard Picard and Scott close behind him. Teilani came to his side, reached down for his hand, still enshrouded in its bulky bandages. She looked at him for the explanation there had been no time to give while they'd been on the run. He shook his head at her, letting her know this still wasn't the time.

"It is a transporter," Spock said. He was at the security/ tactical station, looking somber.

"Och, you're mad," Scott said. "No one can build a transporter that big."

"More to the point, Mr. Scott, it makes no *sense* for anyone to build a transporter that big. Why transport a starship which is itself a method of transportation? Unless the point of the exercise is not to move a ship from one place to another . . ."

"But from one *universe* to another," Kirk said. As threatening as that device was, the solution for dealing with it was elegantly simple to him. "Blow it up, Spock."

Janeway came up to Kirk, and he could see her face already showed the stress of command. "No use. We've already run the numbers. The device is drawing power from the *Enterprise* now, and is completely shielded by her. This ship doesn't have the firepower to make a dent in it. We can't even ram it and be sure we'd take it out."

"We can't just stand here and watch them steal it," Kirk countered.

"But we *have* run out of options," Spock said.

Kirk looked at Picard. "If we can get you on board, could you trigger the self-destruct?"

Picard looked to Spock. "How much time do we have?"

"Ten minutes at most."

Picard looked back to Kirk. "How do I get on board?"

Kirk's mind raced. "First, we focus all our firepower on one key spot on the shields. If we can concentrate enough energy on an area of overlap, we can make the shield reset itself and—"

"Captain Kirk," Scott said gently. "That particular design flaw was corrected thirty years ago. It can't be done any longer."

"Oh," Kirk said. He rocked back on his heels, forced once more to remember he was a man out of time.

"What if we go *with* it?" Janeway suddenly asked. "After the *Enterprise* goes through, could we go through as well?"

"We have no idea how the device operates," Spock said. "And at the rate the asteroids are closing, we will have no time to learn."

They stood in silence on the bridge as the green light bathing the *Enterprise* intensified.

Then Kirk realized what was wrong. "Where's the *Sovereign?"*

T'Val looked back at him from the helm. "We have her stationkeeping at one hundred thousand kilometers. She's not approaching."

Kirk's grin was triumphant. "Because that ship *is* powerful enough to get through the *Enterprise*'s shields and stop that thing."

Scott almost jumped up and down in his excitement. "Of course. That's it. All we need to do is t' get her here."

The engineer's enthusiasm was contagious. Kirk went to his friend, eager to know the next step. "And then what, Scotty?"

Scott beamed. "Well, sir, I *was* her chief engineer. And I've got a few more tricks that Admiral Nechayev won't know anything about."

Spock stepped forward. "Whatever you plan to do, gentlemen, I remind you that time is of the essence."

"When is it not?" Kirk said. He looked at Janeway. "Start your attack run on the *Enterprise."*

Janeway widened her eyes. "Kirk, this ship is no match for the *Sovereign.* If your plan doesn't work, we're finished."

"In this universe—and I doubt that this has changed—that's what we call an all-or-nothing scenario," Kirk told her.

Teilani had been right all along. Challenge would always be a part of his life. Wherever he was in the universe.

His challenge was not clearing fields and pulling stumps.

But making a difference when no one else could.

And if he didn't make a difference this time, he knew he would have no chance to ever try again.

THIRTY-ONE

―――――――――――― ☆ ――――――――――――

The *Voyager* rushed past the *Enterprise* at one-quarter impulse, throwing all her firepower on the one section above the aft hull that Scott had identified as a potential weak point in her forcefield pattern—one that Starfleet had recently identified and was quickly redesigning.

On the *Voyager*'s main screen, the phaser fire smeared into a sphere of scintillation around the *Enterprise,* marking the perimeter of her shields, and clearly having no effect.

Except for the one Kirk had planned.

"The *Sovereign* is powering up her engines," T'Val announced. "They know about the weak spot."

Kirk glanced at Scott. The engineer was at the communications post. "You're sure you can get this to work, Scotty?"

"D'ye really think this is the time to be asking me that?"

Janeway had T'Val bring the *Voyager* around for another pass. Spock calculated that the *Enterprise* would be completely within the crossover device—the immense transporter—within three minutes. Picard was at weapons control. La Forge and Data were in engineering, in case a hasty retreat was required. And McCoy, Beverly Crusher, and Deanna, as well as the two Spocks, remained on the bridge. Waiting.

Picard fired the phasers at will, concentrating everything the small ship had on Scotty's coordinates.

"The *Sovereign* is accelerating. Phasers coming online," T'Val said.

"Full power to shields," Janeway ordered. "Let's keep the *Enterprise* between us."

The bridge pitched as T'Val brought the ship into a tight turn around the crossover device, just escaping the first blast of phasers from the *Sovereign*.

"Clean miss," Picard said.

"They're following," T'Val reported.

"Here we go," Kirk said. "Open a channel."

Spock sent the hailing frequency from an auxiliary control panel and the *Sovereign*'s response was immediate.

The *Voyager*'s main screen suddenly showed the mirror counterpart who had replaced Fleet Admiral Alynna Nechayev. She sat in the command chair of the *Sovereign*, fully recovered from her last encounter with Kirk. Beside her, the Cardassian, Glinn Arkat, stood with folded arms and murderous rage in his eyes.

"Aren't you dead yet?" Nechayev said.

Kirk knew all he had to do for the moment was to keep the admiral distracted. He could see Scott working frantically at communications. Thirty seconds, the engineer had promised. Kirk took that to mean it would take him all of fifteen. It had taken many years, but he had finally figured out why Scotty always managed to complete his work ahead of schedule—he always doubled his time estimate.

"I'd like to propose a deal," Kirk said.

Nechayev exchanged a look of astonishment with Arkat. "Your ship can't stand up to mine. It can't even outrun mine. Why don't I just blow you out of space now and save us both a lot of time?"

"You want our advanced technology," Kirk said.

"I've already got your advanced technology. Two ships' worth."

Kirk settled back in the executive officer's chair and looked skeptical. "The Sovereign class is obsolete," he said. "None of those ships can withstand Starfleet's newest weapon."

Kirk leaned forward, resisting the impulse to look at Scotty. "Corbomite," he said. Then he resisted the impulse to look back at McCoy as McCoy groaned.

Arkat leaned down and whispered something in Nechayev's ear.

"Corbomite?" Nechayev mused. "Let me see . . . would this be something required for the construction of *polyphasic disruptors?*"

"Never heard of them," Kirk said.

"Target the *Voyager,*" Nechayev said.

"They're locked on us," T'Val announced.

Kirk looked quickly to the side. "Scotty . . . ?"

Scott shook his head in frustration. "This isn't like the old days. Ships today . . . they're . . . too damn complicated."

Kirk had one last option. "Admiral, surrender now and I will be able to put in a good word for you during your trial."

The admiral's eyes actually bulged as she burst into disbelieving laughter. Even Arkat smiled beside her. *"You want me to surrender?"*

"Otherwise," Kirk said with a straight face, "you might get hurt."

The admiral laughed so hard she appeared to be having difficulty breathing.

"Kirk, I will actually miss you . . ." she finally gasped. And then she said, "Fire."

Kirk felt Teilani's hand squeeze his shoulder.

"Got 'er!" Scott said.

The *Voyager* hung in space, no phaser fire directed at her at all.

Kirk watched the look of disbelief grow on Admiral Nechayev's face as she realized that the *Voyager* continued to exist in defiance of her orders.

"Now we do this . . ." Scott said happily.

On the screen, the admiral's disbelief turned to panic as the *Sovereign*'s computer announced that a warp-core breach was in progress.

Picard looked back in Scott's direction. "Mr. Scott, are you able to do this to any Sovereign-class vessel?"

"Only the ones I've rigged for remote-control," Scott said modestly. "Now we change her orientation."

"Forward view," Janeway said.

The commotion on Nechayev's bridge was replaced by an exterior image of the admiral's ship as all the port-side maneuvering thrusters fired in a balanced burst, spinning the ship on her axis. A second series of firings stopped her so her ventral surface was parallel to the second asteroid.

"And now . . ." Scott said. "We let the safety systems take over and . . ."

On the screen, there was a small puff of white smoke as explosive bolts blew off a hull plate on the ship's belly. Then, in a streak of flashing blue light, the *Sovereign*'s long, slender warp core self-ejected.

"Mr. Scott," Kirk said, "that is a work of sheer beauty."

"Aye," Scott said as the glowing cylinder of the warp core tumbled toward the second asteroid. "That's one way to look at it." He jabbed another control at his station and the *Sovereign* suddenly pulled away at half-impulse.

"She'll be halfway to Vulcan before they get past my lockouts," Scott said in satisfaction.

But Kirk's sense of victory was short-lived. "The *Enterprise* is now completely within the crossover device," Spock announced. "I am detecting a power-up sequence consistent with transporter-beam generation."

"Time to warp-core impact?" Janeway asked.

"Fifteen seconds," Scott said.

"Unfortunately," Spock said, "transport will begin in ten seconds."

Kirk turned to Janeway. "We just need to delay the process.

Fire phasers. See if we can get the transport sequence to interrupt itself."

Janeway stood up. "Let's do it," she said to T'Val.

The *Voyager's* bridge thrummed with the discharge of the ship's phasers.

"Transport in five seconds," Spock said.

"Impact in ten," Scott added.

The glowing shell of energy that protected the *Enterprise* and the crossover device flickered and flashed with the power the *Voyager* poured into it.

"I am detecting a transport anomaly," Spock reported. "The device is attempting to compensate. Transport in three. . . ."

"Impact in eight . . . seven . . ."

". . . two . . . one . . . Transport sequence has initiated and—"

There was a flash of green light, almost blinding.

Kirk threw his arm in front of his eyes, seething with the knowledge that he had lost.

But when he removed his arm, the *Enterprise* was still there.

"Transport has failed," Spock said.

Everyone but Kirk cheered. He waited to be sure.

Then there was a flash of blue light from another section of the screen.

"The warp core has just exploded on the second asteroid's surface," Scott said. "Shock wave in three seconds."

Janeway wasted no time. "Get us out of here, T'Val."

For a second, the plasma storms of the Goldin Discontinuity smeared across the screen; then the angle of the forward sensors changed so Kirk could see the two asteroids—with one beginning to spin because of the enormous blue explosion that had obscured one side of it.

"The asteroid is being diverted," Spock announced. "Extrapolating new trajectory. . . ." Spock turned to Kirk. They might as well have been on the bridge of the old *Enterprise.*

The first *Enterprise*. "Captain, the second asteroid will clear the first by two hundred meters. The next chance for impact will be in seventeen days. More than enough time to complete the evacuation of the camp survivors."

Kirk allowed himself the luxury of a deep breath. It had all come together—the crew, the technology, the will to win.

He felt the touch of Teilani's hand on his shoulder.

But then Kirk saw Picard staring up at the screen, and knew there was still one last mission to complete.

"We have to go back," he said to Janeway, "and see what shape the *Enterprise* is in."

Janeway nodded. "Let's do it," she said.

THIRTY-TWO

☆

The *Enterprise* hung dead in space, surrounded by the floating ruin of the crossover device, like an ancient sunken vessel shrouded in kelp and debris.

The mighty ship's running lights were out. Her nacelles were dark. But she was intact, and her batteries were keeping life-support at minimal levels.

Kirk and Picard stood together before the *Voyager*'s main screen. Spock and Teilani were with them.

"Jean-Luc, I'm sorry," Kirk said. And he meant it. Among a handful of beings, he truly knew the force that bound a captain to his ship. He knew what must be in his friend's heart as Picard gazed upon the battered hulk before them.

"Don't be," Picard said. He flashed a smile at Kirk. A small one, but one that said he could see light shining through this dark hour. "I still have her. We saved her."

Kirk went to give Picard his hand, but both men stared awkwardly at the bandages that protected Kirk's damaged flesh. Picard put his own hands on Kirk's shoulders instead. *"You* saved her," he said. "And I thank you."

Then La Forge spoke up from an aft sensor station. "Captain?"

Both Kirk and Picard turned as one and said, "Yes?"

367

La Forge smiled. "Captain *Picard*. Scotty and I have completed our structural analysis. She's not showing any sign of transporter misalignment."

"That's a relief," Picard said. Kirk understood why. The subspace shock wave generated by the *Sovereign*'s warp-core explosion had shut down the transporter effect intended to beam the *Enterprise* to the mirror universe. If the shock wave had hit too late, while transport was already in progress, the huge ship might not have been properly reassembled when she had rematerialized. But all was well. Another victory to add to all the others.

But Spock, apparently, did not think so. "Curious," he said. "I was certain I detected a full transporter-field effect before the warp-core detonation."

Kirk smiled at his old friend. "We've never seen a transporter this big before, Spock. There're bound to be engineering differences we know nothing about."

"Perhaps," Spock said, but he didn't sound convinced.

Picard looked down at his Klingon armor, as if suddenly realizing he still had it on. "I suppose I should clean up. The relief vessels will be here in two hours and . . . I imagine there's a great deal of work to be done over there."

Picard walked back to the turbolift, that small smile still on his face.

Kirk watched him go, pleased his friend still had his starship, but glad that he, himself, had other missions to attend to now.

Then Teilani hugged him. "And I want to get you down to Dr. McCoy to get those dressings changed."

Kirk looked at his bandages. Still the least of his concerns. "I'll be fine," he said.

"You'd better be," Teilani told him. "I'm not going to change all the diapers by myself."

Kirk grinned at the thought of that one new mission in particular. He couldn't wait for it to begin. Then he saw Spock look back at T'Val, and knew his friend was also distracted by thoughts of children and parents. Of paths not taken. It pained him to think that Spock might be in distress. Kirk changed the subject.

"Spock, just when the *Voyager* came in on the attack, you said you and your counterpart had worked out what made the two universes diverge."

Spock returned his attention to the here-and-now. "Not the event," he clarified. "The time period. Approximately three hundred years ago. About the time of First Contact between humans and Vulcans. Kate Janeway gave us a clue when she referred to Lake Sloane on Alpha Centauri IV being called Lake Riker in her universe."

"One name made the difference?" Kirk asked.

"No, but it is one of the earliest signs of divergence my counterpart and I could identify. The fact that the lake was named by Zefram Cochrane, following his move from Earth to the colony he founded on that world, made us focus on the time of First Contact."

"There was First Contact in both universes, though?" Kirk asked.

"Yes. And to the best of our abilities to recall history, that event in both universes was the same. Cochrane's first warp flight attracted the attention of a Vulcan ship and the next day, contact was made." Spock's long face took on a thoughtful expression.

"But . . . ?" Kirk prompted.

"It is the events *after* First Contact that somehow seem to be at odds in the two universes. There is nothing conclusive. No key document or incident we can point to. But in one universe, our universe, humans and Vulcans shared an optimistic dream of combining their resources to seek out new life. In the mirror universe, the same cooperation followed, the same early expeditions took place, but there was a decidedly military aspect to their nature. Almost as if, somehow, those responsible for First Contact believed some grave threat was waiting for them among the stars. As if they had secret knowledge of the future and the conflicts to come."

"What kind of conflicts?" Kirk asked.

Spock folded his hands behind his back. "Again, the differences could merely be an artifact of how history is recorded. None of this might be true. But . . . in the mirror universe . . . when the Borg were first detected, far earlier than they were in our history . . . it was almost as if the Terran Empire had been expecting to find them. The Borg did not remain a threat there."

"How could that be?" Teilani asked.

"I do not know," Spock said. "And even if it is true, the explanation of that truth might always elude us."

Kirk looked back at the screen and the *Enterprise*. There were enough mysteries in this universe for him to struggle with. He would leave the mirror universe to others. Janeway and T'Val would return to their war with all the technical information that Kirk could provide them. The mirror Spock would be treated for Bendii here, and given sanctuary until T'Val judged it was safe for him to return. And then, Kirk would return to his own life.

"What are you thinking, James?"

Kirk smiled at the woman with whom he had created life. "Will you marry me?" he asked.

Teilani looked at him with eyes that saw into his soul. He could have no secrets from her and he was glad of it.

"What are you going to do about that stump on Chal?"

"Phaser it out of existence," Kirk promised. "I'll borrow one from Memlon's mother."

Teilani laughed. The sweetest sound Kirk had heard in weeks.

"And then what?" she asked. "After you've planted the clearing and built us a house?" She looked to the screen, past the ship and the storms, to where the stars waited. "What about . . . out there?"

Kirk looked out as well, not through space, but through time.

He could have no secrets from her. He could tell her no lies.

"I don't know," he said. "Maybe I'll farm. Maybe we can breed that horse Jean-Luc sent me. And maybe, I'll buy a starship and we can find out how many other Chals are out there. You, me, and our son."

"Or our daughter."

"All our children," Kirk said with a smile, and he pulled her closer to him, so she could rest her head on his shoulder. "I don't know what I'll do, Teilani, or where I'll go. But what I do know, without question, without doubt, is that whatever waits for me, I'm going to face it with you."

Teilani smiled at him, and in the love she shared with him, Kirk knew he had found what she had sent him out to discover.

His place in the universe.

It was not a world. Not a time. Not any physical place at all.

Instead, it was every place and every time. As long as he was at her side.

"I love you," she whispered, next to his cheek.

"I love you," he whispered back.

A perfect moment.

And then an alarm blared on the bridge.

Instantly Kirk and Teilani broke apart.

"What is it?" Kirk demanded.

"Weapons lock!" T'Val said.

Janeway was on her feet, reading the tactical boards. "It's the *Enterprise!* All systems . . . they're coming back online."

"What?" Kirk said. "How can that be possible?"

"We're being hailed," T'Val called out.

"Onscreen," Janeway said.

All eyes went to the main screen as the image of the drifting *Enterprise* winked out, to be replaced by a transmission from that ship's bridge.

It was fully staffed. All consoles lit and active.

But none of that mattered.

Because of the man who sat in her center chair.

If there were gasps on the bridge of the *Voyager,* Kirk didn't hear them.

If Teilani grabbed his arm in fear, he did not feel her grip.

His heart thundered in his ears.

His breath caught in his throat.

Every thought in his mind was banished, replaced by a primal dread that lived deep in the darkness of his mind.

Because when he looked at the man in the center chair—

—the face he saw was his own.

And that face laughed at him.

"James T. Kirk," the man in the center chair said. "I've heard so much about you. I owe you . . . so much more."

"They are powering phasers," T'Val said.

Kirk struggled through his shock to find his voice. "Who . . . are you?" Though he already knew the answer.

The man in the center chair leaned forward, and the smile that split his face was the grin of the devil.

"You can call me . . . Tiberius."

Kirk leaned against the helm console for support. "Why are you here?"

His mirror counterpart answered as if it were the most obvious question ever asked. "You stole a universe from me, James. And now I'm here to do the same to you."

"Never," Kirk said.

"The choice is yours. Lower your shields and surrender. Or you will die. You have ten seconds to comply."

Then the Emperor Tiberius sat back in the center chair of the *Enterprise.*

The waiting began.

James T. Kirk will return in

Star Trek: Dark Victory

For further information about William Shatner, science fiction, new technologies, and upcoming William Shatner books, log on to www.futurecall.com.

SF
SBA